Twelve military heroes.
Twelve indomitable heroines.
*One **UNIFORMLY HOT!** miniseries.*

Harlequin Blaze's bestselling miniseries continues with another year of irresistible soldiers from all branches of the armed forces.

Don't miss

THE RULE-BREAKER
by Rhonda Nelson
April 2013

NORTHERN REBEL
by Jennifer LaBrecque
May 2013

ALL THE RIGHT MOVES
by Jo Leigh
June 2013

FREE FALL
by Karen Foley
July 2013

Uniformly Hot!
The Few. The Proud. The Sexy as Hell.

Available wherever Harlequin books are sold.

D0179458

Blaze®

Dear Reader,

I'm so glad you decided to join me in Good Riddance, Alaska, whether you're back for this seventh book in the series or if it's your first visit here.

Love is a strange animal—confusing, disturbing, unexpected, misconstrued and, more often than not, downright inconvenient. Take Marine Sgt. Lars Reinhardt and nurse Delphi Reynolds. Neither one is looking for love. In fact, it's precisely what neither one wants. However, they do want one another and things get all inconvenient and complicated when they fall in love, despite their best intentions.

The other confounding thing about love is that it strikes regardless of season or location. In my first Harlequin Blaze book, *Daring in the Dark* (and the second story in this collection), Simon and Tawny are stuck in a Manhattan blackout. She's his best friend's former fiancée and Tawny's convinced Simon despises her. But add a little darkness and a lot of sexual tension and see how fast things change....

I hope you enjoy these tales of inconvenient love. I'd love to hear from you. Drop by and say hello at www.jenniferlabrecque.com.

As always, happy reading!

Jennifer LaBrecque

Northern Rebel
&
Daring in the Dark
—
Jennifer LaBrecque

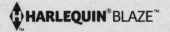

ISBN-13: 978-0-373-79752-3

NORTHERN REBEL

Copyright © 2013 by Harlequin Books S.A.

The publisher acknowledges the copyright holder of the individual works as follows:

NORTHERN REBEL
Copyright © 2013 by Jennifer LaBrecque

DARING IN THE DARK
Copyright © 2005 by Jennifer LaBrecque

Recycling programs for this product may not exist in your area.

This edition published by arrangement with Harlequin Books S.A.

For questions and comments about the quality of this book, please contact us at CustomerService@Harlequin.com.

® and TM are trademarks of Harlequin Enterprises Limited or its corporate affiliates. Trademarks indicated with ® are registered in the United States Patent and Trademark Office, the Canadian Trade Marks Office and in other countries.

HARLEQUIN®

Printed in U.S.A.

www.Harlequin.com

CONTENTS

ABOUT THE AUTHOR

After a varied career path that included barbecue-joint waitress, corporate number-cruncher and bug-business maven, Jennifer LaBrecque has found her true calling writing contemporary romance. Named 2001 Notable New Author of the Year and 2002 winner of a prestigious Maggie Award for Excellence, she is also a two-time RITA® Award finalist. Jennifer lives in suburban Atlanta with a Chihuahua and a cat named Cat.

Books by Jennifer LaBrecque

HARLEQUIN BLAZE

To get the inside scoop on Harlequin Blaze and its talented writers, be sure to check out blazeauthors.com.

All backlist available in ebook. Don't miss any of our special offers. Write to us at the following address for information on our newest releases.

Harlequin Reader Service
U.S.: 3010 Walden Ave., P.O. Box 1325, Buffalo, NY 14269
Canadian: P.O. Box 609, Fort Erie, Ont. L2A 5X3

JENNIFER LaBRECQUE

NORTHERN REBEL

To Brenda Chin, long-term partner in crime.

1

DELPHI REYNOLDS SLUNG her purse over her shoulder and headed down the hall of the now-silent medical office. She was ready to get home, pull off her nursing "scrubs" and put her feet up. It had been one hectic day.

Dr. DeWitt Zellers stepped into the open door of his office, a ready smile on his face. Delphi had been thrilled when she'd secured a position with the senior Dr. Zellers straight out of nursing school. He had a well-deserved reputation as one of the South's finest surgeons. A year ago, his son DeWitt had taken over the practice when his father retired. DeWitt Zellers was charming, paid his employees well and was highly regarded, both personally and professionally, much as his father had been. In the past year Delphi and DeWitt had chatted often. The young doctor was more than personable.

While she was always aware that she worked for him, they'd become friends. He'd consulted with her on his anniversary present for his wife and invited Delphi to his daughter's third birthday party. Likewise he'd given her advice on dating and men. Delphi liked and trusted him. DeWitt was sort of like the big brother she'd never had.

"You got a minute before you head out?" he said.

"Sure."

"Come on in." He waved her into his office, closing the door behind her. Everyone else had left for the day but they'd gotten into the habit of chatting after hours, usually just a quick few minutes. However, today he looked fairly intense. "I wanted to talk to you about something."

He rounded his desk and sank into his Moroccan-leather chair.

DeWitt had gone with her suggestion on Macy's anniversary gift a couple of months ago. His wife was short with dark hair. She carried some extra weight and had thick, heavy features but you couldn't beat her devotion to her husband. The romantic side of Delphi loved the fact that the handsome doctor was so enamored with his rather plain wife. Delphi liked Macy well enough, but they didn't have a common lifestyle. Macy was a socialite. Delphi was a worker bee. But Macy had loved the piece of jewelry Delphi had suggested so maybe there were a few similarities after all.

DeWitt's office was well-appointed functionality. His diplomas, accreditations and accolades, all tastefully framed and matted, nearly filled the wall above his credenza. Along with his medical journals, an assortment of beautifully framed photos shared the credenza: him receiving his diploma, flanked by his mother and a beaming Macy; and DeWitt, Macy and their daughter, Chesney, on the beach, a smiling trio surrounded by sea grass and sand.

His office portrayed professional success and familial devotion. One glance at that wall said it all—Dr. DeWitt Zellers was a great guy.

Delphi stood behind one of the "guest" chairs opposite his desk. It had been an incredibly busy day and she was ready to go home and relax. DeWitt, however, didn't seem to be in any hurry. He sat, his fingers templed in front of his mouth. It was the look he always had when he'd figured out something important or made a decision. She couldn't exactly put her finger on it, but something had been sort of "off" about DeWitt lately. Maybe he was just stressed out. She hadn't pressed him because sooner or later he'd tell her if he wanted to. However, she was sensing a weird vibe from him now.

He rose, rounded his desk and stood behind her, close behind her, as in she could feel his breath against her neck. It was a little creepy. Laughing uncomfortably, Delphi stepped to the right, since the chair blocked her way forward and he blocked her from behind. She turned, laughing again with a mixture of surprise and a little nervousness. "What's up?"

He closed the distance she'd put between them. "Delphi, this is driving me crazy. We just can't fight it any longer."

She was totally lost. Were they still talking about a present for Macy? What was driving him crazy? "Huh?"

He leaned in closer. His breath smelled like the hot dogs Barb had ran out to the corner deli to grab at lunch, and breath mints. It wasn't a good combination. "There's no need to play coy. I know how you feel about me and I feel the same about you." He reached for her and she sidestepped him.

Holy hell. He was…acting nuts. "DeWitt…Dr.

Zellers…." Pulling in his professional title seemed a really good idea right now. "We're friends—"

"We both know it's so much more than that—"

What? "No, it's not."

"Baby, there's no need to keep hiding it. God, I'm going crazy wanting you, thinking about you."

"But Macy…Chesney…." He definitely needed to be reminded of his wife and child right now because he obviously wasn't thinking clearly.

He caught Delphi's hand in his. "I can't leave her. Her father has too much influence. He wouldn't ruin my career but he could—and would—do some damage." Delphi tried shaking off his hand but he had quite a grip going. A seed of panic bloomed in her chest. "Besides, Macy would screw me out of everything and ream me on child support for the next fifteen years. But that doesn't mean we can't be together." The sly glimmer in his eyes was as disconcerting as his words. "I've found this great condo between the office and my house. I could set you up there. The title would be in your name, but I'd cover the payment…."

She finally regained her voice. "You want to set me up as your mistress?"

"I know it's not the same as being married, but it would be just for a few years, until I'm more firmly established and Chesney's a little older."

He thought her outrage was because he wouldn't marry her? "You already have a wife."

"That's what I'm saying. We can work around it."

It? "You're so missing the point."

"I know the condo isn't as big as where Macy and I live." He'd taken on a supercilious tone, much as if he was the mighty physician trying to explain a complicated illness to a simpleton. "But it's bigger and much nicer than where you are now—"

"Really?"

He reached over onto his desk and handed her a color brochure. "I think you'll like it. Gated. Great location. A sound investment."

Stupefied, she took the brochure and glanced at the property while he prattled on about them buying furniture together. It was definitely nicer than where she was now.

"DeWitt, I—"

"I know." Before she could stop him, he had pulled her to him and was kissing her frantically, plunging his tongue into her mouth.

After a moment of shocked paralysis, she used all of her strength to shove him away. "Stop!"

Her hands were shaking. Her trusted employer and friend had turned into someone she didn't know…and didn't want to know.

As he reached for her again, she darted around the second guest chair, putting it between them. "Delphi? What's wrong?"

He looked wounded and confused, as if she'd slapped him in the face.

"DeWitt, I thought we were friends. Why would you even think I was interested in anything more?"

"Delphi, we don't have to play this game. You don't have to be coy." Impatience threaded his voice.

There was that word again—*coy.* "I'm being honest. Outside of work, we're friends. Nothing more. You're *married.*"

"I told you, baby, Macy won't be a problem. You'll see."

He just wasn't getting it. "The only thing I see is that you're not the man I thought you were."

He shrugged. "What's the big deal?" An arrogant smugness settled on his face. "All powerful men have a mistress—it's part of the personality of leaders, men of importance. Macy knows she's lucky to have me."

He was serious. Delphi felt physically sick to her stomach. It was one thing if that was how he saw the world, but that he'd think she would feel the same way...

He and his idea were repugnant.

She wanted to tell him that was the most ignorant, obnoxious thing she'd ever heard come out of a man's mouth. He was, however, her employer. She chose her words carefully. "DeWitt, I'm not interested in you that way. And even if I were, I'd still never act on it because you're married and that means something to me."

"Do you understand what I'm offering you?"

"It has become crystal clear. And I hope it's crystal clear how I feel about your offer." She moved toward the door, her heart thunking hard in her chest.

"Sleep on it."

"I don't have to sleep on it." She opened the door.

"You're making a mistake."

She was so upset she ignored the not-so-veiled threat in his words. "The only mistake I've made was thinking you were someone else. I feel sorry for Macy. She deserves better than you."

She closed the door behind her, quickly and quietly exiting the office suite.

DELPHI WALKED THROUGH the employee entrance the next morning, greeted by the familiar scent of antiseptic.

Despite exhaustion, she was resolved. She'd hardly slept, if at all. She'd tossed and turned, looking at it from every angle. Had she inadvertently led him on? Had she misconstrued their conversation yesterday? Regardless, there was still only one course of action. She would quietly give her two-months' notice. Given the nursing shortage, she should be able to easily find another job in that time frame and it would give the practice some time to replace her, as well, without disrupting the flow of the office. She'd keep what had happened between the two of them quiet, even though at one point she'd considered telling Macy about it. In the end, she'd decided it was better to keep it to herself.

If Macy ever came to Delphi and asked her about anything, Delphi wouldn't lie, but she wouldn't approach Macy Zeller either.

She hadn't finished putting her purse away when Debbie, the receptionist, put her head around the door. "Doc wants you in his office. He said for you to come as soon as you got in."

She thought she'd made it clear last night where she stood. But it was just as well. She'd tender her resignation verbally and give it to him in writing tomorrow. While being friends was no longer an option, she didn't want to leave on a sour note. She'd end things amicably and they'd each go on as if that unfortunate kiss and proposition had never happened.

She gave a cursory knock and opened his office door. Delphi drew up short, slowly closing the door behind her, her mind racing. Macy stood beside DeWitt, who was seated behind his desk.

Her stomach clenched. "Good morning."

"Have a seat, Delphi," DeWitt said, his stern tone remonstrative.

She would've liked to have refused, but her legs were shaking so much, sitting was probably a good idea. She sat.

"This is very difficult to do," he said again in that austere tone underlaid by a weary patience, "but you've really left me no choice. Here are your separation papers. You'll be escorted from the premises."

"You're firing me? I've left you no choice…?" Forget protecting Macy. "You came on to me. I was going to offer my resignation this morning anyway. I can't work with you."

"You said she'd try to turn it around," Macy said, placing her hand on DeWitt's shoulder. He placed his hand over hers. The devoted, loving husband. "Your ploy isn't going to work, Delphi. DeWitt told me everything last night. I feel sorry for you, we both do, but we simply can't let you get away with this."

"What is it that I'm trying to get away with?" Her mouth was so dry she could barely get the words out.

"When he refused to leave me for you, you demanded he buy you your own place…" She wielded the condo brochure like a prosecutor presenting evidence to the jury. "…or you'd come to me with some lies to try to break us up. You're sick, Delphi. You need help. But you've picked the wrong couple to extort. You won't break up our family."

It was like being in the middle of a nightmare and not being able to wake up. She couldn't quite believe what she was hearing.

"Macy, I've known you both for seven years. Do you really think I'd do this?"

Delphi saw it, for just a moment, the bleakness in the other woman's eyes. If Delphi wasn't the bad guy, then it had to be her husband. And if it was her husband… "DeWitt wouldn't lie to me."

Macy couldn't see the small smirk that curved her husband's mouth. Delphi eyed the other woman with compassion. "You have to believe what you have to believe."

DeWitt picked up his phone and hit a button. "Debbie, if you'll call security to my office. They need to oversee Ms. Reynolds collecting her personal effects and escort her from the building."

2

Six months later...

"WHY DON'T YOU come to Good Riddance? I'm desperate."

Delphi laughed, although her laugh felt rusty from disuse. "Thanks a lot."

"I didn't mean it that way." Delphi's long-standing college friend, Dr. Skye Shanahan, laughed on the other end of the phone. Delphi had moved into nursing while Skye had become a general practice physician. Delphi had been somewhere on the other side of surprised two years ago when Skye had given up her thriving Atlanta practice to move to a remote Alaska town. She'd married a bush pilot and hung her shingle out in a little spot called Good Riddance. Now, Skye's long-standing assistant was taking off for medical school. "Well, actually, I guess I did mean it that way because I am desperate. But I wasn't asking you as a last choice. Still, you've never even expressed an interest in Alaska since I moved here, and now, suddenly it's a possibility. It's not that bad, you know…"

Delphi shivered simply thinking about it. "Yeah, but I don't like the cold."

Skye chuckled. "I know. We've covered that a couple of times. You're the one who's always talked about getting married in Jamaica."

"Yep. Sun and sand is my idea of paradise."

"We don't have any sandy beaches but it's sunny here and the days are going to get longer still. If you could help me out for three months, that should give us time to find a permanent replacement. It won't be exactly balmy, but it will be warm and we have really long hours of daylight. I promise, you won't see any snow while you're here."

A steady late-May rain drummed against the roof of Delphi's loft as she absently looked out over Atlanta's soggy skyline. "So, you're saying the person you had lined up bailed at the last minute?" she asked. Even though Skye had told her that very thing, she was buying time as she turned the option over in her head. It wasn't an option she'd ever considered, but maybe that was exactly what she needed. A real change.

"Unfortunately, yes. Nelson leaves in two weeks and that's etched in stone. It took us months to find someone and now, well, we don't have a prayer of lining up someone else on such short notice. And I didn't mean to be presumptuous. I was just thinking that I need help and I'd love to see you and you need…" She drifted off awkwardly. "Well, I shouldn't have assumed anything. Have you found something?"

The only thing she'd found was her savings down to triple digits and every medical job application a dead end. Her only experience had been in Zellers's practice and he wasn't giving her a good reference. And

Macy Zellers had spread her version of the truth to all her cronies.

Few doctors in the city would hire Delphi and the ones who might were looking for more than a nurse. She had been thoroughly, undeniably blackballed.

"No, I haven't found anything." She leaned her forehead against the cool windowpane. She didn't mention the waitressing job she'd started, because that wasn't what Skye was talking about. "I know there are other people a whole lot worse off than me, but this has been incredibly demoralizing." Not to mention a financial disaster. She refused to dip into her 401(k).

"Delphi, it just infuriates me that he's been able to do this to you. It's just so wrong."

She'd mercifully gone from anger to a sanity-preserving numbness. "And they say hell hath no fury like a woman scorned. Men have just as much trouble hearing the word 'no.' And his vindictive wife has been just as bad. I keep clinging to the thought that karma is a bitch."

"DeWitt can't get away with this."

"Well, it sure looks like he has."

"So, why don't you come here and take a break from the Atlanta scene. When you leave, you'll have a glowing recommendation from your most recent job." Skye named a figure that was substantially higher than what Delphi had been making. "We have to pay premium because we're so remote. And we provide free housing."

Delphi looked at Mr. Spock swimming in his glass bowl. She supposed her sister Cam would look after the blue-and-red betta and the houseplants. The best part of the whole thing, however, would be not being on the receiving end of those pitying looks from her family and scornful glances from the medical community. Not that she saw them often but she ran into more than she thought she would. Alaska wasn't on her list of places she'd ever wanted to go but getting away for three months might be the best thing she could do. "A change of scenery, a fresh start…"

"Exactly." Delphi hadn't realized she'd spoken aloud until Skye responded. "How soon could you get here? Next Friday is Nelson's last day."

Delphi did some quick calculations. It was late Tuesday now. "I could leave Thursday evening or Friday morning."

"Yes, yes, yes! You are a godsend! I can't wait to see you! Thank you so much, Delphi. I'll let Merrilee— she's the mayor and she runs the airstrip—know and she'll make your flight arrangements. Should she email them to you?"

This was moving quickly. "Sure."

"Great. Let me call her. She'll get in touch with you directly."

They exchanged goodbyes and hung up the phone.

Night had set in while she and Skye had been talking and now her reflection stared back at her in the dark, rain-spattered window.

The woman who looked back at her still looked trusting, fairly innocent. But she was no longer that woman.

A different place, a change of pace…

She marched over to the kitchen junk drawer and pulled out a pair of scissors.

In the bathroom she faced herself in the mirror and grabbed a hank of hair. Chop. Again, chop. Over and over until most of her hair was scattered on the floor, leaving only short spikes on her head.

LARS REINHARDT SHOULDERED his duffel bag and made his way through the Anchorage airport. He'd had a bellyful of planes, having been traveling for nearly two days now to get to Good Riddance, Alaska, from Riyadh, Saudi Arabia. This, however, was the final leg—a puddle jumper out to the little bush town in central Alaska where his uncle, cousin and older brother lived. Liam, his twin, was technically older by a whopping five minutes.

Liam had obviously suffered a brain fart. It was the only reasonable explanation for his plan to sign on for marriage…again.

Lars had liked Natalie, Liam's first wife, well enough and he was sure Tansy was nice. But Lars just didn't get the whole marriage thing. Hadn't Liam learned anything the first time around—as in, don't go there again? It had only taken Lars once in the broken-heart arena to learn and that hadn't even involved tying the knot.

He was what his teachers had always termed a quick study. He picked up on things fast. Show him once, and he usually had it down pat. So, after the first time he got dumped on, he knew it was something he wouldn't let happen again. From that day on, Lars made sure he never got too involved, never let a woman matter too much. And when it sometimes seemed as though a relationship might move beyond that, Lars rotated out.

He hoped things worked out for his older brother. He really did. However, he couldn't help but wonder if his twin would've been so quick to marry again if he hadn't been discharged from the Marines. They'd exchanged emails and Lars had a good sense of where his brother's head was…and wasn't. Liam had been at a total loss as to what to do with himself and his life for a while. Not only had they corresponded, but they were twins. He couldn't read his brother's mind, but there were times, all throughout their lives, when he'd just had a feeling, a feeling that wasn't his own, but his brother's. Lars had *known* how empty his brother had felt. Was Liam just trying to plug a hole in his life by getting married? He hoped to hell not.

A brunette holding a placard with *Reinhardt* printed on it caught his eye.

"I'm Lars Reinhardt," he said as he walked up to her.

"Juliette Sorenson." They exchanged a brief handshake. "I'm your pilot."

He'd been expecting a male pilot. He didn't know why and the fact of the matter was he really didn't care who ran the plane. But somehow, he just figured bush pilots were supposed to be guys. "Okay then, Juliette Sorenson, let's get this done. I'm ready for a hot meal and a hot bath and I'm not particular about the order."

She laughed. "In about an hour, both should be available. In the meantime, let's get you there. Is that your only bag?" She nodded toward the duffel thrown over his shoulder.

"Yes, ma'am. I travel light."

She smiled, turning. Lars followed her through Anchorage's airport. They stepped out onto the tarmac, a light, fresh wind and sunshine greeting them. They crossed to the small plane. The air was crisp and cool, even though it was May—but at least the sun was out. He didn't think he'd dig the hours of darkness that came with full-blown winter, early spring and late fall.

Juliette opened the door to the plane and motioned with her head for him to climb in. Two steps into the plane, he pulled up short. A shock wave reverberated through him. A woman with short blond hair sat already strapped into one of the seats. He wasn't expecting to see another passenger, but it was more than that. Women didn't generally stop him in his tracks—well, never, as a matter of fact.

And it wasn't as if she was the most beautiful woman he'd ever seen, but nonetheless, something about her slammed into him, leaving him slightly dazed by the impact. She glanced his way, then deliberately looked back out the window at the runway activity, dismissing him.

Squeezing past him, the pilot said, "Pick any seat while I secure your bag and we'll be on our way."

He passed her his duffel, almost absentmindedly, still arrested by the woman sitting inside.

Juliette introduced them from the back of the plane, where she was stowing his bag. "Delphi, meet Sergeant Lars Reinhardt. Sergeant Reinhardt, Delphi Reynolds."

"Hi," Lars said.

She dipped her chin in a quick nod and once again turned away without speaking. A large part of him had never been able to ignore a challenge. His dad used to say Liam came out easy while Lars had come out fighting all the way. And where the blonde was concerned, there was no small measure of ego involved. Lars wasn't used to being ignored or dismissed.

Therefore, he plopped his ass into the seat right beside Delphi Reynolds.

He felt her tense.

The fatigue he'd felt trudging through yet another airport fell off of him like an old shirt. Her "no trespassing" body language acted like a red flag being waved at a bull.

He could have basically ignored her, the same as she was ignoring him. That, however, went against everything inside him. It was the same thing that drove him to work in the demolitions section of the Marines. It was the allure of danger, the challenge. To ignore her would be like ignoring an unexploded mortar—and that wasn't going to happen. Besides, there was the issue that he wanted to know more about her—even more than he wanted that hot meal and hot bath…and that was damn saying something.

SHE JUST WANTED to be left alone. Since the guy didn't appear mentally challenged, he was obviously, deliberately attempting to engage her by sitting right next to her. He was good-looking, and she was certain he wasn't used to being ignored. But although he couldn't possibly know it, this wasn't personal.

She was still numb inside, a state that had actually been really useful in getting through packing and off-loading plants and a fish, as well as explaining to her folks why she was leaving in a couple of days to live in Alaska for three months. That had certainly been a conversation. So, numb and drugged—she'd dosed herself with motion sickness pills in the hope that she wouldn't throw up in flight—she really just wanted to keep to herself. And there was the little matter that trusting—and being wrong—about a friend had turned her life upside down. From here on out, she was keeping her circle small.

"So, what brings you to Good Riddance?"

She answered without turning her head to look at him. "Work."

He waited a second and then asked, "Which would be?"

"I'm a nurse."

Juliette secured the door. Delphi didn't miss the pilot's subtle double take that Lars Reinhardt had chosen to sit right next to Delphi when there were three other seats readily available. "Okay, if everybody's buckled in, we'll be on our way."

"When do we get our peanuts and drink of choice?" Lars said.

The pilot laughed. "Wrong airline," she said.

A hint of a reluctant smile tugged at Delphi's lips as she steadfastly stared out the window. It had been kind of funny, she grudgingly admitted to herself. Except she didn't want to be amused. Dammit, she'd made a commitment to being miserable. Well, not exactly miserable but aloof…yeah, that was a good word choice. She didn't want to be sharing a laugh or information with some stranger.

The plane roared to life and the dog that had been curled up in the front of the plane rose and walked toward the back. She sat and placed her chin on Delphi's knee, eyeing her with a mixture of curiosity and what Delphi could've sworn was sympathy. It was the craziest thing but it was as if the dog sensed her mood and emotions and related.

What? Was she unwittingly giving out some please-invade-my-space vibe? Because that sure wasn't how she felt.

"If Baby's bothering you," Juliette said, rather absently over her shoulder as she ran through an instrument check, "I can call her back up here. She's absolutely harmless."

"She's fine," Delphi said. The soldier, however…he

was a different matter. Maybe Juliette could call *him* up there, she thought with a quirk of humor.

Delphi put her hand out. The dog delicately sniffed it and then nudged Delphi's fingers with her wet muzzle. Knowing she'd been accepted, Delphi scratched the canine behind her ears, her fingers sinking into the soft, thick fur.

"She's a sweetheart, isn't she?" the man next to her said, but it was in one of those talking-to-the-dog voices.

"Do you have a dog?" he asked her. She could hear the smile in his voice.

She did not want to be charmed by this stranger, smiling voice or not. "No."

"Are you always so talkative?"

Dammit, she refused to laugh and be charmed. She'd decided that minding her own business would be the best course of action. She'd still have her old job if she'd had enough sense not to be chatty and friendly with DeWitt. "No."

Okay, time for a tactical change. Obviously monosyllable responses weren't going to shut him down or freeze him out. And he was dangerously charming.

She turned to face him…and he was right there. His eyes were the most unusual shade of brown—depths of brown but translucent at the same time, like stained glass backlit by the sun. She'd guess the fine lines bracketing those arresting eyes were compliments of duty tours in the Middle East, but it wasn't her business and it certainly wasn't the business at hand. "Okay, Sergeant, I have no idea why you feel compelled to sit right next to me, but since you seem to demand my attention, you've got it. So, go ahead. Regale me with your charm. Wow me with your life story. Obviously I'm a captive audience."

He paused for a second and then laughed. "I'm not particularly charming—" *right,* she thought "—and my life story isn't so interesting." She didn't believe he actually thought that for a hot minute. "I suppose I'm just curious as to why you're so antisocial."

"I'm not antisocial. I simply want to be left alone. It's not so difficult, is it? Wait, apparently it is for you. You certainly don't follow social niceties."

"How's that?"

"You're practically sitting in my lap when you could've chosen any one of three other seats. Because I'm a decent human being, I'm going to let you know that I suffer from motion sickness. I took medication but I've never actually traveled in an aircraft this small so there's no guarantee I'm not going to lose my lunch."

In a moment of spectacular timing, Juliette spoke to them over her right shoulder. "We've been cleared for takeoff. So, you'll need to put on your headsets." She sent a glance of inquiry Delphi's way. "You okay? You ready?"

Delphi picked up the small barf bag Juliette had provided earlier. "Ready."

Lars piped up. "Give me a second to switch seats." He moved across the aisle, rebuckled and gave Juliette the thumbs-up. "Thanks," he said to Delphi.

"No, thank *you.*" She turned her attention to the window again, closing her eyes as Juliette throttled forward. It was always better if she didn't have to watch everything whiz by.

What seemed like a short lifetime later, but was really only a matter of probably a few minutes, Delphi released her death grip on the armrests. Thank goodness for motion sickness meds.

"You okay?" Juliette asked again, her voice coming through the headset. Kind of weird, that.

"Yes, thanks. Being in the air is usually okay. It's the takeoffs and landings that get me."

Baby sat up and rested her head on Delphi's knee, gazing at her with sympathetic eyes. She had a sweet masked face. Delphi didn't know a whole lot about dogs but this one looked like a small version of what she thought of as a "sled dog."

Juliette glanced over her shoulder. "Just push her away if she's bugging you."

"She's fine," Delphi said. She could easily grow attached to this animal.

"Malamute?" Lars asked, startling Delphi. They were all tuned in to the same frequency so his voice, with its hint of gravel, sounded right in her ear.

"Husky," Juliette said. "She's my copilot. She's been flying with me ever since I got her."

Delphi swore the dog smiled at that point.

"So," Juliette said, "we can finally have a wedding now that you're here."

Delphi should be minding her own business but she had to admit her curiosity was piqued. This man was flying all the way to Alaska to get married? She wasn't quite sure why that should surprise her so much, other than the fact that she'd thought he was flirting with her earlier. Perhaps because she'd felt more than a little bit of sexual interest from him. Then again, she'd probably misread him. Honest to Pete, her judgment seemed to have thoroughly deserted her.

"Tansy's been incredibly patient. My leave's been

jerked around a couple of times," he said. It was really silly that hearing him talk about his wedding to the unknown Tansy should make her feel kind of queasy. So, he was yet another man who wanted to flirt with her while his woman waited in the wings. They all made her sick.

"So actually, planning the wedding has been a nightmare. But I'm here now. And the ball and chain ceremony is tomorrow. I'm kind of surprised she didn't decide to have it at the airstrip when the plane lands."

Ball and chain ceremony? She felt a load of sympathy for the unknown Tansy if that was how he felt about marrying her.

"My brother's been trying to get married for almost a year now," he said to Delphi in explanation.

An inexplicable sense of relief trickled through her. Ah, okay, the ball and chain comment wasn't quite as offensive and the bride-to-be was no longer a woman to be pitied, at least not based on Delphi's current knowledge.

"We're twins and I'm the best man but the military kept deciding otherwise," he continued with a grin, which caused Delphi's toes to tingle. "I think his fiancée will actually believe the wedding's on when she sees me step off the plane."

"She knows you're on board," Juliette said, saving Delphi from answering. So, he was coming for his brother's wedding. Okay.

Delphi looked out the window. Even though it was mid-May, snow still capped the mountains. The view was fantastic at this altitude. Still, she hadn't come for the scenery. What she'd craved was some solitude to get her life together and a job in her chosen profession. When Merrilee Swenson contacted her with the travel arrangements, Delphi had noticed the town tagline on the correspondence—*Good Riddance, where you get to leave behind what ails you.* That sounded very good to her.

"I brought your mother in yesterday," Juliette offered, still obviously interested in the wedding details.

"I'm sorry," Lars said, and if Delphi wasn't so determined to be engaged by the soldier, she might've smiled. Once upon a time, she would've laughed outright. However, she simply looked out the window.

"Hey, how'd you like to be my date for the wedding?" Was there no end to what would come out of the man's mouth? Now he was hitting on the pilot, knowing full well Delphi was listening in. Oh, brother.

"Hey, Blondie, I'm talking to you."

Delphi was so startled she whipped her head around. Surely, Blondie? What the...? "Are you talking to *me?*"

A snort of laughter, which Juliette quickly tried to mask with a manufactured cough, resounded through the headset.

"Of course I'm talking to you. Juliette and her husband might object. You're the only blonde on board and I forgot your name so... What do you say? Wanna be my date? It's a great way to meet everyone in town and besides, you're the only woman I've ever met who's prickly enough to deal with my mother. She scares most women to death. Hell, she scares me to death." He eyed her appraisingly across the aisle. "But you know, I think you could hold your own with Janie. So, what do you say?"

For one second she thought her head might explode. He'd answered her unspoken question. Apparently there was no limit to what he would say. She was momentarily rendered speechless. Her mind, however, raced. She was prickly enough to deal with his mother? It was small wonder the man was reduced to asking a total stranger to accompany him. She wouldn't go with him to, well, anywhere.

She glanced over at him. If she hadn't been so annoyed with him—and under different circumstances—she might have found his brash approach charming in a humorous sort of way. But it would be a tremendous mistake to give this man even a toehold because he'd just steamroller on through and that wasn't part of her plan. She decided instead on consistency and merely uttered, "No, thanks."

Juliette suffered another "coughing" paroxysm.

Delphi turned her head once again to look out the window, ready for this endless plane ride to end. And saying no was much easier when she wasn't looking into his brown eyes alight with devilishness. It was nearly impossible to maintain a vestige of gloom, much less wallow in it, in the company of such an outrageous man.

He was altogether too much.

SHE'D ALMOST DETONATED. He'd almost set her off. He had to admit that Delphi Reynolds—of course he remembered her name—had livened up the last leg of his seemingly endless journey immeasurably. Calling her Blondie had been a stroke of genius.

He had, however, kind of meant it when he'd invited her along to the wedding. He'd figured there was a fifty-fifty chance. She'd either accept as a means of calling his bluff or she'd tell him to stuff it. Her "no, thanks" had been the abbreviated version of shove-it-where-the-sun-don't-shine-buddy.

What he should want was a soft warm woman with a ready welcoming smile to take the edge off. He'd been deployed the past several months and his upcoming assignment, which was still up in the air, was sure to include hot sun and desert sand, as that was the hot-bed region now. But, in keeping with his contrary na-ture, he'd taken one look at the blonde with the spiked hair, cool demeanor and even colder dismissal…and he'd wanted her. She was a challenge. She was the un-detonated device who silently dared him to approach at his own risk.

His mother, however… He knew some shit would go down at the wedding. Seeing as how the nuptials were scheduled to commence less than twenty-four hours after they were all reunited in one spot, Lars sup-posed there was a fighting chance the caca wouldn't hit the fan until after the newlyweds rode off into the honeymoon sunset. However, the odds were against it. His mother had to be the center of attention—all day, every day—so he really didn't see her making it all the way through a wedding and reception where Liam and Tansy were the focal point. At least his younger brother, Jack, wouldn't be here to witness any "inci-dents." And he was sure there would be several.

His mother would either wig out and stomp off in a snit or suffer some medical malady. Given the num-ber of people around, he'd lay money on the illness. That was usually her M.O., not that he could do any-thing about it. He'd learned evasive maneuvers a long time ago. It all just worked out best to avoid any kind of skirmish with Janie Reinhardt.

The sound of the engines, more of a drone with the headset on, were soothing. Blondie was hell-bent on staring out the window. The dog was snoozing—definitely the right idea. He might as well catch a few winks before they landed.

Settling his head against the window, he drifted off to the engine's lullaby.

He awoke instantly, courtesy of years of training, when the pilot spoke. "We'll be landing in five minutes."

His forty-five-minute catnap had literally flown by. Righting himself, he looked outside.

Evergreens rushed by in slow motion against a backdrop of blue sky and mountains. Lars glanced across the aisle. Delphi Reynolds maintained her position, her shoulders stiff, her eyes trained on the scenery outside.

His eyes were drawn to the expanse of her neck, the graceful curve of her shoulder. When, not *if* but *when,* he got her alone, he would trace those lines with his finger and then tease his lips along the same path. Something about her struck a chord in him, resonated, drew him in. He would have her. But since he was here only for a week, sooner rather than later would be better.

Within minutes they were on the ground. "Nice landing," he said to Juliette.

"Thanks." After the plane had rolled to a stop, they all unbuckled and stood up in the cramped quarters, stretching their legs. Even though he was closest to the door, Lars hung back. He made a sweeping gesture with his hand. "Ladies first."

"Thanks." Delphi squeezed past him in the tight quarters. She smelled good. Her arm and shoulder brushed against his chest and her hip jostled his. "Sorry. Excuse me."

The effect of her touch was like being zapped with a low-voltage stun gun.

"Tomorrow," he said. "Eleven a.m. See you then."

She tossed him a glance over her shoulder. "Goodbye, Sergeant. Good riddance."

"We are indeed here," he said, deliberately misunderstanding her. She turned her back to him again. "And, Blondie—" she didn't turn around, but paused momentarily on the plane's threshold "—it's not goodbye—it's au revoir."

3

DELPHI SIDESTEPPED THE GROUP of people hotfooting it toward the plane, smiling and waving at the man behind her. She would forget about him, or at the least, ignore him, his twinkling brown eyes and charming prattle, as well as the zing of sexual awareness that had arrowed through her when she touched him. Now that they were out of the airplane's close confines, she'd go her way and he could go his.

She looked around as she walked across the expanse separating the landing strip from the office, soaking in her surroundings. She'd been so intent on getting away from where she was that she hadn't thought too hard about where she was going.

There was a freshness here that seemed more marked than Atlanta. The sky appeared bluer, the clouds punctuating it whiter. The air was cleaner. She swatted at her arm. And holy hell, the mosquitoes were bigger—much bigger.

Stepping into the airstrip office, the scent of wood, coffee and cookies greeted her even before the person at the desk did. The woman stood, a welcoming smile wreathing her face and lighting her eyes. Medium-length blondish-gray hair, blue eyes, mid-to-late fifties, pressed jeans and a flannel shirt trimmed in lace, she had to be Merrilee Swenson, the founder and town mayor. Skye had told Delphi all about Merrilee.

She took Delphi's hand in hers. "Welcome to Good Riddance, Delphi, where you get to leave behind what ails you. I'm Merrilee." Yep, she'd known it. "Skye is swamped so she couldn't be here to meet you. But we're going to get you over to the clinic right after we get you settled."

It was impossible not to smile back at this warm woman. "It's nice to meet you."

"Now, honey, I don't want you to worry, but there's been a little snag in getting your cabin ready." When they'd spoken earlier, she had told her they'd house her in a little cabin near the clinic. "You'll find that happens here and we just have to go with it. But we should have you in there by next week. In the meantime, you'll be in one of the rooms upstairs." At this point, it didn't matter to Delphi where she stayed. As long as she had a bed and could close the door on the world for a while, she'd be happy. "Right next door, through that door in fact—" she gestured to a door on the right-hand wall "—is Gus's Restaurant and Bar. We'll comp your meals until you're in your own place. We really appreciate you coming here to help us out."

Merrilee Swenson finally paused to take a breath and Delphi chuckled—really chuckled for what felt like the first time in months. "That all sounds good. I'm glad to be here." She hadn't realized just how ready she had been for a change.

Before Merrilee could respond, the back door

opened and the group she'd passed on her way out piled into the room, Lars in tow.

Merrilee beamed at him. "Lars, it's so good to see you again." She closed the gap and they exchanged a hug.

Merrilee turned to Delphi. "Let's get you introduced around."

"Everyone, this is Delphi Reynolds. Delphi's helping us out for a couple of months while we find a replacement for Nelson's replacement. And as for this motley crew…" She turned to Delphi. "Of course you've met Lars."

Delphi smiled and nodded but avoided eye contact with the disconcerting man. "Well, this is Liam, his twin." She touched the shoulder of a man who bore a striking resemblance to Lars, but wasn't as big and broad. "Liam runs a survival training camp north of here."

"I'm the older brother by five minutes," he said with a slight smile and a firm handshake.

Delphi laughed. "I see." Liam was nice but he wasn't as handsome—or sexy—as his younger-by-five-minutes brother.

Merrilee indicated the woman at Liam's side. "And this is Tansy Wellington, the bride-to-be. Tansy's a love guru."

Tansy was a petite, curvy brunette with happy eyes behind black-rimmed specs.

"Love guru?" Delphi said, intrigued.

"I write a column, a blog, and my first book just came out. I give relationship advice."

A day late and a dollar short—she could've used some of that half a year ago. *Dear Tansy, My boss is obsessed with me. Please advise.* Delphi kept her smile firmly affixed. "Wow, impressive."

"I don't know about that, but it's fun. Nice to meet you." She also had a nice, firm handshake. Handshakes said something about people, at least in Delphi's book they did.

Merrilee nodded toward a woman with shoulder-length salt-and-pepper hair and glasses. She was even shorter than Tansy. "This is the mother of the groom and my sister-in-law, Janie Reinhardt."

"It's actually Dr. Reinhardt. I'm a professor of sociology." She shook Delphi's hand as if it was a chore to make contact. "And I prefer Jane."

"Sorry," Merrilee said, "I'm just used to—"

"I know my brother insists on using that childish name."

"Nice to meet you," Delphi said. So, maybe Lars wasn't too far wrong about his mother. She certainly wasn't warm and fuzzy.

"And this is Dirk Swenson, the boys' cousin," Merrilee said, continuing the introductions. Delphi shot a quick glance at the arrogant Lars, smirking at Merrilee's designation of him as a boy. He grinned and winked at her. Really, that man… "Dirk is also Liam's second-in-command at the training camp."

While Lars and Liam weren't small by any means, Dirk stood a good two inches taller and probably outweighed Lars by thirty pounds. "Pleased to meet you."

She was beginning to sound like a parrot. There was no way she'd ever remember all of these names.

Dirk's hand engulfed Delphi's, but she noticed he was careful not to exert too much pressure. She pegged him as a gentle giant kind of guy.

"Pleased to meet you, as well," she said.

"And last, but definitely not least, is my better half, Janie...I mean, Jane's brother, and the guys' uncle, Bull Swenson."

Bull bore a striking resemblance to Jane and, to a lesser extent, Dirk. Although he stood a full head shorter than the other men in the group, it didn't matter. Bull Swenson had a presence about him. The medical professional in Delphi immediately noted the scars on his neck. They looked old and painfully gained. There was a story there.

"Hello."

Before she wrapped up the introductions, Merrilee motioned to the two older gentlemen who sat in rocking chairs across the room. They flanked a chess set. "That's Dwight Simmons on your left and Jefferson Monroe to your right."

Both men nodded in her direction. In the midst of the meet-and-greet, Delphi couldn't shake her awareness of Lars Reinhardt. It was as if a part of her attention was stuck on him. She'd done her damnedest to ignore him on the plane and now when she had all of these people tugging at her attention, a part of her was still caught up in him. He was a man who simply couldn't be ignored.

"Don't worry, honey, we're not going to quiz you on names anytime soon," Merrilee said and then chuckled. "Now let's get y'all settled upstairs. Lars is in room three and, Delphi, you're in four." Merrilee patted her hand. "You're closest to the bathroom."

"Thank you." Delphi spoke automatically but her brain remained stuck on the idea of having *him* in the room next to her. A shiver raced through her.

"And of course you're invited to the wedding," Tansy said, beaming. "The whole town will be there. Now that you're a part of Good Riddance, of course we want you to come, as well."

"Absolutely," Merrilee chimed in. "It's a great way for you to meet everyone. And it'll just plain out be fun."

Delphi didn't dare look at Lars. She didn't have to. She could feel his smirk. It was one thing to turn him down, but how did you tell a bride-to-be you didn't want to have anything to do with her big day?

She frantically searched for an excuse. It wasn't as if she could say she had another commitment. There was nothing to do here and no one to do it with, not with everyone planning to attend the nuptials.

She grabbed on to the universal female out. Smiling weakly she demurred, "I didn't pack anything suitable—"

"Pshaw." Merrilee cut her off, waving her hand as if brushing aside the matter. "You'll see a little bit of everything there. There'll be plenty of blue jeans, shorts and everything in between."

Lars spoke up. "I already invited her."

Merrilee gave a little clap. "Perfect. Now you both have an escort."

Just shoot her.

It looked as if she was going to a wedding—with Lars Reinhardt—unless she developed a headache. Although the very thought of sharing a room next to him already gave her a headache.

And, unfortunately, a bit of a thrill.

LARS CLIMBED THE STAIRS leading to the rooms above the airstrip, bringing up the rear behind Merrilee and Delphi. Blondie had a cute little butt. He'd noticed when she deplaned ahead of him and it was impossible not to notice now. Her tush was trim and cute, just like the rest of her.

She brought home to him just how long it had been since he'd enjoyed the company of a woman. Of course, it had been a damn long time since he'd been on leave, too. But it wasn't as if Delphi was simply handy and convenient. She'd tripped his trigger switch the moment he'd laid eyes on her. Instant attraction was a potent thing.

She'd pulled out the "nothing to wear" excuse but if she really hadn't wanted to go with him, she'd have invented some fictitious boyfriend back home or some other chick excuse. He'd been around enough women to know the fairer gender didn't go anywhere with a man if they really didn't want to.

Carrying Delphi's luggage—he hadn't taken no for an answer—he continued up the stairs until they turned right and traversed the short hallway.

"Here ya go, Lars." Merrilee opened the door and he walked in. Merrilee lowered her voice. "I thought you'd rest easier if you knew that we put your mother at the new bed-and-breakfast at the other end of town. We figured it might work out better that way and Alyce could use the business."

"Good call." He put down one of Delphi's suitcases and slid his duffel bag off his shoulder, dropping it on the bed.

The room was pretty much the way he remembered it sixteen—wait, it was more like seventeen or eighteen—years ago, when they'd come to visit one summer. It was old-fashioned and welcoming. Log walls, flannel and lace curtains, a braided rug against the wooden floor and a quilt thrown over the bed.

He picked up her suitcase again. "It's still nice."

Merrilee smiled. "You're a sweetie." She walked next door and he followed with the luggage. "And here you are, Delphi. I hope you find it comfortable."

"It's lovely." The expression on her face tugged at something undefined inside him, something he hadn't even known was there. It was as if she found the room comforting.

He noticed a door in the wall. Closed and locked now, it connected their rooms.

This was working out well enough. He couldn't have requested a better setup.

DELPHI PATTED HER FACE dry and quickly touched up her makeup, which was minimal anyway. She'd traded her travel clothes for a pair of casual black slacks and a nylon/spandex top. She'd probably be overdressed but she wasn't comfortable showing up at the clinic in jeans, at least not the first time.

She gazed longingly at the claw-foot tub. It practically begged for a long soak with bath salts and bubbles, her leaning against Lars's chest, nestled between his thighs, his kisses against her neck, his hands on her—

No, no and no. There, it was living proof that he was trouble. She'd met him on the plane, he'd carried up her suitcases…and she was already fantasizing about an erotic bath experience with him. She'd never experienced this kind of chemistry—the heat, the anticipation she felt around him.

Work. She needed to focus on work. She was here for R&R—résumé and reputation repair.

Gathering her stuff, she opened the bathroom door. Lars stood leaning casually against the wall outside, his shaving kit tucked under one arm. A guilty flush engulfed her face but she reassured herself he had no way of knowing she'd just been thinking about sharing some naughty tub time with him.

"Oh," she said. She felt breathless, flustered. "It's all yours."

She stepped into the dimly lit passageway and stopped when she was even with him. There was no reason in the world that she couldn't just keep moving. There was room to pass. Her bedroom was four, maybe five steps away. Her brain said go. Her body said stay.

The smoldering heat in his eyes rooted her. His warmth, his energy tugged at her like an invisible cord.

"I wasn't sure if I wanted a hot shower," he said, "or a hot meal first. The shower won out." *Would you like to scrub my back?*

"The tub is great. Well, it looks great." *I was thinking about you.*

"Sweet." His glance dropped to her lips and it was almost as if she could feel him touching her, tracing the curve of her mouth.

"You look nice," he said. His low voice slid over her like a caress.

He looked dark and sexy, with stubble shadowing his jaw and those faint lines radiating from his eyes. Her breath seemed stuck in her throat, her feet glued to the floorboards. She must be more tired than she thought to be so shaken by a compliment. She found her voice, if not the full measure of her wits. "Thanks."

He shifted slightly on his feet, pushing away from the wall. Her heart pounded against her ribs and she curled her fingers into her palm. Tension, anticipation, desire thickened the air and flowed through her. She swayed slightly.

Lars raised his hand, reaching for her. It was a measured, controlled movement that matched the look in his eyes, part question, part challenge. He had signaled his intent. Now it was her move. He gave her time to advance, retreat or stand her ground. She stood.

Her heart thunking against her ribs so hard she could swear she heard it, she awaited his touch. His nearness warmed her cheek, a precursor to the feathering of his fingers against her skin. His touch, so gentle, so light, melted her inside. Tilting her face up to his with his finger beneath her chin, Lars brushed his lips against hers in the lightest of kisses. It was so tantalizing, so sweet, so inflaming. She leaned into him and returned his gossamer kiss.

He cupped the back of her neck with his big hand as he deepened the kiss. It was tentative, yet sure, as contradictory and intriguing as the man himself.

He broke the kiss and dropped his hand back to his side. Magic seemed to enfold them, join them, in the hallway even after they were no longer touching. She felt suspended in the air, in that moment.

"Let's get a move on." A man's strident voice from downstairs pierced the air. Delphi's feet were once again firmly on the ground.

She took a step toward her room and Lars moved toward the bathroom.

"I'll catch you later," he said.

She knew how he meant it, but it held a ring of warning that what had transpired between them wasn't finished. It would be revisited…and taken further.

"Not if I can help it," she said with a breathless, only kind-of-teasing note.

Lars turned, a decidedly wicked grin quirking his lips. "Blondie, make no mistake about it. I will definitely catch you later. But I always practice catch and release."

"But what if I don't want to be caught?"

He laughed. "What if you don't want to be released?"

Arrogant. "I can't imagine that particular scenario."

He laughed once again, winked at her and closed the bathroom door.

Delphi turned on her heel and marched to her room, torn between exasperation and infatuation. She closed her bedroom door and leaned against it.

What if she didn't want to be released? That wink?

Little did he know that she'd returned his kiss to satisfy her curiosity and nothing more. Now her curiosity was satisfied, but was she? She still simply wanted to be left alone. Didn't she?

"WOULD YOU LIKE someone to walk you down to the clinic?" Merrilee asked.

"Thanks, but I'd prefer to just go at my own pace and get a feel for the town." Delphi had dropped her clothes on the bed and hurried downstairs when she heard the water running in the claw-foot tub next door. She'd put her shift away later. She didn't want to think about Lars stripping down in the next room. She didn't want to think about him naked…and if she stayed a minute longer, it would be inevitable. Actually, it was already too late—those had been the very thoughts chasing through her head as she'd hurried down the hall and stairs. Her mind had painted a picture of broad shoulders, muscular chest, a sprinkling of hair narrowing as it arrowed over a flat belly to a package that did him proud. Perhaps if she put enough distance between her and him, she could get the image out of her head. She could leave that kiss behind, as well. But she needed a few minutes in the fresh air alone to collect herself. She didn't want to have to make small talk with anyone right now.

"I understand," Merrilee said. Delphi sincerely hoped not, but Merrilee had a way of looking at you as if she could see past the facade and know what was really going on. "Out the front door and take a left. You can't miss it."

Delphi stepped out into the mild afternoon. Despite the sun, a cool breeze sifted through her hair and against her skin. She started down the sidewalk, noting that most of the vehicles driving by were older-model trucks or SUVs. She only saw one car and it was a station wagon. All of the vehicles bore a dulling coat of dust.

Skye had summed up the town as a place that met simple needs. There was no Starbucks. No dry cleaners. No car dealerships. A single street ran through the center of town, with businesses flanking either side of the unpaved roadway. A sign on the front window across the street caught her eye—Curl's Taxidermy/Barber Shop/Mortuary. Wow, talk about one-stop shopping.

She passed a shop that billed itself as a video rental/screening room/internet café. Additionally there was a dry goods store, a bank, a shop with a collection of snowmobiles and other machinery with a sign advertising small-engine repair, a hardware store and in the distance a large log building with a sign proclaiming it the community center. The newer business additions were in the opposite direction, at the other end of town.

A few minutes later, she finally arrived at the Health Center. Through the large plate-glass window, the waiting room was jam-packed. How in the world could this many people be sick in such a small place? Skye had told her that sometimes she only saw three people in a day. But now, it looked as if half the town's population was crammed into the office.

Was there an epidemic unfolding? An outbreak of sorts? She opened the door and stepped inside, a bell jangling overhead.

As if someone had pressed a mute button, the room instantly quieted. All eyes trained on Delphi. A man, his long black hair pulled back in a queue, stepped forward. This had to be Nelson, the guy starting med school. A serene smile tilted his mouth and lit his dark eyes. "Hi, I'm Nelson Sisnuket, and you must be Delphi."

"I am." They shook hands while the waiting room looked on like theatergoers enthralled in a stage production. "I'm so pleased to meet you."

"Not nearly as pleased as I am to see you. It was getting down to the wire."

A murmur rippled through the patients and then they resumed their conversations.

Delphi and Nelson walked in unison toward the desk situated next to the short hallway. It was the first medical office she'd ever been in where there was no door that closed off the hallway leading to the exam rooms and the doctor's office.

"Bull's installing a door next week," he said.

"Oh, okay." Either she was incredibly transparent or Nelson was a little psychic. It was kind of freaky.

"I saw you looking at the hallway," he said with a smile. "Skye's been waiting for you, but she just couldn't get away."

Delphi glanced around the crowded waiting room. "No kidding. I take it this isn't typical."

"It's because I'm only here until next week. Change, even good change, throws people off. How about the quick tour while Skye finishes up with Norris?"

"Sure. Sounds good to me."

Two exam rooms, a supply closet, a bathroom and Skye's office comprised the back. The equipment and furniture were obviously dated. Delphi heard the murmur of Skye's voice from behind the closed exam room door.

"Want to wait in here or would you rather go back up front? I need to get back to it."

"How about I wait in here and then I'll join you up front after I see Skye."

"That works."

The room looked as if it had been furnished with military salvage furniture from World War II. She sat in a barrel-backed wooden chair and waited. It was rather nice to be back in a medical office, even one that had taken a step back in time. Back in a familiar environment, her mind drifted.

Lars. The smoky look in his eyes, his taste, his touch. The thought of him climbing into that claw-foot tub naked, her scrubbing his back, him pulling her in with him, clothes and all…

She tried redirecting her thoughts, but he kept inserting himself in them. He was handsome and sexy in a worn, rugged way. The kind of guy her dad would call a man's man, which fit with his marine background.

Mercifully Skye opened the door and entered the office, dispelling all fantasies of Lars. Other than sporadic email updates, they hadn't seen each other in several years. They exchanged a quick hug.

"You look fantastic!" Delphi said, stepping back and taking a good look at her friend. And Skye did. Her long red curly hair, which had almost always been straightened and subdued into a fairly severe chignon, was now pulled back into a simple ponytail at the nape of her neck, allowing tendrils to curl around her face. But her sparkling eyes were the most telling. Obviously Good Riddance and/or being married agreed with her.

"Thanks. I like it here. Actually, I love it here. I'm happy doing what I'm doing and my husband is beyond wonderful, so no complaints." That answered that—it was a combination of man and place.

Skye studied Delphi. "Your hair looks great. When did you cut it?"

"When I accepted your offer."

"It looks good. You look good." Voices sounded in the hall outside. Nelson was obviously bringing back another patient. "How was the trip?"

"Long but uneventful." Well, that wasn't exactly true. Lars was an event. "No problems." Even if he was a bit of a problem to her peace of mind.

"Don't let the crowd in the waiting room scare you. Everybody is here because Nelson's leaving. And I'd better get back to it or we're never going to get out of here today. Do you want to spend about forty-five minutes with Nelson going over how things are organized and then get settled in at the bed-and-breakfast? And how about dinner at our house tonight? We'll get takeout at Gus's—that's the restaurant attached to the airstrip. It's the only restaurant in town. I'd make something, but I don't cook on a good day—" she waved toward the waiting room "—and this isn't a particularly good day. We can eat there but people will be curious about you and I know you have to be tired. Besides, I'd really like for you to see our house."

"That sounds good. I can't wait to see your place."

"Dalton and I will drop by for you around 6:45, if that's okay."

"Perfect. I'm looking forward to meeting him."

"I'm glad you're here."

Once again, Lars flashed through her brain. "So am I."

And oddly enough, she was.

4

DIRK SWENSON SAT at the bar in Gus's, nursing a beer. He'd begged off going somewhere—he didn't even know what they were going to do—with Bull, Tansy, Liam and Aunt Janie. Aunt Janie rubbed him the wrong way, but then again, she rubbed most people the wrong way.

Lars was upstairs next door, settling in. It was good to see him. Dirk hadn't realized just how much he'd missed his cousin. Sure enough Dirk worked with Liam every day and you'd figure with Liam and Lars being twins, one would do as well as the other, but it wasn't the same. He respected both of his cousins, but Lars had always been warmer and more accessible. In Dirk's mind, he'd been more of a brother than simply a cousin. And it'd been too damn long since he'd seen him.

Dirk figured he might as well drown his sorrows in a beer, although it would take more than one to drown anything.

Outside the sun was shining. Inside the room was buzzing with excitement over tomorrow's wedding, some upbeat tune was playing on the jukebox and Dirk was one miserable son of a bitch. He'd tried, really tried, to get Liam's ex-wife, Natalie, out of his head and he couldn't. It was all so mixed up he didn't see how it could ever all be sorted out.

He'd grown up next door to Natalie. Hell, he'd been in love with her for as long as he could remember. And he'd never had the nerve to tell her. He'd always been huge compared to the other guys, his grades had left something to be desired and he was kind of shy around girls, especially Natalie. Still, it had been a terrible moment when he found out she was going to marry his cousin Liam. He'd been pissed at Liam for years, especially when they divorced.

He and Liam had covered it—after Dirk punched Liam in the face—and it was okay now. Liam hadn't mistreated Natalie or been unfaithful. They'd just wanted different things.

Dirk was working with Liam now as the second-in-command at the survival training camp. The camp was primarily accessible by air. So, he not only worked with Liam, he lived a stone's throw from Liam and Tansy.

Dirk had tried a lot of different things but hadn't stuck with any of them for very long. He'd done construction work, truck driving, house painting and had even worked in the oil fields. Finally, for the first time in his life, he felt as if he'd found his place and actually had a purpose. Only he was still in a stew over Natalie.

Dirk polished off his beer and stood, feeling a sense of resolve in the middle of all of his confusion. He knew one thing he could do that he hadn't been able to do before—talk about it.

He pushed through the connecting door to the airfield office, passing one of Gus's waitresses as she came back into the restaurant. Merrilee looked up from where she was filling out paperwork at her desk. "Hey, Dirk. What can I do you for?"

He liked Bull's old lady. She was nice. "Lars upstairs?"

She also had a nice smile. "He sure is. Room three." She grabbed a take-out box from the corner of her desk. "His meal just came. Would you mind taking it up with you?"

"Sure thing."

Dirk climbed the stairs and knocked on the door of room three. Nothing. Then he heard whistling in the bathroom. That was definitely Lars's whistle.

Dirk opened the bedroom door and went in, closing it behind him. He'd wait. Once he made up his mind about something, that was it. He just wished it didn't take so damn long sometimes to make up his mind.

He placed the food on the nightstand. Hell, he might as well relax until Lars finished up in the john. Dirk stretched out diagonally on the blanket. He fit better that way and his boots weren't on the bed. He'd almost drifted off to la-la land when the door opened.

Lars, wearing jeans and a T-shirt, pulled up short. "What the hell? Well, hey, Big D, make yourself at home."

"Just checking out the bed for you." Dirk grinned as he sat up. "It's comfy."

"Well, that's good news." Lars closed the door behind him and dropped his dirty laundry over in a corner.

"I delivered your chow for you."

"That's even better news." He grabbed the foam box off the nightstand. "So, what's up?"

Dirk leaned forward, bracing his forearms on his knees. "I thought I might talk to you for a few minutes." Lars was usually easy to talk to. Liam was so dead-ass serious about everything.

Lars swallowed and paused between bites. "Uh, sure thing. What's on your mind?"

"Natalie." Dirk didn't see a whole lot of point in pussyfooting around the subject.

"Natalie who?" Lars asked around a mouthful of stew.

"Do we both know more than one? Natalie Reinhardt." He'd learned that she hadn't changed her name when she and Liam had split.

"Liam's ex?" Dirk nodded and Lars looked surprised. Liam must've not mentioned the whole thing to Lars, which suited Dirk just fine. Liam was a man who knew how to keep his mouth shut. "Okay, what about her?"

"Well, I'm not sure what to do." Lars listened attentively while Dirk filled him in. "So, how do I get over her?"

Lars placed the now-empty container on the nightstand and propped against the wall. "You've dated other chicks, right?"

"Some." There'd only been a handful.

"And that didn't work out for you?"

They'd all been a total wash. "If it had, I wouldn't be sitting here bellyaching now."

"Then maybe you need to be figuring out how to *get* her instead of *get over* her. Hell, you've never even kissed her." Lars shook his head as if Dirk was a lost cause. "You might sleep with her and find out she doesn't really float your boat."

Dirk stood, curling his right hand into a fist. He liked Lars, so the guy at least deserved some warning. But he needed to understand when enough was enough. "Be mindful that you're respectful when you talk about her."

"Easy there, Big Guy." Lars gestured for him to calm down. "There's not a damn thing disrespectful about sex. I like Natalie so let's just get it straight that I haven't and I wouldn't disrespect her."

Dirk relaxed his fist. "Okay. It's just, you know…" He trailed off.

Lars shrugged. "No, I can't say that I do. I haven't carried a torch like that."

"What about Denise Palmer?" It had been no secret that Lars had been crazy about Denise and he'd been pretty torn up when she'd broken up with him.

"I got over her and learned my lesson. But I'm damn sure not still carrying anything for her. But then, I don't really understand why Liam has to marry Tansy." He shook his head and shrugged again. "But I don't have to get it. All I can tell you is if you're going to be miserable without her, you better figure out how not to be without her."

Dirk sank back onto the mattress and once again rested his arms on his outspread knees and studied the floor. "Well, I don't know how that's going to work out. I like my job with Liam and I'm here and she's there—"

Lars cut him off. "So, invite her here."

Dirk looked up. He hadn't expected that. "Don't you think it would be awkward, considering she and Liam were married once and now Liam's going to have a new wife?"

Lars grinned. "There's only one way to find out.

Ask her and see what happens. It's not as if she and Liam parted on bad terms."

"What if she says no?" The thought of it tied Dirk's guts in a knot.

"Why would she?"

Lars made it sound so simple. "Why wouldn't she? And what if she's only coming because she wants to see Liam again and check out Tansy?"

"Liam hasn't exactly been in hiding. If she'd wanted to see him again, she'd have shown up sometime in the last year."

That was true enough. It was time to lay out on the table what was really eating at him. "What if she comes and she doesn't, you know, like me?"

"Then that's the way it rolls. But at least you'll know. It's a chance you have to take. And you know, there's an equal chance she will like you."

"But I'm not like Liam. I'm big and rough around the edges." He laughed and shrugged self-consciously. "I've never accomplished much of anything."

Lars thought about it for a few seconds and then spoke. "You know you are what you are, Big D. But I don't see how you can say you haven't accomplished anything. You support yourself and you do what you want to do. There's not a damn thing wrong with that. And as for you not being Liam… Well, that's probably a damn good thing 'cause that didn't exactly work out for either of them."

Dirk had never looked at it that way. Feeling better than he had in a long time, he got up. Maybe he did stand a chance with Natalie after all.

LARS HAD JUST finished putting away his gear when a knock sounded on his door. Liam had said he'd come up in a few minutes. They'd, of course, seen one another all evening during the rehearsal and rehearsal dinner afterward but there hadn't been any time for them to just hang out with one another. Now it was time to connect with his brother.

He opened the door and Liam stood in the hall, two longnecks in his hand.

"Thanks," Lars said, grabbing one of the beers as he stood aside for Liam to enter.

"Thought you might be ready for a cold one before the bachelor party starts."

The bachelor party consisted of a get-together downstairs at Gus's to shoot pool and throw darts in about an hour. Gus's had also been the site of the rehearsal dinner earlier tonight. The place reminded Lars of the base rec room.

"You thought right." He hoisted the bottle in Liam's general direction. "Here's to ya."

Liam grinned and returned the gesture. "Here's to you."

They'd been doing that since they were kids. Lars took a long pull of the barley pop. It was smooth and cool going down.

"So, what do you think of Tansy?" Liam asked, settling on the bed and propping up against the headboard. You'd think it was his room.

Lars pulled out the straight-back chair, turned it around and straddled it.

"I like her. She's classy and spunky." Lars grinned. "She'll keep your ass in line." It would've been impossible for him to lie to his brother about something so important so he was relieved he honestly liked the little brunette.

"Yep, she is and she does."

Liam was happy, and for a kind of serious dude, that wasn't said lightly. Lars had never seen his brother like this. He could "feel" his brother's joy.

"It's all good, then," Lars said. "It sounds like your business is rocking. When I checked out your website, hell, I wanted to sign up for a week."

Liam laughed. "No need. You're still living it. How's work going?"

Lars filled him in on the job-related stuff that couldn't be discussed via email. And neither one of them was big on video chat.

They'd emailed, talked on the phone a couple of times, but this was something that had needed to wait until they were face-to-face. To be a marine was all either of them had ever wanted. Liam had married when it was something Lars had no interest in but they'd both always been marines at their core. Liam's discharge had been the first time Lars couldn't really relate to what was going on with his twin. Now was the time to talk.

"You miss it?" Lars asked. There was no need to define "it."

Liam shook his head. "At first I did, but now…no, man. I've adjusted. In fact, now that some time has passed, I'd say it's the best thing that could've happened to me. Life goes on and you can go on with it or not. I like running the survival camp. Every group that comes through presents a new challenge. Dirk's doing a damn fine job as my second-in-command. And, of course, Tansy's great." He took a swig from his bottle. "You sound as if you're still happy in the corp."

Lars felt temporarily disappointed. That was it? Apparently so if they were back to talking about him. And why wouldn't Lars still be happy in the Marines?

"I am." Still, he felt better about Liam now. "I've just been concerned about you."

"I'm not going to lie." Liam shook his head. "I was madder than hell when I showed up here. Bull helped me through a lot of it and so did Tansy. Tansy's the one who came up with the idea of putting together survival camp." Liam had told him that before. "She wasn't about to let me wallow in anything."

"No, she doesn't strike me as the type that would." Lars broached the next topic even more cautiously than the first. It, too, was one of those things you had to discuss man-to-man. "And speaking of Tansy… Don't get me wrong, she seems like a great gal. But marriage? I mean, you tried that once before and it didn't exactly work out. If it was anyone other than you, I'd keep my mouth shut but…"

"We've always had a different attitude about women. You know that crap with you and Denise went down a long time ago. You've got to let it go."

He didn't know what Liam was thinking, but if he thought Lars was still holding on to the pain he'd felt when Denise dumped him…uh, no, not by a long shot. "I have let it go. I let it go back in the day years ago. But I won't make the same mistake again." And he didn't want to talk about himself. This was about Liam. "You look happy and content. I guess I didn't expect to find you this way."

"Yeah? You thought I'd be miserable right before I got married?" Good thing he knew Liam, because his brother didn't crack a smile.

Lars shrugged.

"You should've seen my sorry ass when I first showed up here. That's probably the guy you were expecting to find."

"I'm just as glad I missed that part. You gonna be able to handle those dark winters here?" That would be Lars's undoing.

"It'll make it interesting. I've already got bookings for the 'extreme survival trip' in dark, cold conditions. I've been working with a guy you need to meet before you leave. His name is Clint Sinuket. He's a trail guide and a wilderness expert. I've learned a lot from him. He's out on a trip right now, but you should run into him sometime in the next week."

"Sure thing. I'll look him up."

Liam continued. "This is what I figured out. When I was in the military, it was great and it totally defined me. By God, I was a Marine sharpshooter. Nuff said. But after losing all of that…I had to dig deep and figure who and what I was beyond the military. I found out there's a whole lot more to me and a whole lot more out in the world."

That was all good. Whatever Liam needed to do to work through his discharge, Lars was all for it. "You're different. I'll give you that."

Luckily for Lars, he didn't need to go through all of that. He knew exactly who he was and what he was…. He was a marine and it was enough.

"And as for marriage…" Liam shot him a level look. "Some of the best advice I'd ever heard came from Bull. He said that when you find a good woman, you hold on to her."

Something twisted and shifted inside Lars and it wasn't a particularly comfortable feeling. An image of

Delphi flashed through his thoughts. Liam was getting way too intense for Lars. Time to lighten things up. "I do, all night long."

"Okay, Ace." Liam laughed. "I'm just going to sit back and watch because your time is coming."

It was a helluva time for Delphi to come to mind again.

"It's beautiful," Delphi said to Skye and Dalton as she stood in their home and looked around. The open floor plan boasted pale wood floors, linen-tinted walls and an off-white leather sectional with a companion recliner. It could've been boring but it wasn't. The varying shades of off-white were soothing. Framed prints on the wall provided the room's color. Delphi walked over for a closer look. "These are fantastic."

"It's a hobby," Dalton said with his ready grin. It had taken all of two minutes for Delphi to see just how perfect Dalton and Skye were together. Skye's somewhat brash husband had loosened her up. Delphi had always liked Skye and gotten along well with her, but the other woman had been buttoned up tight, compliments of an overachieving family with impossibly high expectations. Good Riddance and Dalton had been the best things in the world for her friend.

"If you ladies will excuse me, I've got a project I need to check on out back and I'll leave you two to gossip…uh, I mean, catch up before dinner." He dropped a casual kiss on the top of Skye's head and headed for the back door with a spring in his step. The simple exchange filled Delphi with a longing for the same thing. She thought of the kiss she'd shared with Lars. He, too, was brash. However, while Dalton was cute, Lars was dangerously sexy.

"He's a nice guy," Delphi said to Skye as the door closed behind Dalton.

Skye plugged in an electric kettle for tea.

"He's a thorough pain sometimes," Skye said, while her indulgent smile and sparkling eyes proclaimed her thoroughly smitten, "but he is wonderful. I thought he was the most obnoxious man on the planet when I first met him."

"How's that?" Lars again popped into the front of her mind, which made him doubly annoying—she couldn't totally put him out of her mind.

"Green tea?"

"Sounds good to me."

"He was arrogant," Skye continued as she prepared the cups, "and bold, and personal boundaries…forget it." Yes, yes and yes. Skye smiled. "And too sexy for words."

Double yes. Skye could've been talking about Lars. Delphi pushed aside the thought. "Well, that certainly turned around for you, didn't it?"

Skye laughed. "Dalton can be pretty persuasive, kind of like a steamroller. And, of course, he had the hot factor in spades."

Delphi could certainly relate to all of that. "How does he get along with your parents?"

"Believe it or not, they like him." Skye laughed as she poured the hot water. "I know my parents are snobs." Oops, Delphi's thoughts must've been showing on her face. "They didn't take to him at first but they came around pretty quickly. How'd your parents handle you coming here?"

She and Skye had joked a couple of times that if their respective parents could be blended to meet somewhere in the middle, they'd be the perfect parental unit. Skye's mom and dad were neurosurgeons who'd looked down on their daughter being a lowly general practitioner. On the other hand, Delphi's folks were blue-collar all the way and were constantly cautioning her not to "get above her raising." Her redneck familial roots ran deep. "I never told them about the whole thing with DeWitt. It would've been a disaster."

"Your daddy would've wanted to settle it with a double-barrel."

"You got that right. So they think I've come here to experience the splendors of the Alaskan wilderness instead. They vaguely approve of the idea because they've seen all those reality TV shows about the truck drivers on ice and the one about the Alaskan town. Daddy said at least I was coming to a place where there are 'real people,' which is kind of ironic considering he's basing that on scripted television, but whatever."

"Well, you've come to the right place. You've left all of that behind for a while and you can regroup here. But you do need to be prepared for the onslaught of men that will come calling. Make no mistake, age won't matter. They'll beat down your door—all shapes, sizes and age, once they know you're available. Trust me. You won't know a moment's peace until you've told each of them no innumerable times. At the clinic, we'll have a rush of men once you start, simply because you're new, pretty and single."

"You're kidding."

"Nope. Expect to deal with feigned illnesses from

men from twenty to eighty-six so they can check you out and ask you out. It's just as well you'll be at the bed-and-breakfast for the first week or so. That'll keep them from peering in the windows."

Skye passed her the cup filled with steeping tea. "What?"

"The first time Dalton and I were, you know, getting intimate, I looked up and a would-be suitor was looking through the window. It scared the life out of me."

Delphi laughed. Skye had always been so reserved and the idea… Oh, my goodness. "You didn't mention that when you were telling me about this place."

"I'd really sort of forgotten about it. It was when I first got here. Men were lining up until Dalton was kind enough to sacrifice himself by pretending we were together." She rolled her eyes. "One thing led to another and pretty soon we weren't pretending."

"Which is when the man looked through the window?" Delphi pulled out the tea bag.

"Exactly. And then he killed and dressed out a moose and had it delivered to Dalton as remuneration for poaching."

Delphi had never, ever actually heard anyone use the term *remuneration* in a sentence. "Fantastic," she said regarding the moose payment.

"You'll see soon enough."

"About going to the wedding tomorrow—"

"It's great timing. It'll be fun. Liam is Merrilee and Bull's nephew and with Merrilee the town founder and mayor, well, they're the version of Good Riddance royalty. Everyone will be there."

"All I have is a very casual dress."

"That's all you need. You can meet everyone and

you'll see dishes there you never imagined—moose stew, caribou jerky, smoked halibut. You must be exhausted with the travel and the time change. I'll run you back into town after dinner so you can get some rest. Tomorrow's going to be another big day for you."

Apparently it would be. Because apparently Delphi was going to a wedding.

5

DELPHI SHIFTED ON the wood pew to get a better look around.

It was the oddest thing to be sitting at a wedding of people she'd only just met, surrounded by people she mostly didn't know. She'd been given accurate information—there was a wide range of dress attire, from jeans and T-shirts to formal dresses and coat and tie. It was, however, all lovely.

The nondenominational church was very simple. No stained glass graced the windows. The pews, obviously hand-hewn, boasted clean lines. The gleaming wood floors were dirt-free but worn, complimenting the white-washed walls. There was no choir loft or ornamentation. A plain wooden pulpit stood in the front of the room. To its right sat a highly polished ebony Steinway baby grand piano.

She leaned in close to Skye and murmured, "A baby grand? Really?"

"It's beautiful, isn't it? It was donated by a wealthy tourist who spent last summer fishing here. He also foots the bill on having a piano tuner flown out every three months to keep it sounding perfect."

"Wow."

"I know. But it gets a lot of use. Jefferson gives free piano lessons on Tuesday nights."

The piano should have looked incongruous. Instead it flowed beautifully with the room's simplicity. It was as if everything else was deliberately void of ornamentation to showcase the instrument's elegance.

The room imparted a soothing tranquillity, which had been absent from so many of the churches Delphi had been in over the years. A spirit of peace prevailed.

Two pillar candles at the front, flanking boughs of evergreens, carried the theme of simplicity. Delphi caught the occasional scent of jasmine. Above the quiet murmur of voices in the church, the sound of birdsong drifted through the windows, carried on the breeze that ruffled through the room.

A well-dressed man whom she recognized as one of the older gentlemen playing chess in the airstrip office yesterday made his way to the piano and sat down.

Skye leaned over and whispered in Delphi's ear. "Jefferson is a former jazz player. His instrument of choice is the saxophone but he plays the piano and cello, as well."

Good Riddance certainly had an interesting array of people. He glanced over his shoulder and smiled at everyone. The room quieted. Outside, however, the birds were impervious and continued their own songs.

Flexing his fingers, Jefferson ran through a series of notes or chords or whatever—Delphi was piano illiterate—in what was obviously a warm-up. He segued into the song known to Delphi as a tune she'd heard numerous times at her gran's. In her head she could hear Sinatra crooning about fairy tales coming true as he sang "Young at Heart."

And in the back of her mind, ever since they'd shown up at the church, she'd been wondering and waiting to see Lars. She'd heard him moving about in his room last night and this morning but rather incredibly, considering their rooms were right next to one another and given the size of the town, they hadn't bumped into one another. She'd heard him but hadn't seen him since yesterday evening's kiss.

Beside her, Skye whispered, "Aw, that's sweet. Tansy's book is about finding your fairy tale romance."

"Appropriate." Delphi thought it was a nice sentiment, but thus far the fairy tale that had transpired in her life was more along the lines of the Brothers Grimm.

A very colorful, to put it politely, woman with bright red hair, turquoise eye shadow and melon-colored lipstick walked up the front. She wore a vintage pink satin evening gown and matching turban with bedraggled pink and orange feathers adorning the turban's front. Settling one hand on the piano, she faced the group and smiled. She was missing a few teeth and was seventy if she was a day.

"Alberta is a gypsy queen, fortune-teller and matchmaker," Skye offered in a whisper.

No teasing smile or twinkle in Skye's eyes indicated she was anything but serious. Delphi nodded. Alberta looked like a gypsy queen.

A woman with steel-gray hair and a severe gray dress replaced Jefferson at the Steinway. After retrieving a saxophone, he positioned himself to the left of the piano.

The ensemble waited while a thin man with owlish glasses followed by Liam and Lars Reinhardt walked to the front and took up the customary wedding places. Skye had told her earlier that Mack Darcy officiated at most of the funerals and weddings.

Mack, Liam and Lars faced the congregation. Delphi's heart began to race and her breath seemed trapped somewhere in her chest. Lars quite literally stole her breath. She'd thought he was handsome before but in his dress blues...

Mr. Darcy motioned for everyone to stand. The musicians began playing and thanks once again to her gran, Delphi recognized the opening notes of "It Had to Be You" even before the gypsy queen clad in pink satin began to sing.

Delphi fought against her mouth gaping open. Nothing had ever been more unexpected than the slightly husky, smooth notes coming from Alberta's orange-hued mouth.

An extremely well-endowed blonde wearing a light blue silk shantung tea-length sheath preceded the bride and her father. Tansy seemed to float along in a wedding gown that was tiers of tulle and organza and a veil that trailed down her back. She carried a simple bouquet of blue flowers tied with a flowing white ribbon. Delphi was pretty sure the flowers were forget-me-nots. She recognized it as the state flower from reading online about Alaska. They were delicate and it was a great sentiment for a wedding.

Even though she was still on her father's arm, Tansy

and Liam only had eyes for one another as the song continued.

Despite herself, Delphi's gaze was drawn to Lars. He was looking at her. It was as if everyone in the church faded to nothing and it was just the two of them watching one another across the room.

A torrent of attraction engulfed Delphi. The moments spun out like a magical spell—the saxophone, the words, the man.

The song ended and she shook her head slightly to clear it. She brought her attention back to where it should be instead of making goo-goo eyes at a man she was starting to want so much, but wasn't sure she actually liked. It all made her feel rather crazy.

Of course, it was no more surreal than being caught up in one of the biggest occasions in the lives of people she didn't know. Why not find herself enthralled with a man she didn't want to be enthralled with?

Tansy's father handed her over. The busty matron of honor wept openly, but it was obviously tears of joy. The exchange of vows was brief and simple, yet sincere. At one point, Delphi blinked back a tear or two. The devotion on the bride's and groom's faces moved her. It was a glimpse of something precious and pure, but real.

Delphi had never been one to sit around dreaming about her wedding day. She knew plenty of women who had the dress and ring picked out long before an actual groom showed up on the scene. She'd never quite understood it. She'd been so focused on her career and establishing her own path that marriage had been put on the back burner…and it still was there.

However, this wedding struck her as what a wedding

should be—a public vow of devotion, a sharing of their mutual love with friends and family…and a stranger.

Mr. Darcy declared them married and the room erupted into clapping and even a whistle or two. Liam kissed Tansy and once again, Delphi couldn't keep her glance from straying to Lars. Delphi felt as if she was falling down the proverbial rabbit hole.

A few more people made their way to the front, picked up instruments and gathered in front of the couple. The musicians broke into a rousing rendition of "When the Saints Come Marching In" as they made their way down the aisle, followed by the couple. Everyone stood and began dancing. After a moment's hesitation, Delphi joined in. It was the strangest music choice, particularly for a wedding, but it was fun.

She realized as she danced along with the crowd into the dazzling sunshine that she'd forgotten all about being miserable.

THE RECEPTION WAS just cranking up when he saw Delphi sashay through the community center door with her posse. She and the town doc were tight and there were a couple of other women and men with them. He'd been watching for her to arrive, waiting. She was rocking a green-and-white sundress, or more accurately, she was rocking him.

She saw him, too. For a second their gazes were enmeshed, just like earlier at the church, then she looked away. He pushed away from the wall and crossed the room, through the people who thronged in the center. He could swear the whole town had shown up for the reception.

And he wasn't the only one approaching Delphi with

intent. There was one guy incoming at 0500 and another one at 0900. He cut hard to the right, maneuvering past a small group in his way. He was damn near neck and neck with the enemy approaching from the 0500 position. He made a tactical split decision and zigged, forcing the other guy to zag. That zag put Lars's opposing force behind a group of older Native ladies. As to the incoming from 0900, that guy was simply too slow.

Lars reached Delphi first, just as her posse scattered. She obviously had no idea she'd been the target of the two other maneuvers.

"Hi, Blondie."

Over her shoulder he saw the other guy retreat… for now.

A small smile curved her lips. "Hello, Marine. Nice wedding."

"I suppose." The best thing about it had been the brevity. And his brother and Tansy had looked pretty happy about getting hitched. "Better Liam than me."

"I'm sure the bride thinks so, as well," she said with a smart-ass smile.

"Undoubtedly." He grinned. "That makes it a win-win all the way around."

"I take it you're not big on marriage."

"Actually, I'm allergic."

"Allergies can be debilitating," she said. She smelled good. He wished they were alone. He would see if that spot on the side of her neck was as sweet as he imagined it would be, as sweet as her lips had been. "You should seek help for that."

"I have. I steer clear. Avoidance is the safest course of action. For a woman with nothing to wear, you look…nice." He leaned in closer, putting his lips next to her ear, her shoulder brushing against his. He murmured for her ears only, "Although that dress is slightly wicked and leads to not entirely nice thoughts."

Even though it wasn't overtly sexy, the top hugged her breasts and followed the lean line of her body to the curve of her hips. The green and white was cool, like spring grass, but it made him think of heat and the tantalizing parts that lay beneath the innocuous fabric.

She turned her head and spoke softly in his ear. Her breath against his skin sent a shiver through him, tightening parts and hardening others. "Does that line usually work for you?" she said.

A couple jostled them as they passed, and she was momentarily pushed against him. He caught her…and held on. "I don't know—I've never used it before. Is it working?"

She smiled as she slipped out of his grasp. "How easily they forget," she murmured. She said to him, "Remember? I'm immune."

"Is that so?" He'd be just as happy to skip the former boyfriend bashing, just like he had no interest in divulging his relationship history. He kept it light and flirtatious. "But then new strains come along and are resistant. Defenses, antibiotics, vaccinations, none of those work." He nodded toward the crush of people dancing in the middle of the room. "We should dance. If you continue to stand this close to me, people are going to talk."

Of course, he didn't give a rat's ass what anyone thought but teasing her and flirting with her was fun. And dancing was a good excuse to hold her close.

"Worried about your reputation, Sergeant?"

"I do have to consider it."

"Morally compromised?"

He laughed. "Always." He formally bowed from the waist and held out his hand. "Shall we?"

"Why am I sure I'm going to regret this?" Nonetheless she placed her hand in his.

He took her into his arms and swung her out onto the dance floor. She felt good and right next to him. "You know moral compromise is highly contagious."

She tilted her head back to look up at him, her eyes alight with challenge and humor. "I told you I have a strong immune system."

He simply smiled. Not only was he well versed in mounting the offensive, he thrived on it.

And last night's reconnaissance kiss had sealed it for both of them. For the next six days, she was his primary objective.

NELSON WAS THE DJ of the evening. Apparently Tansy had a thing for nostalgic music, since "All of Me" was playing. Delphi laughed with exhilaration as Lars expertly twirled her around the dance floor. She'd never danced to this kind of music and she'd never been with a partner who possessed his skill level. He was a man of surprises.

Slightly breathless from the exertion and the man himself, she said, "Where'd you learn to dance like this?"

"I took lessons in high school. I like to dance."

It was different, that was for sure, but then he was pretty darn different. He excelled at ballroom dance, and he detonated bombs, and he kissed like heaven. "You're good at it."

"I'm good at lots of things."

Even his slight smirk held an element of charm. "Is that a fact or an opinion?"

"Some of both."

"I'll take your word for it."

"I could show you my certificates."

"Oh, you're certified. Impressive."

"I don't carry them around with me so I guess I'll just have to let you decide for yourself."

"That's okay. I'll take your word for it."

"Ah. So you trust me." The music segued into a slower number. He pulled her closer against him.

She gave a carefree laugh. "Hardly." And the beauty of it was that whatever went on between them didn't require any degree of trust.

"I'm wounded."

Right. And she was the Queen of England. She giggled. His lighthearted flirtation was impossible to resist. And the press of her breasts against his chest went a long way in fixing everything, except the sensual ache that was growing more and more intense.

"Don't take it personally," she tossed back at him, in the same lighthearted flirtatious vein.

"Does that mean you don't trust anyone?" He dipped her, his arm strong and sure behind her back, his left hand firm on her waist while his other hand clasped hers. Within seconds he'd righted her. It had all happened so quickly and been rather thrilling.

"A select few."

"Ah. Cautious." He rested his chin against her hair, tucking her in against him. She felt simultaneously secure and vulnerable, which was as unsettling as the thud of his heart against hers.

"Hard-won lessons."

"I understand."

She doubted it, but who was she to argue? "If you say so."

He pulled back to peer down at her, a smile crinkling the corners of his eyes. "You're a difficult woman to have a conversation with."

"I am? You seem to have plenty to say." She was only half teasing him. The man never seemed at a loss for words.

"Case in point. I have to do all the talking."

"That's easy enough." She leaned back and looked up at him. "Find another conversational partner." The minute the words left her mouth, she knew it wasn't what she really wanted.

"Ah, but I don't want to have a conversation with someone else. I want to talk to you."

"And you want to talk to me why?"

"You intrigue me."

She laughed. "No, I don't."

His expression said she'd caught him by surprise. "Hmm. Then why do you think I want to be with you?"

"You only want to talk to me because I'm not interested. I'm not wowed by your good looks or your charm." Well, they both knew that wasn't the absolute truth.

"You're not? Damn."

"I told you I was immune."

"So, let's talk. Then we'll see whether I'm still interested. Either way you're only out a few hours, right?"

"Hmm." She was shamelessly teasing him by pretending to think about it.

"Given how talkative you are, I think you just said,

'You're right, Lars. I think that's a spectacular experiment. Let's give it a try.'"

All her resolve and good sense seemed to flee in the face of the fun she was having. She laughed at him.

Delphi didn't know who was more foolish—him with his disarming charm, or her for being so unwillingly but easily disarmed.

DELPHI HADN'T EXPECTED to have so much fun. She'd anticipated staying just long enough to make a decent appearance and then head back to her room. Instead she'd been dancing, eating cake, drinking punch and meeting so many people her head was spinning. She'd never remember all their names.

And the entire time she'd been aware of Lars Reinhardt's exact location. Most of the time he'd been at her side. And when he wasn't with her, he'd catch her eye across the room. He was attentive, she'd give him that, and actually it had worked out fairly well that she'd been his "date." The last thing she needed or wanted was the local single men jockeying for her attention. She didn't want even a hint of scandal associated with her in this new position.

The men and women had been divided on opposite sides of the room. All the single men gathered in one spot. It didn't escape Tansy's notice that Lars positioned himself with the married group, the same as Delphi stood on the fringe of all the married women. The crowd counted in unison, "One...two...three...."

Facing the women, Liam tossed the garter over his shoulder into the crowd of single guys. Curl caught it. A cacophony of catcalls and whistles and a few good-natured rumblings from the men accompanied the catch.

Tansy faced the men across the room. Once again there was the communal countdown and Tansy threw the bouquet high and wide. A woman with a long dark braid down her back who looked distinctly Inuit caught the flowers. The room really broke into cheering then.

"This should be interesting."

Delphi glanced beside and slightly behind her. It was Alberta, the woman in the pink satin and turban. "That's Luellen Sisnuket, Nelson and Clint's cousin. She and Curl have been an on-again, off-again item for a while now. I've got a feeling they're about to be permanently on."

Delphi laughed. "They're in trouble now."

6

It HAD STARTED out as a glimmer and then blossomed into a smile, which gave way to laughter. It was a bit like watching the sun emerge over the horizon in the morning.

"Okay, so I'll *pretend* I'm interested in talking to you."

"Blondie, I'm not sure if I can handle all this ego-stroking," he said, leading them off of the dance floor.

"Marine, I'm so sure your ego is just fine."

Here they were in the midst of a small mob and he wanted to kiss her again. In fact, he was starting to feel a little desperate with the need. He was, however, sure that would reverse all the progress he'd made with Delphi.

"Would you like something to—"

Before he could finish his sentence, the music ended and the DJ spoke into the microphone. "If I can have your attention, Liam and Tansy are about to cut the cake and they'd like for everyone to enjoy a piece." He smiled out at the crowd. "And afterwards, could all the women move to one side of the room and all the men to the other? They'll be tossing the bouquet and the garter soon afterwards."

"I'm amazed he's lasted this long," Lars said to Delphi in an undertone. "Liam isn't one for either crowds or parties."

She leaned in closer and her breast glanced against his arm, sending another surge of heat through him. "Well, it's not as if he gets married every day." Her breath was warm against his cheek.

He suddenly felt as if his shirt collar had grown too tight. "He must love her to go through this."

There was a musical note to Delphi's laugh. "I'd hope he loves her. He's marrying her."

"I hope so, too."

They both hung back as everyone moved toward the front. They had a good view of Liam and Tansy from where they stood. His brother and new sister-in-law laughed together and exchanged a look as they both held on to the knife and cut a piece of cake.

"Did you see the way they looked at one another during the ceremony?" Delphi said. Lars wondered if she heard the note of wistfulness in her voice. He doubted it.

"I could only see Tansy." But he saw both of them now as they fed cake to one another, and he had to admit it'd be nice to have a woman look at him like that. Of course, the expression on Liam's face left absolutely no doubt as to how he felt about his wife. It was there for everyone in the room to see—fierce protection tempered by tenderness, love and joy. It was the oddest sensation to know that of all the experiences he and Liam had shared as brothers and twins, this was a moment Lars had never had. An awareness rippled through him that he brushed aside.

"It was quite lovely."

Delphi was quite lovely, too, even with the internal scars she obviously carried. He'd seen far too many soldiers who had suffered a lapse of one kind or another—he recognized the look of pain. Awareness rippled through him again. He dragged his attention back to Liam and Tansy. "Liam looks at her differently than he did his ex-wife."

"I didn't realize he'd been married before."

"They aborted that mission. Luckily there were no casualties."

"Have you ever been married?"

"Nope. I never answered that particular call of duty. You?"

"Call of duty. Do you think of everything in military terms?"

"Pretty much. Conditioning." Was she avoiding the question? "So, do you have an ex floating around somewhere?"

"Nope. I've had other priorities."

"Such as?" It wasn't a challenge, as much as curiosity. Not that every woman he'd dated had been marriage-oriented, but there was something different about Delphi. She just didn't seem to fall into any neat categorization.

"Hold that thought. I want a piece of cake."

"How about you snag me a piece, too, and I'll recon two glasses of punch?"

"It's a deal. I'm parched."

She didn't look parched at all. She looked lush and vibrant—flushed cheeks, sparkling eyes, full lips, ripe breasts teasing at the top of her sundress.

Lars gave in to temptation and pulled her to him, kissing her hard and fast. Her eyes were wide as he released her.

"Sorry. I…" He trailed off, for once finding himself at a loss for words.

She ran the tip of her tongue along her lower lip. "No apology necessary, Marine."

He was one second away from suggesting they skip out and create their own private festivities when a situation developed at the front of the room. Lars didn't even have to look to know.

The only thing that surprised him was how long it had taken.

THE CRASH STARTLED Delphi out of her stupor of desire—that was really the only way to describe it. It also threw her immediately into medical mode. In the back of her head, as she hurried toward the crash, she wondered at Lars's muttered comment. He was surprised it had taken so long.

Delphi moved quickly through the crowd. Thank goodness people had enough sense to get out of her way. Janie Reinhardt lay crumpled on the floor amid overturned chairs, a rumpled tablecloth and spilled table contents. Delphi quickly scanned the room for Skye and Nelson but didn't see either one of them.

Lars's mom's color was good, Delphi noted as she leaned down. Normal, not clammy and sweaty.

Visual stimuli? Delphi waved her hand in front of the woman's face. No response.

Auditory stimuli? "Dr. Reinhardt? Jane? Can you hear me?" No response.

Delphi checked her pulse. It was a little accelerated, but not bad.

The room was eerily quiet considering how many people were packed in. Jane still appeared unconscious. There was really nothing she could do now—she didn't want to move her in case of a head or spinal injury.

Pain stimuli. Placing her knuckles midway on Jane's sternum, Delphi rubbed.

Jane Reinhardt nearly howled as she slapped at Delphi's hand. "Are you trying to kill me?"

Okay, the patient was no longer unconscious. "No, ma'am. I was checking your response to stimuli. And I see you're conscious now."

Jane's attitude mellowed and she looked around in bewilderment. "What happened?"

Murmurs rippled through the group.

"You passed out. Has this kind of thing happened before?"

"Oh, dear. I suppose the excitement was simply too much. It happens sometimes when I get too excited."

Jane began to sit up and Delphi gently but firmly restrained her with a hand to her shoulder. "Let me check you out before you try to move."

She did a brief, but thorough, exam on the older woman's reflexes and visual responses. She checked Jane's head for any obvious concussive swelling. There was also no blood anywhere. Everything seemed in order. In fact, Delphi was a bit surprised Jane didn't exhibit any bruising or swelling considering her fall and the items she'd taken down with her. She was one lucky lady.

"I think you're fine. Do you hurt anywhere? Any blurred vision, dizziness or nausea?"

"Well, of course I hurt," Jane snapped. "I fell."

Delphi let the comments roll off of her. She had plenty of experience with difficult patients. "Is it just a general soreness or one area specifically?"

Delphi saw the exact moment when Jane bit back a caustic comment and switched to pathos. "I'm sorry, it's just a general soreness." She glanced pointedly at the debris surrounding her. "But then I guess I took a pretty hard fall."

Delphi kept an impassive, professional smile on her face as she slipped one arm behind Jane's back for support, and grasped her under the elbow with her other hand. "Let's just go slow getting up."

Jane tried, and even though Delphi had her firmly, she sank back to the floor. Oddly, she actually exerted pressure against Delphi's arm to return to the floor.

"I think perhaps a couple of the men might be able to help me better. I don't want to fall again."

A couple of men stepped forward at the same time, ready to help.

Lars's cryptic comment on the plane, that Delphi could perhaps handle his mother, came to mind. Delphi, in that instant, totally got it. She smiled at the men and shook her head, declining their unspoken offer. She said to Jane, "No. You and I are doing just fine. Work as hard at getting up this time as you just worked at going back down."

That earned her a baleful look, which quickly shifted to long-suffering as Delphi kept her arm firmly in place. "Okay. I'll try again."

They both stood on the second try, although Jane wobbled once she'd regained her feet and reached out and grabbed one of the men's arms. "Thank you."

Jane's thanks were directed at the man, not Delphi. However, that didn't surprise Delphi in the least. She'd thwarted Jane and held her to a line. She was fairly certain that didn't happen very often with Dr. Reinhardt.

In her brief scanning of the room for Nelson, Delphi had noticed the set, hard look on Lars's face—definitely an expression she hadn't seen before. Now she noted that none of Jane's family—Liam, Lars, Dirk or Bull—moved to help her, but instead simply stood by watching. For that matter, Merrilee and Tansy were doing the same. Hmm.

Delphi rechecked Jane's vitals after she was escorted to one of the chairs and seated. The mother of the groom seemed fine.

Once again, everyone turned to focus on the newly-weds' tossing of the bouquet and garter and subsequent exit, but the energy had shifted. Tansy and Liam's departure felt fairly anticlimatic following Jane's fainting spell.

Lars materialized by her side. He was still wearing that hard look. "I'm surprised it took that long. I was holding my breath all through the wedding. But it kind of makes sense that she waited that long."

By unspoken consent, she and Lars stepped to the side, away from the others. "Are you saying that fainting spell was deliberate?"

She'd suspected as much given that Jane had ostensibly taken quite a fall but had no bumps or bruising. It had been a little too staged.

He crossed his arms over his chest, radiating annoyance. "One hundred percent."

"Okay…." Delphi was a bit at a loss as to what to say. She was in uncharted territory here.

"Did she break anything? Was there a knot on her head where it hit? Of course not, because she didn't really faint. She's been pulling that stunt since we were kids. Mom just can't stand it when she's not the center of attention, so she 'faints' and lo and behold, everyone suddenly focuses on her."

"That's—"

He cut her off before she could say she'd come to the same conclusion. "Narcissitic? Self-involved? Yes and yes. And the best thing to do is simply ignore it or at the most, downplay it. She plays to an audience, which is why lecturing in front of a captive audience as a professor works so well for her."

It seemed a little harsh but it also held a ring of truth. Jane Reinhardt's pupils hadn't indicated even temporary unconsciousness. "Which is why none of you stepped forward to help?" It was part observation, part question, but it was devoid of censure.

"Exactly. We might look unfeeling to everyone but it escalates if any of us react."

The best way to defuse drama for the sake of drama was to ignore it. "I get it."

"You do, don't you?"

"What's not to get?"

"This one chick…girl…I mean, woman, told me I just didn't understand my mom and I should be more sympathetic. She thought I was a jerk."

All the unfair, unwarranted accusations and all the lies that had been believed about her came rushing back at her. "Some people want to offer an opinion when it really doesn't have anything to do with them."

Narrowing his eyes, he subjected her to a questioning look. "True, but rather cryptic."

She suddenly craved the privacy of her room. "It was fun. I'm going to head back now."

"I'll walk you back."

"There's no need."

"I want to."

"Maybe I don't want you to."

"Suck it up, Blondie. My reputation would be shot to hell and back if I let my date wander back escort-less."

It hovered on the tip of her tongue that his reputation wasn't her business or her responsibility, but arguing with Lars was proving useless. He just charmingly ran roughshod over you or argued a point that was really convoluted but seemed to make perfect sense while it was coming out of his sexy mouth. And what did it matter in the scheme of things?

"Okay."

"Be reasonable—"

"I said okay."

He grinned sheepishly, which was an altogether attractive look on him. Of course, she had yet to see him looking unattractive. He elevated handsome to a knee-weakening, mind-numbing state in his dress uniform.

"Then...well...okay, let's head out." He formally offered the crook of his arm as if they were at a gala. In a moment of carefree silliness that she hadn't known in a long time, she slipped her arm through his. "Why, thank you, sir."

"Damn, Blondie, you're slipping. You were just nice to me."

"No worries. It was a momentary slip. You shouldn't get used to it."

And neither should she. The one thing she knew for certain about Lars Reinhardt was that he was temporary.

"Thanks, Dirk," Merrilee said as he put the last table back in place in the community center.

"No problem." He'd offered to hang around and help with the cleanup after the party, well, actually the reception, was over. Once Tansy and Liam hightailed it out, the joint had cleared as quick as a honky-tonky bar fight when the cops rolled in. He'd been glad to stay behind and help Merrilee.

It wasn't as if he had anywhere to go, anything to do or anyone to see. Liam and Tansy were honeymooning at some undisclosed destination, but he was pretty sure they were holed up at Shadow Lake, where they both stayed when they got together. Lars and that new nurse, Delphi, had been cozying up during the party and left afterward. He and Merrilee were the last two left in the building. Bull had gotten stuck taking Aunt Janie back to the new bed-and-breakfast where she was staying. His uncle had definitely got the short end of that stick. Dirk would rather mud-wrestle an alligator than hang with Aunt Janie. The gator was nicer.

On Monday, he and Lars were flying out to the camp. Lars would spend the day checking it out and then the bush pilot would swing back around and pick him up. Staying at the camp alone for the rest of the week suited Dirk well enough. He had some things to get ready for the next training session, which would start a week from Monday. And seeing as how he *felt* alone all the time, he figured he might as well *be* alone.

"I think that about does it," Merrilee said, looking

around the room to make sure they hadn't missed any-thing. It looked fine to him. "It was a nice wedding, wasn't it? Liam and Tansy are a good match."

"Better'n him and Natalie." Damn, that just sort of slipped out. But he wasn't surprised—Natalie was al-ways on his mind. Kind of like one of those brain-eating parasites he'd seen on some TV show.

Merrilee gave him what he always thought of as a "sorting out" look. After a second or so, she said, "I never met Natalie, but it's hard to imagine anyone suiting Liam more than Tansy. What's Natalie like?"

"She's nice. Real pretty. Kinda bubbly. She's a schoolteacher. We grew up next to one another."

"I take it you two have stayed friends and keep in touch?"

"Not really, well, not that much. I hadn't talked to her for years until Tansy and Liam got together. Since then, we've emailed a couple of times."

"Oh. I see." The heat of a dull flush climbed his neck to his face. Hopefully Merrilee wouldn't notice. Her tone and her smile said she did. She knew he was miserably in love with Natalie.

He tucked a chair more firmly under the table and stared at it. If Merrilee looked at him as if he was a joke, he really didn't want to see it—but he didn't think she'd do that.

"I was thinking of inviting her out here for a visit," he said quickly, adding, "Lars said I should. It was his idea." He figured it wouldn't hurt to get a woman's opinion on the idea, but there was no way he'd bring it up to his own mother—he'd never hear the end of it. Merrilee was a good choice.

She didn't hesitate. "Sure. Why not? It's beautiful

here and since she and Liam parted on good terms, it shouldn't be too awkward. Invite her, if that's what you want to do."

"When do you think I should ask her to come?" he mumbled. Just thinking about it made him feel as if he had a cement block in his gut.

"I didn't catch that, honey."

He repeated his question, making sure he spoke up.

Merrilee smiled and rubbed his arm reassuringly. "There's no time like the present. If she's a school-teacher, she's about to be out for summer break."

"I'd forgotten about that." Really, all he'd been able to think about was the chance that she'd say no—that is, if he actually got up the courage to ask her in the first place. He shoved his hands in his pockets.

"The days are nice and long now. We can put her up at either my place or Alyce's. One of us should have a room available."

Both Merrilee and Lars made it sound so simple. "So, what should I say? I'm not very good at this kind of thing."

"Have you ever mentioned it when you emailed her?"

He shifted from one foot to the other. "No. Not really."

"What does 'not really' mean?"

"Well, she's said a couple of times that it sounds real nice here." He had a quarter and two dimes in his pocket. He could feel the shapes with his fingers.

"It sounds to me like she's been waiting on you to invite her."

"You think? I figured she was just being polite."

"I don't know her so it's hard to say. But if she's

brought it up a couple of times, she'd probably be up for a visit."

He rubbed at the back of his neck, feeling an itch starting there at the thought of what to say and how to say it. Maybe he'd just wait a while longer. "Um… okay."

"Dirk, I hope I'm not out of line with this, but would you like for me to help you write to Natalie?"

She hoped she wasn't out of line! Was she nuts? He was always so damn nervous and said so little in his emails. The less he wrote, the less room there was for goof-ups. Natalie was so damn smart and Dirk had always struggled. He was a whiz at math, but reading and writing stumped him. He'd always been in the "special" class, and "special" hadn't meant the smartest. "If you'd just write it for me, that's even better."

Merrilee laughed but not unkindly. "No. The message needs to be in your own words." That, right there, was the problem. He sucked at words.

"But I could help you with it."

There was hope. Well, at least hope that he wouldn't screw up the letter-writing part of it.

"Okay."

"Let's hop on it."

"You mean now?" He suddenly felt kind of sick.

Merrilee slipped her arm through his and winked at him. "There's no time like the present."

If she said so.

7

LARS GLANCED AT the woman walking along next to him, seeing her in a different light—and it wasn't just because they were outside in the sun.

It was strange, definitely unexpected. That one simple exchange with Delphi about his mom had changed things. Delphi got it in a way no one outside of his family did. It was private and personal and pretty much no one else's damn business. He wasn't quite sure why he had gone into it with her.

Her look was slightly probing. "You okay?"

They'd already passed the airstrip/bed-and-breakfast and kept walking. Despite the people out and about, it was as if he and Delphi were separated apart from everyone else.

"Of course. I'm fine." It was unnerving how well she seemed to read him.

She looked unconvinced but lightened things, nonetheless, with a sly smile. "You've just gotten quiet. That seems an unnatural state of being for you."

Mark it down. Miss Aloof was teasing him. However, he still couldn't quite shake the heaviness that descended on him every time his mother had one of her "episodes."

What the hell? She'd understood his mother faking illness—he might as well lay it all out on the table.

"I just hate when she pulls that crap," he said, shaking his head. "It just… I don't know.…" He petered off, not even sure of what he was trying to say. Liam and Jack had always shrugged their mother's ways off more easily than Lars had. He tried, but it stuck to him like stink on shit.

Although Delphi hesitated a moment before she spoke, her step didn't falter and she kept pace with him. "Maybe it's because she's being manipulative. Being on the receiving end of manipulation generally makes people angry. Then you feel guilty for being angry because obviously there's something inside of her that can't just enjoy and allow others to enjoy?"

Lars considered it. That was it exactly. "Yep. That about nails it. So, all of us just steer clear. Why do you think Liam came to Alaska?"

They reached the end of the sidewalk, then turned to cross the road.

"Oh," Delphi said. "Your brother didn't come here to start a wilderness survival camp?"

"Nope. He was just angry and didn't know what to do with himself when he got a medical discharge. He needed somewhere to go and sort himself out, so he came here."

"And now you're here…temporarily," she said.

They waited until a four-wheeler and a pickup passed and then crossed the street.

"Yep." He opened the airstrip/bed-and-breakfast

door and waited on Delphi to enter before him. "Just like you, only I'm even more short-term."

As they mounted the stairs to their rooms, a teasing smile hovered about her lips and glinted in her eyes. "I suspect truer words were never spoken."

The conversation had moved to a different realm, which was fine with him.

"I can confirm that for you." They stopped outside her door and Lars stepped in closer. "So, there, we have something in common." She smelled like sunshine and fresh air. "We're both short-term. Maybe you don't trust me—which isn't personal because you don't trust anyone—but you don't have to trust me. I'm not making any promises. I don't want anything beyond the chance to enjoy your company for the next five days. And I'm not offering anything outside of the next five days."

She leaned against the wall, looking up at him, the expression in her eyes indiscernible in the dim light. "What if I'm not interested in the next five days?"

He wanted to kiss her lips, mingle her breath with his, bury his face in her neck, and he would gladly, easily take her in the hallway against the wall. However, now was not the time.

Nonetheless, he shrugged. "Then you're not interested. I have my leave, which won't be quite as good as it could be, and then I go back on active duty."

"And what if I want more than the next five days?"

She was definitely playing devil's advocate.

"Delphi, my job, my life, depends on my ability to assess a situation, the risk and the most likely outcome. It's highly unlikely you'll want more than the next five days—not because we won't hit it off, but I don't think either of us are in that headspace."

There was a slow, sultry quality to her smile. This woman certainly set his charge. "I think you've said that once or twice before," she said.

"Readily admitted. I like to be straight up. I'm attracted to the kind of woman who isn't looking to fall in love. You strike me that way. The last thing I want is to break anyone's heart."

"If I say no? What happens then? Some men don't take no very well."

He thought they'd just covered that. Apparently somewhere along the line, and he'd guess recently, someone hadn't taken her refusal in stride. "Then I'll be disappointed, but that's that. I'm attracted to you, but I'm not desperate. If you say no…well, then you've said no." He took a step backward and leaned against the wall, as well, giving her more room. "I'm not some whack job like the chick who tried to take Tansy out so she could have Liam."

"What?!"

He forgot she'd only just arrived and wouldn't know about the incident last year. "Some military historian followed Liam here and said she wanted to write his story. Little did he guess that she was obsessed with him. He and Tansy flew out to check on the land for the survival camp. Mallory stalked them and tried to kill Tansy."

Delphi looked both horrified and fascinated. "You're not kidding, are you?"

Lars shook his head. "I wouldn't kid something like that. He'd turned her down and she decided it was Tansy's fault. In her mind the best way to get Liam was to eliminate the competition."

"Oh, my—"

"I know."

"What happened?"

"Liam disabled her."

"How?"

"He had no idea who the shooter was. He only knew someone was trying to hurt Tansy. Liam neutralized the threat with a shot to the shoulder."

"Wow." Delphi tilted her head to one side, the wheels obviously turning. "Depending on how and where it hit, she might've needed rods and joint replacement."

Lars simply stared at Delphi for a moment then laughed. Desire and amusement made an interesting combination.

"What's so funny about that?"

"Mallory was damn lucky Liam wanted answers. He's a sharpshooter. He could've easily killed her if he'd wanted to. And all you can talk about are rods and artificial joints."

She shrugged. "Hey. I see things in medical terms. So shoot me. Wait, that's the wrong thing to say to you guys, isn't it?"

Lars laughed, appreciating her quirky humor.

"You're safe enough—even if you say no."

She crossed her arms over her chest and studied him for a moment. "Have you ever actually been turned down?"

Was that sarcasm or was she really curious? Hell if he knew, but it prompted a chuckle. "Of course. I'd like to show you something."

She mockingly widened her eyes. "Now, that *is* moving a little fast…"

He laughed again. Yep, he'd definitely like to show her *that*. "I wanted to show you Mirror Lake. It's a thermal lake, so it never freezes over, and it's an eagle haven. All in all, it's a pretty cool place. I was thinking a late evening outing and a swim."

"I didn't bring a bathing suit."

He grinned. "Me neither."

"You are a bad influence."

"I gave you fair warning. Moral corruption is contagious."

"You may be right."

He grinned. "I'm always right." They both knew it was bullshit but it was fun. "Nine o'clock?"

She hesitated so long he thought he might just turn him down yet. Finally, she spoke. "Nine works."

"Should I knock on your door?"

"I can meet you on the sidewalk."

"Sure. If that's what you want."

He'd won that skirmish and gained ground.

DELPHI FLOPPED BACK on the quilt-covered bed in her room and stared at the tongue-in-groove ceiling. Obviously the wedding and the fun at the reception had gotten to her because she'd agreed to go out with Lars Reinhardt. He'd made it seem so natural. And once she'd agreed, she'd realized just how much she'd wanted to say yes.

What had happened to finding him brash and annoying? Well, he was fairly brash, but really not so annoying once you got used to him. She'd had such a great time at the reception. She'd never, ever danced like that—whirling and twirling and then being held close. And then there'd been the flirting and the simmering sexuality between them.

Delphi had been so alternately angry and numb following the incident with DeWitt that she hadn't experienced the least ounce of sexual desire since. Lars had changed that. She definitely wasn't numb anymore. And, she realized with a start, she wasn't nearly as angry as she had been. The touch of his palm against hers, the feathering of his breath against her neck as they danced and again when they talked in the hallway, the sheer masculinity of his size and his very maleness…

The entire afternoon had been heady and romantic with an undeniable sexuality.

He was, however, a virtual stranger and she'd agreed to go to some lake with him.

She called Skye on her cell and cut straight to the chase after the perfunctory greetings. "So, I lost my mind and agreed to go to Mirror Lake with Lars Reinhardt this evening. Do you know anything about him?"

She sensed Skye's hesitation on the other end of the phone. "I only know he's Bull's nephew. Liam is a great guy but I don't know much about him. Any other man here I could vouch for or warn you off, but Lars is an unknown quantity."

Worrying her lip between her teeth, Delphi rolled to her side. "I don't want to start off here on the same sour note I left in Atlanta."

"I don't see how that could possibly happen. In fact, maybe a few dates with Lars will erase some of the lingering…ick—" Delphi smiled at the use of the word from the highly educated, fairly formal Skye "—of the whole DeWitt debacle," Skye reasoned. "I understand your reasons for wanting to keep the whole thing quiet, but he deserves to be reported to the board for his actions."

Her reasons boiled down to one thing: it would be further hell to go through. At the most DeWitt would get a slap on the wrist. He'd still come out on top while she remained unemployed. "Yep. But that falls into the gap between an ideal world and the real world."

"I know. So perhaps escaping into an ideal world with a good-looking, well-built man for a little while is a good thing. Are you attracted to him?"

A shiver ran through Delphi at the memory of his nearness. "Is the sky blue today?" She laughed at herself. "Yesterday I wasn't so sure I liked him, but he's sort of growing on me."

Skye laughed. "That has a familiar ring." She had expressed a similar sentiment in regards to Dalton. "I say go and enjoy. Even if Lars is a dud, Mirror Lake is pretty amazing."

"Okay. I'll go and proceed with caution. Extreme caution. By the way, is there any place in town where I can find a bathing suit?"

"Good Riddance isn't exactly brimming with fashion stores." Delphi had always appreciated Skye's dry sense of humor. "You'd have to order something like that." Skye hesitated. "I have two if you want to try them on. They've been washed and I haven't worn them since last year."

There was no way she was going swimming without a suit. "You're sure?"

"Positive. Dalton is running by Donna's place later

to pick up a tool. He'll drop them off, if that's okay with you."

"You're a lifesaver, Skye."

"It's my job," her friend deadpanned on the other end of the phone.

"Ha. Seriously, thanks for asking me to come and thanks for lending me a bathing suit. I haven't felt this good in a long time. Today was fun."

"I'm glad you like it here. Have fun tonight."

"That's the plan."

Full-steam ahead…for five days. And while Delphi no longer trusted her own judgment, Skye couldn't be wrong.

LARS SHIFTED IN HIS SEAT, impatient for dinner to be over. Thank God Merrilee and Bull were here, too, and he wasn't stuck with only his mother. They were all sitting at the kitchen table in Bull and Merrilee's kitchen above the hardware store. Merrilee's spaghetti with a salad and bread was incredible.

Despite Merrilee's best attempts, Dr. Jane Reinhardt had commandeered the conversation from the get-go. Actually, there was no conversation involved—it was strictly a one-woman monologue. As usual, his mom was playing to a captive audience.

"So, I very quickly told the dean that I wouldn't be a part of…"

Blah, blah and blah…who gave a righteous crap? He didn't. It was the same shit, just a different day. Lars's mind drifted to later on tonight—to moonlight, warm water and the cool blonde who had felt anything but cool in his arms as they'd danced away the afternoon.

"Lars would you care to join us?" his mother said

with her famous quelling glance, her tone sharp. Both warning signs were ones he knew all too well, having learned them at an early age. Tread carefully, or Mom would explode and it wouldn't be pretty.

Damn, she got under his skin. "Present."

"I beg to differ," she said. "I see you so seldom, you'd think you could actually be here instead of Lars Land."

Damn if she couldn't reduce him in a few seconds to being eight years old again. From the time he was a kid and had ever let his mind wander while she was prattling on, she'd disdainfully referred to his daydreaming as Lars Land. Damn, he hated that term.

So he, Liam and Jack went out of their way to avoid her because nobody ever knew what was going to set her off. And whenever Dirk spent time with them, he seriously walked around on his tiptoes. Lars could detonate bombs all day, every day. He could set off Delphi. But he'd go out of his way to avoid setting off his mother. Even now, dead-ass silence reigned at the table. You could've heard a flea fart.

Enough. He was thirty-two years old. He had a successful career. He'd had too many years of walking on eggshells around her.

So Lars called his mother out.

"Okay, Mom, you've got my undivided attention. You've got *everyone's* undivided attention, which is what is always required." He nudged his plate away and leaned back in his chair, crossing his arms over his chest. "Please, continue."

"Sarcasm is totally uncalled for, son. But, as I was saying, I took *my* curriculum change to the dean—"

"When are you leaving?" Lars interrupted his

mother with the question, even though he knew the answer. If she was going to treat him as if he was eight, then dammit, he'd act like it.

She graced him with a scathing look. "Tomorrow morning, which of course you know, which is why we planned this dinner tonight so we'd have an opportunity to spend some time together before I left."

Lars nodded. It probably wouldn't change a thing but he was going to say what he wanted to say and the consequences be damned. He was fed up holding his tongue. "You know, Mom, last night you talked about your gardening, your trip to Spain, the book you've decided to work on and how you've had to set the new member of your teaching staff straight."

She appeared somewhat mollified. "Okay. I suppose you do pay attention."

He continued, even though he knew she wasn't going to like what he had to say. "Not once did you ask Liam or Tansy about their work." And he knew she hadn't—Liam and Tansy had mentioned it. "Did you ask Merrilee and Bull about their businesses? Did you tell them you were happy for them?" He shook his head. "I've been here more than twenty-four hours and not once have you brought up my job or even my life, for that matter. Maybe you're saving it all for the eleventh hour, but it's getting a little late in the day for you to pretend you actually give a damn about anyone except for yourself."

His mother rose to her feet. "I don't have to listen to this." She grasped the edge of the table, swaying.

"What? Are you going to pass out again? Make sure you don't fall into the meat sauce." His mother sat back down forcefully and Lars turned to Merrilee. "Which is exceptional, by the way."

"Thank you." Merrilee remained totally together. "It's my grandmother's recipe."

His mother, however, did not. "How dare you speak to me that way?" Her voice quivered with indignation. Tears sparkled in her eyes. "I don't believe in prying into my children's lives or the lives of others, for that matter, which is why I've not subjected anyone to an inquisition."

Bullshit. She didn't ask because she didn't care about anybody but herself. "Mom, asking someone how they are, how they've been, doesn't come close to being an inquisition."

Her eyes glittered with heavier tears, which might have been manufactured or genuine or a bit of both. "I'm damned if I do and damned if I don't." She rose to her feet again. "If you'll excuse me, my flight is rather early in the morning. I think I'll get back to my room."

Merrilee pushed back and stood, as well. "I'll walk with you, if you don't mind. I could use the exercise and that way Bull and Lars can attend to the dishes."

For a second Lars almost felt sorry for his mom. For a fleeting instant she looked lost and hurt, but then it passed. "It's not necessary, but if you want the exercise, by all means."

Lars stood. "Mom, I apologize for being rude."

"That's all you have to say?"

He ran his hand over his head. Lars knew what she wanted him to say, but he couldn't apologize for telling the truth. "I love you. Get a good night's rest and I'll see you in the morning."

"Only if it's not too much trouble for you to see me

before I leave." When he was a kid her sarcasm had always cut deep. "Perhaps you can drop off a script so I know the right thing to say."

Okay, so he didn't feel quite so bad anymore.

"I'll be back in a bit," Merrilee said.

"We've got the dishes covered," Bull said, beginning to stack the plates.

Merrilee pressed a quick kiss to his cheek. "Thanks, love."

"Night, Janie-Girl," Bull said to his sister.

"Good night."

For a long minute, only the clink of dishes and silverware filled the silence in the room after the door closed behind the women. Bull, never a big talker, was apparently waiting to hear what Lars had to say. Bull ran dishwater in the sink.

"Was I too harsh with her?" Lars finally said. He'd never spoken to his mother that way. He gathered the glasses.

Bull shrugged as he carried the plates over to the counter. "You might have been a little hard, but you didn't say anything that wasn't true."

For the first time in his life, Lars paused and thought of his mother as a whole person and not just his mother. "Was she like this when she was a girl?"

"Janie's always had to be the center of attention, just like she's always at odds with someone." Lars couldn't recall a time when his mom wasn't fighting with someone in the family or in her professional circle. "She doesn't want to know what's going on in your life as much as she wants to tell you what you should do." Bull began to run water in the sink as Lars brought over the pasta bowls. "It's gotten worse as she's gotten older.

Maybe she needed to hear that tonight. It doesn't really matter—it's said. I doubt it'll do any good, but it won't do any harm either. What's harmful is keeping all that bottled up inside you."

Lars hadn't realized his misery had been all bottled up inside until his earlier conversation with Delphi. It was as if she'd recognized something he was too close to see in himself. "Well, I guess it's not now."

Bull plunged his hands into the soapy water. Lars positioned himself to rinse and dry. That was one thing his mom had in common with her brothers. None of them believed in dishwashers. Bull called it "quality time."

"If it makes you feel better, say it. But don't expect your mom to change. It's pretty unlikely at this stage of the game."

Lars hadn't thought it through. He'd simply had enough and blown his cool. "You're right. It just felt like it was time to call her out. She may not change, but I don't have to play her game anymore. Mom is incredibly manipulative."

Bull nodded. "Yep." He scrubbed at a pot. "Of course, not all women are like your mom."

Had the comment come from anyone other than Bull, Lars would've offered a sarcastic rejoinder. As it was, he simply said, "I know."

"Good. I'm going out on a limb here. If you feel rejected by Janie…well, it's not you—it's her."

Lars's knee-jerk reaction was to deny he felt rejected by his mother. Only he realized he couldn't, as he finally pegged the nameless feeling he'd always had. He'd considered her difficult and alternately demanding and remote, but it took Bull's labeling it as rejection for it to hit home.

All these years… It was as if he'd finally found the buried trip wire he'd been searching for with dread all this time.

"You know, you're right." He felt damn good. "Can I take you up on that offer to use your truck while I'm here? I've got a date tonight."

"Delphi? Mirror Lake?"

"Yeah and yeah." Lars was a little disconcerted. "How'd you know it was Delphi and Mirror Lake?" He rinsed the pots and pans and placed them in the dish drainer.

Bull grinned. "I remember how much you liked it when you were here before. And Delphi—well, that was easy enough to figure out. You two seemed to be having a good time at the reception."

"She's different."

"Different is good."

"Yeah, I think so, too."

"Merrilee is one of a kind." Funny, Delphi struck him that way, as well. "When you find a good one, you hold on to her."

As he'd told his brother, he planned to do just that. At least until it was time to rotate out.

8

THE SUN WAS still making itself known when Delphi stepped out onto the sidewalk in front of the bed-and-breakfast. She wouldn't like the long hours of dark and cold in the winter, but she liked these extended daylight hours now. The sun warmed her face and neck.

A jovial mix of music, conversation and laughter floated on the air from the bar and restaurant next door, along with the smell of burgers and fries. From further down the street, children's squeals of delight mingled with dogs barking. Skye had pointed out an empty lot that served as the local "sandlot" baseball field. A couple strolled arm in arm down the sidewalk across the street.

Out of nowhere the thought floated through her mind that she could like it here, really like it. Funny. She'd simply wanted to get away from her situation and regroup. Actually *liking* Good Riddance hadn't been part of her plan.

The bed-and-breakfast door opened behind her and her heart began to thud. She turned to greet Lars…except it wasn't Lars.

"Your honey'll be along soon enough," Alberta said with a cackle. "Don't mind us. My studmuffin napped through the party today so Jefferson's gonna play dis horn so we can dance."

"That sounds like fun." And it did.

Alberta still wore her pink evening gown complete with feathered turban while her studmuffin wore the same pair of denim overalls with flannel shirt he'd had on yesterday. Nonetheless, he beamed at Alberta. "She's a regular doll, isn't she?"

"Yessir, she is," Delphi said.

The gypsy queen put her head against his shoulder and smiled up at him, her eyelashes fluttering like a young girl awaiting her first kiss. The look that passed between them was similar to the one between Tansy and Liam earlier. Skye and Dalton also had the same way of looking at each other, heedless of onlookers.

Jefferson nodded his saxophone toward Delphi by way of greeting. "Alberta wants to dance to 'Moonlight Serenade.'"

She cackled once again. "That's right. Gotta dance to it now, since me and my boys can never make it up till midnight any longer." A three-legged cat hopped along with them. "Lord Byron loves music."

Jefferson took up a spot on the corner of the sidewalk and began to play, the saxophone's notes weaving through the night air, sultry and buttery rather than piercing. Alberta and her husband danced in Good Riddance's dusty street. Further down, the couple who ran the dry goods store drifted out and began to dance, as well. The man and woman who'd been walking on the opposite sidewalk took advantage of the music, too, as Jefferson segued into another song.

There was a romantic, surreal element to it all. The dusty street in the middle of the Alaskan bush, the notes of the saxophone weaving a spell, the dancing couples, some in evening wear, some in work gear, snow-topped mountains and evergreens serving as a backdrop.

A truck pulled to a stop in front of her, startling her until she realized Lars sat behind the wheel. He got out and rounded the front. Sunlight glinted in his short, military-cut hair. He'd exchanged his dress uniform for blue jeans and a Super Bowl T-shirt from a couple of years ago. It was rather disconcerting how simply seeing him set her heart rate galloping. Was it those broad shoulders or that wicked glint in his eyes when he smiled? Or perhaps it was just that general sense of attraction she'd felt for him from the very beginning. Either way, her pulse had moved into hyper mode.

"Hey, you," he said, and for some goofy reason, it struck her as incredibly romantic.

"Hey." She felt lost in his gaze, but lost in a good way.

"Street dance?" he said, nodding toward Jefferson and the couples.

"It's turned into that." Good Lord, but she wanted to kiss him again.

He motioned with his right hand. "Would you rather stay? We could check out Mirror Lake another time."

"No. This is great but I'm looking forward to seeing Mirror Lake."

He smiled and her tummy seemed to somersault. "Me, too. Ready to roll?"

"Yeah, let's go."

He opened the passenger door for her.

She stepped off of the sidewalk and climbed in. "I don't know what I was thinking," she said when he got back in the cab, "but I wasn't expecting you to be driving."

He flashed a grin her way. "It's a bit far out of town to walk, so I borrowed Bull's truck. He offered to let me use it while I was visiting."

"Nice." The sun slanted through the windshield, illuminating the fine lines bracketing his eyes. A small scar ran along his jawline. A light dusting of hair ran along his forearms. His biceps bulged impressively. However, it was the man himself, his air, the whole package, that sent a prickle of gooseflesh dancing over her skin. Excitement...anticipation hovered between them.

A delicious tension pulsed in the cab. *Slow down,* she reminded herself. She threw out a safe topic. "How was dinner?"

Trained to notice details, as details often meant the difference between life and death, Delphi saw his smile take on a tense edge. "I don't know."

His response surprised her. So much for dinner being safe. "Didn't you eat with your family?" At least that's what he'd said he was doing.

"Sure did."

He wasn't making sense. "So, how can you not know how it went? Have you been drinking?" She had to ask. She didn't ride with anyone who'd been drinking. She'd seen too many drunk driving victims come in on ambulance stretchers.

They left the town behind, evergreens flanking the road before them. His driving *seemed* fine but she could easily walk back if she needed to. They both could if he'd overindulged. For that matter, she was fully capable of driving.

He shot her a sidelong look, a frown furrowing his brow. "Of course not. I have more discipline than that."

"No need to get all huffy. I just don't get how you wouldn't know if something was good or bad."

He rubbed his hand over his head. "What the heck? You already know more about my family than you probably wanted to." She waited. "You know how we talked about my mom earlier?"

"Yes."

"Tonight at dinner was more of the same—it was all about her. Not once has she asked about me. And she won't. She'll offer an opinion on what I should do and how I should do it but it's all based on bullshit. Because she doesn't know a damn thing about me. Sorry, it just pisses me off."

She understood his vehemence. It really sucked to be manipulated. "No apology necessary. What happened?" If he told her it was none of her business, well, then it was none of her business.

"Tonight at dinner, I called her out on her behavior. I'm tired of letting her get away with this crap."

"And…?"

"It kind of felt good, but it was also awkward as hell. She got up and left."

That didn't surprise Delphi at all. Anyone who would "faint" to garner attention would certainly go for a dramatic exit. However, she merely said, "I'm sure it was a little awkward."

"So, there you have it. The food was good and then it got weird. So I don't really know how the evening was."

"You okay? We don't have to go." She didn't want

him to feel as if she was an obligation. "You're here all week. We can go some other time."

"No. I want to go now. It's no big deal. I just couldn't tell you if it was good or bad."

That made sense. "Okay."

"You're easy to talk to," he said.

She laughed. "Make up your mind. You told me earlier it was difficult to have a conversation with me."

He grinned at her and her heart rate instantly doubled. That smile was like a shot of epinephrine. "There's a difference in talking to someone and actually having a conversation."

"Ah, okay. I see. Well, you certainly can talk."

He laughed. "I'm not sure that was a compliment."

"It wasn't an insult. It was more of an observation." And she'd been teasing him a little.

"If you say so."

"So, now that the wedding's over, what are you up to the rest of the week?"

He turned left off of the main road.

"Monday I'm flying out to Liam's camp to check it out. I'm going out with Dirk in the morning and Dalton's going to swing back by and pick me up in the afternoon. Then I'm going to get in some fishing, hiking and reading. What about you? Do you jump right into work?"

"Pretty much. Nelson will still be here next week so I'll shadow him, meet the patients and get a feel for how Skye works. We're friends but we've never worked together before." They topped a rise and over to the left lay a spectacular lake. "This is really beautiful!" Delphi nearly squealed like a kid with excitement. "Lars, look. Eagles. Oh, my goodness, they're incredible."

Two of the birds perched atop trees while another one soared against the backdrop of a flawless blue sky. "I've never seen anything quite so beautiful in my life," she said.

"I'm inclined to agree." However, he was looking at her rather than the landscape and it felt like a visual caress.

He stopped the truck, putting it in Park. He killed the engine and they sat, letting the tranquillity of the place wash over them. An eagle called out but rather than shatter the peace, the cry became part of the ambience.

Lars broke the silence. "How did all of this work out? You just quit your job to come here for a couple of months?"

She looked out the window at the trees etched against the sky. Should she trust him? He was nothing to her, really. Except he had let her in on his family's problems, ones she suspected he didn't share often, if ever. And he was temporary, which, in a way, made the nightmare she'd been through easier to talk about. She looked at him. "It's not a secret, but I don't particularly want it broadcasted."

"I'm not a broadcasting kind of guy."

"For all that you like to talk, no, you don't strike me that way."

They were silent for a few minutes. He waited patiently. "I've been unemployed for six months because I got fired from my last job."

"Okay."

One word. Nothing more, nothing less. He was still waiting. She continued, keeping it as simple as possible. "My employer made a pass at me. I turned him down. He blackballed me. Because it was my word against his, I haven't been able to find a job."

He sat silently. She wondered not just how, but if, he was going to respond. Finally, he said, "That's bullshit."

She felt sick to her stomach. He was just like all the rest. She didn't know why she'd been stupid enough to think—

He interrupted her mental rant. "He shouldn't be allowed to get away with something like that. Was he some old fart?"

Relief washed over her. His "bullshit" hadn't been aimed at questioning her story. "No. He was young, not even close to old-fart designation—thirty-six, married, handsome and charming."

"So, of course, why would you turn him down? Bastard. What'd he do, beat you to the punch by firing you?"

She was so relieved she almost wanted to cry. With the exception of a few, most of her friends had felt compelled to quiz her as to whether she'd been attracted to him, had she given him some signal, as if they were looking for something she did to encourage or excuse him. It had been insulting and demoralizing, and had just heaped insult on injury. However, Lars had immediately believed her and his hazarded guess was on target.

She ran her fingertip over the ridge of the upholstery. "I went in the next morning prepared to give my two-months' notice and not ever mention what had happened to anyone. He was two steps ahead of me." She shook her head at her naïveté, her stupidity. "He called me into his office and his wife was in there with him. He'd told her I'd propositioned him and when he turned me down, I'd threatened to make trouble. He fired me on the spot. His wife took care of blackballing me with all the other doctors' wives. The few offers I did get, afterwards, included more than a job."

"Son of a bitch."

"I agree. I've called him and the rest of them that and more. The good old boy network is still alive and well in the Doctors' Club. They all have one another's back." She glanced out the window at the proud bird, fierce and beautiful, on the branch, etched against a sky bearing streaks of pink and orange. "And you know, from their perspective it made perfect sense. Doctors are considered quite a catch by a lot of women, by a lot of nurses, in fact. He's a handsome, fit man so why wouldn't they believe I'd make a play for him? What I've never figured out is why he'd do something like that. I thought they were a happy couple. I *admired* that they were a happy couple. And even if he wanted to stray, he could pretty much have any woman he desired. So why me? I don't get it."

"I get it," Lars said softly. "There's something about you."

She turned to face him, trying to understand. "There is? What?"

"I don't know how to explain it to you."

And it was there in his eyes—not just lust, but something that said that she stood out from other women. His words and his look acknowledged her uniqueness. She felt a warmth inside her she wasn't sure she'd ever felt before.

"I didn't lead him on. I didn't flirt with him. I never thought of him that way. He was married, and married is married in my book."

"And that might've been just the problem—you didn't see him that way. That sucks. I can see why Good Riddance appealed to you. I also understand now why you just wanted to be left alone."

She could've kissed him for his attitude, his understanding. Actually, she could also kiss him simply because she liked kissing him and because she wanted to. In fact, she thought she'd do just that.

He opened his mouth to speak and she cut him off. The man could definitely talk. "Come here, Marine."

"I'm right here, Blondie." He was a devilish tease.

"Scared?" she said.

"Why would I be afraid of an itty-bitty little thing like you?"

"You tell me. All I know is I invited you to kiss me and you're still over there and I'm over here."

He leaned in closer and inhaled her scent, his breath warm. The energy of his skin mingled against hers, although they didn't touch. She felt drunk from his nearness, the smell of him. He murmured into her ear, "I didn't realize that was the mission."

She felt like a temptress. "Are you up to the assignment?" she whispered, brushing her cheek against the faint beard shadowing his jaw. A tremor ran through her at the slight, yet intimate contact.

"There's only one way to find out. First order of any mission is intel and recon." He nuzzled along her neck and jaw, a leisurely exploration that left her breathless and hungry for more.

His mouth found hers but instead of the kiss she so eagerly anticipated, he continued his reconnaissance. He focused on her lower lip. Nipping, licking, sucking, sending her spiraling into a vortex of desire. His mouth was warm, his stubble a delicious abrasion. He was driving her mad. She tried to lure him into an actual kiss. He chuckled against her as he evaded her. It was sensual play rather than rejection. "I'm leading this mission, Blondie."

He lazily traced the line of her upper lip with the tip of his tongue and she shuddered. She wrapped her hands around his biceps, holding on, feeling the play and bunching of muscle beneath her palms and fingers.

"Okay, Marine. You're in charge."

His lazy, sensual, arrogant laugh reverberated against her mouth. "There can only be one squad leader."

That wouldn't work for her long-term, but long-term wasn't what this was about. All that mattered was here and now.

"All right, already. Just shut up and kiss me." She slid her hand up to cup his neck.

He splayed his fingers against her scalp. "Gross insubordination," he said, even as his mouth finally captured hers.

It was as if her senses had been starved for this… for him. The firm command of his lips on hers, the demand, the taking. Sweet and hot, his tongue delved into the recesses of her mouth and she welcomed him.

Satisfaction coursed through her, catching her breath up in her pounding heartbeat.

They broke apart and he leaned his forehead against hers. The seconds dragged out as they remained, forehead to forehead, their ragged breathing the only sound as heat swirled around them. Delphi kept her eyes closed, savoring the moment.

She opened them when Lars lifted his head. He

withdrew his hold on her and paused for a second, as if to caress her cheek, but didn't.

"Want to walk down and check out the lake?" he said.

"Absolutely."

The air between them seemed to echo the throb inside her. As wonderful as the kiss had been, it hadn't been enough, not nearly enough. But there was more to come between them physically, much more.

That kiss was merely the prelude.

9

"You heading back to Atlanta when your stint is up here?" he asked as she shrugged into her light day-pack. His was already on his back.

"It's nice to reconnect with Skye and this seems like a great place, but yeah. I'll be heading back to Atlanta in September. I understand myself well enough to know that I won't be able to take the winters or the isolation." Packs in place, they set off down the gentle slope leading to the tranquil green-tinted water.

"I hear you on the winters."

She nodded, the waning sun highlighting a smattering of freckles across her nose and the fine hairs along her jaw.

"But all of that aside, I won't let my former employer get away with this. I'll regain my life in Atlanta, which includes a solid career. I'm not going to be run out of town with my tail between my legs. The dust will settle. I'll have a new reference and I'll have my life back. He and his wife can kiss my grits."

Her Southern drawl became more pronounced on

the last bit. It was cute. He admired her spunk. "Atta girl. That's the spirit."

She slanted a sideways glance his way. "Most everyone back in Atlanta said I was crazy."

She was bringing out protective instincts in him he didn't even know he had. Maybe it was her independence, her need to handle her own problems. Or because she'd tapped into his situation and therefore he felt equally tapped into hers. It was more likely good old-fashioned testosterone because Lars was itching to put a beat-down on that jerk of a doctor.

"Maybe it's time for you to find a new set of friends."

She smiled. "Maybe it is."

"So, there's no boyfriend to kick that doctor's ass? You didn't leave a brokenhearted man behind in Atlanta?"

It shouldn't matter what she'd left behind. He was out of here at the end of the week. He didn't want to think too hard about why he needed to know so badly.

"No. It's hard to talk about dating when my career was swirling down the toilet. But I left a fish with my sister."

A fish? Lars cracked up.

They'd reached the lake's edge and stopped. Delphi looked at him as if he'd lost his mind. "What's so funny about a fish?"

"It was the lack of transition. I asked about a man—" he was incredibly glad there wasn't one "—and you told me about a fish."

She laughed, her eyes sparkling. "I guess that came a little off the cuff. If there's one thing I've learned, it's that life isn't predictable. I certainly never saw myself in this situation."

Lars wasn't sure whether he was just lucky or behind the curve, because he was precisely where he'd planned to be. They began walking along the shoreline, accompanied by the water's rhythmic lapping. "That's the same thing Liam said. He was madder than hell at the time, but he swears it's all worked out for the best. Something about one door closing and another one opening."

"Yeah. I've heard that, too. It's kind of hard to swallow, though, when you're in it. Do things ever take you by surprise?"

He'd been caught off guard once, but he'd learned quickly. "Not anymore. I can't afford any surprises in my work. So I've learned to be thorough and anticipate every possible angle."

"So, what exactly do you do in the Marines? What's your job?"

"I'm a demolitions expert. If it's designed to blow up and hasn't, I go in and either blow it up or defuse it."

"No margin for error there."

"Exactly. That's why I work hard to ensure no unanticipated events."

Delphi uttered a sound of delight. "Oh, Lars, look!"

For a moment he stood transfixed by the look of childlike enchantment on her face. It reflected unguarded, unfettered joy. Hard to believe this was the same woman who'd been so closed off on the plane the day before. "The dragonflies—aren't they incredible?"

He dragged his attention away from her. A dozen dragonflies, give or take a few, skimmed the water and flew in figure eights over the bank. "That's too cool.

It's been a long time since I've seen dragonflies." They simply hadn't been part of the world where he'd been.

"It's almost like magic," she said, a breathless note in her voice.

He almost laughed, and then something about the place, the woman, the moment, struck him as other-worldly. As if she, this, was some kind of magic. He shook his head slightly to clear the notion. He'd obviously needed more of a recharge than he'd realized if he was susceptible to that kind of thinking, even momentarily.

"Yeah." Magic didn't exist, but chemistry was a very real aspect of his world. The chemistry behind explosives. The chemistry between him and Delphi. That was real and tangible. The sexual response arcing between them, drawing them to one another, even now, was real and physical. So, the dragonflies were nice but he wasn't buying into any magic thinking. "Since this is a magical spot—" the look she shot him said she knew he was indulging her and scoffing a bit but she'd indulge him because she was right "—we can watch the sunset from the shore. Or did you want to go for a swim?" The sun was steadily sinking toward the horizon. It wouldn't be long before it was dark. "I brought a couple of towels. We can sit on them if you go with option one, or use them to dry off afterwards if you want to check out the water."

She wore a slightly dreamy expression, her face bathed in the glow of the last vestiges of the day. And he knew the same way he'd known with Liam that he was seeing a glimpse of the woman she'd been before her trust and career had been wrecked. She'd been a stranger before, because he knew. That knowing rattled him.

Delphi slid her backpack from her shoulders. "I think the water would be nice. It's not every day that you can swim in a thermal lake at sunset in the middle of Alaska with dragonflies dancing around you. Let's go for it."

He'd thought they were just flying around doing what a dragonfly did, but okay. She began to undress very matter-of-factly. By the time Lars dropped his backpack and pulled out the towels, Delphi had her shoes and socks off.

He shouldn't stare, but he couldn't seem to look away as she unzipped her jeans. Her bright green panties surprised him, but it was her pale shapely legs that knotted his gut. She stepped out of her pants and pulled her T-shirt up and over her head in one fell swoop. Damn!

"Voilà," she said with a bit of a smirk.

Once again, she'd caught him by surprise. She stood there in a modest one-piece bathing suit. He had been expecting a bra and panties and the little devil knew it.

That blew his "anticipate and not be caught unaware" mantra all to hell.

"I thought you didn't have a bathing suit with you." Somehow it was disappointing to think that she'd lied to him, even if it was just a trivial matter of clothing.

"I didn't." She flashed a smile his way. "I borrowed one of Skye's."

"Ah." She was talking about her friend, the town doc. Skye was the redhead married to the pilot. "It's very conservative."

It was the same cut competitive swimmers wore, no

plunging necklines or ruffles. And oddly enough, that made it all the more of a turn-on. It didn't scream *look at me,* which made him look all the harder. She was compact and not exactly thin but curvy. He fisted his hand by his side, trying to keep from reaching for her. If he touched her now, they'd never make it into the water, and she wanted to experience the lake.

"It is fairly conservative, but that's Skye."

"What about you? Would this suit be what you had if you'd packed your own?"

"No. This isn't anything like my bathing suit at home, but it's probably not a bad idea to dial myself back."

He knew she was talking about her experience with her former employer. For the short period of time he'd known her, he was already positive that none of the blame had been hers. "You have to be true to whoever and whatever you are."

"Agreed." She dipped her toe into the water. "Although sometimes things get so mixed up, you lose sight of just who you are." She circled her foot into the lake, sending ripples farther out. "Ah, this is nice."

A breeze kicked in and she crossed her arms as she waded out, moving tentatively. "I'm thinking there's a drop-off…yes, here it is." She began to tread water. She slipped below the surface momentarily and then emerged, her already short hair plastered to her scalp. She turned to him, laughing, exhilaration shining on her face. "Aren't you coming in? This was your idea, after all."

Lars stood, drinking in the sight—her laughing eyes, the smile curving her lips, her sleekness surrounded by water and highlighted by the setting sun.

He snapped out of his momentary stupor. "It *was* my idea, wasn't it? I guess that means I should go in."

He pulled off his T-shirt and Delphi turned her back to him, facing the open expanse of water and the opposite shore. "What are you doing?" he said as he took off his shoes.

"Giving you some privacy."

"I'm coming out in the water with you." He shucked his jeans.

"I know, but—"

"You're a nurse." He pulled down his jeans. "Haven't you seen it all?"

"But you're not in a bed—"

"Why didn't you say so sooner?" He cut her off, deliberately misconstruing her comment, teasing her, as he joined her in the lake. "That can easily be arranged."

They both knew a bed was where they were going to wind up. The way she'd returned his kiss, the look in her eyes…

She laughed. "I meant a hospital bed. In an exam room." She splashed him, yet one more time taking him unawares. He hadn't counted on her playfulness. Her aim was surprisingly good—the water caught him on his lower face and shoulders.

"You'll pay for that," he said, as he wiped away the droplets, joining in her game.

"You're going to get wet anyway."

"We'll see how you feel about that in a few seconds." He advanced on her.

She backstroked farther out, watching him. "But I'm already wet, so there's no need for you to do anything."

Everything tightened, thickened and quickened inside him at their double entendre exchange. "Oh, but I want to make sure you're really wet."

Her glance challenged him. "I've taken care of it."

"It's just not the same. Be ready."

"You have to catch me first." She glided out away from him, toward the center of the lake.

"No problem. I was a competitive swimmer in high school."

She stopped, treading water. "What? Are you serious?"

It was just the edge he needed. He caught up to her. "Nope. Psych."

"That's not fair." Despite her protest, her eyes smiled at him.

"I know." He caught her and pulled her to him. She put her hands on his shoulders, holding on. Wet skin against wet skin, her curves fit against him, causing his breath to catch.

"You're shameless." She, too, seemed breathless and he knew it was him, them, not the exertion.

"I like that," he said. "Shameless goes right along with amoral. Now prepare to get wet."

"Look. See. Already wet." She pointed to her hair slicked against her head, as well as the fact that she was immersed in water up to her shoulders.

Nonetheless, he tightened his hands on her waist. "Take a deep breath. On three, you're going under. One…"

She looked up at him, laughing, daring him to follow through. "You wouldn't—"

"Two…"

"Lars—"

"Three." He dunked her. She squealed just as she went down.

He pulled her back up. She broke the surface sputtering. "You really—"

"Uh-huh. I told you."

She swiped the water away from her eyes. "I thought you were just psyching me again." She pursed her delectable lips in a pout.

"You aren't really mad, are you?"

She slid her hands to the back of his neck, cupping her palms. "I should be."

"But you aren't, are you?"

"I'm trying to decide."

Good God, but he wanted her. He'd been pathetically happy simply to rest his hands on her waist, to feel the flare of her hips beneath his fingers. How could he not kiss her, here in the lake, at sunset in the middle of Alaska, a place neither of them belonged? "Well, if you're waffling, I guess I might as well go ahead. It'll probably tilt the scales, one way or another."

She narrowed her eyes at him. She wrapped her legs around his waist, which brought her in even closer proximity. "If you dunk me again, you're going under, too."

He was already under her spell. Maybe the idea of magic wasn't so far-fetched after all. With one arm wrapped around her, he managed to do a one-armed backstroke until he felt the lake bottom beneath his bare feet. "That wasn't what I had in mind."

As with the dunking, her eyes widened as he lowered his head to hers.

Warm water, crisp air, hot kiss.

She sighed into his mouth and kissed him back.

Once again, it was like kissing in a dream, but this was real. It was the most incredible experience, buoyed by the water, floating weightless, the heat of his mouth, the press of his body. Just when she thought it couldn't get any better, it did. This kiss was like no other.

His skin was sleek beneath her arms and legs, his chest hard against her breasts. She curled her fingers against his neck, feeling the prickle of his short hair beneath her fingertips. His tongue, like a warm velvet probe, teased against her lips. Hungry for more of him, she opened her mouth. She feasted on his taste and the stroke of his tongue against her own.

Finally they broke apart, both gasping for air as surely as if they'd been underwater.

"We missed the sunset," he said, as he swept his hands down her back to cup her buttocks.

She didn't care. For the first time in a long time, she felt free to enjoy her sexuality. For the first time in a long time she wanted a man, this man in particular. "It seems that we did."

The column of his throat was strong and tanned. Droplets of water clung to his skin. She leaned in closer and licked the moisture from his neck.

A shudder rippled through him and his warm breath stirred against her cheek as he sighed. "Delphi…"

He'd apparently moved far enough back so that his feet touched the ground. Hers, however, were still suspended, but he held her up.

She rested her head against his broad chest and shoulder. "This is nice."

She felt peaceful and content in the moment. She felt like a desirable woman, something she hadn't felt—or wanted to feel—since that episode with DeWitt. Even more important, she felt very real, very hot desire for the very tempting, very temporary Lars Reinhardt.

Something that had been dancing in the back of her consciousness ever since their embrace. She ran her hand down his side and sure enough, sleek skin gave way to fabric. Bathing suit trunk fabric. She laughed as she shook her head. "You told me you didn't have a bathing suit either. Was that another psych?"

"I was teasing you." He squeezed her buttocks, lifting, separating, and she felt the warm water against her bottom. He'd wanted to make sure she was wet. She definitely was.

"I see." She dipped her finger beneath the top band of his trunks.

"Are you teasing me?" he said, even as he pulled her bathing suit bottoms up to meet in the middle, a temporary thong. He filled his big hands with her bared cheeks.

"It depends on your definition of teasing. If you're asking am I toying with you? Not yet. Am I being playful? Absolutely. Am I insincere? Not in the least."

"That sounds good to me." Lars kissed her shoulder as he continued to knead and massage her skin.

His hardened penis pressed against her, between her thigh and her belly. "Actually, that *feels* pretty good to me...."

She hadn't flirted like this since the incident. But she'd questioned herself a hundred times—had she said or done something that DeWitt had misconstrued? Had she possibly led him on?

Now it was as if she'd found a part of herself again—the fun-loving, flirtatious Delphi. That had been why she'd been so annoyed by Lars on the plane.

She'd wanted to stay in her funk because her funk was safe, but Lars was clearly anything but safe. And now that she'd accepted that, it felt good to get back to the woman she really was. And he felt good, all six feet plus of him.

She pushed aside all the thoughts of DeWitt and the incident and brought herself firmly back to the moment.

He kissed the length of her neck and at the same time slipped his finger past the elastic of her bottoms and along her desire-slicked channel. Heat exploded inside her. She moaned and dropped her head back and to the side, giving him more access, even as she pressed downward on his marauding digit.

"And that *feels* really good," she said.

Delphi was momentarily bereft when he withdrew his finger but was quickly mollified when he took her breasts in his hands.

As he rolled her nipples between his fingers, a sweet heat that had nothing to do with the lake and everything to do with the man and his touch coursed through her, culminating into a sleek want between her thighs.

The thought floated through the back of her head that she'd just met him yesterday. But it was quickly chased by the thought that it didn't matter. All that was important was how wonderful this felt, how alive and vibrant she felt with his hands and mouth and big hard body on her and against her.

She reached between them and cupped his erection through his trunks. His breathing grew even heavier, his touch more intense.

The medical professional in her surfaced. "Lars, I've tested safe and I have a birth control implant. If you have issues, then let's find a condom." It wasn't a deal breaker, they just had to take precautions.

"No issues. All my tests are clear."

"Then let's take off our suits," she said. "Can you throw them to the bank from here?"

"No problem. Let me help you get yours off."

"You're so thoughtful," she said, laughing.

He slid the straps over her shoulders. "That's my personal mission, to be thoughtful and helpful." He tugged them down farther and she pulled her arms out. He left it at her waist and cupped her breasts in his hands. Fire raced through her, stoked by the sensation of his calloused palms and the smooth-as-silk lapping of the lake.

Taking a deep breath, he sank beneath the water and tugged the suit down and over her hips, skimming it down her legs. She raised her right foot to lift it out of the suit. Lars braced his hand on her hip and propped her knee on his shoulder, opening her thighs.

She nearly came when he exhaled, sending air bubbles rushing against her clit. It was unlike anything she'd ever felt before. Another onslaught of bubbles rushed against her but this time he followed it with an intimate underwater "kiss."

Delphi gasped and arched against his mouth. He pulled the suit down and off of her left foot and then resurfaced.

She could barely find her voice. "Lars…" She was at a loss for words. She gathered herself and said, "I can help you with your trunks but I don't know that underwater trick."

"Hold on." He pulled off his swim trunks and within

less than a minute both bathing suits had landed on the shore with a wet thunk. "Now…"

He skimmed her shoulders with his hands and pulled her to him. She fit against him perfectly. His hard nakedness, along with the warm water, created a sublime arousal unlike anything she'd ever experienced.

Cupping her scalp in his big palm, he found her lips with his while he wrapped his other arm about her waist. Their mouths fused together, their tongues stroking, exploring. Delphi couldn't get close enough to him. She sucked on his tongue as she wound her leg around his lean hip, rubbing herself against his erection.

"Mmm," she moaned into his mouth, straining against him.

He moved his hands to her hips and nudged at her slick opening with the head of his penis. Oh, my God, he felt good. She wrapped her other leg around him, taking him inside her, stretching to accommodate the width and length of him.

Delphi was frantic for more. She felt elemental and raw. Wanton. He thrust into her and she ground down onto him. His grip on her tightened and she dug her fingers into his skin, nudging him deeper and harder inside her with her feet against his backside.

A storm of desire raged inside her. Every fiber, every cell needed him to satisfy the craving he'd awakened.

Higher, tighter, she felt it coming. Her orgasm crashed through her, over her. And as if he'd been waiting for her, Lars followed.

10

LARS STOOD IN the aftermath of what qualified as the best sex of his life and tried to regain his breathing and his sanity.

"Mirror Lake is definitely my favorite place now."

Delphi rested her head against his chest and shoulder, her ragged breath warm against his skin. "I knew when you said you wanted to show me something…"

He chuckled. "That wasn't exactly what I meant."

"I don't know that I believe that, but I'm not complaining."

He laughed, smoothing his fingers over the ridge of her shoulder blade to the indentation of her spine. "No complaints is good. In fact, it was incredible. I could swear the earth moved under my feet."

"I'm flattered—"

What the hell? There it was again, stronger, more intense.

"Delphi," he cut her off. "It just happened again. The ground shifted. And the water is warmer. That means seismic activity. We need to get the hell out of here."

She didn't panic as they headed toward the shore.

In fact, her face reflected more curiosity than alarm. "Seismic activity?"

"Yeah. The lake is fed by a hot spring."

He saw the moment it clicked for her in her expression. "Which is tied into volcanic activity," she said. "So when the ground shakes and there's a surge in the lake temperature, you know something is going on with the magma below."

"Yep, you got it."

They climbed out of the lake and toweled off. Quickly, efficiently, they pulled on their clothes without further discussion. Lars shoved their two wet swimsuits into Delphi's pack and the towels into his. The hike back to the truck was short and easy.

Lars looked at her as he turned the ignition. "You okay?"

She looked calm but the hand she ran through her short hair was slightly unsteady. "Fine."

Lars leaned over and planted a swift hard kiss on her mouth. "It's probably not a big deal, but just in case, we need to let people know."

"Right." He fully appreciated her calmness. Obviously, she'd been trained for emergency situations. He wasn't so good with women prone to histrionics. "It seems that exploding things are following you."

Lars drove down the potholed trail to the main road, a smile curving his mouth at her dark humor. "A bomb is one thing but I don't want to tangle with an earthquake or a volcano."

"Me either. I hate to sound stupid but I never really thought about why there would be a hot springs there."

"That makes two of us." His headlights picked up gleaming eyes in the dark ahead of them, and then they were gone. Probably a wolf. "I bet most of the people who swim in the lake haven't given it much thought either."

As they got closer to town, buildings replaced the towering evergreens. Nothing seemed amiss. He pulled up in front of the airstrip bed-and-breakfast. "Here you go."

"You aren't coming in?"

Lars shook his head. "I'm going over to Bull and Merrilee's. I know it's late but they need to know what just happened. Better safe than sorry. I thought you might not want to go since you've got an early morning ahead of you."

It was her turn to shake her head. "I'm revved up right now. I'll go. If I don't, I'll just be wondering all night what's going on."

He grinned. He liked that she hadn't freaked out. She obviously had a sense of adventure. He backed out and headed to Bull's. "All right, then."

They pulled up in front of the hardware store. While the store was dark, a light glowed on the second floor. Lars parked the truck and said to Delphi as they climbed out, "This way." He led her along the side of the building. "They live above the store. They've got outside access as well as stairs inside."

"I noticed that at the restaurant next door to the B&B," she said as they mounted the stairs.

"Most of the business owners live above their shops." When they reached the top landing, Lars rapped on the wood door. In a minute or so, the light was switched on and Bull opened the door.

"Is there something wrong over at the bed-and-breakfast?" Bull cut straight to the chase.

"Everything's fine there but there's something we thought we should pass along," Lars said.

"Come on in." Bull stood aside and Lars ushered Delphi in ahead of him.

It was difficult to believe he'd been sitting at the kitchen table less than six hours ago. A lot had happened. Maybe some things had changed. Whichever way he looked at it, it felt more like a lifetime ago.

DELPHI GLANCED AROUND while Lars recounted the rumbling ground and temperature surge. The kitchen, while not overly large, was comfortable. Cast-iron cookware hung from hooks on one wall, and in the middle hung an assortment of wooden utensils, much like a display of functional art.

The kitchen table was a clean design and since Bull owned the lumber shop downstairs, she suspected he'd made the table himself. Instead of backed chairs, each seat was an individual bench with buttock indentions.

And the whole time, all she could think about was Lars's knee against hers and his scent on her skin.

Lars wrapped it up. It had only taken him a minute or so to brief Merrilee and Bull about what he'd experienced at the lake. Merrilee spoke up. "The activity has increased in the last year but it's being monitored. So far, they've told us it's not anything to be concerned about. I'll check in with them in the morning. If there's an alert status, the department will contact me here at home."

Lars nodded matter-of-factly. "Good deal." He stood and Delphi followed suit. "We'll let you guys get back to bed."

"Stop in anytime, especially if you've got a concern," Bull said. Delphi had noticed he was a fairly quiet man. Not shy, simply quiet. It was an important distinction. He watched, processed and was very much self-contained. It struck her suddenly that for all his forwardness and joviality, Lars was a bit similar. While he was much more verbose than Bull, he also observed, processed and possessed more than a measure of self-containment. Delphi knew without a doubt that the discussion they'd had concerning his mother was a rare event for Lars.

She and Lars walked toward the door. He looked at Delphi. "Feel like walking back to the bed-and-breakfast?"

"Of course." She was invigorated and full of energy in a way she hadn't been in a long, long time.

Lars nodded and said to Bull, "We'll leave the truck here and walk back. Thanks for letting me use it."

"Sure. Anytime."

They made their way down the stairs and stopped by the truck to pick up their backpacks. The town enveloped them in its silence. When they'd both shrugged into their backpacks, Liam slung an arm around her shoulders and pulled her against his side as they began walking in the direction of the B&B.

A thrill shot through her at the weight of his arm around her, the heat of being held against his solid side. The feeling of being protected—almost cherished— floated through her, like the fleet passing of a wraith on the periphery of one's vision, vanishing equally quickly.

"It's been quite the day, hasn't it?" Liam broke the quiet between them.

The wedding and reception, the lake, sex, the mini-quake… Yeah, it had definitely been quite a day. "That's an understatement."

On a whim she wrapped her arm around his waist and rested her head in the crook of his shoulder. The darkness was different here than back home. Despite the absence of streetlights, the evening's veil held no menace. It was a place out of time. No cars cruised down the street. No radios or TVs blared behind closed doors. There was only the sifting of the wind through the evergreens and the hum of mosquitoes. An owl hooted in the distance. A sense of safety enveloped her.

Her words flowed out of her feelings. "Doesn't it feel peaceful here?"

"Yeah. It's great. But I'm so conditioned to noise and activity that it takes some getting used to. I'm generally on alert."

An internal sigh rippled through her. She didn't want to think about Lars being any place except in Good Riddance. She didn't want to picture him in battle gear, in danger. She pushed aside the thought. "It's good for the soul."

"I couldn't agree more."

They strolled along, a quiet harmony flowing between them. Their sexual energy was definitely part of that flow.

They covered the remaining distance in silence. A sudden exhaustion swept through Delphi. It *had* been quite a day.

"Tired?" Lars asked. It was funny how he picked up on her mood shift. She hadn't said anything.

She laughed, a bit disconcerted that he'd tapped into her feelings. "Exhausted. It just hit me."

"I'm not surprised. It's the aftermath of all that adrenaline."

"My feet and legs have turned to bricks."

"Do you want me to carry you?"

He was serious. She almost laughed, but she was too tired to laugh…and she didn't want to hurt his feelings. It was actually very gallant of him to suggest it. And she needed the energy to tackle the stairs leading to the bedrooms above. "That's sweet but I'm fine."

Exhaustion weighted her, tugged at her, but she put one foot in front of the other until she gained the upper floor landing. A heavy snoring resonated through the hall from one of the two rooms at the top of the stairs. She didn't know who the other guests were but one of them was sleeping well.

"Need me to tuck you in?" Lars whispered.

She smiled in the dark hallway and whispered back, mindful of the late hour and the other guests, "I have to take a shower first. Lake water."

"Gotcha." They stopped outside of her bedroom door. Lars's hand was warm against the small of her back. "Go in and get your stuff together and I'll hook you up in the bathroom."

Jet lag, tension, excitement, sex—it had all caught up with her. She seriously felt as if she could just drop on the spot. There wasn't an ounce of hanky-panky left in her right now. "Lars, I'm too tired."

"Delphi, I don't think I'd be much good anyway. I'm pretty tired myself. I'm just going to start the water for you. It takes a couple of minutes for it to actually get hot. Get your things together and I'll let you know when the shower's warm."

She was pretty much too tired to even think but that sounded right enough. "Okay. Thanks."

She went into her room and in no time had clean panties and her nightie and robe. She weaved on her feet as she glanced at the clock. She knew she wasn't supposed to be switching back and forth in her head, but with the time difference it was 5:00 a.m. back home. She'd just sit on the edge of the bed, just at the bottom until Lars knocked.

That wonderful, sexy, arrogant, sweet marine....

LARS TAPPED AT Delphi's door. The water was finally warm. Dead silence on the other side. He tapped again. Nothing.

He eased open the door. "Delphi?"

She was fast asleep on the end of the bed. He called her name again. "Delphi…"

She didn't budge. The water was still running. He'd hop in and shower and then try to wake her again. She'd either be refreshed from her nap or she was down for the count. He was fairly certain it was the latter.

He dropped by his room and grabbed clean underwear, sweats and a T-shirt. Back in the bathroom, he stripped and stepped under the stream of warm water.

It had been an incredible day with Delphi. Not just the sex—although that had been damn good—but the whole thing. They'd danced, laughed and flirted. It had been just what he needed.

Used to efficient, fast showers, he was finished after a few minutes. When he was done, he returned to Delphi's room. The bedside lamp threw a soft light over her features. She was so cautious when she was awake. He stood for a moment studying her as she slept. He brushed aside a shadow of guilt at watching her in an unguarded state.

Her mouth gaped slightly open. Her lashes cast faint shadows on her lightly freckled cheeks. She looked soft and sweet in sleep.

He trailed his finger over her cheek. Her soft skin bore a fine dusting of baby down along her jawline. She murmured softly, turning her face into his touch.

He had fully intended to try to wake her, but she was hard and fast asleep. He couldn't just leave her like this. If she woke up as he was putting her to bed and wanted to shower, then so be it. Lars turned back the covers on one side.

Working methodically, but carefully, he undressed her and put her in the nightie he found on the bed next to her. He transferred her to the turned-down side of the bed and tucked the covers around her.

He flipped off the bedside light, plunging the room into darkness. Pausing, he stood momentarily stilled by indecision. He could go next door to his own bed or he could climb in with her. There was a fifty-fifty chance she'd be pissed when she woke up and found him in her bed, but, dammit, he spent plenty of nights alone in bed and he'd be a fool not to enjoy the pleasure of her warmth while he could. Better to ask forgiveness tomorrow morning than wait for permission.

Shucking his sweatpants, he climbed into the other side of the bed. He wrapped his arm around her and she rolled into him, snuggling. With a quiet satisfaction, Lars closed his eyes.

DIRK STARED AT the blinking cursor on the computer screen. Done. He'd dawdled around and done everything else he could possibly think of since he'd gotten back to his room. He'd even shined his boots. But this couldn't be put off any longer. Merrilee would corner him tomorrow and harass his ass to make sure he'd actually sent the damn invitation. He should've just kept his big mouth shut. Now he was stuck.

Finally he'd plopped down and typed out the invitation he and Merrilee, mostly Merrilee, had put together. Now all that was left to do was to press the send button.

He ran his hand over his head. Shit. As long as he didn't send it, she couldn't say no.

Natalie, I hope things are good with you and your family. The weather is really nice in Alaska now. There's a lot of fishing and hiking and other fun things to do. Plus it's really pretty, if you like wildflowers and mountains and nature, which I think you do. There is also a nice spa here you might like, too. It is a great time to come if you haven't already made vacation plans. So, do you think you'd like to come out for a visit? Your friend, Dirk.

Merrilee had said he had to flat out ask her if she wanted to visit. Damnation. And she'd told him to take out the part he'd written about the kind of fish that were biting and instead mention the spa. Spas just weren't on his radar, but Merrilee knew the kind of things a woman would like.

He shook his head. He had to send the damn thing before the next morning so he might as well get it over with. He took a deep breath, stabbed the button with his finger and exhaled as it zipped through the internet.

He pulled off his jeans—he never could email Natalie when he was sitting around in his boxers; it just didn't seem right—and pulled off his socks.

Dirk walked back over to the laptop to close it down and his heart started thumping hard and fast. Natalie had emailed him back. He stood there in indecision. If she'd said yes, he'd be too excited and wound up to sleep. If she said no, well, he'd be pretty wrecked. And if he didn't open it and find out one way or another, the wondering would gnaw at him all night. Any way it turned out, he was screwed.

He opened the file. He read it twice, then once again for good measure. Natalie was coming. Here. To see him.

Holy hell.

11

DELPHI BURROWED CLOSER to the warmth. She felt him, smelled him, and memory and a measure of confusion crowded in on her. She blinked her eyes open. Lars was snoozing, his head on the pillow next to her.

She was missing something. The last thing she remembered, she was waiting on the shower. She looked down at herself. She was in her nightgown. Either she'd done a grand job of sleepwalking or he'd undressed her and slipped on her nightclothes. Since she'd never sleepwalked in her life, it was unlikely she'd started now.

She didn't know why the notion of him undressing her was so disconcerting, but it was. They'd had a sexual encounter. In her job, she routinely undressed patients and thought nothing of it. However, there was an intimacy to being undressed by a man you'd had sex with and then sharing a bed when it wasn't necessary. Perhaps that was what had her so off-center—finding him in her bed. He had a perfectly good room next door. There hadn't been any "action" going on, so it had been fairly pointless for him to climb into bed with her.

She reminded herself that intimacy didn't matter. He was still leaving at the end of the week, so there was nothing at stake. It gave her a sense of freedom. There was no power struggle, no opportunity for him to misconstrue anything she said or did. And if he did, well, his mistake wouldn't get her fired and blackballed.

He was an interesting man, she'd give him that. A man who set off bombs and could dance like nobody's business. A man who put his life on the line in his job, but was also vulnerable to his mother's antics. And she'd watched and paid attention yesterday.

If you took impressions at face value, Liam came across as the serious twin. Even at the reception, there had been a solemnity to him. Therefore, in contrast, Lars, with his ready smile, twinkling eyes and teasing manner, came across as if he was a bit of a lightweight and not to be taken seriously. However, there was depth to Lars that wasn't apparent at first glance. And it wasn't as if he was putting on an act. Those qualities seemed to be genuine facets of Lars. His devilishness was as much a part of him as his intensity about his mom.

He slept on his side, his back to her, one arm flung above his head. The back of his neck was brown above the ribbing of his T-shirt. Spooned behind him, Delphi felt the weight of his bare legs against her thighs.

She lay there, content to feel the rhythm of his breathing against her chest and belly, to languish in his warmth and his masculine scent and feel.

His resting heart rate was probably fifty or a little lower and she was certain he had a BMI of around twenty-four. The man was fit. When she'd first seen him on the plane, she'd thought he was attractive but tiresome. However, he had actually been fun and thoughtful yesterday and last night. And the sex in the lake had been earth-shattering.

Desire, like the hot spring that fed the lake, infused her with warmth. Sharing the bed with him, curled up next to him, she experienced her own seismic activity. Now seemed as good a time as any to find out whether he was a morning person or not.

She slid her hand beneath the edge of his T-shirt. He woke up instantly. He didn't move, but she felt it in his body tension.

They both remained silent as Delphi continued her exploration. Trailing her fingers over his taut belly, she followed the fine trail of hair to the edge of his briefs.

His swift intake of breath was audible in the room's silence. She delved beneath the elastic and encountered the velvet hardness of his erection.

She made an approving noise and wrapped her hand around his penis. "This is your wake-up call, soldier."

He arched against her hand and chuckled low in his throat. "Is this reveille?"

She fingered the smooth head, catching a pearl of moisture on her fingertip. "Aren't you supposed to blow reveille?"

"That's generally how it goes." He rolled onto his back, a rakish smile tugging at his sensuous lips.

With a low laugh, she ducked beneath the covers. The scent of arousal, both hers and his, surrounded her. Wriggling farther down the bed, she tugged his briefs down his hips, freeing his penis. She licked up the length of his velvety shaft and he sighed. He put his left hand beneath the covers and stroked her hair.

Delphi took him in her mouth and "rode" him with

her mouth and hand. Her arousal intensified with each slip and slide of his penis.

Releasing him, she pressed kisses along his thighs and his lower belly. Lars grasped her arms and pulled her out from beneath the covers and onto her side.

"Now, that was a wake-up call," he said. Lars pressed kisses along her shoulder and neck, his unshaven jaw prickling against her skin. He leaned slightly back and away. "I don't want to kiss you any closer because I haven't brushed my teeth."

"I'm in the same boat." She didn't want to get in his face with her morning breath either. Nothing like a little early a.m. halitosis to kill a mood.

"I'm not inclined to step out into the hall this way." He indicated his erection.

Delphi giggled, imagining him running into one of the other guests with his "flagpole" tenting his clothes. "That's probably best."

He growled. "You think that's funny, do you? You'll pay for that...."

He kissed along her collarbone and then down the front of her gown. Her breath caught in her throat; her heart rate accelerated. Then he lowered his head even farther and mouthed her nipple. She bit back a cry as she heard someone walking down the hall outside the door. Instead she dug her fingertips into his scalp. Closing his mouth around her breast, he sucked harder. She pulled him closer, pressing herself up and into him. His warm mouth against her with the wet material... She bit her lip to keep quiet. Knowing others were awake and moving around right outside the door brought another level of excitement to their sexual play.

He moved to the other breast, leaving the cooler air

to "kiss" the side that was now wet. He reached between them and pushed aside the crotch of her panties. While he taunted her nipple with his tongue, teeth and mouth, he teased his finger through her pubic hair and dipped into her oh-so-wet-and-eager channel. She gasped. The combination was like a charge of electricity through her.

Oh. Yes. She fisted her hand into the sheet, holding on. Again and again he fingered her while he moved from one breast to the other until she thought she couldn't possibly stand it another second longer.

As if he knew what she needed and how she needed it, he pulled her to him so that her mouth was against his shoulder, muffling her cry as she came.

LARS SMILED TO himself. That was one hell of a wake-up call…and they weren't done yet. Delphi was about to find out what detonation was all about. He was aching for release, as well.

She kissed his shoulder and sagged limply against him. He pressed a kiss to her temple. "Catch your breath, Blondie."

Her eyes widened and then glimmered with interest and excitement. "Caught."

He got up and stood by the bed. Outside the bedroom the bathroom door opened and the measured tread of another guest echoed against the hall's wood floor.

The footsteps stopped one door over. "Myrtle, you're going to have to get a move on, woman, We're due to go fishing in half an hour."

"I told you it was a mistake to go our first day here.

My body's still on Pennsylvania time. Don't rush me, Lamar."

Lars and Delphi exchanged a look. She put her index finger over her lips in a "quiet" sign. He winked at her and twirled his finger and hand in a turn-over-and-around gesture. She rolled over onto her belly and looked over her shoulder at him.

Outside, the couple went back and forth.

Lars crooked his finger, beckoning her. She moved an almost-indecipherable amount. He grinned, liking her game. He grabbed both of her ankles and dragged her across the mattress, almost to the edge of the bed. She opened her mouth in mock surprise. He silently laughed, tapped her lightly on the ass and pointed his thumb up.

Delphi got on her knees and all the joking was over because there wasn't a damn thing funny about her rounded rump thrust in the air and the sweet pink of her glistening sex tempting him.

He gently pushed down on her shoulders until her cheek rested again the sheet. Oh, yeah. He stepped up behind her and wrapped his hands around her hips, holding her in place. He slid the head of his cock against her slick opening. She made a low mewling noise in the back of her throat and his cock quivered.

He entered her slowly and she snatched a pillow and buried her face in it. They set up a rhythm. He pushed into her and she thrust back on him. It was hot, hot, hot to watch his cock slide in and out of her, to feel her warm, wet sex wrap around him.

He could feel her climax coming. Lars gave in to his orgasm, coming right along with her. He lay back down on the bed with her, and she simply lay there as if she were boneless.

He still wore his T-shirt. She still had on her night-gown. She was facing the opposite direction and he pressed a kiss to the nape of her neck.

"Feel free to wake me up that way any day, anytime," he said.

She made a murmur of amusement.

It was a good thing his day had started on such a good note. He braced himself for what was to come and rolled away from her, sitting up. "I'm afraid I have to run. My mom is leaving this morning and I need to show up. Try not to miss me."

She made a sound.

"That sounded suspiciously like a snort."

"Mmm."

She was cracking him up. It was a bit of an ego booster that he'd sexed her into such a relaxed state.

"Begging me not to leave won't do any good. I've got to go, Blondie."

She looked at him, heavy-lidded, obviously sated. "You're an idiot, Reinhardt."

"Oh, yeah? Would you let an idiot do this?" He raised the hem of her gown and kissed her plump butt cheek as he got out of bed.

She laughed in surprise and rolled over on her back. "Thanks."

"For?" Was she thanking him for sex? For leaving? For literally kissing her ass?

"For, well, everything. Yesterday was fun. And thanks for putting me to bed last night. And this morning…well, that was good."

"I'm just going to see my mother off," he said. If

she was trying to give him a kiss-off, she'd have to be more direct than that. "I'll be back."

She offered a teasing smile. "I was counting on it."

He loved her smiles. They weren't all the same. There was her smart-ass smile, her haughty smile and her I-just-got-sexed-into-bliss smile.

"Okay," he said, oddly reluctant to leave her.

"Go. Before I drag you back to bed."

He stood, pulling on his pants before he blew his mother off.

He stopped at the door and looked back at her. She was all tousled and inviting stretched out on the white sheets. She wore an I-want-more-of-you smile—definitely his favorite so far.

MERRILEE HESITATED, which was something she very seldom did with her husband. Bull had been not only her lover but her best friend for twenty-five years now, but when it came to blood relations, folks could be peculiar. Her husband was no exception. But she needed to talk to someone and he was the one. She would choose her words carefully.

He worked at the chunk of wood with his whittling knife and beat her to the conversational punch.

"What's on your mind? You've been looking like you were ready to bust all morning. What gives?"

He knew her well, sometimes too well. It made getting away with anything darn near impossible. She'd left the airstrip to come over and talk to him.

"Well, yesterday—"

"I know. I've been waiting for you to bring up the business with Janie." They hadn't talked about it last night. She'd seen Bull's mind going over it when she'd gotten back from walking Janie to Alyce's bed-and-breakfast yesterday. But instead, they'd talked about the wedding and how much fun everyone had at the reception afterward. Light and easy conversation. The one thing she'd learned was it didn't matter if you were lovers or husband and wife or best friends or a combination thereof, things needed to be discussed in the right time and space. Sometimes banal conversation cleared the air and paved the way for weightier issues later. And, while it wasn't what she'd wanted to discuss with him, he obviously wanted to talk about his crazy sister now. Merrilee tried to keep a compassionate mind and heart open to Janie, but Janie made it difficult.

"Okay," she said, opening the door for him to say what was obviously on *his* mind.

He shook his head, a frown planting grooves across his forehead. "I didn't realize until last night just how Janie's peculiarities…have affected her boys. I did a lot of thinking last night. I've been busy with my own life and haven't really spent any time around the boys since they were teenagers. But I think her behavior has had a negative impact on Lars. I think her madness is the reason he went into bomb disposal—*and* the reason he won't get serious with a woman."

She'd been so focused on Dirk's problems, she hadn't thought about Lars.

"How's that?"

"I have a theory that Lars likes to detonate bombs because then he's the one who controls the explosions going on around him."

"You're probably right." Bull was right about most things, although she hated to admit it sometimes.

He nodded. "I remember what it was like growing up with her. And I was her brother, not her kid. The least little thing could set Janie off and when she exploded…well, it wasn't pretty." He sighed. "I bet you got an earful tonight walking her back."

"I did. I just listened and my only comment was about how weddings could be fun but they could also be very tense. Really, anything I said wasn't going to make a difference."

"That's for damn sure. I told Lars the same thing tonight. He can say what he needs to say to make himself feel better but it won't change Janie. What do you make of him and Delphi?"

Merrilee knew Bull well enough to know he wasn't so much switching topics as focusing on something that was unfolding. Janie was who and what she was. "There's chemistry for sure, and I'd say some pretty high walls, as well."

"You know we Swenson men like a challenge. Their last name might be Reinhardt, but by blood, they're Swensons."

"Well, there is that." Merrilee was impatient to get this off of her chest. "Speaking of challenges, I wanted to talk to you about Dirk."

Her husband looked momentarily taken aback, which was most unlike Bull. "Damn, here I was thinking it was Janie and Lars on your mind and I've been rattling on about them. What's up with Dirk?"

"I'm pretty sure he can barely read and write."

Very little shocked Bull, but this definitely took him by surprise. "You mean he's illiterate?"

"I think he's semiliterate, maybe at a second- or

third-grade level. At least, what would've been third-grade level when you and I were in school."

"How'd this come up?" Bull suddenly looked old and rather weary and Merrilee realized they weren't spring chickens anymore. "He say something to you?"

"No. He wouldn't. And I think he's done a great job of compensating and hiding it over the years. But I was helping him write an email, which is another story, and it was pretty apparent."

"Hmm."

"I know you tell me to mind my own business most of the time."

"Which you ignore most of the time. But this is one time you shouldn't."

"I'm glad you feel that way. I'm just not sure how to approach it because there are self-esteem issues involved. I think it needs to come from you."

"I'm thinking we should both sit down with him. But we need to have a game plan in place to present to him as an option."

"Okay." Merrilee could pull together a plan. She was good at that.

"Do you think Liam or Tansy know?" Bull continued. "They both work with him."

"I don't think they have a clue. It's not anything either of them would ignore." Merrilee gave way to the component that had made her angry ever since she'd recognized Dirk's handicap last night. "Damn, his mom was a teacher, for crying out loud. How did Laurie not notice?"

How did a mother who taught English for a living not realize her son was practically illiterate?

"Probably because Dirk was always more interested

in outdoor stuff—hunting or riding a four-wheeler and skipping school. I think she finally threw her hands up and let him do what he wanted to do."

Merrilee wanted to cry for Dirk. "Yeah, you'd skip school, too, if you couldn't read at the same level everyone else in your class could."

"On top of it all, he's always been awkwardly bigger than everyone else," Bull said. And yeah, that would just make not reading all the worse. "Maybe it'd be best coming from Lars. They've always been close."

"I don't know. He's going to know it came from me. That's at least three of us who will know his secret."

"Things become overwhelming when you keep a secret bottled up. Not that he needs to take an ad out in the paper, but I think it might actually be a relief to him if he's aware that the three of us know."

"You're a good man, Bull Swenson."

"I know." She swatted playfully at him. "I'm one lucky son of a bitch."

12

SHE SHOULD GET UP. She should do something. Instead she just lay there after Lars left, luxuriating in feeling so good.

The sheets, rumpled beneath her cheek and the rest of her body, bore his scent, while the air smelled like sex. And what sex! It had been intense, fun, naughty with people right outside the door…and incredibly satisfying.

She smiled into the pillow. This must be what a crack addict felt like. Because as good as it had been, she wanted it again. He was just a man, but what a man he was!

Lars had looked at her as if she was off her rocker when she thanked him, but he had no idea what he'd given her. She laughed and stretched, enjoying the soreness between her legs. While the back-to-back orgasms had been truly noteworthy and fantastic, he'd given her something better still. He'd helped her find something she hadn't known she'd lost.

He'd restored her sexual sense of self. Heck, he hadn't just restored it, he'd uncovered a depth to it unknown to her until now. It was as if her sexuality had roared back to life and was running rampant.

She was faintly horrified when she realized she'd just been intimate with lake water dried on her. She wasn't germaphobic, but as a nurse she was cognizant of good hygiene. That roused her out of bed.

The original plan had been that she'd arrive on Friday afternoon and have the weekend to unpack and set up her cabin. But since she wouldn't be in that cabin until later in the week, her day was wide open.

She knew firsthand that the other guests were out on a fishing trip. It was the perfect time and opportunity to relax in the claw-foot tub next door.

Twenty minutes later she was shoulder deep in fragrant water and bubbles. She closed her eyes and let the warm water work its magic on her recently used muscles.

She'd fantasized about Lars in this very room. She sighed and smiled. The man was so much better than the fantasy. She'd fully expected him to have other plans today, but apparently his only obligation was seeing his mother for breakfast and then saying his goodbyes to her. He'd said he'd be back and she would be ready and waiting.

GIVEN A CHOICE, Lars would prefer to detonate a field strewn with land mines than deal with his mother in this mood. And her mood was evident in her very stance. He had figured out early on how to read her body language. She was, as the saying went, loaded for bear.

She stood in the airstrip office, studying the wall of photographs behind the two old chess players. He paused for a moment at the bottom step, studying her, trying to see her differently than he'd always seen her—simply his mom.

As always, she stood ramrod straight. Even though she couldn't have been more than five feet and a few inches, she was imposing. Her salt-and-pepper bob was immaculate as always. She wore a pair of black travel slacks and one of her signature shawls around her shoulders.

He knew that she knew he was watching her. But if there was any doubt, Dwight announced in his megaphone volume indicative of his deafness, "Your boy's here."

At thirty-two, with thirty-three fast approaching, it had been a long time since anyone had referred to him as a "boy." It pulled a smile from him as he descended the last step.

She turned and peered at him over the top of her black-rimmed glasses.

"Good morning, Mother," he said, his smile taking on a forced quality in the face of her censorious gaze.

"Lars." She acknowledged him with an abbreviated nod. Apparently it wasn't a good morning on her end.

His mom should try getting laid. It had done him a world of good.

"Ready for some breakfast?" he said.

"So, you're up to suffering through another meal with me?"

Okay, so everyone had always put up with her shit. Hell, so had he, but he wasn't known as the family rebel for nothing. It was the same feeling he'd had last night. Enough. She was his mother and he owed her a measure of respect, but he would not stand for her manipulations any longer.

"Here's the deal, Mom. I'd like to have breakfast with you." Satisfaction glimmered in her eyes. "I would not, however, like to listen to passive-aggressive comments for the next hour."

Dead silence filled the room. Overhead a floorboard squeaked. Delphi.

"I will not tolerate you speaking to me that way." The indignation in her eyes and her ice-cold tone underscored her words.

He was infinitely weary of what felt like a battle that had been going on his entire life. "Let's just try to have breakfast together without hostility and hurt feelings, Mom."

"I simply made a statement."

Bull had warned him last night not to expect anything different. That assessment was spot-on. So Lars had two choices. He could go to breakfast with her and endure an hour of this bullshit or tell her goodbye now and skip the sixty minutes of misery.

As a kid, there'd been no option. Even as an adult, up to now, he hadn't seen the latter as an alternative. It was as if the conversation with Delphi had unlocked something inside him.

"I love you, Mom. Have a safe trip back and take care of yourself."

"You're...you mean...you're not going to breakfast?" She was totally flummoxed, but then why wouldn't she be? After thirty-two years Lars had just changed the tapes.

He shook his head. "I'm not."

"I'm sorry you seem to think I always say the wrong thing."

It wasn't the first time he'd heard that. This time, however, he heard it with fresh ears. Even her "apology" put him at fault. His mom was one unhappy human being.

It was time to put his exit strategy into play because the next move would be her lapse into pathos. When disdainful outrage didn't work, she fell back into histrionics and physical malady.

"And I'm sorry you feel that way." He grabbed her and gave her a quick, tight hug. He couldn't say he liked her, but she was his mom and he did love her. He took a step back. "Be safe."

He was halfway across the room when she called out to him.

"Where are you going?" She sounded so bewildered, he almost relented, but if he did, she'd just pick up where she'd left off.

"It's a nice morning for a walk." His mom would make a scene in here, but she wouldn't follow him down the street. If he went back upstairs, she'd follow him and bad would just turn to worse. "Love you, Mom." He couldn't in good conscience tell her it'd been nice to see her.

He walked out the front door. His leaving wasn't a turn-tail-and-run move. It was more of a strategic retreat, a decision not to return enemy fire. He wasn't getting into a firefight.

The mild sun on his face felt great as he walked down the sidewalk. Not allowing his mom to bully him felt even better.

His cousin materialized out of seemingly nowhere.

But then again, Lars had been so consumed in his thoughts he could've stepped on top of Dirk and not known it.

"Hey, Big D. How's it going?"

"She's coming."

What the hell? Lars whipped his head around to look over his shoulder. His mother wasn't back there. "Mom's not back there."

"Why would she be?" Dirk looked at him as if he'd lost it. "I thought she was leaving today."

They walked on.

"She is."

"Oh, okay. Then why'd you bring her up?"

"Never mind," Lars said. "Let's start this all over. Who's coming?"

"Natalie."

Right. Okay. They'd talked about her on Friday night. "Cool. That's great. Way to go, Big D. When's she coming?"

"I'm not sure yet." The familiarity of the look on Dirk's face slammed Lars in the gut. Lars had seen his share of men die, and there was a look in their eyes, a look of inevitability, of resignation, of giving up the fight. Dirk wore the same look. What in the hell was going on with his cousin?

They'd run out of sidewalk. A group of kids, plus a couple of dogs, were playing dodgeball in the sandy lot to the left. Lars propped against a tree. Dirk shoved his hands deep in his pockets and looked around. Lars suddenly realized Dirk hadn't just happened to run into him. He'd been waiting outside for him.

"What gives?" Dirk apparently needed to get something off of his chest.

Dirk shuffled from one foot to the other. "I shouldn't have asked her. I shouldn't have ever looked her up." The look of self-loathing on Dirk's face shocked Lars. "I'm not good enough for her. I—"

"Whoa, whoa, whoa. What's this all about, Dirk? So you're not Liam? That's a damn good thing. You're a great guy, a hard worker. What the hell do you mean you're not good enough for her?" He quickly ran back through their conversation. Dirk had never gotten too caught up with women. But he was definitely straight. Otherwise, he wouldn't be miserable over Natalie in the first place. That left only one other option he could think of. "You know, if you've got a problem getting worked up, a doctor can prescribe something."

Dirk turned beet-red and for a second Lars didn't know if Dirk was going to punch him or cry—either one would suck. "I get it up. What the hell?"

"Exactly, what the hell? If you're not into guys and you can get it up, why are you acting so crazy?" Well, that was a thought. Maybe mental issues ran in the family—his mom was certainly a head case. "Hell, I'm sure there's medicine for whatever's ailing you. You can take a pill for just about anything these days."

"Yeah?" Dirk looked as if he wanted to hit something. "Do they make a pill for stupid?"

Dirk wasn't going to be recruited for the space program but he wasn't stupid either. "You're not stupid. Why would you say that?"

Dirk's face took on a mulish expression and Lars sucked in a deep breath and prayed for some patience. Dirk got that expression when he was digging in his heels on something.

Lars's morning had gotten off to such a damned

good start. He'd woken up to explosively fantastic sex with a great woman. It was a beautiful sunny day and no one was likely to get blown up or killed here. What could go wrong? But the day seemed to be steadily going downhill.

"Look, D. I'm not your mama and I'm not your shrink. If you want to talk, then talk. But you've got to tell me what you're dealing with or just shut the hell up. So what's it gonna be?"

For what felt like a full minute, Dirk glared at him, obviously mulling it over.

"I can't…" The last bit was an indecipherable mumble.

"You can't what? Dammit, talk man."

"I can't read so good."

"So?" Was it just the day for family drama? "I sucked at history. That's not a big deal."

"Yeah, okay. Thanks." Dirk turned to leave. It was the echo of hopeless resignation on his cousin's face that led Lars to reach out and stop him.

"Hold on. Rewind here. Just how bad is your reading?"

Dirk tried to shake Lars's hand off. "Forget I mentioned it. It's no big deal."

It was obviously a huge deal and Lars felt like an ass. "If it bothers you, it's a big deal."

"I shouldn't have said anything."

The very fact that he had said something meant that Lars shouldn't have blown him off. "It's definitely a problem, but not one that can't be overcome."

"Oh, yeah? I had teachers shoving shit in my face for twelve years and I just don't get it. Sometimes the words get all tangled."

"That sucks. But something can be done about it. You're obviously not stupid. How do you do your job with Liam? Don't you have to keep supply lists and inventories and stuff?"

"Yeah. I can count." Lars figured Dirk was entitled to that bit of sarcasm. He shrugged. "I memorize the list and recognize the words from going over them with Liam and Tansy."

"Do they know?"

"No one knows." He looked at the ground and then looked up at Lars. The pain in his eyes reminded Lars of a wounded animal. "Look at me. I'm huge. People already think I'm dumb as an ox. What woman wants a dumb man?"

Lars threw a thought out. "Is that why you change jobs and move locations?"

"Pretty much." Another shrug. "You keep moving and it doesn't catch up with you. But if you stay in one place too long with the same people, sooner or later someone's bound to figure it out."

Lars floundered, totally out of his realm. Jesus, Dirk's mom had been an English teacher. "Okay, look, we'll figure this out. I don't know jack about this, but I know someone who would. Let's talk to Merrilee."

"She's nice. She helped me write the note to Natalie after the reception."

"Look, Dirk, I can guarantee she can help. How about we go together to see her. Or would you rather talk to her alone?"

"It doesn't matter." Dirk's shrug said otherwise. "You've probably got stuff to do."

Lars said, "Look, my day's wide open. Let's give

my mom time to get on that plane and then we'll sit down with Merrilee and put together a plan of attack."

"Okay." Some of the tension eased from Dirk's face. "But we'll definitely wait until Aunt Jane rolls on out. Your mom is tough."

"Tell me about it. We can hang out here, until the plane lifts off, and then we'll track Merrilee down." Lars figured it had taken a lot of courage for Dirk to bring up the subject to him in the first place—he didn't want his cousin to back out before they did something about it.

"Sounds good to me. Thanks for taking the time to help me out. You know, I already feel better."

"No problem. That's what family is for, right? You're going to be fine."

He and Dirk hung out talking about football and dissecting the last Super Bowl and how it could've been different. More than a couple of townies stopped by to chat and tell Lars what a great guy Liam was and how awesome Tansy was and what an outstanding couple they were. It made him proud. Liam was a good man and Lars was damn happy his brother had found a good woman to share his life with. Oddly enough, Liam's marriage gig was beginning to make some kind of sense to him.

Eventually, the little bush plane rose into the sky.

"The coast is clear," Dirk said.

"Let's go find Merrilee."

"We could just do it Monday or wait until we get back from the camp."

"Well, that'd work, except you're not coming back to Good Riddance. Nice try, though, D." Lars stood and held out his hand to pull Dirk to his feet. "Now, get off your ass and let's go get this thing done."

Dirk lumbered to his feet and they headed toward the airstrip office.

And speaking of good women…sooner or later he'd get back to Delphi.

13

DIRK SERIOUSLY THOUGHT about bolting. But he and Lars had grown up together and Lars would just drag him back and make him finish this thing. Dirk should've kept his mouth shut, except he'd been in a damn panic ever since he got Natalie's note. He'd thought she'd say no. And then he started thinking of all the ways she might find out just how dumb he was and those thoughts had all made him feel as if he was sinking in quicksand. Not that he'd ever been in quicksand, but he'd seen a couple of horror movies and he figured that was close to what it would feel like.

Lars paused at the door and for a second Dirk thought his older cousin might give him a break.

"Okay, I'm here for moral support, but this is your show to run."

No such luck. Dirk nodded, manned up and opened the door.

Merrilee looked up from her desk. "Ah, two of my favorite nephews."

Yep. That was nice.

"Hey, Merrilee, you think we could talk to you for a few minutes?" The words rushed out of Dirk's mouth.

"Of course." She picked up a plate of muffins and held them out, offering them to him and Lars. Dirk passed since he sort of felt like puking, but Lars grabbed one. "What's up, boys?"

"Maybe it'd be a good idea to take a walk or something," Dirk said, glancing over at Dwight and Jefferson. Dwight was half-deaf but Jefferson's hearing was just fine.

"Sure thing." She put the plate of muffins back and picked up her coffee cup. "Hey, would you guys hold down the fort for a bit?" Jefferson nodded and she turned back to Lars and Dirk. "Picnic tables okay or do you want to go over to the house?"

"Picnic tables," Dirk said. Given a choice, he always liked it better outside. Maybe it was because he was so damn big, but he always felt hemmed in indoors.

They dipped out the back door and crossed the landing strip clearing to a couple of picnic tables at the edge of the trees.

Merrilee perched on the table top, her feet on the bench seat. Lars sat down on the other end of the bench, leaning his back against the table edge, his legs stretched out in front of him.

Dirk paced. There was no way in hell he could sit down. The birds were chirping, over on the sandlot kids were playing ball, and there were background noises everywhere. But here, with just the three of them, it was quiet. Merrilee and Lars waited.

Lars studied the sky as if there was a message in the clouds. He was probably just making sure the plane didn't turn around and bring his mom back. Dirk had been nice when he'd said Aunt Janie was tough. She was a horrible woman. But he didn't want to put Lars in the position of having to kick his ass defending his mom, even if Dirk's words were true. Some things you just didn't say about another guy's mom.

Shit. He was just standing here bullshitting in his own head to put off spilling his guts.

Merrilee waited patiently. She looked as though she could wait until next week, if that's how long it took.

He felt the heat rising in his face. The longer he put this off, the harder it would be.

Screwing up his courage, Dirk looked Merrilee in the eye. He might be a dummy, but he wasn't a coward. "I have a little trouble with reading. Sometimes, a lot of times, the words get mixed up. I mean, I *can* read, but…" He trailed off. There was no sugarcoating it.

Merrilee shrugged. "Okay."

He saw it in her eyes. There wasn't even a flicker of surprise. "You knew?"

"I guessed last night. You just beat me to the draw on bringing it up."

Dirk sat on the ground. He wasn't sure his legs would hold him up. Merrilee hadn't looked at him with impatience the way his teachers had, or pity like that one woman had when he'd had to ask for help. He only saw kindness.

"Well," Merrilee said, "then I'll teach you. We'll work together and you'll get better at it."

She made it sound so simple. She'd teach him and he'd learn. Just like all the other kids. The teachers taught and they learned. He'd sat there with the rest of the kids in those classes, paying attention, but he'd never caught on. What made him think it would be any different this time? Maybe it would be the same—

"Don't even let your brain go there," Merrilee said. "Everyone can learn. You're everyone."

Dirk swiped at his eyes, at the tears he couldn't hold back. "Damn bugs."

She'd said *we*—he wasn't in this alone. He wasn't hopeless. And maybe, just maybe, he really wasn't stupid. There must be some hope.

Lars thought there was and now if Merrilee said it, it must be so.

DELPHI PULLED ON a T-shirt and bike shorts, feeling pretty dumb. She'd finished her leisurely bath, spritzed on some perfume and scoped out the sexiest thing she'd brought with her. It had been slim pickings, considering she'd come here to work and hadn't been in a sexy frame of mind when she was packing.

She'd donned black lace panties and a matching push-up bra. She'd put on makeup, tidied the bed and turned back the covers invitingly.

Her heart had started beating double-time when she'd heard the plane take off. She'd waited. And waited. And waited.

She hadn't asked Lars to come back. She'd thanked him and sort of left the offer open, figuring they'd see one another when they saw one another. *He* was the one who'd said something about coming back. She couldn't recall his exact words but he'd clearly intimated he'd be back shortly. At least that's the way she'd taken it when he said he just had to see his mother off.

But that had been half an hour ago. Under normal circumstances, that wasn't such a long time, but this was Good Riddance. There were no traffic jams. For goodness sake, Jane Reinhardt had taken off just out the door.

Delphi would be damned if she was going to waste another minute sitting around waiting.

Her instincts had been wrong again. At least there were no disastrous consequences like before. Now she just had a little wounded feminine pride. She'd also be damned if she'd let him know she'd sat up here waiting—and wanting. She tied her shoes and stood.

And while she was on her little inner rant, obviously the sex hadn't been as mind-blowing, hot, incredible for him as it had been for her or he'd want more of it, the same way she did. Uh, make that *had,* as she *had wanted.* Past tense. She didn't anymore.

Nope. Lars had done an adequate job scratching her itch. So, thank you, Marine. Now she'd simply go about her business. Much the way she'd been going about her business before he had bowled her over with that smile and charm and wound up sending her into orgasmic oblivion. So, there you go. It was a win-win situation. He'd gotten laid. She'd gotten laid. She'd had a good time yesterday, last night and this morning. Nothing more, nothing less.

It was all about expectations and managing those expectations. And moving forward, she wouldn't expect anything.

So, now to get on with her day. She'd shipped her mountain bike out ahead of her. Merrilee had shown Delphi where it was but there'd been absolutely no time to pull it out. Now she had time in spades and it was a gorgeous day for a bike ride.

Putting on her happy face, she left her room. Jefferson and Alberta's husband, Dwight, turned to her as she came downstairs.

She flashed them a friendly smile. "Good morning, gentlemen."

"Morning," Jefferson said with a gentlemanly nod.

"If you're looking for him, your boyfriend's out there," Dwight said. Actually, it was more of a shout.

Despite herself, she glanced in the direction he'd pointed. The window afforded a view of the landing strip. Merrilee, Dirk and Lars were hanging out at a picnic table on the other side of the runway.

"He's not my boyfriend." Delphi felt obligated to correct what was obviously a wrong impression.

Dwight winked at her and chortled. "Alberta calls me that, too—a boy toy."

Jefferson shook his head at his chess partner. "She didn't call him her boy toy."

Dwight crossed his arms over his bony chest, a belligerent frown beetling his unruly eyebrows. "She does too call me that," he said to Jefferson, and then he looked back at Delphi with a toothless smile. "Calls me her studmuffin, too. He's just jealous 'cause he's sexually frustrated. He ain't found a girlfriend yet." He ended that bit of too-much-information with a sage nod.

Jefferson rolled his eyes. "Don't pay him any attention," Jefferson said in a normal tone. "He's deaf as a post," he said much louder. Then louder still, "And he hears better than he plays chess."

"No worries." Delphi laughed at the deliberate baiting. Laughing eased some of her tension. It made her feel a little stupid that she'd been waiting upstairs in an admittedly aroused state while he was out, going on with his day. He hadn't even had to be present. Simply thinking about Lars and what they'd done and what she wanted to do again with him had been enough to leave her panties wet and her body aching. And he was just hanging out.

"Don't let me keep you from your game. I'm just going to get my bike put together over here."

She tuned out the two men's good-natured bickering as she unpacked her bike. Merrilee had stowed it in the area by the front door where a couple of small bistro tables were set up.

Delphi was adjusting her seat post when the back door opened and Lars walked in. She focused 100 percent on the bike.

"Your girlfriend's over there," Dwight said in his megaphone voice.

Determined to play it cool—she'd be damned if she let him know she'd been annoyed in the least—she looked up and shook her head at Dwight's well-intentioned but misguided announcements.

Lars nodded and strolled over to where she was.

"Hey, you," he said with that smile that kind of made her feel like a chocolate bar in the summertime, all gooey inside. Even when she was out of sorts with herself and him, he still had the effect on her. It must be an involuntary central nervous system response to him because in her current frame of mind she wouldn't willingly feel this way. "I was afraid you'd given up on me." He brushed his hand over his head. "I got tied up on something."

"No problem." She smiled as sweetly as she could manage. She straightened.

"Nice bike."

She leaned it against the wall. It was ready. "Thanks. Do you ride?"

She packed away her tools.

Lars shook his head, watching her, his eyes taking on a hot sexual gleam that sparked the same in her. "No, but I recognize first-class equipment when I see it." His statement was chock-full of double entendre she would've appreciated some other time. Nonetheless, her body tightened and her nipples pebbled at the heat in his eyes. "Were you heading out for a ride now?"

He looked down at her bike shorts and a knowing smile tilted the corners of his sexy mouth when he saw her stiff points outlined against her shirt.

She tried to ignore the sexual energy bouncing all around them. "Yep. It's a nice day so I'm going for a ride."

Lars glanced over his shoulder at the two old men and then back to her. Jefferson and Alberta's husband weren't even pretending to play their game. They openly watched her and Lars.

"Could I have a private moment with you, upstairs, before you head out?"

She didn't owe him an audience and her first inclination was to smile sweetly and say she'd chat with him when she returned. Whatever she did—if she just walked out the door with her bike or if she went back upstairs with Lars—they were going to be gossip fodder. However, now that she'd cooled down, she wanted to hear just what he had to say.

"Sure, I've got five minutes before I head out."

LARS CLIMBED THE STAIRS behind her, enjoying the swish of her ass, which was enticingly right in front of him.

She could smile all she wanted to, but Ms. Delphi Reynolds was pissed off.

He didn't owe her any further explanation outside of that he'd gotten tied up. But he'd wonder if he was in her place. And he'd seen the way her nipples pearled and decided then and there that she might ride her bike later, but she was going for an altogether different ride now.

Besides, it had been a hell of a morning with his mom and then Dirk. He could use a little recreational relaxation.

His room was before hers. He slipped ahead of her and opened the door. "Ladies first."

She stepped into the room and busied herself looking around as if she was checking out the furnishings. She stood with her arms wrapped around her waist. Lars closed the door behind them.

Damn, it was as if they'd passed Go and then he'd been sent all the way back to the beginning. Her body language screamed the same message it had when he'd boarded the plane on Friday—Off Limits: No Trespassing.

He leaned against the door, giving her space. "There was a family emergency."

"No problem. I understand."

No problem, his ass. And her *I understand* rang hollow. "Look, I can't go into it, but I got back as soon as I could."

She nodded as she walked over to look more closely at the framed print on the wall. She spoke without turning around. "It's fine, Lars. Really. Last night and this morning was fun, but you don't owe me anything and I don't owe you anything."

"You're right we don't owe each other anything. But you got part of that wrong, Blondie. This morning was incredible."

She tossed him a cool look. "It was good."

"Incredible."

"How was breakfast with your mother?" she said, changing the topic. Fine. He'd made his point.

"It didn't happen. It was pretty plain it was going to be another hour of her trying to get me back in line, so I left. I didn't come back upstairs because she would've followed me to get the last word. So, I walked out the front door, ran into Dirk and the rest, as they say, is history."

"I see." She clasped her hands primly in front of her.

He hated to break it to her but her obviously erect nipples ruined the whole prim setup.

"Do you? You were definitely the best part of my morning." He took a step toward her. "I'd like for you to be the best part of my afternoon."

She sidestepped his advance. "That's sweet, but I told you I'm going for a ride."

Regroup. Reload with fresh ammo and try a different assault tactic. "How was your morning? What'd you do?"

She walked over to the antique desk on the wall opposite his bed. Running her fingers over the wood, she answered him. "I had a nice long soak in the tub, tidied my room and went downstairs. The rest, as you say, is history, since you saw me working on my bike when you came in."

"I see." What he saw was unless she'd spent enough time in the tub to turn into a prune, that hadn't filled all of her time. She'd been waiting on him. He bit back a satisfied smile.

"Are you mocking me?"

"Not even remotely." He was simply glad to know why she was so pissed. He hadn't gotten back when he thought he would…and she'd been waiting on him in bed. He knew it.

He looked down at her sweet nipples teasing him through her shirt and then deliberately looked back up into her eyes. "Come here, Blondie."

"I'm going for a ride, Marine."

"That's exactly what I'd like, too." He just happened to have a different kind of ride in mind. "Great minds think alike."

"On my mountain bike."

"I was thinking of something a little more personal."

"Maybe later."

"Well, would you take pity on a poor soldier and tide me over with a kiss?"

"That's a bad idea."

"I'm striking out here. I can't come up with anything that works for you. No rides. No kisses. Work with me, Blondie."

"You're on your own, soldier."

"But I'm wounded. I had a really rough morning. A hug? Just a hug? I'm appealing to the caregiver professional here."

She crossed her arms over her chest, her eyes full of reproving skepticism…and a glimmer of humor. She was beginning to crack. "So, I'm supposed to believe you went from wanting a ride to a kiss, then to a hug and only a hug? I'm a caregiver professional, but I'm not an idiot."

He pulled out his last bit of ammunition, which was the white flag of surrender. "You're the squad leader, here, Blondie. I just wanted to talk to you—" She snorted and he shrugged sheepishly. "Okay, busted. I was hoping for more than talk, that's true—but you gave me the five minutes I asked for, so now it's up to you."

"I don't trust you."

He held out his hands, palms up, a classic show of no weapons in hand. "I don't have any hidden agenda here." He dropped his hands and arms back to his sides. His shrug was a tad self-conscious. He had never worked so hard for a woman's temporary affections. And crazily, he'd never wanted a woman's temporary affections the way he wanted hers—the way he wanted her. "I want you. You turn me on. I've been up front with you from the beginning." He bowed from the waist. "And the next move is yours, Blondie."

"So, I can walk out that door and go for my bike ride and there will be no hard feelings?"

"None whatsoever. It's not my feelings that are hard."

She nodded, still considering.

Lars spoke again. "But can I make a request?"

"Sure. It doesn't mean it'll be granted, but go ahead."

"Before I leave, the next time we're together, would you wear that outfit?"

That took her aback. "My biking gear?"

Apparently she didn't have a clue the way the tight shorts showcased her thighs and booty. "It's hot."

"This?" The look on her face was priceless. She was

so confounded he almost laughed. Except how much he wanted her was no laughing matter.

"Walking up the stairs behind you…yeah. Trust me."

Famous last words….

14

SHE COULD WALK out the door, hop on her bike and get in a ten- or twenty-mile ride. And she could also stick a pin in her eye.

Lars waited patiently for her decision. There was a quietness about him as he stood, broad-shouldered, lean-hipped, his usually laughing eyes serious in his lean face. Her entire body tingled at just the sight of him. She felt a quickening in her womb, the slick wet between her thighs, the ache in her breasts.

She looked away from him, hoping to clear her thoughts. How was she supposed to think while they were standing in a bedroom together?

She worried her lower lip between her teeth. Perhaps she'd overreacted a bit earlier. Her bike would be here with her for the next three months while her... whoa, not *her* but *the* marine would be shipping out in a few short days.

There was caution, and then there was stupidity. She'd never been with a man who turned her on the way Lars Reinhardt did...and apparently she did the same thing for him.

She smoothed her hands down her thighs. "I suppose I could spare a hug."

He opened his arms and it felt like so much more than a simple invitation to hug him. It was a hug and he was just another man, she reminded herself as she closed the distance between them. She stepped into his outstretched arms and embraced him. She closed her eyes and rested her head against his chest, hearing his heart thudding beneath her ear. She inhaled his scent—a combination of sun, man and their earlier sex.

She nestled closer, her arms still wrapped around him. His arms tightened around her, but not hard, more as if she were a delicate treasure he didn't want to let go.

His chest was hard against her tender nipples. His quiet sigh seemed to ripple from his body into hers on a wavelength of shared desire. Her whole body was a little tender, a little sore, merely heightening her sensitivity.

Lars rested his head against her hair. It occurred to her that this was the longest he'd been quiet since she'd met him. It was another side to the man who was spinning her world into something temporarily fantastic.

His lips brushed against her scalp as his penis pressed against her, evident despite the layers of their clothes.

Like a match tossed amid dry tinder, desire engulfed her in its flames.

There was something powerful in the silence between them. She wrapped her hands around his biceps and turned him around. Three steps behind him was the mattress. Walking him backward, she pushed lightly and he went down like a mighty oak.

He lay on the bed, looking at her like a man who'd just won the lottery.

Foolish man.

He held out his hands to her. "Delphi?"

She stepped between his open legs and placed her hands in his. Palm to palm, kneeling on the bed, she lowered herself to him.

Foolish her.

"Do you think everyone downstairs will know what we're doing up here?" she said.

"Doubtlessly." It wasn't particularly what she wanted to hear, but at least it was truthful. And wasn't that what she wanted? "But it's okay. I think they've all had sex before."

She laughed. "I think you're right." Besides, the whole town could know, and she wasn't getting up and walking away now.

She smoothed her fingertips over the fine lines near his eye.

"Too many days spent squinting in the sun. Sunglasses only help so much."

"The Middle East?"

"Yep." He caught her hand and brought her fingers to his lips, pressing a soft kiss against them.

He didn't want to talk about work and neither did she. It wasn't the time.

She smiled, an unexpected tenderness welling inside her. "I like them. They add character."

"I'd like to think I manage to have character on my own, Delphi." Despite his teasing tone, a seriousness underscored his words. "These lines don't mean anything except I've spent too much time in the sun.

I could be the biggest bastard in the world and still have these."

So she might've overreacted to his prolonged absence earlier, but he was definitely overreacting to this. Perhaps she unsettled him the way he unsettled her. She hoped so. And she truly didn't want to overthink any of this—she just wanted to experience him…them, if he'd just quit talking. "Lars…"

"Yes?"

"Sometimes you don't know when to shut up."

"You're in charge. I've got a couple of ideas as to how you could shut me up."

She picked up a pillow, brandishing it as if she was going to put it over his face. Lars laughed lazily and grabbed her butt. Most men would've grabbed her hand or arm. Lars grabbed her ass. Which was just fine with her. She liked the way his big hands caught and held her rear cheeks.

"That wasn't exactly what I had in mind. Delphi…"

She tossed the pillow aside and shifted on him, bringing her pubic area into direct contact with his erection.

Lars groaned. "Oh, woman, you are driving me…"

She hoped to distraction, because that's how she felt.

Fully aware of how to satisfactorily shut him up, Delphi wriggled farther up his big, hard body until she saw her reflection in his irises.

She kissed him. Letting herself go, she indulged every kissing whim she felt. Tiny little butterfly touches of lip against lip. Sharp little nibbles. Slow, lazy glides.

He hadn't shaved and his faint beard rubbed against her mouth and cheek. Her skin would be red afterward. Who cared? His mouth was too delectable and he seemed to enjoy kissing as much as she did. He alternately stroked her back and massaged her buttocks.

She tugged at his T-shirt and he nodded. There was simply no need for words. Together they stood, undressing without fanfare. Delphi was fairly certain it had something to do with their respective professions. He was used to being methodical and so was she. However, when she reached for the waist of her bike shorts, he caught her hand in his, shaking his head. "Leave them on. Please," he tacked on as an afterthought. That's right—she was the one in charge of this particular operation. She indulged him and left her bike shorts on. Who'd have thought those would be sexy? But apparently it really did something for him, judging by his jutting penis and the hot gleam in his eyes. And when a man looked at a woman the way Lars was looking at her, she'd feel sexy in a cloth sack. Woohoo for bike shorts!

Of course she'd seen him naked before, but last night, they had been at the lake. The sun had been going down and she'd just been too flustered to pay attention to details. And well, this morning, she'd had her head under the covers and then she'd been on her belly.

But now, now she had plenty of time and the sun was beaming in over the top of the lower café curtain.

She was fascinated by what she saw.

"Delphi?" He looked at her quizzically. "What's wrong?"

She found a boldness she'd never known she possessed. It wasn't as if they were dating or even had a potential future. She dragged her gaze up to his face. He really didn't know?

"Lars Reinhardt, it's a crime against women for a man to look this good. You were at the head of the line when they were handing out beautiful male bodies." And she fully appreciated the amount of work he must put into maintaining his muscled, honed physique.

"Damn, Delphi…" he said. Good grief, he was turning a dull shade of red. Now it was her, however, who couldn't seem to shut up. "If you were a patient, every nurse and female technician, as well as Rodney, who swings the other way, would be lining up to get a look."

Shaking his head, he touched his hand to his temple. "Woman, please." Nonetheless, she could see he was pleased, even if he was a little embarrassed. And it certainly hadn't diminished that impressive joystick of his. "It's not as if you haven't been naked with me before."

"Yeah, well…" She just didn't need to go through the rest of that. "Good God."

He grinned, his arrogance pushing aside his earlier embarrassment. "Well, *I* wouldn't go that far, but if *you* insist."

He sat on the edge of the bed and pulled her between his legs. In one smooth motion, he stretched out on the bed, pulling her along with him, on top of him. "Now find a better use for that mouth instead of talking me to death."

"Ha. You're one to talk…literally. Anyway, you can't tell me what to do. I'm in charge of this mission." She'd never been so lighthearted when she was naked with a man. It was usually pretty serious stuff, but with Lars, it was as if some dam inside her had given way.

"Look, Blondie, you can't designate me a god and then still be in charge."

"Oh, yes, I can. Those were the terms of this particular engagement. You can't change the rules in the middle."

He sighed as if he was being tested to his limits even as he traced the slightly puckered outer edge of her areola. The lightest of touches created a mind-blowing sensation that shot all the way through her. She sucked in her breath.

"Speaking of…" he drawled. "I'd say you've got all the makings of a goddess." He caught her breasts up in his palms and seemed to weigh them, catching the tender points between his thumb and forefinger. "Definitely a goddess. That means you can be in charge of a god."

It was all so silly, but erotic at the same time. She supposed that made her the goddess of bicycle shorts.

She ran her hand over his pecs. "If I'm in charge, why are you making all the rules?"

"Because I'm in charge of you being in charge."

He was impossible, in a totally wonderful way. "Shut up, Lars."

"I was about to tell you the same thing."

Delphi knew just the thing to shut him up.

She caught the tip of his earlobe between her teeth, following the nip with a swirl of her tongue.

She whispered against his skin, "Two rules—"

"Rules?"

"Yep. The first one is that you can't talk."

"Dammit, woman."

"I can always pack up my toys and go home if you don't want to play." She made a pretense of moving off of him. They both knew she wasn't going anywhere.

"Okay, I won't talk. What else?"

"You have to just lay there and let me do what I want to do, when I want to do it and how I want to do it."

"You're powertripping, Blondie."

"Trust me, Marine."

She thought he might give her the no-go, but he finally offered a tight nod.

He was 100 percent correct. She was powertripping…and she loved it.

She licked, sucked, nipped and kissed down the column of his strong brown throat. Her breath was ragged as she pressed openmouthed kisses along his shoulder. The man's skin was like silk.

She devoured him, ravishing every inch of him. She swirled her tongue over his male nipples. His areolae were large and dark. She teased her tongue around the rim of his belly button.

She tasted his hip, inner thigh, the length of his velvety penis, the heavy weight of his sac, the heavily muscled quads. And with each touch of her mouth and hands, she felt him grow more and more tense, until his breath echoed harshly in the room and his big hands were tightened into fists.

Delphi straddled his hips and positioned herself against his cock, shorts and all. She cupped him in her palm. Hand on one side and her spandex-covered sex on the other, she "rode" him. She was barely in control of herself as she pushed harder and faster, her breasts bouncing with the rhythm she set. She had long ago drenched the crotch of her shorts with arousal. She knew he felt her slick juices and the fabric with each slide against his cock. And with each slide, her clit was stimulated, over and over and over.

Lars's face grew rigid and she thought each stroke

would send him over the edge, but it wasn't until she found her own pinnacle of pleasure that he came.

Delphi collapsed somewhat inelegantly on top of him. Something had just happened that was outside the realm of recreational sexual pleasure. Later, she'd think about all of it.

Lars tapped her shoulder. She dragged her head up to look at him. A fine sheen of sweat coated his face. He quirked an eyebrow. Still dazed, it took her a second to figure it out.

"You can talk." Good luck to him. She barely got that out.

"You can be in charge anytime."

Delphi smiled as she closed her eyes and rested on his chest.

Yeah, it had been that good.

Thank goodness he was temporary, she thought sleepily. Otherwise she'd be in trouble. Serious trouble.

LARS LOOKED OVER at the woman who was conked out in his bed. He resisted the urge to touch her face. She was obviously wiped out. He'd caught a quick nap himself but he was damn near starving now.

He eased out of bed and dressed. She hadn't stirred. He started out the door and then reconsidered. He found a piece of paper and a pen. No more misunderstandings like the one earlier today.

Picking up chow next door. Back soon.

He propped the note on the bedside table and eased out the door. Downstairs Jefferson and Dwight were exactly where he'd left them. He idly wondered if they ever got up to pee.

Dwight shot him a sly glance. "That was some five minutes there."

Delphi might be pissed if she'd heard, but she was asleep upstairs, so no harm, no foul. Lars grinned. "Yessir, it was."

He pushed through the connecting door to the restaurant/bar next door. Gus's, the only chow line in town, was hopping. But then again, as far as he could tell, Gus's was always hopping.

Bull, Merrilee and Dirk were sharing a table to the right of the pick-up counter. Lars waved but went and put in his order first. He had no idea what Delphi liked to eat, but he liked the moose burger and fries, so he ordered two. If she didn't like it, he'd eat hers, too.

He wandered over to his people's table and dropped into the empty chair. He was damn tired and all he'd done was lie there this time around. But a man should never underestimate the energy required to hold on until his woman came.

Merrilee looked at him, laughter dancing in her eyes. "Lean forward, hon." He leaned and she plucked a white feather from his hair, or what little hair he had. It was from the pillow.

"Napping?" She laughed at her own joke and Dirk grinned like an ass. Bull shot Lars a sympathetic look, but he, too, had a glimmer of amusement in his usually somber eyes.

"Yep. Picking up some chow and then I'm just going to lay low this afternoon."

"Catching up on some…rest?" Dirk smirked.

Damn, now that Big D wasn't moping, he was full of himself.

"Since I'm spending tomorrow with your sorry ass, I figured I better rest today."

"How's Delphi?" Merrilee asked. "I haven't seen her today."

"She's fine. She's resting, too."

Merrilee smiled. "Rest does a body good. And I think that young lady needed to catch up on hers. You boys have an early flight tomorrow morning. Y'all are leaving at eight. We've got a plane down and we're waiting on the part, so Dalton's got a busy day. He'll swing back by the camp and pick you up somewhere around seven."

"That works," Lars said.

A pretty little redheaded waitress, aptly named Ruby according to her nametag, brought over his to-go boxes and two longnecks.

"I put extra ketchup in the boxes," Ruby said, smoothing a hand over her apron front. "Liam likes lots of ketchup with his fries. I thought, you being twins and all, you might, too."

"Good call. I like ketchup even more than Liam does. Thanks." Lars smiled at her and a blush swooshed over her fair skin.

"No problem," she said and hurried away, her face now bright red.

Delphi's compliments on his physique came to mind and then he blushed.

"Still killing the ladies," Dirk said without a whit of envy.

"Yeah, well, someone's got to uphold the family name. Liam's taken and you're doing a piss-poor job, so it's all on me." Poor sot. Dirk was so hung up on Natalie, he didn't even see other women.

A man would have to be blind to miss how pretty Ruby was. Lars didn't want to think what would happen if Natalie's visit was a bust, or worse yet, she canceled on Dirk's lovesick ass.

He pushed away from the table and stood. "Okay, I'm starving, so I'll see you all later." He pointed at Dirk. "And I will definitely see you at 0800."

The pretty little waitress smiled at him shyly on his way out and he smiled back, but it was purely a smile of thanks. He guessed Dirk wasn't the only poor sot too hung up on another woman to be interested in Ruby Red Breast.

He willingly admitted it—to himself—as he climbed the stairs. Hell, yeah, he was hung up on Delphi. He'd never been so *taken* with a woman before.

And obviously he'd lost a few brain cells in their back-to-back sexual exploits. Because if he was thinking with all his faculties, he'd slow himself down, dial himself back. However, not only did he not want to, he wasn't too damn sure that he could.

He opened the bedroom door and despite him being quiet, Delphi rolled over as the door clicked closed. She smiled sleepily, her eyes at half-mast, her face glowing pink. She sat up, the sheet falling to her waist, leaving her rose-tipped breasts bare. She tugged the sheet back up.

"Do I smell food?"

"Moose burgers and fries." He held them aloft like a trophy. "And a couple of brews."

A smile wreathed her face. "You *are* a god."

And in that exact moment, he felt like a god. And he got it. He understood why his brother had married

Tansy. He understood why Dirk couldn't see past Natalie, a woman he hadn't seen in years.

Lars understood because he'd found his goddess.

He was ass over end in love with Delphi Reynolds.

15

THE SOUND OF Nelson locking the front door of the clinic was music to Delphi's ears. It had been a very long day. And it wasn't over yet. The two exam rooms had to be readied for tomorrow, which was another packed day.

"So, what'd you think?" Skye asked, slipping off her white lab coat. If anyone had told Delphi her friend would willingly, openly refer to herself as Dr. Skye she'd have laughed. But it suited Skye now. She was like a brighter, happier version of the friend Delphi had known throughout college. *Vibrant.* That was the word. Vibrant described Skye these days. With her mass of wild red curls and glowing happiness, she was positively radiant.

The three of them began prepping the first exam room.

"What do I think? I think I'm amazed at how much work you guys do." Delphi was ready to drop.

"It won't be this busy all the time," Nelson said as he replenished the bandage drawer.

"I know. I'm the new girl in town and everyone's sad to see you go. Well, happy for your opportunity, but they'll miss you." Delphi could easily understand why Nelson was so beloved in this community. Quiet, he possessed an extremely dry sense of humor. If you weren't paying attention his wry observations would go right over your head.

And Skye had told her he was the shaman-in-training for his clan. It had taken all kinds of special dispensations for him to work out going away to medical school without giving up his shaman status. Delphi didn't understand all of it but she was glad it had all worked out for him.

He was a nice guy, and his wife had stopped by with his lunch earlier today. She was beautiful in an equally quiet way. Seeing the two of them together had been like watching the flow of a river—quiet, strong but deep.

She'd seen the two of them and thought about Lars. It was easier to pinpoint the few times that she hadn't thought about Lars. Let's see…none. It was as if he'd been simmering on the back burner of her brain all day. You'd think with the office being so busy and all the things Delphi needed to assimilate to take over from Nelson, she wouldn't have had the mind space to spare him a thought. Er, no, he'd parked his fine self on some prime brain real estate in her head. It was quite disconcerting.

Delphi couldn't wait to stretch out in that claw-foot tub and let the water soak away her aches.

"I'm going to make some quick notes on the charts while you guys finish up the second room, if you don't mind," Skye said, putting her hand in the small of her back and stretching.

"No problem."

"Sure."

They moved into the second exam room. There were only the two. Delphi wasn't quite sure if she would get used to the giant smiley faces painted on the walls. But then again, she didn't have to. Three months would fly by before she knew it.

"How'd you like Mirror Lake?" Nelson said.

He laughed at her start of surprise. "Everyone knows most everything that goes on in Good Riddance," he added.

"It's one of the coolest places I've ever been." She told him about the dragonflies swarming at the water's edge. "I'd never seen anything like that before."

He regarded her solemnly with his coal-black eyes. "It's a message."

"Huh? A message? What kind of message?"

"Dragonflies are a powerful totem. Animals appear to us with messages. Sometimes we must figure out what message the animal carries. However, the dragonfly carries the message of change. Change is coming to you."

"Well, I am here."

"It is not Good Riddance. It is far more fundamental to you, internal to you. And the change will bring peace, harmony, purity with it." He nodded. "And the lake bottom trembled while you were there, also, did it not?"

Okay, everybody was truly up in everyone else's business here. "Yes, it did."

"Yet more change. Your messages are clear and strong."

Delphi wasn't sure she was exactly comfortable with being pegged with change messages. "Lars Reinhardt was there, as well." Not that she needed to tell Nelson—she was sure that was common knowledge, as well. "Maybe the messages were for him."

"You were there together?" She nodded. "The messages are for both of you."

"Um, okay."

He touched her arm and something powerful seemed to course through her, an energy. It wasn't the sexuality that raged rampant between her and Lars. This was, she didn't know, different. It certainly got her attention.

"It's important that you understand. The changes, they are deep. The very crust of the earth spoke to you. But your changes are tied in with Lars. And his changes are tied in with you."

Nelson was a nice guy, but he just didn't get it. "Well, you know Lars is only here for a few more days and, well, it's just a holiday romance."

His smile held a curious note of amusement. "It has nothing to do with me, Delphi. The universe has spoken. You can heed its message or not."

Okay. She'd roll with the *not* option.

"It won't matter," he said, guessing her thoughts. "Because the events have already been put in motion. Just think of it as a cosmic 'heads-up.'"

Just think about it as a bunch of nonsense. She found it rather surprising that Nelson bought into all of that with his medical background.

"It is the way of my people," he said. "You do not have to believe. You will find it is so, regardless."

Okay, that was creepy. He'd responded to her thoughts. More than likely, her skepticism had shown. She tended to wear her emotions on her sleeve.

They were just finishing up the room when she heard the drone of the bush plane. Lars was back.

She couldn't keep a smile from blossoming on her face. And why should she? She was in lust. Heck, she could even be silly and say she was temporarily in love. That was fun.

"You guys have a minute?" Skye called out from her office.

Delphi curbed her impatience. Lars would be there when she got off. It wasn't as if he was going anywhere, at least not for a couple of days.

Skye was sitting behind her desk. Delphi settled in one of the chairs on the "patient" side. Nelson took the other.

Skye looked from Delphi to Nelson and back to Delphi. Finally she spoke. "Delphi, we've been friends a long time. I love you like a sister. I know I like you better than my sister. And Nelson, you have been both coworker and friend and I just think the world of both of you." Tears gathered in Skye's eyes and spilled down her cheeks. She sniffed.

Delphi and Nelson exchanged a puzzled, concerned glance. Skye had loosened up considerably, but she was still one of the most composed women Delphi knew. Regardless of how much she'd loosened up, Skye didn't cry. Now, however, was an exception. The waterworks really cut loose.

Delphi waited, her heart lodged in her throat as Skye dashed at her tears. What could possibly reduce Skye to this?

"Oh, my, I'm crying."

Delphi looked questioningly at Nelson. However, he no longer looked confused or concerned. A quiet smile curved his mouth. Okay…obviously he'd figured out something Delphi hadn't.

Delphi couldn't stand it a second longer. "Okay, you're killing me here. Why are you crying? What's wrong?"

Skye shook her head and opened her mouth, but a wail came out. Nelson nodded sagely and Delphi was wound so tight she thought she might reach over and shake him until he told her what the hell was going on.

Nelson passed a handful of tissues across the desk and Skye took them, mopping at her face. Mascara left raccoon rings around her blue eyes. Finally, Skye got her tears under control. Her smile was watery as she beamed at them across the desk. "I'm *expectiinnngg.*" The last word came out as another wail and she promptly burst into tears again.

"Are you happy or sad?" Delphi said. Skye had smiled, but with all the wailing and tears, it was rather confusing—mixed signals.

"Happy, of course." She hiccuped from all the waterworks. "My hormones are all out of whack. And I'm so tired, I can hardly move at the end of the day."

A baby. Oh, my. Skye and Dalton were going to have a baby.

"How far along are you?" Nelson said. At least one of them had the presence of mind to ask a sensible question.

"Right at twelve weeks. We wanted to wait. At least until we knew for sure."

Delphi got up and rounded the desk, hugging her friend. Tears slid down her cheeks. Great! Now she was crying, too. Laughing through their tears, Delphi and

Skye looked at Nelson. "You might as well cry, too," Skye said with a sniffle.

Delphi sat back down.

Nelson smiled. "I'm going to leave that to you two. Thanks, though. So, you're due…" He trailed off, mentally calculating.

"The babies are due in November."

"Babies?" Delphi was sure she'd heard a plural, as in more than one.

"Babies. There are two heartbeats—both strong, thank goodness. Twins. My due date is Thanksiving." She laughed. "If I make it that far with two of them. It'll be quite something to be thankful for."

Babies. Twins. Delphi tried to shut down the imagery that popped into her brain, but it was a losing battle. Her and Lars with their own set of twins. One blond like her, one darker like him.

And that was some truly insane thinking when she'd only known the man a few days. She must be more tired than she'd realized…and more temporarily besotted than she cared to admit.

"HI, MERRILEE," LARS said as entered the back door of the airstrip office.

He didn't stop to chat but headed immediately for the stairs.

Merrilee called out to him. "Good evening to you, too, Lars. She's not in yet."

"Oh." He stopped and pivoted around. He walked back over to Merrilee's desk. "How are you?"

Merrilee laughed, shaking her head. "You've got it bad, haven't you?"

There was no point in denying it. "Yep."

"That seems to be the way you Swenson men do it. It hits you like a truck and that's it. Quick and hard and there's no going back. Bull waited twenty-five years for me. Dirk's been carrying a torch for Natalie since they were kids." Yes, Dirk was fixated, all right. He had talked about her all damn day. Merrilee continued her rundown of the Swenson men in love. "Liam tried, but he couldn't deny Tansy. Now it's you. I'm glad you're being sensible about it."

"Do you know how crazy that sounds? You're saying it's sensible that I'm in love with a woman I've only known three days?" He laughed.

She quirked an amused eyebrow at him. "Are you asking me to reassure you or are you reassuring me that it can't be so?"

It was pretty damn hard to fathom. "I think the former."

"Oh, good, because I couldn't deliver on the latter."

And she had a point. The Swenson men did tend to love immediately, and it was usually hard and fast. Well, there had been Liam and Natalie, but they'd never been in love. They'd just been friends who were confused and wound up getting hitched.

"I really don't know what to do about Delphi. I don't want to freak her out, but I'm out of here in a couple of days. You know our whole relationship was based on it being short-term, but now… Hell, I don't know. That's a lie. I do know. She's going to trip. It's the damnedest thing—Liam and I have always shared this…I'm not sure how to explain it. It's not like I can read his mind or 'see' what's going on with him, but there are just some things I know—and when I know—it's his stuff, not mine. Well, I'm getting flashes of that same knowing with Delphi. Trust me when I say she's going to flip."

Merrilee appeared totally unconcerned with his up-coming battle with Delphi. "Well, I guess it's a good thing you're trained in mounting offensives and deto-nating explosives without getting blown to bits, isn't it?"

BY THE TIME she'd walked back to the bed-and-breakfast, Delphi was in a near state of panic. Everything had turned upside down on her. She heard Lars whistling under his breath as she got to the landing. She paused, but then decided against knocking. She needed a few minutes to herself to decompress from the day, from the weekend, from him.

She walked into her bedroom. The connecting door between their rooms stood open. Damn, she'd forgot-ten about that. They'd been going back and forth yes-terday and this morning and it just made more sense than bopping out in the hall. They'd left it open when they both headed out this morning.

She walked over to the opening. Lars was stretched out on his bed, his hands folded beneath his head.

"Hi," she said. "How was your visit out to the camp? What'd you think of it?"

Oh, God, she was awash in joy at simply seeing him, his smile. It was terrifying, especially in light of her conversation with Nelson.

"It was great." His voice washed over her and she soaked up its cadence like a surgical sponge. "Liam has a cool operation set up out there. On one of your days off, you should check it out. And it's a nice flight out. Definitely some pretty country."

"Great idea." She nodded politely. "I'll have to do that before I go back."

Lars tilted his head to one side and eyed her as if he knew she was freaking out inside. "How about your day? How was it?"

"Busy. It's hard to believe there are that many people in this area, much less that they all need medical attention. Of course I'd say a third of them were there to see me, a third to bid Nelson farewell and only the last third were actually sick."

"It's going to be a week for you." He patted the bed. "Take a load off, Blondie, and I'll give you a back rub."

Distance. Walls. Boundaries. "I appreciate the offer but I'm going to blow the cobwebs out with a bike ride."

He nodded slowly. "I see."

Dammit, he did see. "Lars, I..."

"Let's talk about it, Delphi."

"You do like to talk, Lars." It wasn't a compliment. Not the way she felt now.

"Don't. And yeah, I tend to think that most things can be resolved with a decent conversation." He sat up against the headboard and she noted just how impossibly wide his shoulders were. And she remembered how they'd felt and tasted when she'd kissed him on that very bed yesterday. "Of course there are cases like my mother where it doesn't make a damn bit of difference, but then you're not my mother."

"No. I'm not." She wanted to push him away. It was all too much, too fast. "I don't even like your mother." While it was true enough, she'd never been so rude in her life.

"You are spoiling for a fight, aren't you, Blondie?" God, she hated it that he knew. "News flash—no one likes my mother. Mainly because she doesn't like herself. It's sad, but that's the way it is. Now what's got your nose so out of joint?"

"Nothing." She crossed her arms over her chest and glared at him. This was all his fault. She'd been minding her business on the plane. Why couldn't he have just minded his? "Everything."

"I'd say that about covers it and then some."

"Skye's pregnant."

"That's cool." He looked at her face. "Isn't it?"

"Of course. When a deliriously happy married couple are expecting, why wouldn't they be excited?"

He just sat on the bed, waiting.

"She's having twins."

It started out as a smile and morphed into a full-blown grin.

"There's no need for you to grin like a jackass."

"That's what has you so tweaked, isn't it? And I bet you thought about me all day."

He was unbearable. "You know, just because I told you how good you looked naked yesterday, there's no reason for you to arrogantly assume far too much today."

"Yep. You're in love with me and it's got you tweaked."

"I am not in love with you. I love having sex with you. There's a huge difference."

"Yeah, you got that right. There is a huge difference, but lucky for us we've got both going."

"Lars, I swear, you are not going to talk me to death on this."

He stood up, standing next to the bed, his hands on

his lean hips. "Didn't you hear what I just indirectly said, woman? I love you. I'm in love with you."

And he'd better just damn stay over there by the bed. She took a step back, feeling the press of the wall against her spine. "What happened to the rational man I made a deal with a couple of days ago?" She did her best to imitate him. "'I'm temporary, Blondie. Five days and nothing more.' Now you want to drag out love like it's some prize. This is so *not* what we agreed to."

"You're right. We did not cut a deal up front to fall in love. I don't think most people do."

"We are not in love."

"Speak for yourself."

"Okay. I am not in love with you, Marine."

"Bullshit."

"What? Do you think you're so irresistible that every woman who stumbles over you has to fall at your feet?"

"Nope. Just you."

She felt desperate. He literally had her back against the wall.

"Don't tell me how I do or don't feel."

"You know what your problem is, Blondie?"

"I have no interest in hearing your summation of my problems, Marine."

"TDB—"

"I'm not versed in your military acronyms, Sergeant."

"TDB. Too damn bad."

"Oh."

"Yeah, *oh* is right. You're going to hear it because I'm in charge of this particular operation." She opened her mouth and he arrogantly shushed her. *Shushed* her. "I'm not through."

"I don't care." The jackass shushed her so it was her turn to talk. "What you fail to understand is that on a temporary basis, you're okay. But there are a lot of things I don't like about you."

"Like what? Name one thing."

"You talk too much."

He shrugged it off. "Name two things."

"Easy. You always have to be in charge."

"Bet you can't name a third," he said, riding roughshod over her very valid issues. "So, out of my many positive attributes, you can only come up with two things you don't like about me."

"Oh, I could come up with more, if you'd quit talking circles around me. How can I think when I can't get a word in edgewise? And on top of it, I'm looking at you. I can't think when I'm looking at you."

She realized the error of her admission the moment the words left her mouth.

"You can't think when you look at me?" He was even handsome when he smirked. "The problem isn't that you don't trust me or us. You don't trust *you*, Delphi. You're letting that doctor still screw up your life."

"How can I trust you? You've changed the rules." Just like DeWitt. "You can't just arbitrarily decide to rewrite the terms."

"Okay, then I have a proposal."

"I will not marry you. You've really lost it."

"Easy, Blondie, I'd have to ask you first."

Ouch. That was kind of embarrassing—not that she'd *wanted* him to ask her to marry him. That would be even worse than him saying they were in love. "What do you propose?"

"We scrap it all and start from scratch. Wipe out the last three days. We start fresh with different terms."

"That's silly."

As usual he ignored her. "So, Blondie. I'm here for the next few days. I'm looking for a wife and I'm also all for having some really hot, mind-blowing sex. Falling in love is fully admissible and so is establishing a long-term, ongoing relationship." See, that's what she was talking about.

"Look, Marine, that worked with me one time but I'm a quick study. I'm not falling for that bowl-me-over-with-your-charm ruse."

"Oh, is that what I did? I had no idea you found me charming."

God, she was so frustrated it was all she could do not to stamp her foot at him. Instead she turned on her heel and marched back through the connecting door. "I should've ignored you from the beginning on the plane. I should've stood my ground then and I wouldn't be in this predicament now."

"And exactly what predicament are you in, Blondie?"

Damn him, she very nearly tripped up and blurted out that she'd fallen in love with him. But she didn't.

"I'm going for a bike ride."

"Hmm. You know how I love those shorts on you."

She didn't stamp her foot, but she did slam the connecting door…and derived great satisfaction from it.

Unfortunately, she could still *hear* him. "I'll pick you up for dinner and a movie around nine."

She paused in the middle of taking off her scrubs. Dinner and a movie? There was no movie theater here.

The man was crazy. And annoying. And altogether charmingly mad.

He'd almost convinced her that for them to have fallen in love in three short days was not only plausible, but probable.

Being wrong about DeWitt had wrecked her career.

Being wrong about Lars would wreck her heart.

He was a most dangerous man.

16

AND SHE THOUGHT he'd been relentless before.... Delphi had no idea what was in store for her. It was terrible when you had to turn a woman against herself in order to straighten her out. Lars just needed the woman to figure out that she loved him, and then trust herself that it was the right thing.

Only she was scared to trust how she felt about him. And he'd be damned if he'd just sit on his ass and wait on her to figure it out. That simply wasn't his way. Never had been.

He took the last two steps in one leap. Merrilee and her posse were hard at work in the airstrip office. Luckily, Delphi was tied up at work. Not that it would really make any difference, but an element of surprise always made an offensive maneuver more effective.

Alberta; Merrilee; Ruby; Juliette; Tansy's sister Jenna; Norris, a former newspaper reporter; Nancy, who ran the dry goods store with her husband; and a couple of other women he didn't recognize had quite the assembly line going.

Even the men had pitched in. Dwight and Jefferson had foregone their chess game to work alongside Bull, Dirk and a tall fellow with a shock of red hair named Rooster.

Talk about community spirit. It was something you'd only see in Good Riddance.

Lars peeled off a C-note and slid it across the table to Rooster. Rooster was the bookie. He'd take a bet on most anything. "Who'd you want to put your money on?"

Lars leveled a you've-got-to-be-kidding-me look Rooster's way.

The man held out his hands, palms up. "I have to ask. And hell, you might even want to go with the long shot."

"I'm putting my money on me."

Rooster grinned. "So is everyone else." He lowered his voice as if he was sharing a confidence, even though everyone in the room could clearly hear him… well, except for Dwight. "I put a few bucks on Delphi. I had to. She's such a long shot. Besides, I sort of felt sorry for her. It'd suck to have every bet against you."

"No worries. I just hope you didn't bet too much on her."

"I'm here, ain't I?" Rooster said with a toothy grin.

Lars clapped Rooster on the back. "Yep. And I sure appreciate it." He looked to Merrilee for instructions. "What can I do?"

"We're finishing up the last hundred now. You can take these over to the businesses. Start with Alyce's bed-and-breakfast and work your way up one side of the street and then down the other. And of course, no one wears them until tomorrow morning. We're cutting it close. It only gives you two days."

"Yeah, but it's two days of relentless attack."

Bull smiled quietly. He knew that you never went into battle doubting the outcome. You went in to win.

"She'll dig in her heels and put up a good fight," Lars said. "I wouldn't love her if she didn't. But I'll win."

"And if you don't?" Merrilee asked the question quietly.

"Then I've lost this particular battle, but I will ultimately win the war." He almost felt sorry for Delphi, but it was for her own good. The woman was going to be miserable without him. And he was damn sure going to be miserable without her. He was just trying to save them both a lot of misery. Hell, one of them had to be in charge.

Juliette laughed at him across the table. "You sure changed your tune fast for a man who, just a few days ago, was referring to marriage as a ball and chain."

"I'm a quick study. When faced with Delphi, why would I be stupid and ignore the obvious? The woman obviously is crazy about me. And I'm obviously crazy about her."

"Lars always has been a rebel," Dirk said. He looked at the buttons covering the table. "This suits you."

"It's unorthodox, that's for sure," Norris said, her admiration clear.

Delphi loves Lars. Simple. Direct. And maybe if she saw it often enough she'd realize it was the truth.

DELPHI DIDN'T WANT TO be paranoid, but it felt as if the whole town was watching her...and waiting for something.

She knocked on Skye's door. They had a few minutes before the day started. Skye sat behind her desk sipping a cup of decaf. No more high-test for her.

"Can I talk to you for a second?"

"Sure."

"Uh, I don't want to sound paranoid and I know you've lived here for a couple of years and you love it, but I'm getting this really weird vibe. I don't know— it's hard to explain."

Skye, usually so composed, squirmed in her chair. "You know Good Riddance is a very involved community, Delphi. It's a totally different culture than where we come from. People in Atlanta are friendly enough but they don't get involved the way people here do."

"Okay." Delphi waited on the rest.

Finally Skye spoke again. "If you don't want that pumpkin muffin, do you mind if I have it?"

That was it? "Sure. I mean, no problem. I don't mind."

Skye was pretty much inhaling anything that wasn't tied down or wouldn't fight back. Those twins of hers were ravenous.

"Skye…"

She looked up from peeling the paper off the bottom of the muffin. "Yeah?"

"You were talking about the sense of community and involvement in Good Riddance…." Delphi trailed off, hoping Skye would pick up the conversational thread.

"Uh-huh. That was it."

That was it. Apparently the twins were sucking out her brain cells, as well, because her advice had been a bunch of nothing. And it seemed to her that Skye was avoiding her.

Fine. She'd landed in some Alaskan bush version of *The Twilight Zone*. Whatever. They had another jam-packed day. And the day after tomorrow was Nelson's last day.

It was also the day that Lars left. She couldn't wait. It couldn't come fast enough. She would be so seriously glad to hear that plane take off on Friday and know that he was on it. So, he'd go back to wherever. She'd finish her three months here, then go back to Atlanta. He'd become a distant memory. A handsome, dashing, charming arrogant soldier who'd swept her off her feet. And possibly at some point in the future, perhaps in a couple of years, she could laugh when recounting her brief fling with Lars Reinhardt. It had been fun and silly and wildly romantic. But in the end, she'd had the good sense to put the necessary boundaries in place. One day she'd tell her girlfriends about the man who'd been built like a god and who thought they could possibly be in love after a few days. One day, she would. But for now, she was counting the hours and the very minutes until he left.

The days weren't so bad. They were so busy. The nights were nearly unbearable. Knowing he was on the other side of the wall. Knowing she only had to open the door. Knowing he wanted her. Knowing the magic to be found in his arms. But it was easier this way. He'd changed things up and that's when she'd cut things off.

She heard Nelson unlocking the waiting room door and the chorus of greetings as patients filed in. There was nothing else to do but jump into the day with a smile.

Delphi walked into the waiting room and immediately noticed that everyone was wearing a button or a badge. A tingle ran down her spine. What was going on? And then she got close enough to actually read the button.

Really? She was momentarily speechless. Everyone, and she meant every single person in the waiting room, was wearing one. She did a double take. Even Nelson?

He held up his hands in a gesture of peace and surrender. "I can't argue with the messages. The dragonflies and the earth delivered the message."

Delphi marched back down the hall, a suspicion niggling at her. Sure enough, Skye had one on her lab coat.

"Et tu Brute?"

"What can I say, Delphi? I knew when you came over to the house on Friday night."

"How could you know? I didn't even know then. I don't even know now. I mean, I do know now. I'm attracted to him. I'm grateful to him and maybe I fancied myself a little bit in love with him but this is nothing more than a holiday fling. It won't stand up to the test of time."

"How are you so sure?"

"I don't even know his favorite color. What if he leaves the seat up in the bathroom?"

"Give me a second." Skye picked up the phone and punched in a number. Someone answered almost immediately on the other end. "Morning, Merrilee. Is Lars anywhere around? No, I don't need to talk to him. You can just ask him for me. I need to know his favorite color and if he leaves the seat up or down in the bathroom. Sure. I'll hold for a minute." Skye held up a finger indicating Delphi should give her a minute. "Merrilee's checking now. Yeah? Okay. Thanks." She hung up the phone.

"His favorite color is orange and, yes, he leaves the seat up. So, there, now you know. What else?"

"I'm not wild about the color orange," Delphi muttered. "And who could live with a man who leaves the toilet seat up?"

"I totally understand. Those are both deal-breakers. They're both good, sound reasons to throw away the best thing that's ever happened to you."

Skye had always favored sarcasm. "I didn't know that's how you saw it. You never said anything."

"You didn't ask."

"I know Mrs. Watkins is waiting in room one—" *with her button on* "—so we don't have much time. But do you really think he's the best thing that ever happened to me?"

"Of course. I don't say things like that if I don't mean it. Actually, I don't say anything I don't mean. It's a waste of breath and time."

"But how?"

"Because I saw how you two were at the wedding and then at the reception. He looks at you the way Dalton looks at me. And you look at him the way I look at Dalton. And then there's the fact that you were positively glowing until you found out about the twins. And then you got all freaked out because how could he possibly be so important to you, so soon? How can you trust it? How can you trust that you're not off the mark the way you were with DeWitt, even if that was a totally different situation? It's all very clear to everyone here. And since you seem confused, we're all helping you figure it out."

Skye. Even Skye had defected. Lars was Rasputin. Delphi nodded, feeling the tug of tears at her eyes.

She sucked it up. She'd be damned if she'd cry just because an entire town, who didn't know her, didn't understand where she was coming from, had ganged up on her. They just treated her life as if it was some communal joke. And if Lars thought she'd be bowled over or think this was anything other than blatant disrespect for her, as if she was too stupid to know her own heart, her own emotions... If he thought she'd be swayed by this, he had another think coming. If anything, it made her more resolute to stand up for herself. And if she had to stand alone, well, then she'd stand alone.

She was torn between wanting to burst into tears and itching to march over to the B&B and give Lars a piece of her mind. However, she was a professional, so she did neither.

By the end of the day, she'd perfected smiling at the patients while steadfastly ignoring the buttons.

Her nerves were seriously on edge by the end of the day. She finished her duties as quickly as possible and left.

Merrilee, with her button on, was closing up the airstrip office when Delphi came in. She took one look at Delphi's face and reached up and removed her button.

"I'm sorry," Merrilee said, and Delphi felt a small measure better. "He was desperate. Desperate men take desperate measures."

Delphi simply nodded. If she spoke, it was altogether likely her voice would be filled with the tears that had been clogging the back of her throat all afternoon.

"I'll order you a dinner to go from Gus's."

Delphi managed a thanks and a quick nod and went upstairs. He'd turned her into the laughingstock of Good Riddance. She had to work here for the next three months. She would never forgive him for this. Granted, he could be brash and run a little roughshod over people, but this? This was so far over the top. It simply made her realize just how right her decision had been.

Skye was wrong. He wasn't the best thing that had ever happened to her. He couldn't be.

She'd feel better once she ate something. And she'd choke down some of whatever came from next door. She'd skipped breakfast, and lunch hadn't even been a remote option.

She smelled the food just before the knock sounded on her door. She opened it, expecting Merrilee or perhaps Ruby—really anyone other than the man outside her door. She immediately recognized him. They might bear a resemblance, but each man was uniquely his own person.

Liam Reinhardt held out the box containing her dinner. "I'd understand if you say no, but I'd appreciate a few minutes of your time."

There was a somber intimidation to Liam that wasn't part of Lars's makeup. She hesitated but then found it impossible to refuse. She didn't think many people said no to Liam. She wasn't looking to start a trend. It was all too easy to imagine him sighting a target and squeezing off a kill shot.

She stood aside. "Come in. Did Lars send you?" She recognized the inherent foolishness of her question the moment it left her mouth. No one would send Liam anywhere. He wasn't a man to answer to others. However, she refused to be intimidated.

"No. He doesn't know I'm here. I heard there was a family emergency so we cut our honeymoon short."

"You cut your honeymoon short to talk to me?"

"Sit down. Eat."

Bossiness seemed to be a family trait. As much as she resented being ordered around by this unsmiling facsimile of Lars, she sat and, opening the take-out box, she ate.

She ate in silence.

Liam waited in silence.

When she'd somewhat assuaged the hunger pangs, she pushed the take-out box aside. She had no interest in eating her entire meal with this austere man looking on. The sooner he stated his business and left, the better.

"That button is the dumbest thing my brother has ever done," he stated baldly.

Hmm. Maybe he wasn't as bad as he initially seemed. It struck her as pretty dumb, too. "Well, that's one thing we agree on."

"I think there's probably quite a lot we'd agree on." Amazing how a simple quirk of his mouth transformed him into a normal human.

Whatever. "Perhaps."

"I'll keep it brief. I'm sure it's been a long day."

"Yes."

"Depending on your point of view and the circumstances, Swenson men are either cursed or blessed. When we fall in love, it's a done deal. It's been that way for generations. We're one-woman men. If your woman feels the same about you, it's a blessing. There have been a few unfortunate males in our family who weren't lucky enough to have their feelings reciprocated. I'm sure they considered it a curse. I made a serious mistake when I married my first wife. Natalie and I were friends but we weren't in love. You haven't been here long so you might not be aware. Do you know Merrilee and Bull's story?"

"No." Her throat felt tight. Uttering the one-syllable response was a challenge.

"Bull met Merrilee twentysomething years ago. He was one of the first people to move here when she founded the town. He was in his late forties and had never been married. He took one look at her and he knew. He was done. They were together from that day forward, but she wouldn't marry him. He bought a ring and held on to it for twenty-five years. There had never been anyone else for him then and there never will be anyone else. That's how I feel about Tansy. I've just learned that Dirk's been in love with Natalie for years. If I'd known, I'd have never looked twice at her because it means Dirk's been left to wander alone. And now there's you and Lars. Regardless of how you feel about him, he's stuck with you."

"That's not very flattering."

Liam shrugged, unrepentant. "Sorry, but that's just calling it what it is. I'm stuck with Tansy. It's the way we roll, as Dirk would say."

Liam continued. "Making the buttons was a dumb move on Lars's part, but it was a desperate move. For God's sake, don't pretend to feel anything for him that you don't. In the end, that doesn't do anyone any good. However, his heart will always be yours for the taking."

And without further comments or pleasantries, he headed for her door. His hand was on the knob when Delphi spoke. "Thank you for coming."

"I came for Lars. My brother's hurting. I didn't come to plead his case. I came to give you the facts, so you can make an informed decision."

"I didn't want him to fall in love with me."

"It doesn't matter. You didn't have any more control over it than he did. And trust me, if we could choose who we fall in love with, don't you think Tansy would've done better? I'm not exactly a lovable guy but my wife sees something in me." He grinned and shook his head. "I'm one lucky son of a bitch while she got the short end of the stick. But it is what it is."

Her mouth was still sort of gaping over him saying that Tansy wouldn't have voluntarily fallen in love with him. Maybe Liam wasn't so bad after all. But he did scare the hell out of her. He didn't have Lars's slight outrageousness.

Liam's little talk cast a whole different slant on Lars's button campaign. He hadn't been trying to humiliate or ride roughshod over her. Well, maybe he was trying to ride roughshod a bit, but it was because he would always approach a problem with ingenuity. The man thought outside the box. That was what it took to defuse bombs. And to sweep her off her feet. He was the kind of man who would love her for the rest of his life whether she ever came to her senses or not.

They'd have to talk about that toilet seat. There was a lot they needed to talk about. But as he had very wisely pointed out, and she'd been too scared to listen, talking could take care of a lot of things. If that was the case, then he was the master handler, because he could certainly talk.

And what she had to do now had never been clearer.

So, THAT HAD BEEN a bust. He'd been across the street talking with the Native guide Clint Sisnuket when he spotted Delphi coming in from the clinic. One look at her face had said it all. His button campaign was a fail.

It was more than a fail. She wasn't just angry—she was humiliated. It was a calculated risk, which had ended badly. Hell, maybe he needed to slip Rooster a C-note to put on Delphi, since his odds now appeared greatly diminished. As Merrilee had pointed out, he was running short on time.

Not much got him down, but he was pretty damn down. Dirk heralded him from the front entrance into Gus's, waving him to come over. Lars shook his head and went into the B&B. He just wanted to hang in his room. He was as much a lovesick fool as Dirk.

At least if he was in his room, Delphi would be on the other side of the door. Granted, she wouldn't talk to him, wouldn't see him, but at least he could sit on the other side of the damn door, feeling her presence.... He was pathetic. Love was pathetic. It sucked.

Delphi wanted to get all bent out of shape and accuse him of changing the rules on her. What the hell? He'd just been looking to sleep with her and have a couple of laughs. He damn sure hadn't expected to fall in love.

But his ship had been torpedoed the moment he boarded the plane and saw her sitting there. Direct hit. And with every day, every kiss, every touch, his ship took on water. By the time he realized it, there wasn't a damn thing he could do. His ship was sunk—by a little blonde spitfire.

He closed his door and stretched out on the bed. She was quiet, but nonetheless he heard her moving around next door. He was sort of drifting, trying to clear his mind, when her knock startled him into an upright position.

No doubt she wanted to give him hell about the button campaign. He really was a poor bastard that he'd rather have her bitching at him than not have any contact with her at all.

Pa-the-tic.

"Come on in."

She opened the door and stepped through. She had on the dress she'd worn to Liam and Tansy's wedding. And on the right side of her dress, where the strap met the bodice, she'd pinned on one of his buttons.

He fisted his hands at his sides to keep from reaching for her.

"Hey, you."

"Hi."

"So, I see you picked up a new fashion accessory."

"Yeah, it seems to be all the rage. Apparently a whole lot of people are smarter than I am."

He took a step toward her. "Woman, it's not that you lack brains—you're just misguided sometimes. That's why you need me to tell you what to do."

"Is that a fact?" She deliberately took a step forward, encroaching on his territory.

"It is."

"Well, I think the terms have to be renegotiated," she said. "I get to be the squad leader half the time."

"A third. You're smaller than me."

"Half."

He couldn't stand it any longer. He put his hands on her waist. "You drive a hard bargain, Blondie, but okay, half."

She slipped her arms around his neck, linking her hands at the top of his spine. Her touch sent a shiver through him.

"I love you."

Her words sent his happy meter soaring. He grinned. "I know. I'm the one who told you."

"Oh, yeah." She rested her head against his chest and he nuzzled her head. "You know there's a whole lot we don't know about each other. And a lot that has to be worked out." She leaned back and looked up into his face.

"Yep. But we've got the main points covered." Speaking of main points, he slid his hands down her back and grabbed her delectable ass. "You love me."

She made a pouty face. "Well, let's not forget that you love me, too."

He slid the dress strap off her shoulder and blazed a trail of kisses along her skin. She smelled good and tasted even better. "That was never the question, Blondie." He nipped her.

"There is one other point while we're negotiating, Marine." Oh, hell, he knew what was coming. Sure enough she reached down between them and palmed his dick. Yep, she was bringing out the big guns by handling his big gun. "That toilet seat—"

"I'll work on it." She'd nag him relentlessly. He'd just have to distract her. "So, the button campaign wasn't a total wash."

"Has anyone ever told you you talk too much, Marine?"

He chuckled and shifted, bringing her hand into harder contact with his dick. Hey, if she was going to handle his equipment, far be it from him to complain.

"As a matter of fact, there's this hot little blonde chick I met on a plane—"

"Lars—"

"Yeah?" They were going to have so much fun… for a long time.

"Shut up and kiss me."

* * * * *

HARLEQUIN® READER SERVICE—Here's How It Works:

Accepting your 2 free books and 2 free gifts (gifts valued at approximately $10.00) places you under no obligation to buy anything. You may keep the books and gifts and return the shipping statement marked "cancel." If you do not cancel, about a month later we'll send you 6 additional books and bill you just $4.74 each in the U.S. or $4.96 each in Canada. That's a savings of at least 14% off the cover price. It's quite a bargain! Shipping and handling is just 50¢ per book in the U.S. and 75¢ per book in Canada.* You may cancel at any time, but if you choose to continue, every month we'll send you 6 more books, which you may either purchase at the discount price or return to us and cancel your subscription.

*Terms and prices subject to change without notice. Prices do not include applicable taxes. Sales tax applicable in N.Y. Canadian residents will be charged applicable taxes. Offer not valid in Quebec. All orders subject to credit approval. Credit or debit balances in a customer's account(s) may be offset by any other outstanding balance owed by or to the customer. Please allow 4 to 6 weeks for delivery. Offer available while quantities last.

NO POSTAGE
NECESSARY
IF MAILED
IN THE
UNITED STATES

BUSINESS REPLY MAIL
FIRST-CLASS MAIL   PERMIT NO. 717   BUFFALO, NY

POSTAGE WILL BE PAID BY ADDRESSEE

HARLEQUIN READER SERVICE
PO BOX 1867
BUFFALO NY 14240-9952

If offer card is missing write to: Harlequin Reader Service, P.O. Box 1867, Buffalo NY 14240-1867 or visit www.ReaderService.com

HB-L71-05/13

GET FREE BOOKS and FREE GIFTS
WHEN YOU PLAY THE...

Just scratch off the silver box with a coin. Then check below to see the gifts you get!

SLOT MACHINE GAME!

YES! I have scratched off the silver box. Please send me the 2 free Harlequin® Blaze™ books and 2 free gifts for which I qualify. I understand I am under no obligation to purchase any books, as explained on the back of this card.

151/351 HDL FV7L

FIRST NAME   LAST NAME

ADDRESS

APT.#   CITY

STATE/PROV.   ZIP/POSTAL CODE

7 7 7 **Worth TWO FREE BOOKS plus 2 FREE Mystery Gifts!**

Worth TWO FREE BOOKS!

Worth ONE FREE BOOK!

TRY AGAIN!

Visit us at: www.ReaderService.com

HB-L7-05/13

JENNIFER LaBRECQUE

DARING IN THE DARK

1

HER HEAD DROPPED to his shoulder, but still she watched the mirror. She knew not to look away. Every time she stopped looking, he stopped touching...and his touch drove her crazy. And yes, watching in the mirror made it so much more intense, so much hotter. His fathomless eyes met hers in the reflection. Her, on his lap, her back against his chest, her legs spread. He reached between her thighs and his long fingers parted her, opening her to his touch and his pleasure. His fingers were dark against her bare, pink flesh, sliding into her yawning, hungry portal...oh, yes...felt so good...please don't stop...watching...wanting...oh, almost there....

The shrill ring of the bedside phone shattered the moment, pulling her out of the dream. Her body tight, her thighs wet, Tawny groped for the phone. "Hello."

"Were you napping?" Elliott said, his normally cheery voice sounding just a bit forced. Of course, she could just be transferring the tension that lingered from being poised on the brink of orgasm in her dream. Or it could be Elliott criticizing her, which seemed to happen

more and more frequently. It was almost like spending
time with her parents.

"Hmm." As an event planner for a group of Mid-
town attorneys, her hours weren't nine to five, Monday
through Friday. "Last night was the cocktail party for
that German client, remember? Then the partners had
a lovely working breakfast at six-thirty this morning.
Just what I wanted to do, crawl out of bed at four-thirty
on a Saturday. Anyway, there's no sin in an afternoon
nap." Intense sexual arousal and guilt lent her voice a
husky note. "Did you work very late last night?" Elliott invested incredible hours in his art gallery, but it
was paying off with a growing reputation and clientele.

"Late enough." He sounded uncharacteristically
terse.

Maybe it really was just her. She was wound so
tight and ached so badly she wanted to cry. Or come.
She should laugh, confess to her husband-to-be that
she'd just been having the most awesome dream sex
and that she still desperately needed to come and ask
him to help her out.

Once upon a time she would've thought laid-back,
easygoing Elliott would get off on a round of afternoon phone sex and talking her into an orgasm. But
she wasn't so sure anymore. Lately he'd been neither
laid-back nor easygoing. And what if somewhere along
the way she revealed he wasn't the man spreading her
thighs and leading her to ecstasy in her dreams? And
what if the man she'd agreed to marry "till death they
did part" couldn't pick up where the dream left off and
get her to that magical place?

He continued and the opportunity was gone. "I

thought I'd come over after the gallery closes this evening."

"That's fine as long as you bring dinner and we stay in." If he called this late in the day, she sure wasn't cooking. Elliott was more into clubbing and being seen than she was. A quiet night at home suited her.

"Staying in works. I wanted to talk to you."

Tawny propped up on her pillow. She and Elliott talked often, but when someone announced they *wanted* to talk... "What?"

"It's too complicated to go into over the phone."

"That's a lousy thing to do. Bring it up and leave me hanging."

"Sorry. But let's leave it till tonight." It wasn't her imagination. He definitcly sounded strained.

"Okay..." Sex. It must be about sex. Of course at this point her brain *was* one-tracking.

"Thai sound okay?"

"Sure. You know what I like." Elliott couldn't possibly miss her flirtatious innuendo. Maybe he'd initiate a little phone sex without her asking.

Elliott cleared his throat, as if her teasing left him uncomfortable. "Um, yeah, I'll pick up chicken curry."

Nix the phone sex. "Chicken curry sounds good."

He cleared his throat again. He was either nervous or coming down with something. "I thought I'd bring Simon along."

Her hand tightened on the phone even as her internal temperature slid up the sizzle scale. "Simon?" She licked her suddenly dry lips and rolled over onto her belly. "Why would he want to come to my apartment? He's avoided me like the plague ever since the photo shoot. He obviously dislikcs me."

"He's a busy guy. I don't think he dislikes you. Simon's just…"

"Dark. Brooding. Cynical. Intense. I think that about covers it." And sexy in a shiver-down-her-spine, her-head-needed-to-be-examined kind of way. But that didn't seem the most prudent observation to make about her fiancé's best friend.

Elliott laughed and Tawny was thankful it didn't bother him that she obviously rubbed Simon the wrong way. Sometimes she wondered if Elliott didn't prefer it that way, but she'd dismissed the notion as unworthy of Elliott.

"Simon's just Simon," he said. "Can he come, too?"

Could he come? She grew wetter still, her whole body flushing and her nipples pebbling harder. Intense, brooding Simon, with his faint British accent, had been the one in her dream.

"Tawny?" Elliott prompted on the other end of the line.

She squirmed on the hard mattress. "No. I don't mind if he comes." Simply saying it aroused her even more. Guilt and shame fed the dark lust Simon inspired in her on a nearly nightly basis. Now it was getting even worse—she'd only taken an afternoon nap. He was her fiancé's best friend, he despised her and every night he was the source of soul-shattering sex in her dreams.

"We'll see you a little after nine, then."

She hung up and closed her eyes. Why was Simon coming with Elliott? Why the three of them? What would they do?

With her body strung tight and humming with arousal, a dark fantasy bloomed in her. The three of them, here in her bedroom. Elliott, golden haired and fair, Simon, dark. Two sexy men intent on touching and tasting every inch of her, all with the singular purpose of pleasuring her.

She blinked her eyes open and reached into the drawer of her bedside table, pulling out her vibrator. She couldn't go through the afternoon this way.

Elliott was her fiancé. He was funny and generous and warm, most of the time. She might not have control of her dreams, but she was wide-awake now.

Despite her best efforts to focus on Elliott, it was Simon she came for as she shuddered her way to an orgasm.

"You look like hell," Simon Thackeray said as he carefully placed his camera case in an orange vinyl chair in Elliott's inner sanctum and sat in the matching chair.

Blond, good-looking, outgoing and possessing a sense of style that always left him looking as if he'd just stepped off the pages of *GQ,* Elliott turned heads in a crowd. A girl in college had once likened the two best friends to Apollo and Hades. They were foils in both looks and personality. Elliott, sunny and outgoing, Simon, dark, quiet, withdrawn. But Elliott had sounded weary and worried on the phone when he'd asked Simon to stop by. He didn't look any better than he'd sounded. "What's going on?"

Elliott perched on the edge of the stainless-steel desk and swung one leg. "We've been friends a long time."

Simon nodded at the obvious. They'd met in a photography class in junior high, where they'd discovered a shared love of art and a friendship that had weathered the years. Elliott had thrown out a lifeline that saved Simon from drowning in his own loneliness. Conversely Simon had anchored Elliott, provided him with some much-needed stability. Elliott's parents were warm and outgoing, but volatile.

He wasn't so sure he would've pursued a career in photography if Elliott hadn't believed in him and pushed him. And Simon had provided invaluable contacts when Elliott had decided to open a small gallery.

"You know you're the brother I never had," Elliott continued. "I've always thought I could tell you anything. Share anything." Once upon a time Simon had felt the same way. Until he'd discovered that there were some things you couldn't share with your best friend. Like being in love with his fiancée. "I hope you'll always be my friend."

Simon sighed at Elliott's penchant for melodrama. If Elliott hadn't parlayed his art-history degree and eye for art into owning a gallery, he could've given Broadway a run. "Elliott, unless you've ax-murdered a little old lady, I'm going to always be your friend." Simon shrugged. "I'd probably be your friend even then. Why don't you just tell me what this is all about?"

"I'm gay."

"Right."

First Elliott had called him in and gave him the big friendship spiel, and now he was fooling around when Simon had a photo shoot scheduled in forty-five minutes. Elliott had a warped sense of humor and a piss-poor sense of timing.

Elliott knotted his hands together. "This isn't a joke. I'm serious. I'm gay."

Simon sat, stunned. Elliott was…gay? How was that possible? They'd been best friends for over a decade.

Simon was the odd straight guy in a profession that attracted homosexuals like a homing device, yet he'd never once suspected Elliott of anything but blatant heterosexuality.

For God's sake, Elliott was engaged to Tawny, slept with her on a regular basis, and he'd just announced he was gay? "When...how...?"

"Perhaps *bisexual* is a better estimation." Elliott ran his manicured hand through his short blond hair. "I've found myself increasingly attracted to men over the last several years." He shook his head and offered a harsh laugh lacking in humor. "Don't worry. Not you."

Quite frankly Simon could give a toss if Elliott was attracted to him or not. Well...maybe he was a bit relieved Elliott hadn't professed undying love or lust for him, but he'd definitely missed something along the way.

Simon clearly recalled the first time he'd seen Tawny. It'd been here in the gallery, outside Elliott's office. Simon had dropped by during a private event—a cocktail party and private viewing Tawny had arranged for her company. She'd been engrossed in an animated discussion with the caterer. One look at her and his world had shifted into sharper focus. Then she'd disappeared and he'd sought out Elliott, intent on discovering who she was, only to learn Elliott had beat him to the punch. Before Simon had opened his mouth, Elliott had announced he'd met his dream woman and arranged a date with her. Intuitively Simon had known it was the same woman. And he'd been right.

"What was this six months ago when you told me you'd just met the woman of your dreams?" he asked.

"She was hot and sexy and so different from the other women in New York, I thought she might *cure* me."

She'd been a bloody cure?

Simon pushed to his feet and walked over to the window overlooking the street, needing to look at something other than the friend he wasn't sure he knew any longer. Elliott had always been a bit self-absorbed, but this...

Outside, Manhattanites shared the sidewalk with tourists. Customers thronged from the electronics store across the street to the corner falafel stand and the shops in between. A cabbie flipped off a delivery van that cut him off.

Like a strip of negatives laid out before him, he saw in his head photos, moments in time committed to memory. He'd wagered the more he was around Tawny, the more he knew of her, the more his attraction would diminish. Instead with every encounter he'd found himself increasingly drawn to her, discovering that her spirit, her wit, her spunk, ran even deeper and surer than her physical beauty.

And he'd held himself increasingly aloof. Afraid he'd betray himself with a careless glance, a misplaced remark, he hid behind sardonic comments. He'd still held out hope for himself, for a recovery, even after Elliott proposed. He'd get over her.

It had been the photo shoot, the day he'd spent photographing Tawny, at Elliott's request, that he knew he was deeply, irrevocably in love with her. He gripped the windowsill and rocked on the balls of his feet, looking inward instead of at the busy street outside. It was the only time he'd ever spent alone with her and he'd glimpsed something so sweet, so elusive, that to end that day had bordered on physical pain.

And she'd been a bloody cure for Elliott. He turned around to face Elliott, struggling for an even tone. "And was asking her to marry you part of the cure or did you consider yourself cured at that juncture? I'm a bit confused. Is this a twelve-step program?"

"Does it make you feel good to be such a sarcastic bastard?"

"Not particularly." Simon felt a foreign urge to pound Elliott's head against the cinnamon-colored wall. "You asked her to marry you when you knew you felt this way? When you knew you were attracted to men?"

Elliott colored at Simon's censure. "But I'm also attracted to her. I thought if I threw myself into the relationship enough these feelings would go away." He stood and shoved his hands into his pockets. He began to pace the room.

"But they didn't and you cheated on Tawny?"

Elliott squared his shoulders defensively. "Just once. Last night. You know Richard, the acrylics painter we're featuring? I've caught him looking at me, watching me a couple of times. Anyway, we were working late last night, shared a bottle of wine and one thing led to another."

Perhaps this was one big mistake Elliott was blowing out of proportion through guilt. Elliott was also a bit of a dramatist, and guilt distorted the clearest picture, as Simon well knew. "Did you have too much wine? Were you drunk?"

His blue eyes solemn, Elliott shook his head. "No. That'd be an easy excuse. I wasn't drunk. I was intrigued. I thought I'd try it and know for sure, one way or the other." He scrubbed his hand over his forehead. "I liked it. I have feelings for Richard."

Simon squelched a frown of distaste. This shouldn't be any different than listening to Elliott talk about a woman. But it was. Vastly different. Simon held up a staying hand. "I neither want nor need details."

"I wasn't offering them. That was merely by way of clarification," Elliott said, clearly put out. "I've got to tell Tawny. She deserves to know."

"Bloody right she deserves to know." The risks associated with homosexuality slammed him in the gut. Concern for both Tawny and Elliott sharpened his tone. "I hope you used a rubber."

"Of course I did." Elliott slumped into a chair and dropped his head onto the back. "That's just one of the reasons I need to tell her. If we stay together—" that knife twisted in Simon's gut "—she has to make an informed decision."

"You like sex with Richard but you're going to sleep with Tawny?" Simon said.

Elliott creased a sheet of paper between his fingers. "I love her. What's not to love? She's sexy, smart, warm and generous. But we're not setting off any fireworks in the bedroom. I'm attracted to her, but it's not as exciting as it is with Richard."

Elliott had just handed him far more information on several fronts than he'd ever wanted. And he was driving Simon mad, fidgeting with that piece of paper. "Would you put the paper down?" Elliott shot him a look but tossed it onto the desk. "So you don't want to break off the engagement?" Simon asked, his head beginning to throb from tension.

"I don't know. She's a great woman. I need some time to think. I guess whether we break off the engagement is up to her." He ran his hand over the back of his neck. "This is going to be a hell of a conversation." Elliott drew a deep breath and whooshed it out. "Come with me to tell her."

"No." This was between Elliott and Tawny. And talk about a conflict of interest. Simon wanted her, but not with a broken heart or as a rebound lover. However, she *would* be available if this went down the way he thought it would.

Elliott braced his hands on the desk and leaned toward Simon. "Please. I need you for moral support. This is going to be one of the hardest things I've ever done."

Elliott hated facing unpleasant tasks alone. From the time they'd met and become fast friends, he'd dragged Simon along to face teachers, professors, his parents. He'd always maintained Simon was stronger than he was. But for once Simon wasn't being dragged into Elliott's mess. This time his friend was flying solo.

He shook his head. "It's private, Elliott."

"You were there when I proposed," Elliott argued.

Simon crossed his arms over his chest. "And if I had known you were going to propose, I wouldn't have been." Outgoing, give-me-an-audience Elliott had chosen a double date to propose. Simon recalled the agony that had ripped through him when Elliott had presented Tawny with a yellow-diamond engagement ring over dessert. Simon's date, Lenore, had thought it quite romantic.

"This is a mess. I need you there when I tell her. I called her and asked to come over tonight after the gallery closes." He stopped pacing and faced Simon, the length of the room separating them. "I told her you were coming, too."

Simon squashed the adolescent urge to ask Elliott what she'd said about him coming round. He and Elliott had always supported each other. They'd always watched one another's back. But he wasn't sure if he could bear to see the hurt and betrayal on Tawny's face. Nor did he have the right to witness that. "You shouldn't have done that."

"Please, Simon."

But he hadn't exactly been coming through for Elliott all the nights Simon had lain in his lonely bed and made love to Tawny in his head. His conscience smote him. He had no business going. He didn't want to go. But he owed Elliott, whether Elliott knew it or not, for every licentious thought he'd ever had about Tawny. For all the times and all the ways he'd had her in his head.

Guilt did crazy things to men—left them agreeing to things they would otherwise run away from.

"Okay, I'll go. But I'll have to meet you there," Simon said. He stood and picked up his equipment bag.

Elliott dropped into his chair, his relief evident. "Nine o'clock. Her place. Do you remember the way?"

He'd dropped her off once with Elliott. "Sure." He shifted the camera bag to his shoulder and turned for the door.

"Simon…" Elliott said.

He turned again to face Elliott.

"You're a good friend."

Righto. He was a good friend to be obsessively, compulsively in love with his best friend's woman.

2

TAWNY GLANCED AT THE CLOCK on her dresser. Fifteen minutes until Elliott and Simon arrived. She discarded her skirt on the closet floor and defiantly pulled on a pair of shorts. She'd gotten home from running errands and had plenty of time to shower and shave her legs. And now she was dithering about what to wear. As if it mattered.

Her fiancé and his best friend, the guy who disliked her intensely, were coming over with take-out Thai. After a year of living here, one of the things she still loved about New York was the variety of fabulous food within blocks, even if a Southern-girl transplant couldn't find grits or sweet tea.

She looked over the clothes in her closet. It wasn't as if they were going anywhere or she was looking to impress anyone. She picked up a faded T-shirt from her very first 5K run and promptly discarded it. Nah, Elliott had a thing about her dressing up, even if they were staying in. And even though she wasn't entering a beauty contest, her Southern upbringing drew the line at having anyone over and wearing *that*.

She laughed at herself. And no, she still couldn't bring herself to wear white after Labor Day or before Easter. She might be living on Manhattan's Upper West Side but she'd always be Tawny Edwards with Savannah, Georgia, sensibilities. Funny, she'd come to New York to find out who she was and what she was about. She smiled. Wouldn't her mother be surprised that the rebellious Edwards family screwup still adhered to the rules of white?

She settled instead on a halter wrap. Casual but sexy. And more important, cool—a major plus considering how stinking hot it was outside. She finished dressing and closed the closet door on the discarded clothes littering the floor. She pulled her hair up and clipped it haphazardly with a giant barrette underneath. Even with the air-conditioning cranked, the sweltering heat seemed to seep inside.

She spritzed perfume behind her ears and, on a defiant whim, sprayed it between her breasts. Simon might not like her, but dammit, he'd at least like the way she smelled.

She sang along with a Roberta Flack remake playing on the radio in the other room. She loved the evening program—*Sensual Songs and Decadent Dedications*—which offered a nice mix of old and new love songs. And who cared if she was off-key?

She tugged at her shorts. She'd skipped her run this morning and she felt it in their snug fit. Some women were blessed with svelte, slender bodies that actually fit into sylphlike fashions. She, however, didn't belong to that club. She'd learned long ago that eating half of what was on her plate and exercising every day was the only thing that kept her from resembling the Pillsbury Doughboy in drag. Petite and curvy all too easily slid into short and fat.

Tawny made the mistake of double-checking her behind in the mirror while she sang about him killing her softly with his song. Ugh. It was still there...all of it and then some. Elliott was right. The last time they were in bed, he'd mentioned that her butt had gotten bigger. Not exactly what she'd wanted to hear, but she supposed the truth sometimes hurt.

She'd seriously considered having her ass liposuctioned with her last bonus, but what if those fat cells relocated to her thighs or some other equally heinous body destination? Unwilling to risk fat-cell transference, she did an extra set of butt-killing donkey lifts every other day. And from the looks of things, it was time to make that a daily habit.

An outraged yowl in the other room diverted her attention from the shortcomings—or rather the overabundance—of her behind. She went into the kitchen and dumped a measure of cat food into the empty bowl by the refrigerator.

"Uh-huh. You're as close to wasting away as I am." She laughed and snatched Peaches up for a quick hug before he squirmed out of her arms. "But I understand. I'm hungry, too." She put him down in front of his food bowl.

Peaches, a five-year-old declawed Maine coon abandoned by his former owner and promptly rescued from the animal shelter on his last day before the big E— as in euthanasia—in no way resembled a peach in either coloring, countenance or personality. However, Tawny had named him that because it reminded her of her Georgia roots without bringing home too close.

Which probably made no sense to the rest of the world but perfect sense to Tawny.

One might reckon that Peaches would be grateful to have been snatched from the jaws of certain death and appropriately fawn over his savior. One would be wrong. It had been Peaches's arrogance in the face of his impending demise that had stolen Tawny's heart and sealed the feline's fate.

The sound of the buzzer reverberated through the apartment and Tawny's heart thudded in her chest. Simon and Elliott. The idea of coming face-to-face with Simon had tormented her all afternoon. She hadn't seen him since he'd begun to invade her dreams, and subsequently her body, in a most satisfying, but totally disquieting, manner.

She swallowed and turned the radio down on her way to the door. Peering through the peephole, her heart hammered even harder as Simon's lean face stared—not at the door but down the hall, as if he'd actually prefer to be anywhere rather than outside her apartment.

On the radio Etta James crooned in a low, sultry voice about her love coming along at last and the end of her lonely days, which did nothing to dispel Tawny's nervousness and the sexual anticipation curling through her.

She mentally slapped herself around. *Get a grip.* So in her dreams she'd had wild monkey sex with Simon. By no stretch of her overactive, oversexed imagination was *he* her own true love coming along.

She squared her shoulders, pasted on her best loaded-with-Southern-charm smile, slipped the locks and opened her door. "Hi, Simon."

"Hullo, Tawny." It was wickedly unfair the way his voice, with its hint of British accent, revved her engine. That was one thing about her dreams—he always talked to her during sex and it always turned her on. This was no dream, but she'd been conditioned and felt a familiar heat stir within her.

She looked past him. "Where's Elliott?"

"I had a shoot today so we came separately," he said without a glimmer of a smile in the depth of his dark eyes.

Tawny stepped aside. "Come in."

His dark hair, cut close and combed back, lent his lean face an ascetic look. She felt his body heat as he stepped past her into the room, his camera equipment slung over his shoulder. This was much worse than she'd anticipated, far more potent than any dream. His clean, subtle scent teased her. In her dreams his scent didn't entice her as it did now. She caught her breath and strove for a light tone.

"How was your photo shoot?"

"Fine. It went quick. I've shot Chloe before," Simon said.

The name evoked an image of a tall, thin, beautiful model. Tawny didn't feel the slightest twinge of remorse at hating the unknown, unsuspecting Chloe— that was the price paid by thin, beautiful women without an ass the size of a principality.

A few weeks ago, after their engagement, Simon had photographed Tawny at Elliott's request. Elliott possessed an eye for art, but he wasn't an artist. Simon, however, was a genius with a camera. She wasn't a professional model and it had taken an entire day of Simon working with her, cajoling her, but her photographs had been fantastic. She'd seen herself in a different way. She'd seen strength, but also a sensual vulnerability.

He'd been patient and almost charming, as if when he got behind the camera he forgot himself or perhaps he could truly be himself.

During the shoot, she'd thought she'd finally reached Elliott's best friend, won him over. It had been a magical day. But then afterward he'd retreated even further behind a wall, cooler and more aloof than ever. Mercifully their paths hadn't crossed since.

Except at night. In her bed. In her dreams. The night following the photo shoot she'd dreamed of erotic, explicit sex with Simon. And every night since. Now the object of her writhing lust stood in her apartment, having spent the day photographing some skinny model. Tawny bit back a bitchy comment.

"I haven't seen you to tell you I thought the photos you took of me were great. Not that I'm great, but the photos were. You're very good at what you do." Whoa. Instant image of him bringing her to orgasm in her dream. "I mean, you're good with your camera." She closed the door. *Tawny, honey, find a brain cell and grab on to it.* She sounded like a dithering idiot.

"You're very photogenic. You have a great smile and good bone structure," he said.

He spoke very matter-of-factly. He could've been discussing the weather. There was absolutely no reason for her heart to pound as if he'd just claimed her beauty equal to that of the legendary Helen of Troy. She felt as gauche as she had when she'd been a third-grader and Henry Turner had pulled her braids. Except she'd liked Henry Turner. And while she might have toe-curling dreams about Simon, she wasn't altogether sure that she liked him.

"Thank you. Your equipment should be safe here." She indicated a spot between the door and the antique cupboard to the right. Hauling *that* monstrosity up when she'd moved last year had been a party. "Would you like a drink while we're waiting on Elliott? Red wine?"

Simon placed his camera and equipment on the floor next to the cupboard with more care and consideration than many mothers with babies. He glanced at her over his shoulder. "Absolutely."

Earth to Tawny. She should stop admiring the way his black T-shirt hugged his shoulders and the lean line of his back. She should also stop eyeing the fit of his jeans over his very fine—make that *extra* fine—ass.

He stood, pivoting to face her in one fluid movement. He arched a questioning brow. "Need any help?"

Don't mind me. I was just checking out your eye candy. "No. Going right now." She indicated the sofa with a flick of her wrist. "Make yourself at home. I'll be right back."

She fled the room, silently urging Elliott to arrive soon. Those dreams were seriously messing with her head. She'd felt as if his gaze, hot and consuming, had licked across her shoulders bared by her halter top and across her buttocks snugged into her shorts.

She leaned against the counter and dragged in a calming breath, dismissing her ridiculous notions. Simon had been his usual remote self since he'd arrived. The only heat she'd felt from him had been a product of her own twisted, overactive, inappropriate imagination.

She reached past Peaches to the small wine rack atop the fridge and pulled out a bottle of cabernet. Peaches, who spent most of his time on top of the refrigerator, offered her a lazy slit-eyed look.

Tawny uncorked the bottle. "You know, normal cats curl up on a bed or in the corner of the sofa or drape themselves across a chair back. Why do you camp out on top of the refrigerator?"

Of course, the cat didn't deign to answer. Tawny pulled three wineglasses out of the cabinet. She personally thought Peaches liked to render himself inaccessible. And what did it say about her that she loved that damn cat? "Don't mind me. I'm leaving now."

She went back into the den.

Simon sat on her purple chenille sofa studying the room. Self-consciousness surged through her, knowing he was seeing her personal space through the eyes of an artist. Her taste tended toward eclectic. She favored reproduction art, the occasional antique and furniture more comfortable than stylish.

She placed the wine and glasses on the bamboo chest that doubled as a coffee table. Simon focused his attention on her, and she wished contrarily that he was eyeing her apartment once again instead. The glow from a stained-glass floor lamp at the corner of the sofa backlit him. Dark hair, dark slashing eyebrows above dark eyes, unsmiling visage, black T-shirt and jeans. He was a dark angel come to torment her.

His eyes snared her. The room shrank to just the few feet separating them. If this was one of her dreams, she'd join him on the couch, where she'd nibble and lick her way past his perpetual reserve until they were both getting naked....

"Do you need any help?" he asked.

"Thanks, I've got it." *Don't mind me while I stand here like some whacked-out nympho and fantasize about taking your clothes off while we wait on Elliott to show up.* She disgusted herself. "Glass of wine coming right up."

She managed to pour two glasses. She handed him one, taking care not to touch him in the exchange.

"Were you talking to someone in the kitchen?" he asked. Surely that wasn't amusement lurking in the austere Simon's eyes.

She sat in the armchair on her side of the coffee table, the farthermost point away from him in the confines of her tiny den. Avoiding even the most casual physical contact seemed a good plan. "My cat."

"And does it talk back?"

Whaddaya know? Simon actually owned a sense of humor. "No. He's a typical male. Selective hearing. He only talks if it concerns his empty belly. Or the remote."

"My kind of cat." Simon's spontaneous grin did crazy things to her insides. He silently held his glass up in a toast and then sipped.

His fingers, long and lean, wrapped around the glass stem and reminded her of her afternoon dream and where his fingers had been then.

Simply thinking about it left her wet and wanton again. Great. She'd sit here across from him, drinking wine, waiting on her future husband to show up, and wind up with a wet spot. *Stop.* She would not sit around fantasizing about this man. It was wrong. Guilt churned in her gut. *Thinking* about Simon turned her on faster and hotter than Elliott's actual touch.

She only had to make it through the evening. A few short hours. And next week she was signing up for therapy. Alison, one of the executive secretaries, saw a therapist weekly. First thing Monday morning she'd ask Alison for a referral. This *thing* for Simon was getting out of hand. God knew what would happen if he offered a smidgen of interest or encouragement. What kind of woman ran around in perpetual lust for her fiancé's best friend? And it had actually started her thinking, quite hard, as to exactly how she felt about Elliott and whether marrying him was such a good idea. She and Elliott were good together. They got along well. They had fun. But it was nothing like the dark passion with Simon that haunted her dreams. Toss in a vague sense of discontent with her bedroom time with Elliott…

Did she break it off with someone based on hot dreams about someone else? Which came first? Her discontent with Elliott or this dark sexual attraction to Simon? Was she truly attracted or just scared of commitment? Definitely time for a therapist.

"Good wine. Thanks," Simon said.

"Sure." Nervous, she swigged her wine instead of sipping and promptly choked. Then choked some more. Dammit, she couldn't catch her breath.

Simon skirted the chest and took her wineglass from her. He knelt down and, as if conditioned by her dreams, she automatically spread her legs to accommodate him. He grabbed her shoulders. "Can you breathe? Nod your head."

She nodded yes. But he didn't take his hands from her bare skin. Finally the choking fit ended. She was left with him kneeling between her thighs, his fingers curled around the curves of her shoulders, her face hot with humiliation, her body hotter still at his proximity.

"I'm…fine," she said, her voice wavering. Not from her choking spell but from his touch, the brush of his body against her bare legs. The reality of his touch was a thousand times more potent than a mere dream. Did his hand tremble against her shoulder or was it her own reaction?

Simon released her and stood abruptly. Still between her legs, he looked down at her. "You might want to save the chugging for Kool-Aid or beer," he drawled. He turned on his heel and picked up his own wineglass to sit once again on the sofa.

Bite me. Tawny hated him at that moment. How could he be so concerned and considerate one minute and then snide and nasty the next? She ignored his comment and focused instead on Elliott. She glanced at her watch. Almost nine-fifteen.

"Elliott should be here soon. I hope so. I'm starving," she said. Yeah. Simon had just spent the day photographing one of the skin-'n'-bones set and she'd just presented her well-padded ass as starving. "Well, not starving, obviously, but hungry." She simply couldn't say or do anything right in front of him.

And then it didn't matter because she wasn't in front of Simon. She was in utter pitch-black darkness and sudden silence.

"What the hell?" Simon said.

Her sentiments exactly.

"Simon?" Panic filled her voice.

"I'm right here," he said. He stood, blind in the dark.

He bumped his shins against the chest. Cautiously he put his wineglass down.

Damn good thing he did because Tawny grabbed on to his arm, startling him, the uncustomary tremor in her voice reflected in her fingers. "I'm sorry. I've got a thing about the dark."

Moving slowly, he felt his way around the furniture until he reached her side. He'd never experienced such absolute darkness. He couldn't see her, but he felt her body heat, smelled her perfume, felt her energy pulsing in her hand on his arm, heard the soft pant of her panic. "A thing?"

"Yeah, I don't like it worth a damn." Her laugh verged on pathetic and tugged at his heartstrings. As if everything she did didn't tug at them. "Curiosity got the better of me and I managed to lock myself in a closet for a couple of hours when I was four. I was terrified. Ever since, the dark freaks me out."

She laughed again, and if he hadn't been so tuned in to the nuances of her voice, he might've missed the nervousness still lurking behind it. Against his better judgment—touching her, as he'd found a few minutes ago, was definitely bad judgment—he caught her hand in his. "It's okay. I'm here. Does your building lose power often?"

"Twice before. But it was always during the day." Her voice sounded surer, less panicked, and her hand was steadier. She tried to pull her hand from his. "I'm fine now."

Her slight breathlessness gave her away. She wasn't fine, but she was doing her best to give that impression. He fought the urge to pull her closer, wrap his arms around her soft vulnerability and reassure her everything was okay. Instead he contented himself with clasping her hand tighter. "Well, I'm not. I'm blind as a bloody bat in here. Where's your flashlight?" he asked.

She turned into him and her cheek brushed against his shoulder, setting his heart racing. It was agony to be so close to her, touch her, smell her.

"I don't have one. It got broken when I moved and I keep forgetting to replace it." Her breath feathered against his neck and her hair teased along his jaw.

"Okay. No flashlight. Move on to plan B. Where's a window?"

Her fingers curled around his. "My bedroom. There's one in the bathroom, but it's small."

"Okay. Lead on to your bedroom." Despite the dark, he closed his eyes when he spoke. Under different circumstances...

"This way." She tugged him by the hand and within seconds he ran into something hard.

"Ow. Damn." Obviously the wall.

"Sorry," she apologized, her disembodied voice beside him.

He rolled his shoulder. "I take it you didn't hit the wall."

"No. I'm in the doorway."

Brilliant. She was laughing at him. Actually banging into walls was rather funny but hard on the shoulder.

"Walking beside you isn't going to work. I'll walk behind you." He braced his hands on her bare shoulders. In the dark he could well imagine her naked. Correction. It was as if she *was* naked, the way he'd imagined her so many times before. Her shoulders were soft, her skin like warm, supple suede. Her scent surrounded him, seduced him. He ached to pull her back into him, to lower his head and kiss the delicate skin at the back of her neck, shower kisses along the curve of her shoulder. He wanted to absorb her heat, her taste, *her.*

Longing pierced his very soul. To have her in his arms but still out of reach was cruel beyond measure. Just one taste of her... He leaned forward and she swayed ever so slightly back into him, tensing beneath his fingertips. Wisps of hair brushed his face. What the hell was he doing? He jerked his head back.

"Simon?" The husky way she said his name always curled heat through him.

"Give me a second to get my bearings." Clothes. He needed to touch clothes. "How about this?" He grasped her full, round hips just below the curve of her waist, the same way he would if they were dancing in a conga line. Yeah, or having sex from behind.

"That's fine." Her voice sounded strained. Or maybe it was just him. This proximity had him near daft.

"Okay. Lead the way." Sod it if he sounded harsh. Better she think him rude than randy.

He walked behind her, keeping a firm grip on her hips, trying to ignore the sweet sway beneath his fingertips. Wouldn't she be impressed? While she fought off a panic attack, he was getting a stiffy from merely touching her and inhaling her scent with every breath he took.

In the room behind them Tawny's cell phone rang. She hesitated, tensing, turning slightly in the direction of the ring. Simon tightened his hold on her. "Just keep going. We don't have a chance of getting to it before it goes to voice mail. Not to mention banging the hell out of us along the way."

They resumed their dark journey. Almost immediately Simon's cell vibrated at his side. "Hold on. Someone's ringing me." He plucked his cell off his side and flipped it open one-handed, keeping the other hand on her hip. "Thackeray here."

"Simon, are you with Tawny?" Elliott asked without preamble.

"Yes. She's right here."

"I just tried to call her and she didn't answer." Elliott's voice held a petulant note.

"It's pitch-black in her apartment. She couldn't get to it in time. Where are you?" Bugger, Elliott. He should be the one here with his hand on Tawny's hip, tortured by the feel of soft flesh and her womanly scent. Except it wouldn't be torture for Elliott because she wasn't off-limits to him.

"I'm at the gallery. We don't have any lights either."

"Why are you there? What's going on?"

"I don't think we're under siege, if that's what you mean. I think it's one of those blackouts like we had a couple of years ago. I was running late. Richard and I had a few things to iron out and then everything shut down."

Simon welcomed the dark. Tawny couldn't see the expression on his face. He didn't give a farthing about Richard and Elliott's details, but if Elliott had been here with take-out Thai as arranged, then Simon wouldn't be holding on to Tawny in the dark. Alone. Tempted nearly beyond measure.

"Excellent. How long do you think it'll take you to get here?" Simon asked, deliberately keeping his voice neutral.

"We're locked in. When the electrical system is

compromised, the security system goes into total lockdown."

This was getting better and better. "You're locked in at the gallery?"

"That's it in a nutshell." Simon heard the murmur of another man's voice in the background followed by Elliott's breathless laughter. "Listen, you don't have to stay with Tawny. I'm sure she'll be okay."

Hot anger lanced him at Elliott's careless, cavalier regard for Tawny. This afternoon he'd been annoyed with Elliott. Now Simon was furious with his friend. Did he not know or simply not care that the woman who met life head-on was terrified of the dark while he was cozied up with his new lover? What the hell had he been doing hanging out with Richard instead of meeting at Tawny's the way he'd set it up? Where did Elliott get off taking that proprietorial tone when he told Simon he didn't have to stay? And there was no way he could say any of that to Elliott with Tawny listening.

"Of course I'll stay with her until the power's back on. I wouldn't dream of leaving her alone."

She moved closer to him, and without thinking he tightened his hand on her hip. They'd both shifted during his phone call and now her left hip nudged his, his hand was still on her other hip, his arm wrapped around the curve of her back. This was bad—very, very bad. How long would he be trapped in this apartment with this woman who drove him crazy? Who touched him somewhere deep inside? Who seemed to slip past every barrier he'd ever erected? His body thought it brilliant; his mind recognized it as a big mistake.

"No. I said you don't need to stay," Elliott snapped.

What the hell? Simon didn't want Tawny to know Elliott was so bloody self-absorbed that he'd have Simon leave her alone in a blackout. Better that his selfish friend appear the considerate fiancé he should be than wound her with the truth. "Don't give it another thought. I won't leave until the electricity's restored."

"Whatever. Go ahead and play Sir Galahad." Elliott, the bastard, actually sounded peevish.

Simon hung up on him and put the phone back on his hip. "That was Elliott. He's fine. He thinks this is a blackout. He's stuck at the gallery with the acrylics painter. In the event of an electrical failure, the security system locks down."

"Apparently Elliott asked you to stay. You don't have to babysit me. I'll be fine."

Piss it all. This was a fine conundrum. He'd never wanted to leave a place more in his life, to flee the hounds of hell nipping at his feet—those beasts of longing and desire that made it nearly unbearable to be in her presence. On the other hand, he didn't think she relished being abandoned during a blackout and he couldn't bring himself to leave her alone. He knew it had been sheer terror and a gut response when she'd clenched his hand earlier but now she didn't want to be an obligation.

"I know I don't have to stay, but I'd rather not have to make my way home without benefit of the subway. Do you mind if I stay until the power's restored?"

"Not at all. I'd like for you to stay if you want to."

He tried to lighten the moment. "Then it's settled You're stuck with me until then." *Please let it be sooner than later.*

Her laughter sounded more relaxed and he knew

he'd done the right thing. "Okay. Looks like we're stuck with one another."

He wasn't sure exactly how it happened, but in that moment...she moved...he moved...in the inky black, and his hand closed over her breast. For several stunned moments he could only stand there, his hand wrapped around her soft breast, her nipple stabbing against his palm through her shirt material.

Like a sudden summer storm, the atmosphere shifted and thickened. A sexual charge pulsed between them. For one daft moment, he could have sworn she leaned into his touch, pushed her pebbled point harder into his hand. Want slammed through him, his universe reduced to the feel of her breast in his palm, the hot desire that left him rigid. She uttered a muted, inarticulate sound. He wasn't sure if it was a moan or a protest, but it served as a dash of cold water.

He yanked his hand away. "I'm sorry. That was an accident."

"Of course it was.... I'm sure...you'd never..."

"How far are we from your bedroom?" he asked, his tone as tense as his body.

"Simon..."

She thought he only had to touch her breast and he was ready to throw her down and have his wicked way with her? Ready to fondle her and taste her until she was so caught up in their passion she'd forget all about the dark? Unfortunately she was right. And if she was his, he'd do just that. But she wasn't his. "The window—that's where the window is, isn't it?"

"Yes." Was that relief or embarrassment or both in that single syllable? He left it alone.

They navigated the short hall to her bedroom, past

the bed and over to the window. Tawny opened the curtains and raised the blinds.

The city lay shrouded in darkness, reminiscent of a well-rendered charcoal sketch, dark skies with the looming shadows of darker buildings against it. In the distance auxiliary-lit buildings stood, glowing sentinels guarding the city. Up and down the street, candles, flashlights and headlamps provided illumination.

Despite the muffled noise of people and the inevitable bleating of car horns, the darkness isolated them, stranded them on the island of her apartment, removed from the rest of civilization.

Dark clouds scudded across the sky, obliterating the bit of light the night sky might have afforded.

"A storm's coming in," she said.

"It looks like it. Do you have any candles?"

"No flashlight, but I have lots of candles."

She released his hand and turned. Her bedside table stood a few feet from the window. She opened the drawer and felt around. She held up a long object. "My flamethrower."

She flicked a long-nosed, handled lighter and lit a candle by her bed. She crossed the room, lighting two wall sconces. They flanked a painting of a semidressed woman reclining on a divan. Very sensual. Like her. Like the room.

A sleigh bed dominated the windowed wall. A comforter in an elegant paisley pattern of bold reds, cinnamon and gold lay atop it. Matching gold fringed pillows were piled against the headboard invitingly. A mirrored dresser filled the wall space between the bed-

room door and wardrobe. Tawny moved over to a large
triple-wicked pillar candle on her dresser.

She turned to face him, smiling. "I told you I had
plenty of candles."

She was even more beautiful with candlelight dancing across her face, flickering over her bare shoulders,
casting the valley between her breasts into a mysterious shadowy place he longed to explore. Her smile
faded and the perfume of the candles wafted around
them, exotic scents that conjured images of hot sex,
that stripped away his reserve and left him a man who
ached for the woman he wanted and couldn't have. Her
lips parted and he could have sworn he glimpsed a re-
ciprocal heat in her eyes.

"You shouldn't burn them all. We don't have any
idea how long the lights will be out." Nothing like a
little censure to dissipate a mood.

"I have plenty. I've got a thing for candles."

"What else do you have a thing for?" he asked, his
tongue moving faster under the circumstances than
his internal censor. And he was only human. They
were alone in her apartment, in candlelight, her bed
was right there and less than five feet separated them.

She wet her lips, as if her mouth was suddenly too
dry, and he felt another stab of familiar guilt—this
time for making her uncomfortable. "That was a joke.
My misguided attempt at humor. Do you have a radio
with batteries so we can find out what's going on out
there?" Definitely time to introduce the real world. He
needed outside stimuli to keep from drifting off into
another fantasy of just the two of them.

"My boom box uses batteries." She opened her
closet door and stepped over the pile of clothes on the

floor. She knelt down and bent over. He should look away, direct his attention to the painting on the wall, check out the dark New York skyline. Hell, watching paint dry would be better, far more noble, than staring at her on her knees with her amazing, enticing, drool-inspiring bum in the air.

She backed out of the closet, boom box in hand, and stood. She flipped the switch. Nothing happened. "Okay. Batteries that aren't dead would be a bonus." She upended the radio on the bed and opened the battery compartment. "Six C-cell batteries. I'll have us fixed up in no time. I keep extras on hand."

She rounded the bed to the bedside drawer, where he stood. She pulled out two batteries and tossed them onto the bed. She dug a bit more, pulling out a third. "Three isn't going to do it."

Her skin glimmered in the soft light, her eyes were soft and luminous, her scent issued a siren's call. He thrust his hands in his pockets to keep from reaching for her. He'd been mad to agree to be here tonight. "No. I'd say it's rather obvious we need three more."

"I've got it covered." Her smile said she was tired of him being a jerk. And he was tired of being a jerk, but it was better than giving in to his impulse to ease her onto the bed, peel her clothes off and become intimately acquainted with every delectable inch of her naked body.

She delved back into the drawer—obviously command central in her bedroom—and pulled out…the biggest vibrator he'd ever seen. Well, actually, he didn't believe he'd ever seen a vibrator firsthand before. It was quite…large.

"Simon, meet Tiny." Tiny was pretty intimidating

from a man's point of view. Not that he suddenly felt inadequate or anything. She unscrewed the bottom, dropped two batteries out and replaced the top. She put it back in the drawer and then pulled out a much smaller dildo with a smaller stem on the top of it. "This is Enrico and Bob." She waved the toy in his general direction.

"Um, I gather the little guy is Bob because he…"

"Yep. You got it. He bobs up and down."

Simon reminded himself to breathe—but not too heavily. This was going great. He should've abandoned her, along with his principles, and gotten the hell out of her apartment when he'd had the opportunity. He'd only thought it was hot before. He was burning up now. "I guess this answers the question as to what else you have a thing for."

She pulled out a single battery and tossed it onto the bed atop the others. "There you go. Six C-cell batteries, and I promise they're all in working order. Why don't you put them in?"

3

MAYBE SHE'D GONE A TAD too far introducing her vibrator boys by name, but she'd had enough of his quiet sarcasm and disapproval. According to Elliott, Simon's demeanor stemmed from being first-generation American. His father, a Brit, had relocated to New York before Simon was born to curate some museum or another. She didn't care if his father was next in line for the British throne, she was tired of Simon's hot-and-cold attitude. And if she was honest with herself, she was none too pleased with herself that he turned her on to the nth degree and annihilated her composure. Around him she couldn't seem to think of anything beyond sex. With him. She'd nearly made a fool of herself when he'd put his hands on her shoulders. And then when he'd touched her breast…she'd come close to begging him to take her then and there, hard and fast, against the wall, in the hallway. Simon brought out a sensuality in her that she'd never known before and in some aspects frightened her with its intensity.

Silently Simon loaded the batteries into her boom box. His hands weren't quite steady as he fumbled with the last one. Maybe the close confines were getting to him, too.

The radio blared to life. "…so, it looks like it's a good old-fashioned blackout brought on by the incredible demand for a little air-conditioned relief from the triple-digit heat. Unfortunately, the lights are out across the tristate area and authorities tell us they're not sure when they'll have the lights back on. It looks like it's going to be a hot night, so just settle down where you are and stay put. In honor of the blackout, we're going to open the lines for requests and dedications that have to do with hot and summer. And I guess we'll be seeing a bunch of newborns nine months from now. Hey, you've got to pass the time somehow. Let's start this set with an oldie, 'Love the One You're With.'" Tawny reached over and turned it off.

Trapped in her apartment with Simon for the night? Tawny bit back her panic. Danger signals exploded in her brain—her, Simon, candlelight—and already it felt as if the temperature in her apartment had increased a few degrees.

"Well, we can forget take-out Thai. Are you hungry?" Sure, leave it to the fat girl to bring up food, but dammit, she was starving. And it took her mind off sex. And Simon. And sex with Simon. Well, probably not, but she was still hungry.

He grinned and she was totally disarmed by the flash of his white teeth in the dim lighting. "I'm famished. I could chew nails."

"I don't keep much food on hand. There's a deli a block and a half away. Do you think it would still be open?"

"It should. During the 2003 blackout, food stores

were selling out because they didn't know how long their power would be out. Better to sell it than let it ruin. I've even got some cash on me. Let's give it a go." He smiled with a touch of self-conscious eagerness. "And I wouldn't mind burning a roll or two of film."

Duh. He was a photographer. Of course he'd like to be taking pictures. And it was incredible how his whole demeanor changed when he talked about photography.

"Sure. Food and photographs. Works for me," she said.

No sooner had the words left her mouth than lightning flashed and thunder boomed overhead. Rain fell in a sudden onslaught. Nothing, it seemed, was subtle or happening in small measure tonight.

"Or not. Okay. That's it. I'm not planning anything else tonight because everything I plan gets trashed," she said with a nervous laugh. They were stuck here. She picked up a small votive to lead the way back down the hall. "I'm not a culinary queen, but nails shouldn't be necessary," she said.

She didn't comment when Simon blew out the other candles in the room before he picked up the radio and followed her. She had enough candles in the closet to carry them for a week, but it wasn't worth arguing the point.

She was more than willing to bury the hatchet between them since they were stuck here together.

She snagged her wineglass on the way into the kitchen. "Good wine is a terrible thing to waste."

"Ah, something we agree on." Tawny waited for Simon to exchange the radio for his glass and the wine bottle. Given the minimum square footage of her apartment, they'd have no trouble hearing the radio from the kitchen. He followed her into the other room. Within a few seconds, several candles illuminated her galley kitchen.

"What's that?" Simon asked. She followed his gaze to the top of the fridge. In the semidarkness, Peaches resembled a blob of prey more than a feline.

"Peaches, my cat. He likes the top of the refrigerator. He's the one with a bad attitude and selective hearing."

"Poor fella. You'd have a bad attitude, too, if you were a guy called Peaches." Simon made a sympathetic noise in the back of his throat and surprised Tawny by reaching up to scratch the cat behind the ears. Peaches promptly hissed and swatted.

"He's not Mister Friendly."

"Neither am I," Simon said with a self-deprecating smile as he leaned back against the counter and crossed his arms over his chest.

"Well, forget it, I'm not adopting you if you find yourself abandoned," she said with a teasing smile, despite the flutter in her tummy at the thought of making Simon her own. "You'd probably be as bad-tempered and ungrateful as he is."

"Duly noted," he said with another smile that doubled her heart rate. "Why do you keep the wretch?"

"Because it was love at first sight on my part." She glanced away from him. That almost sounded as if she had declared herself in love with Simon at first sight. A totally ridiculous notion. "He'll come around sooner or later."

Simon quirked a sardonic brow in the direction of Peaches. "I believe you're an eternal optimist."

"Call me Pollyanna." She opened the refrigerator door and peered into the black hole, considering their limited food options. "The microwave or the oven won't work. I've got leftover pizza. And I can throw together a fruit salad. How does that sound?"

"Better than nails."

Tawny laughed, enjoying his quiet teasing and relaxing into his company. She pulled out the food and closed the fridge door. "Are you always so gracious and enthusiastic?"

"Yes, except when I'm in a bad mood." He sipped his wine, and as if the camaraderie between them was unacceptable, she could almost see him retreating. She wanted him to stay. "It was monumental bad timing that I wasn't the one delayed and Elliott isn't here with you instead."

Elliott. Right. Her fiancé. She twisted her ring with her thumb. Guilt flooded her. She hadn't spared Elliott a nominal thought since his phone call. She shrugged. "It's an emergency. We all do the best we can. I'm sure Elliott would rather not be trapped in the gallery with that acrylics guy. And while you might not be thrilled to be here, it's better than being stuck on the subway."

She pulled out the chopping board, a knife and a bowl.

"And why would you think I'm not thrilled to be here?" he asked.

She went to work chunking the fresh pineapple. She almost said she wasn't as dumb as she must look but thought better of it. "Should I believe you're thrilled to be stuck in this apartment with me?"

"Would you believe me if I told you there was no other place I'd rather be?" Something in the depths of his eyes stole her breath.

She laughed to cover her breathlessness and cored

an apple. "No. I think there's probably a list a mile long of places you'd rather be, but you're too nice to say so."

"Quite. I'm such a nice guy."

"Be honest. Wouldn't you rather be at your girl-friend's? Or if the photo shoot had gone a little longer, you'd be with Chloe." Okay, she admitted it. She was fishing. They'd double-dated several times with Simon. Each time it had been a different woman. But after the photo shoot, Simon had always begged off whenever Elliott invited him along.

She added diced apple to the bowl and reached for a banana. His love life intrigued her. Not that it had anything to do with her. But if she was having head-banging sex with him in her dreams, she could at least know about his love life.

"I don't have a girlfriend and Chloe isn't my type," he said, shrugging. A thin, beautiful model wasn't his type? She looked at him, considering the implications. Maybe he was...

"And no, I don't mean not my type that way. I'm not gay. Chloe's a nice woman, but she doesn't do a thing for me."

Whew! She shouldn't be so relieved. She sectioned an orange. What kind of woman was his type? Who would appeal to a self-contained man like Simon? And why didn't he have a girlfriend? In a dark, fiendish way, he was spine-tingling, toe-curling sexy. "So, what kind of woman does something for you?"

"I've never really thought about it."

"Sure you have. Everyone has a type they go for," she said.

"I don't really have a type."

He seriously needed to loosen up a bit. She mixed

the fruit together. "Sure you do. I bet if you stop and think about it, there's a certain type of woman that attracts you, that makes your blood run a little hotter."

"Is this some kind of game, Tawny? Do you want me to say it's a woman like you?" His voice was low, dangerous in its quiet intensity.

Wasn't that exactly what she wanted? To know that for all the times she'd writhed, screamed his name in the middle of an orgasm, woken up wet and spent, that he wasn't totally immune to her? Yes and no. The only game she was playing was with herself, and it was a dangerous one. She looked away from his dark-eyed gaze, glad to busy herself with getting two bowls out of her cabinet. "Don't be ridiculous. You've made it abundantly clear how you regard me. I'm just surprised you're not still seeing Lenore. You made a nice couple." Lenore had been Simon's date the night Elliott had proposed. The tall, willowy blonde had been a perfect complement to Simon's urbane dark looks.

She divvied out the portions and they sat at the small wrought-iron table she'd tucked in the corner.

Simon shrugged. "Lenore is nice. That's why I quit seeing her. I'm in a bit of an unrequited love and it didn't seem fair to date her when my head and heart were otherwise engaged. Delicious, by the way," he said, indicating the fruit and pizza. "Thank you."

"Glad you like it." His other words slammed into her. A dark jealousy coiled through her at the thought of a woman capturing the distant Simon's heart. This mystery woman must be a paragon. Beautiful, sophisticated, thin, witty, probably a couple of PhDs under her belt. Unwisely, unwittingly, instinctively Tawny hated her. Hated her for capturing his heart and hated her for tossing it aside.

So of course she said, "I'm sorry. That's a hard place to be. Do you want to talk about it? About her? Sometimes talking it over with someone, things aren't as hopeless as they seem." She couldn't seem to shut up, hell-bent on atoning for her lust. "Maybe I could help you figure out a way to win her over—you know, another woman's perspective."

She bit into the pizza, finding something else to do with her mouth other than babble on. Simon regarded her over the rim of his wineglass, his expression indecipherable. "You're offering aid with my dismal love life?"

It could prove to be just the cure she needed to get over this...thing for him. She nodded and swallowed. "Sure. Why not?"

He placed his empty glass on the table. "That's generous, but she's unavailable."

Ouch. "She's married?"

"No. But she's in a serious relationship."

That merely irritated her. Was Simon truly in love or was it the unavailability factor? People, especially men, always wanted what they couldn't have. Put a taboo label on it and they had to have it.

"Until she says *I do,* she's not unavailable. You've got to decide how important she is to you. If you're willing to forego other relationships, she must matter a lot. Wake up, Simon, and smell the coffee. What're you gonna do? Sit around in some weird celibate state—"

"I never mentioned celibacy." Simon tried to pull a haughty look on her.

Tawny rolled her eyes. "Give me a break. If you

won't date a woman because you don't want to be unfair, then you're certainly not sleeping with anyone." Alarming how much that pleased her. So of course she worked even harder to push him. "You're gonna moon around in a celibate state for a couple of years or even the rest of your life because she's in a relationship but not married? How bad do you want her?"

"With every fiber of my being."

His quiet intensity sent a shiver down her spine and pierced her heart. What was wrong with her? Who he wanted and how much he wanted her had nothing to do with Tawny.

"Then it's time for you to fish or cut bait."

"THANKS FOR YOUR ADVICE to the lovelorn. I'll keep the 'fish or cut bait' in mind."

Wasn't that twisted? The object of his unrequited affection—and hence intense guilt, as she was engaged to his best friend—sat across the table, bathed in candlelight, wearing a sexy halter top and shorts and advising him to put a move on her. At least, that's what he'd interpreted her charming colloquialism to mean.

Tawny topped off her wineglass and refilled his at the same time. "Well, I think you should go for it. What have you got to lose?"

What did he have to lose if he went for *her* right now? "Really nothing, other than those small matters of pride and self-esteem."

"It's pretty hard to wrap your arms around those and snuggle up to them. Or enjoy a glass of wine or a candlelit bubble bath with them either."

He struggled to keep his expression one of sardonic amusement while inside her words played out in his head as snapshots of the two of them. The irony of sharing a glass of wine with her in candlelight nearly slayed him. He was an absolute masochist to participate in this conversation. Bugger that, he was a masochist to even *be* here.

"But a glass of wine sooner or later is gone, eventually the candles burn out and the water grows cold, so perhaps one has to make the more long-lasting choice."

"Except that life is fleeting. Tomorrow may not come before the wine stops flowing or the water cools."

"Am I in the company of a hedonist?" he asked, very clearly recalling his recent introduction to Tiny, Enrico and Bob, her on-demand boyfriends.

She tucked a piece of hair behind her ear. "Life is short and it's a shame to waste opportunities. This woman could be the love of your life and you're letting her slip away. And who knows? She may feel the same way about you." He really was a pathetic sod. He was flattered she didn't consider him so repugnant she couldn't imagine a woman attracted to him. "Maybe she just doesn't know it yet. Or she could be shy and afraid to tell you."

Simon laughed. Neither of those came to mind in a Tawny word-association exercise. Other than her aversion to the dark, she'd never displayed either characteristic. "I don't think shy or fear are factors when it comes to my lady."

Tawny leaned her elbow on the table and pursed her lips, tapping one finger against the corner of her mouth as she eyed him consideringly. She had a truly lovely mouth, full but without the collagen bloat so popular these days.

"Well, maybe this is some kind of courtly love." She

snapped her fingers. "That's it. You know, chivalry and all. Knights only loved their ladies from afar. Maybe you're just afraid to declare yourself because you aren't truly physically attracted to her. Maybe you wouldn't know what to do with her if she actually reciprocated your attraction," she said. She crossed her arms as if she'd neatly solved a little puzzle.

His boyhood days of envisioning himself as a bold knight were long gone. There was nothing courtly or chivalrous about the maelstrom of emotion she evoked in him. He absolutely burned for her. And he'd had enough of her speculation. It was time for this conversation to end. He knew one sure way to kill the conversation and prove to her just how far removed he was from her romanticized notions.

He traced his finger along the edge of his glass and smiled at her across the table, offering her a glimpse of the dark passion seething beneath his surface. "I don't know about courtly love." He chose his next words very deliberately—crude and base—to make a point. "I do know I would fuck her senseless for a week, given half a chance."

Her eyes grew huge and she swallowed hard, but she didn't look away. "Oh. Senseless…a week…well, then."

Okay. Perhaps he'd gone a bit over the top there. "I apologize if I shocked you."

She raised her chin. "I'm not shocked at all. I think all that passion is…well, hot. I'm not sure there's a woman alive who wouldn't want to know a man was so hot for her he'd like to—" she paused and emphasized the very words he'd uttered "—fuck her senseless for a week. As long as somewhere in the week he wanted to work a little conversation and getting to know her into the sexathon."

Far from offensive, it sounded sexy and exciting when she threw his words back at him. Especially when she drawled it in that low, honeyed tone with a glint in her eye that spoke more to interest and arousal.

Simon was knee-deep in muck but apparently lacked enough sense to stop wading. "I've never operated solely from a state of lust. Her brain and her personality are half the appeal. Otherwise I'd only want her for half a week. And I wouldn't worry about senseless."

Her naughty smile wrecked him. "You are wicked, Simon Thackeray."

Forget muck. This felt like dangerous sexual flirting and he needed to stop. And he would. Soon. He leaned forward, drawn by the heat in her eyes, lured by her smile. "Perhaps my love languishes unrequited because I'm too wicked to love."

She shifted forward, her knee brushed his and the contact surged through him. A seductive smile curved her lush mouth. "I seriously doubt that. Don't you know that all that wickedness just drives women to distraction?"

All he truly knew was that she drove him beyond distraction. Beyond caution. "Are you speaking from personal experience?"

"The last time I checked, I was a woman, so I suppose so." There was something in her eyes. Something that said she knew how utterly wicked he could be and she liked it, despite herself.

Which was ridiculous because he'd been very careful to limit his exposure to her. He raised his brow in question. As if she suddenly realized what he'd seen in her eyes, she blinked and it vanished. She leaned back into her chair, putting a distance that existed beyond mere space between them. Thank God one of them had some sense. "What do you do with all of that pent-up...energy?"

Egad, the woman was relentlessly curious— no trouble at all believing she got herself locked into a wardrobe—which was yet one more reason he'd taken himself out of her and Elliott's sphere. For one moment he considered telling her he jerked off often, just to see if it would shock her into no more questions, but that tactic had already failed once. And quite simply he couldn't bring himself to be so crude. He opted for the truth.

"I run. A lot. At this point, I'm probably hovering in marathon-training range." He laughed at himself. "And never underestimate the efficiency of the proverbial cold shower."

As it stood now, a cold shower sounded better and better on more than one count. Sweat slicked him and her skin glistened with a fine sheen of moisture. He was a sick beast when a woman sweating struck him as sexy.

"I didn't know you were a runner. I'm nowhere close to marathon training, but I run five days a week."

"Are you sexually frustrated, as well?" He might as well be hung for a sheep as a lamb.

"No. I have a fat ass," she said with a cheeky grin that held a smidgen of self-consciousness. He bit back the protest that her ass was perfect, enticing and far from fat. She went on, "We should run together some time."

Somehow running with her to relieve the stress of

Tawny-induced lust seemed self-defeating and warped. He liked it. "Maybe we should."

"How about tomorrow?" she said.

Depending on how long it took to restore the power, he'd definitely need it.

"It's a date, then." Poor word choice. "I didn't mean a date as in a *date*." Yet another reason he avoided being around her. His brain seemed to become nothing more than rat turds rolling around in his empty head when she was near.

She raised her eyebrows. Amusement at his verbal bumbling danced in her eyes and twitched at her lips. "I knew what you meant."

From the other room her cell phone rang. She scraped her chair back, excusing herself.

Simon stayed in the kitchen to offer her some privacy. He began to clear the table. Without the hum of the refrigerator, the AC and all the other white noise associated with electricity, he couldn't help but overhear her conversation, even with the radio on.

"Yes, Mom, I'm fine.... No, he's not here. He got caught at the gallery.... No. I'm not alone. One of Elliott's friends stopped by.... Yes. He's a photographer.... No, they don't know when they'll have it back on.... No. No sign of looting or vandalism, but yes, we're going to stay in." Her voice lowered. "Mom, improper isn't the same here as it is at home. And I'd rather not be alone.... Yes, I'll call you later."

Elliott had flown down to meet Tawny's parents after the engagement and given Simon an earful afterward. Very conservative, very Southern, very proper. Rarified members of the genteel Savannah blue-blood set, her father was a surgeon and her mother was a lifetime member of the garden club. They'd lunched at the country club.

It took less than a thimbleful of imagination to figure out Mama Edwards had reprimanded Tawny over the impropriety of being alone in her apartment during a blackout with another man. God help them both if her mother had overheard their conversation. And at least her mum called to check on her. Simon doubted he'd even crossed his parents' minds. He'd been off their radar screen since he left home. Who was he fooling? He'd never registered *on* their radar screen.

Tawny walked back into the kitchen just as he finished rinsing and stacking the bowls. "My mother," she confirmed. "They heard about it on CNN." She took in the tidied kitchen. "You cleaned up! If I weren't already taken, I'd keep you for myself."

Her teasing words were a dagger to his heart.

"Ah, but there is Elliott, isn't there?" He deliberately chilled his tone.

"Yes, there is Elliott." She put her cell phone on the counter and turned to him. "But that reminds me, exactly why were you and Elliott coming over this evening?"

4

SIMON HAD GROWN UP IN New York City and had never seen an actual deer caught in headlamps, but he experienced a sudden onset of empathy. Bugger. If he'd been thinking with his whole brain instead of sniffing about after Tawny like some lust-driven horn dog, he would've seen this coming, should've anticipated the question. Instead she'd figuratively caught him with his trousers down. Simon didn't feel like a very bright boy.

"It's a bit of a mystery to me." He was a terrible liar.

"Uh-huh."

She clearly didn't believe him. And he might stretch the truth to protect her from what he perceived to be Elliott's selfishness, but he couldn't knowingly lie to her. However, exactly how Elliott planned to handle this impending fiasco *was* a mystery to him.

She picked up her cell phone. "Let's call Elliott. It's not as if he's busy or anything if he's locked in the gallery without electricity."

Simon winced inside. She'd be devastated to know just how *busy* Elliott might be at the moment.

Tawny speed-dialed the number and drummed her fingers on the counter.

"Hi, Elliott. Everything quiet over there? Fine... Nothing. We ate cold pizza and fruit. I asked Simon what it was you wanted to talk about tonight. Apparently he's as in the dark as I am.... No, I didn't intend that as a pun.... So let's talk now.... I know you wanted to be here, but you might as well tell me over the phone, because you've aroused my curiosity. Don't make me wait. You've got to satisfy me."

Aroused...wait any longer...satisfy me. She talked to Elliott this way and he still got off on someone else? That told Simon all he needed to know about his friend. Since Elliott wasn't dead, he must be gay.

"Yes. He's right here. Okay." She huffed out a breath and handed the phone across to Simon. "He wants to talk to you."

Simon reluctantly took the phone.

Tawny planted her hands on her hips and glared at him. Brilliant. Forget a private conversation. Not that he blamed her. She had to feel jerked around.

Instinct told him he wasn't going to like where this was headed. "Elliott?"

"Tawny wants to know what I wanted to talk to her about." Elliott sounded positively panicked.

Simon leaned against the counter and crossed one foot over the other. "Right."

"I can't tell her over the phone," Elliott said as if Simon had demanded he do that very thing.

Simon braved a glance at Tawny's set features. "I don't believe there's a choice."

"But there is." He recognized Elliott's wheedling enthusiastic tone. Whatever it was, Simon's instincts were already screaming *no*. "The right choice. You tell her."

Simon damn near dropped the phone. "No."

"Yes. The more I think about it, this works out better."

Maybe for Elliott. Cold day in hell and all that.

"Absolutely not."

"Oh, come on, Si. You two already don't like one another. And what else are you going to talk about? What have you got to do stuck there in the dark with one another? This blackout could last several hours."

"Not a chance."

"Think about it. It'd be better this way." Was it only twelve hours ago that he'd declared nothing Elliott did could compromise their friendship? He was rethinking that position. "You don't know Tawny the way I do. She's not going to give up on this until one of us tells her. I can try feeding her some line about wedding plans, but when she finds out the truth, that's just going to make it a thousand times worse."

"I don't see why your conversation can't wait."

"I'm telling you, she's sexy and sweet but beneath those soft curves and big green eyes she's relentless when she wants something. She's a steel magnolia."

Simon recognized that truth. He'd experienced it firsthand when she'd sunk her teeth into the topic of his love life. He considered banging his head against the counter or perhaps the cabinet. Anything solid would do.

Could this night possibly get any better? First he was trapped with a woman he wanted beyond reason. Now said woman was about to hound him to no end for news sure to crush her. And he was the lucky devil doing double duty. Not only was he in the firing line to be shot as the messenger, but who else was around to endure the messy aftermath? And when it was all said and done, he'd wade through hell and back if he thought she needed him.

"I'll take care of it."

"Simon, you are the best friend a man could have."

"We'll talk about that later." This wasn't for Elliott. This was for Tawny. Because she deserved better than hearing the truth over the phone while Elliott was locked in with his new lover. Because it might render him asunder, but he would give her a strong shoulder to cry on and be there for her.

"Okay. I'm grateful. Eternally grateful. Let me talk to Tawny for a minute."

Silently Simon passed the phone back to Tawny.

"Yes?… He is?… Okay. Stay safe and I'll talk to you later," she said. She flipped the cell phone closed, disconnecting the call. She picked up her glass and polished it off. Putting the empty goblet on the counter, she looked at Simon expectantly, some of her former exasperation lingering in her eyes and the set of her mouth.

"I understand you have something to tell me?"

Apprehension knotted Simon's gut. The proverbial shit was about to hit the proverbial fan.

"Let's go in the other room. You'll want to sit down for this."

SIMON LOOKED GRIM. SO MUCH for the let's-all-jump-in-bed ménage-à-trois theory, although she already pretty much knew that was toast. What could possibly warrant that rigid, resigned set to his jaw, and was that a flash of *pity* in his eyes when he looked at her?

The truth slammed her. She sucked in a calming breath. Elliott was dying. He'd been handed down some awful diagnosis and the two of them were going to break the news to her. She was the worst human being possible, having erotic dreams about Simon and wallowing in a private lustfest while poor, brave Elliott faced the specter of death alone.

Simon leaned forward, bracing his arms on his knees, his fingers linked together. He turned to face her. "Elliott should be the one telling you.... I was only coming to lend moral support.... I'm not sure where to begin."

Tawny squared her shoulders and sat straighter on her end of the sofa. She'd be brave. "How long has he known?"

Simon did a double take. "How long have *you* known?"

"Well, just now."

Simon slanted a questioning look her way. "Now?"

"I figured it out and Elliott can count on me to stand by him, even if the wedding doesn't happen." He might be too sick or he just might not have enough time to make it to the altar.

"Tawny, what is it that you think you know?"

"Elliott's dying, isn't he? What is it? Cancer? A tumor? How long does he have? I knew he'd been acting different lately, but I thought..."

Simon waved a hand, stilling her. "Let's back up a bit. You think Elliott's dying?"

"Isn't he? You look like the Grim Reaper."

"I always look like the Grim Reaper." Simon sighed. "As far as I know, Elliott's healthy as a horse." *Whew.* She sagged against the sofa, limp with relief. As long as Elliott was healthy, nothing could… "He's been see-ing someone else."

What? She shot up. "Bastard." She'd kill him. Here she'd been feeling guilty over *dreams,* when all the while Elliott was playing Bury the Bone with some-one else. "Is it someone I know?"

"I think you've met him."

It took a few seconds for the definitive *him* to soak through her haze of shock and anger. "Him? Did you just say *him,* as in Elliott's seeing a *guy?*"

Simon offered a curt nod. "That's what he told me this morning."

"A man? A man! I've been dumped for a freaking man?" Another woman was bad enough, but a man? She'd never been so angry and humiliated in her life. And don't forget betrayed.

The hot press of tears gathered. Dammit. She didn't get really mad that often, but when she did, instead of ranting and raving she cried. It sucked.

Simon shook his head. "I don't think he necessarily wants to break up. He just wanted to come clean. He says it's only been once and he thinks he's bisexual." Simon looked grimmer than ever.

Elliott's nerve floored her. He didn't necessarily want to break up? That was rich. And it fueled her anger. She didn't have anything against homosexu-als, but she wasn't marrying one. She tugged at the ring on her finger. It stuck on her knuckle. That was the final detail that totally unhinged her. Tawny, the family screwup, had once again managed to not get it right. Her anger spilled over in the form of hot tears rolling down her cheeks. She tugged again. Finally she yanked the ring off. She shoved it into Simon's hand.

"I won't be needing this any longer." The last word ended on a sob.

She was so angry she was shaking. And blubbering.

Simon slid across the space separating them. She caught a glimpse of his face. He looked positively stricken. He folded her into his arms, pulling her against the wall of his chest, cradling her, rocking her back and forth. "Please don't cry, Tawny. It's going to be okay."

Stern, austere, sarcastic Simon offered her solace. That this man who didn't like her very well was reduced to having to comfort her went a long way in cooling her anger and stemming her tears. Crying when she was angry had proven a curse of embarrassment since childhood.

That was almost as humiliating as her being inadequate enough to send Elliott to seek male companionship. She ought to have some measure of pride and pull away, but somehow it felt less embarrassing to simply stay where she was, pressed against Simon's chest. Plus it was a very nice chest.

"How amusing for me to offer you advice on your love life when mine was down the toilet and I didn't even have enough sense to know it," she said against his shirt. "How pathetic."

"Tawny, never refer to yourself again as *pathetic*." He cupped her face in his hands and tilted her head back until she looked at him. He gentled away her tears with his thumbs. Her skin tingled beneath his touch. His jeans-clad knee pressed against her bare leg. "There is nothing remotely pathetic about you. You're beautiful and sexy."

Simon could obviously lie with the best of them.

She knew her eyes and nose were swollen from crying. Some women cried prettily. She wasn't one of them. She was fairly certain she wasn't looking her level best. And then there was the little matter of Elliott dipping his wick…definitely where it didn't belong. "Yes, I'm so beautiful and sexy, I drove my fiancé to being gay."

"Right now I'm very pissed with Elliott. And even though he's my friend, he's an idiot." He patted her awkwardly on her shoulder.

Poor Simon. Small wonder he'd been so reluctant to broach this subject. "It was bad enough that he stuck you in the middle. You don't have to say all of this. And don't worry, I'm through crying. When I get angry, I cry. Charming little quirk." She dashed away the last of her tears.

"Elliott is all kinds of a fool."

She sniffled. This was the man she'd seen the day he'd photographed her, the man she'd glimpsed behind the wall of reserve. He really could be very nice. "It's very chivalrous of you to say that."

"I don't have a chivalrous bone in my body. I'm stating the obvious. You're beautiful and sexy and Elliott's an idiot," Simon said.

Tawny opened her mouth to argue the point and Simon interrupted her.

"Perhaps this will convince you," he said, lowering his head and capturing her mouth.

TAWNY TASTED LIKE EXACTLY what she was—forbidden fruit. Sweet, hot, drugging, addictive. He felt her hesitation and surprise, tasted the brine of her tears.

Simon pulled away from her mouth and the temptation to plunder and explore. He raked his hand through his hair. "That was out of line. I apologize."

She shook her head. "No." She linked her arms around his neck and pulled his head back down to hers. "Please don't apologize," she said, her breath warming him. Her lips molded to his and a fantasy came to life. Tawny kissed him, hard and hot.

He knew she was angry with Elliott. Knew he was payback. Knew he should walk away. But while his head said one thing, his heart said another. God help him, he returned her kiss. Six months of pent-up passion unleashed within him. He'd lived with fantasies. And now he held the flesh-and-blood embodiment of those fantasies in his arms.

Her tongue probed at his lips and the last vestige of his resistence deserted him. He buried his hands in her hair and crushed her to him. She strained against him, her anger, her frustration almost palpable. And then it was gone, replaced by something less volatile— and far more dangerous. She softened, her mouth now giving rather than taking. Offering. He took and gave in return.

Simon slid his hands from her hair and stroked down the satin warmth of her bare shoulders. She moaned into his mouth and shuddered against him.

Reason took a holiday. He sank back onto the couch and she followed him, lying against him, between his thighs. Her hips pressed against an erection he couldn't deny. Her fingers winnowed through his hair as he thoroughly explored the hot sweetness of her mouth. He plied his hands along the sexy curve of her back. He would love to photograph the lovely curve of her neck, bared by her upswept hair that led to the sinuous line of her back. He touched her with the reverence of an artist and the appreciation of a man.

The intensity of her kiss shook him. She pressed against his erection in supplication and he groaned into her mouth. He filled his hands with the full roundness of her buttocks and pulled her harder against him. She slid one leg over his, straddling his thigh, opening herself to him.

He ran his fingers along the silk of her thighs, his knuckles brushing against the edge of her panties. Oh, sweet heaven, they were wet.

"Oh, Simon," she moaned into his mouth, "you always make me…"

She provided a voice-activated sanity check. He wrenched away from her and steadied himself on one elbow, although she remained between his thighs. What the hell was he doing? He'd been one second away from slipping his finger beneath the elastic of her panties and touching her intimately. He gulped air and sought some measure of his control that had been woefully missing a few seconds ago.

Tawny remained atop him, her body pressed intimately against his. Her arousal, mingled with her perfume, was a heady scent.

"I'm sorry," he said. And just how sorry was he with one hand still on her delectable bottom? He jerked his hand away and rubbed his brow.

She scooted to the other end of the couch. He sat up, missing the press of her between his thighs, as if a vital part of him had been amputated.

Tears still clung to her lashes. Passion weighted her lids. His kisses had left her lips swollen and ripe.

"I'm really sorry," he repeated. "I didn't mean to… that shouldn't have… I got out of hand."

"Please don't apologize, Simon. You didn't exactly force yourself on me. I crawled on top of you." She looked away from him, throwing the fine line of her nose and the curve of her cheek into shadowy relief. "You must think I'm a slut."

He rubbed the back of his neck, contrite. He had the utmost respect for her—*slut* had never crossed his mind. He'd kissed her to *show* her how desirable she was, because *telling* hadn't worked. Instead he'd further compromised her self-esteem.

"Never. You were upset, I was out of line and it won't happen again. I never meant to take advantage of you."

She shook her head. "You didn't take advantage of me. I was the one out of line." She touched his hand and then jerked back when she realized what she'd done. "I don't want you to be uncomfortable. I won't throw myself at you again."

He almost pointed out that she should have a very good idea of just how much he'd enjoyed it since she had been riding the ridge of his erection. It had left him hard, but it had by no means posed a hardship. His body screamed that she could throw herself at him any day, any way, any time.

Tawny curled up, tucking one foot beneath her. She smoothed her fingers over the back of the couch. "Did you know about Elliott?"

Elliott. Much better than discussing that kiss. "No. On either count. He's never even hinted at being gay or at being interested in someone other than you."

Although maybe the signs had been there but Simon

had been too obtuse to see them. Elliott was a bastard for cheating on her and dragging Simon into it, but Simon believed Elliott cared for Tawny. Right now she was hurt and betrayed, but she must still care for Elliott. As a friend, it was his role to ensure neither Tawny nor Elliott did anything rash regarding their future that they'd later regret. That's how a man of honor would behave.

She huffed out a breath. "I don't feel quite so stupid if you didn't have a clue either."

"I thought he was joking when he first told me."

"Well, I know he couldn't have possibly orchestrated a blackout, but how convenient for him. This way he could stick you with telling me, the scum-sucking son of a bitch."

He bit back a laugh. She definitely had a colorful way with the English language. He didn't want this woman pissed at him. "I know you're hurt. I would be, too. But in the morning you'll feel differently about all of this. You and Elliott can work this out."

She crossed her arms over her chest, which did incredible things to her already pretty damn incredible cleavage, and directed a haughty look his way.

"Why don't you ring him?" Simon tried again. He'd spent enough time around women to know that talking, venting, was a big deal. And Elliott, who avoided confrontation at every opportunity, certainly wasn't going to initiate a conversation. "Talk to him. I'll go in the other room and give you some privacy."

She threw up a staying hand, her nose in the air. "Not going to happen. I have nothing to say to Elliott. Well, maybe a thing or two, but not while he's there with his new lover." She shook her head. "No, thanks.

And I don't even want to think about what they're probably doing right now."

"That makes two of us," Simon said without thinking.

"And what's there to say other than he's a two-timer who better not have given me some communicable disease he picked up while he was out screwing around?"

"He says it was safe sex."

"I hope he's not lying about that," she said.

"No. I asked him bluntly."

"That's a relief. So other than the satisfaction of cussing him out, I don't need to talk to him. There's no going back and there's no going forward. We're playing on a whole different ball field now. I'd had some doubts in the last couple of weeks and this just nailed it."

Had she really been having doubts? His skepticism must've shown.

"I can tell what you're thinking. Sure that's a convenient way for me to save face, but it's true. Ever since I started having—" she stopped as if she'd almost said something she shouldn't "—well, second thoughts. And I've had an increasing sense of Elliott trying to shape me into what he wanted me to be."

Elliott had laughingly said once on a double date that he possessed a better sense of style than Tawny. Simon also recalled another comment that Elliott needed to take her shopping. Both times Simon had thought Elliott out of line and far off the mark. Simon liked her sense of style. He wasn't quite sure what to say. "Elliott has very specific ideas."

"Uh-huh. Trust me. My parents have been trying to

mold me long enough. I recognize the signs. Regardless, Elliott and I are history."

Which left her a free agent and him still constrained by the bounds of friendship.

5

COULD SHE HAVE POSSIBLY made it any clearer than if she'd held up a sign inviting him to kiss her again? And again. And then take it further. To pick up where he'd left off, with his fingers brushing against her wet panties.

They both obviously wanted one another. He'd felt her damp underwear and she'd felt his rock-hard erection. And she'd just told him in no uncertain terms that she no longer had a future with Elliott.

Simon's hair stood up at the crown where she'd run her fingers through it. She rather liked it because it made him much less intimidating and proved him human.

"People say and do a lot of things they don't really mean when they're angry," he said in the tone of a peacemaker.

Was he implying she was irrational and should make allowances for Elliott's wandering penis? Ha. She was very much in touch with rational thought. "I'm not angry."

Simon simply looked at her.

"Okay. Maybe I'm still a little mad that he cheated on me and that it was with a man." She cringed inside, feeling fat, ugly, lacking and unwanted. "How can I even compete when I don't have the same equipment?"

Simon shook his head, a touch of anger marking his face and the movement. "You don't compete. As difficult as it might be to believe, this isn't about you."

Freaking easy for him to say. "Have you ever had a girlfriend tell you she'd discovered her inner lesbian after sex with you?"

"Uh, no."

"I didn't think so. Don't you think that might leave you feeling a little deficient? Like your equipment wasn't up to par or you had some serious operator error going on?"

Simon looked like a man facing a firing squad. "I know it feels that way, but this isn't because there's a problem with you. Elliott's the one with the problem. And I sure as hell wish he'd talked to me before he did something stupid that buggered up his relationship with you."

His vehemence and apparent disapproval of Elliott surprised her. Usually, right or wrong, men stuck together. And she'd always sensed Simon didn't like her, so his reaction doubly surprised her.

She picked a *People* magazine off the bamboo chest and fanned herself. "I'm surprised you don't think it's his lucky day that he's managed to get rid of me."

Simon sat ramrod straight. "I'm sorry you misunderstood my actions that way."

What? As if she was some neurotic she-devil who'd misinterpreted his friendly demeanor? She was pissed and hot and sweaty. He'd picked the wrong day and the wrong gal to pull that holier-than-thou crap. She stood, bracing one knee on the couch, and planted her hands on her hips.

"Whoa. Stop right there. You're sorry I misinterpreted your actions? If you're going to apologize, then do it right. If you're not, then save your breath. But don't even think about giving me some backhanded apology."

He had the grace to look slightly ashamed but still arrogant. And very sexy with the candlelight flickering from the table beside him. "You're right. I've acted like a jerk and I'm still acting like a jerk."

That surprised her. But then again, she never really knew quite what to expect from Simon. "I didn't call you a jerk. Not exactly. Well, maybe that's what I was implying. I've had it with all the prevarication. What's the point? Let's just cut to the chase. You've never liked me. You've barely managed to be civil and I've never known why. I thought that day you photographed me it was different…. I thought…well, never mind. I'm a big girl, and after finding out that my fiancé prefers men, I don't suppose it can get any worse. So while we're sitting here with nothing else to do, why don't you enlighten me? Tell me why you've never liked me. They say confession is good for the soul."

"I don't think…"

"Oh, come on, Simon. Get real. There's something about the dark of night that brings out the daring. You know how it is. Things you'd never think about in the light of day. Things you'd never do or say otherwise somehow seem okay in the dark."

Their hot kiss—her tongue in his mouth and his hands on her ass, pulling her harder into his erection—still lingered between them. She saw it in his face. "We both know I've never had the guts to ask before and I probably won't have the guts to ask again. In fact, after tonight our paths probably won't cross again. So let's get daring in the dark and have a real conversation," she said.

The idea of not seeing Simon again was far more disquieting than the thought of not seeing Elliott again. She was needling Simon, but it was better than flinging herself at him. What she really wanted to do was lose herself in his arms, feel the heavy thud of his heart beneath hers, taste the heat of his passion, wallow in the desire that left her aching, wet and feeling like a desirable woman. She longed to discover firsthand whether the real passion between them was as potent and incredible as her dreams.

"If our paths won't cross again, what could it possibly matter?" he said. The flickering light played tricks on her. For a brief second she could've sworn dismay flashed in his eyes.

"Because it'll bother me until I have an answer. My nickname growing up was Bulldog because I can't let things go. Why you disliked me will niggle at the back of my mind and worry me—unfinished business—until ten years from now I have to track you down and demand an answer so I can take myself off Prozac."

Simon frowned in confusion. "You're on an antidepressant?"

Tawny smiled at him. It was sort of weird trying to charm a man into telling you why he disliked you. But nothing about the feelings Simon stirred in her was normal or comfortable. Between Simon and Elliott, her journey of self-discovery had taken an abrupt turn. "No. But if you don't give me an answer, it'll drive me crazy and I'll have to start taking it. So go ahead and exonerate yourself up front."

He shook his head but seemed to relax, stretching his arm along the couch back. He had nice arms. Just the right amount of muscle and a smattering of dark hair. Who was she kidding? Everything about him registered on her sexy meter. And—woohoo—she didn't have to feel guilty about it anymore. She could lust up front and outright without even a twinge of conscience.

"Does everyone in your family communicate this way?" he asked.

"No." She laughed and tossed the ball right back at him. "Does everyone in your family try to dodge the issue by introducing another topic?"

He grinned and a healthy dose of that guilt-free lust slammed her. "No. They simply don't talk."

It was the most he'd ever said about his family and she was curious to know more. "The British stiff upper lip?"

"Something like that. And their heads are full of ancient artifacts and civilizations." Per Elliott, his father was a museum curator and his mother was an archaeology—or maybe it was anthropology—professor. "They find the modern world something of an inconvenience."

It took a nanosecond for her to feel the loneliness of a little boy who had always hovered on the periphery of his parents' attention. Tawny knew as surely as she knew her name that Simon had been something of an inconvenience, as well. She related. "I wasn't an inconvenience, but I've always been a disappointment."

"I never said I was an inconvenience."

"You didn't have to say it."

He tilted his head to one side. "How could your parents possibly find you a disappointment?"

Okay. So he was probably just looking to shift the conversation from himself, but he seemed genuinely puzzled that she might disappoint Dr. and Mrs. Carlton Jonathan Edwards III.

"It's been all too easy. I'm not exactly the overachiever my sister Sylvia is—magna cum laude from Yale and a rising member of the Savannah bar." Out of nervous habit she started to twist her ring on her finger and realized it was no longer there. Her nail scraped her bare finger. "Betsy, my younger sister, married one of Daddy's partner's sons. She and Tad have a beautiful home on Wilmington Island in a prestigious gated community. Me? I'm not as smart as Sylvia and I'm not as refined and gracious as Betsy. I talk too much, I'm too assertive, I have a master's degree in business but I plan parties for a living. I committed the ultimate sin of leaving Savannah, Georgia. When I came home with Elliott, they were pleased, although he wasn't a Southerner. Now it turns out he's gay."

She was batting a thousand here. And while she was hauling all of her shortcomings out for examination... "Oh, yeah, and Sylvia and Betsy take after my parents, who are tall and thin. Thanks to recessive genes, I take after Grandmother Burdette, short with a big butt." And add talking too much and saying the wrong thing to that list. Why the heck had she mentioned her big ass?

Simon crossed his arms over his chest, restrained strength in lean, sinewy muscle. He leveled an uncompromising look at her from his end. "Are you sure you want the truth, here in the dark?"

Uh-oh. Something in his tone reminded her of Nicholson in *A Few Good Men,* assuring them they couldn't handle the truth. She'd asked for it, but now she wasn't so certain she wanted it. But she'd never run away from things or buried her head in the sand, and she wouldn't start now. "Absolutely."

"If that's really how your parents feel, all of you need to get over it. Lose the pity party and look at things the way they really are. You say you're a party planner as if it's some lesser accomplishment. You're an event planner for a law firm with a hundred and fifty practicing attorneys. According to Elliott, you do an incredible job planning and executing a multitude of functions. That requires tremendous organizational and negotiation skills."

She opened her mouth to point out she had an assistant, but he forestalled her with a raised hand.

"Let me finish and then the floor's yours. I think you came to New York to get away from your parents' censure, but you might as well pack up and go home if you're going to continue to see yourself through their eyes and judge yourself against some mythical standard." *Ouch.* His tone softened. "You'll never be free to be you until you accept and like who you are. I don't know what your sisters look like and I don't care. Your body would drop most men to their knees. Any man with half a dose of testosterone would tell you that you have the perfect behind. I'd like to think men aren't quite so shallow as to fall in love with your behind and overlook all of your other obvious attributes and qualities, but certainly any man would love your derriere. It could drive a man to madness."

Well. It was her turn to talk and she didn't know

what to say. He'd certainly taken her at her word and said a lot. And perhaps he was right. She'd ostensibly moved to the Big Apple to shake off the confines and constraints of Savannah aristocracy, but was she still measuring herself against their standards? And how much of her attraction to Elliott and her subsequent engagement was due to the need for their elusive approval? And she'd think about all of that. Later. Now her fragile, wounded, her-fiancé-succumbed-to-the-charms-of-a-man ego latched on to the part about her body dropping a man to his knees and her ass driving him to madness. "Really? Madness?"

He quirked an eyebrow at her as if to say he knew where she was coming from and then he smiled at her, the first smile she'd ever received from him that actually reached his eyes. Her breath caught in her throat. Even now this smile didn't totally encompass him. She always had a sense of part of him being closed off, as if he held a jealously guarded secret. "At the least, distraction."

In the span of a very brief time her self-perception was changing drastically. The way she saw herself was beginning to unravel. Perhaps it had begun with her dreams about Simon and her reaction to him tonight, the way she saw herself since she'd discovered Elliott's unfaithfulness, the way Simon portrayed her in relation to her parents. In a very short time frame her world had shifted and changed and left her floundering. Perhaps the past year in New York had just been a warm-up, and the closest she'd come to discovering her true self had been in the past few minutes.

And she and Simon were getting real. She'd had a glimpse of the real Simon when he'd photographed her for Elliott. What would she see in herself now, were he to photograph her again? She didn't want him to retreat again. She didn't want to dream about him tonight. Tonight she wanted the flesh-and-blood man in her bed.

An idea began to gel. He was so much more approachable when he was behind the camera. If she could talk him into photographing her, she also had a fairly good chance of getting him into her bed.

"Simon, would you do something for me?"

"It depends on what it entails." Ah, ever cautious, ever reserved Simon wasn't crawling out on a limb blind.

"I'm more than willing to pay you."

A wicked smile set her heart thundering. "You've definitely caught my attention now."

Something dark and sexy underlay the note of droll amusement in his voice that sent a wave of desire washing through her. Attention was good for starters, but she definitely wanted more.

"Would you photograph me while we're waiting on the lights to come on? Not for Elliott this time but for me?"

"I'M NOT FOR HIRE," HE SAID. Agreeing to photograph Tawny would be a combined act of madness and desperation.

"Oh." Her disappointment wasn't feigned.

Who was he kidding? He might as well get real with himself. Photographing her would be a sweet torture. Making love to her with his camera was a dismal substitute for actually touching and tasting her but far safer. And when it came down to it, he was incapable of denying her anything. He'd give her the moon if it was his to offer.

"But I will do it for free."

She shook her head, freeing a few strands of hair that promptly clung to her cheek. She brushed them back. "No. I insist on paying."

"Trust me. I'm a selfish bastard. You're much less likely to cry in front of a camera. It isn't gratis as much as self-preservation."

"I only cry when I'm really angry, so you're safe unless you make me mad." She smiled. "I'm beginning to think you're not a selfish bastard at all but that's the image you like to project." She narrowed her eyes at him. "Then we'll barter. I'll plan a party for you one day."

"Absolutely." Right. He had one friend. Elliott. And he wasn't feeling like throwing a party for him at the moment.

"Or I could set something up more private, for you and your lady if you decided to approach her," she said, as if she'd read his mind.

"You did offer to help me with my sad love life, didn't you?"

"I could set up something very nice and romantic. You really should approach her. You've got so much to offer a woman."

"I've already agreed to photograph you. Blatant lies aren't necessary," Simon said. He laughed to cover his pounding heart.

Tawny smiled and caught him totally off guard when she tossed a small pillow at him and it bounced off of his chest.

"Maybe you need a little dose of your own hard-line truth. Whoever this wonder woman is would be damn lucky to have you. I think you're hiding a very nice guy behind your aloofness. You're smart, occasionally very funny, talented, sexy and I give you high marks in the kissing department."

He didn't know what the hell to say. "Okay."

"At least think about it," she said. "Decide what kind of evening you'd like to have with your own true love. I bet if you ask her, she'll say yes, and I can take care of the rest."

She faced him from the other end of the couch like a luscious piece of fruit just out of reach. Well, unfortunately, closer to his reach than was comfortable. And he didn't have to think about it too hard. He'd want it similar to this. Candlelight. A bottle of wine. Her. Him. Soft, seductive music. He'd sit in a chair and she'd stand just out of reach and slowly peel her clothes off until she was splendidly naked. She'd come closer, close enough for him to touch the velvet of her skin, cup the fullness of her breasts, cull the dew of her desire, inhale the scent of her skin and arousal.... He jerked himself back from the precipice of lust he'd almost plunged over headfirst. "I promise I'll think about it."

"Just let me know when."

"Sure." He levered himself off the couch and crossed to his equipment stored by her door. "Now that we have an agreement, what's your favorite room? Your favorite place? Where do you spend most of your time?"

He pulled out his camera and began setting up the lens. He relaxed into the rote task, pleased to focus on something tangible, something other than his feelings for Tawny.

She hesitated. "The couch is my favorite spot."

He wasn't buying it. She'd thought about it too long for him to believe her.

He looked at her across the candlelit room. She sat perched on her knees, bracing her arms on the sofa back, watching him.

"Come on, Tawny. What happened to honesty in the dark and all that? Let's try this again. What's your favorite place in your flat?"

Her chin rose a notch. Ah, that was his girl. "The tub. It's an old claw-foot. Great for soaking."

Click. Instant photo in his head. Her, hair piled atop her head, steam rising, skin glistening. He swallowed.

"What's your next favorite place?" No way she missed the hoarseness in his voice, but bloody hell, he was only human.

"The bedroom." Only marginally safer than the bathroom, with her big sleigh bed, but at least naked wasn't a given. "And my least favorite room is the kitchen. I don't like to cook and neither the kitchen nor this room has windows. They feel claustrophobic."

"Then let's photograph you in the bedroom." He strove for a professional tone. She'd hit on the perfect solution to his problem. Photographing her, he became a professional engaged in a shoot instead of Simon Thackeray besotted with Tawny Edwards.

"I definitely want to change clothes. I'm hot and sticky."

"Fine. Take your time. I'll finish setting up my equipment."

"It won't take me long." She picked up a candle and hesitated. "Would you, uh, mind just walking me to the bedroom until I light the candles?" That's right, he'd blown them out earlier. "I hate walking into a dark room."

She had major issues with the dark. But then again,

he had major issues with getting too close in relationships. He knew that. Particularly after one of his girlfriends had flung the accusation at him on her way out the door. Everyone had their own neuroses to bear. "Sure. I'll lead the way so you don't have to walk into the dark room."

"Thank you, Simon."

Her soft voice with its honeyed Southern drawl slid beneath his skin. Ridiculous, really, that she looked at him as if he'd just agreed to slay dragons on her behalf. Even more ridiculous how good it made him feel.

"You're welcome, Tawny."

A fat candle in hand, he led the way, aware of her close behind him. Unfortunately for him, he now knew how delicious her mouth tasted, how her curves fit against his body as if she'd been tailor-made for him. Just before he reached her room, she placed her hand lightly on his back. Her touch hummed through him.

"Wait a minute. Let's stop by the bathroom. A nice cold washcloth would be heavenly right now. I bet you could use one, too."

How about a nice icy shower? But he'd get by with a cool cloth. "Sure."

He stepped through the dark doorway to his left, the candle illuminating a rectangular room with a small, high window. A claw-foot tub with a circular shower curtain pushed to one side sat beneath the window. The mirror over the sink reflected his light and brightened the bathroom.

Simon sucked in a deep breath as her hip and breast brushed his side, her fingers sliding along his back as she squeezed past him in the confines.

"Sorry," she muttered.

"No problem."

She placed her votive on a small shelf next to the sink. Thick, fluffy towels and washcloths sat neatly folded in an open cabinet. She plucked two cloths from the stack and held them under the cold-water tap.

Simon waited beside the sink, next to the door. She squeezed excess water from the cloth and passed one to him.

He ran it over his heated face and watched Tawny do the same. She slid the cloth over her neck, rolling her head to one side and then the other. A half moan, half sigh escaped her. "How good does this feel?" she asked, her voice low, husky, intimate.

"It's somewhere past good." Icy droplets trickled down his throat, raising gooseflesh. It wouldn't surprise him to hear the water sizzle on his skin. She definitely had him hot and bothered. The cloth might be cooling him down, but she was heating him right back up.

"Here. Let me wet it again." She took his cloth and held it under the cold faucet. She held it out to him dripping wet.

Simon set his candle on the widest portion of the sink and took the cloth from her, his fingers brushing hers in the exchange. The brief contact fired through him.

"Have you ever been this hot before?" she asked. "If I spontaneously combust, douse me with water to put out the flames."

Simon had no idea where it came from, but he ran with his impulse. "Like this?" he asked. He stepped closer and squeezed the cloth, cascading water over her shoulder.

She gasped, whether at the shock of the cool water or at his audacity or perhaps both, and then laughed. "Oh, you..."

"Or like this?" He sent another round of droplets skittering down her back, bared by her top.

"Maybe more like this." She reached up and squeezed her cloth at the base of this throat, sending a cool stream down the front of his T-shirt.

He laughed and retaliated. She shrieked and didn't bother with the washcloth, cupping her hands beneath the water and tossing it his way. Within seconds they were both drenched. One of them, their aim so bad, doused the big candle. It sputtered out and ended their water play. Only the small votive flickered, plunging them into intimacy.

"Oops," Tawny said. "That was fun."

Her hair hung drunkenly from its clip. Water sparkled against her skin. The cold water had her nipples standing at full attention against the wet material of her shirt. Simon swallowed hard and looked her in the eyes. *Just don't look back down.*

He cleared his throat. "It was fun."

He had no idea he could be so playful. Water fights had never happened in his house. Hell, fun hadn't happened in his house. His parents had taken their jobs and life very seriously. They still did.

She grabbed a towel off of the stack and he reached for it. She bypassed his hand and instead began to rub his wet hair herself.

"I can do that myself," he said.

"I know." She gentled the towel along his jaw, slid the thick, soft cotton down the column of his throat. "But there, I've taken care of it."

She took a step back and, using the same towel, blotted her face. Simon held out his hand and she gave the towel over to him.

"I can do this myself," she said, echoing his earlier declaration.

"I know." He eased the towel over the length of her neck, across the delicate line of her collarbone, into the valley created by her breasts. Simon made sure only the cotton cloth touched her skin. He moved behind her and slowly, carefully dried her shoulders and the expanse of sweet skin along her spine. He knelt on one knee and drew the towel along her thighs, the backs of her knees, her calves.

"Turn around for me."

She pivoted slowly and he once again slid the towel the length of her legs, the material whispering over her skin.

He stood and silently handed her the towel.

"Thank you," she said.

"No problem."

At least there wouldn't be as soon as they got out of this confined space where she smelled too good, looked too good, felt too good. He picked up the candle she'd carried in. The sooner he got her to her room and put his camera between them, the better off they'd both be.

6

SHE WAS IN DEEP DOO-DOO. Something had just happened there in the bathroom, without even a kiss or an overt touch. She'd gone from mere lust to infatuation. Every inch of her knew that it was no longer a matter of *if* they wound up in her bed together tonight but *when*. He couldn't possibly touch her with such tenderness and not want her. And while part of her was keyed up in anticipation, the knowledge also put her somewhat at ease.

Simon lit the last of the candles in her bedroom.

"I have a couple of T-shirts that are big on me. They'd probably be tight on you, but at least they wouldn't be wet." She fished out a shirt she occasionally slept in because it was two sizes too big. "How about this?"

"Thanks."

"I'll just hold on to it until you get out of that wet one." She knew what she wanted and she was going for it. *Him.*

"Were you planning to watch?"

"Unless you object. A girl's got to get her thrills where she can."

"I'm not sure that I qualify as a thrill."

"I'm certain you do."

Simon tugged his T-shirt loose from his jeans and peeled it up and off his body. Sweet mercy, the man had a body to die for. Broad-shouldered, lean-hipped and nicely trim in between. She felt like Goldilocks, who'd just discovered the perfect male. Oh my, that one had been too big and hairy. And oops, that one was too hairless and skinny. But, oh baby, this one was *just* right. And however cliché it was, she found it incredibly sexy the way that dark hair trailed past his navel and disappeared below the waistband of those jeans.

"You, Simon Thackeray, were built to thrill. I'm very…thrilled."

He grinned. Not the arrogant smirk of an overinflated ego but that of a man pleased to be appreciated.

"You want to toss me that shirt you're holding on to?" he said.

She sighed audibly. "I will if I absolutely have to. Don't feel compelled to get dressed on my account." Nonetheless, she tossed it to him.

He caught it single-handedly and sobered. "Are you flirting with me, Tawny?"

"Yes, Simon, I am. Shamelessly."

"Do you think that's a good idea?"

"No. Not really. I think it's probably a very bad idea, but I'm certainly enjoying it. How about you?" she said.

"Am I enjoying it or do I think it's a good idea?"

"Both."

"I have to go with you on both counts. I'm enjoying

it and I'm sure it's a bad idea." He pulled the shirt over his head, hiding that yummy physique.

Spoilsport.

But not to worry, she planned to get it back off of him soon enough.

THERE WAS SOMETHING VERY intimate about being in her candlelit bedroom, knowing she was about to undress. "Hold on a minute. Don't move. I'll be right back."

He sprinted back to the den, snagged his camera and was back in her bedroom within a minute. "I want to capture the moment, the anticipation, the preparation, not just the finished product." Hell, maybe it wasn't a good idea. In fact, he was damn near certain it was a bad idea. But no worse than being here now. And photographing her was safer than kissing her.

When he shot, he became one with the camera. He could be himself behind the lens.

"You want to photograph me changing clothes?"

"Not while you're actually changing but while you're getting ready. Plus it gets you used to being in front of the camera. Just forget I'm here."

She looked across the room, her eyes holding his. It was a look, one breath away from smoldering, that acknowledged him as a man she'd kissed earlier. "I can't do that."

"Can you forget the camera's here?" He was proud of his steady tone. He didn't feel steady.

"I think so."

He fired off a couple of shots, just to get her used to it. She smiled, self-conscious and awkward. "Just relax," he reminded her. If he could keep her talking, a stream of distracting chatter, she'd also relax. "Do you have your hair up because it's cooler that way?"

"Yes. But it's so hot now, I don't think it's going to matter. And I should do something with it anyway." She turned her back to him and pulled the barrette out and let her hair tumble past her shoulders. His shutter whirred. She shook her head and pushed her fingers through it. He shot again. She looked at him in the mirror, a beguiling mixture of longing and uncertainty, and his heart pounded. Was there anything more enchanting, more intimate, than a woman taking her hair down?

"Better?" she asked.

Click. "Perfect. Keep doing what you're doing."

She raised her arms and reached beneath the fall of her hair. "Beautiful. Beautiful delineation of your neck, shoulders and arms. A study in perfection. A work of art."

"You don't have to say those things, you know."

"I know. But it's true." And it would be so much better without the interfering lines of her halter top. "Keep your back to me and take your top off," he said, automatically instructing her in what would give the best shot of her back.

"Is that how you get women to undress for you? A few complimentary phrases?" She glanced over her shoulder, laughing, teasing but with a sexy glint in her eyes.

"You're onto me." His responding laugh was rusty. As a rule, he didn't laugh a lot. "No naughty pictures. I just want to capture the line of your back without the top. Move away from the mirror, keep your back to me, take it off and lift your hair that same way. Wait a second. Here. Stand here." He moved her away from the mirror and positioned the tall triple-wick candle—the one she'd earlier said could go all night—until the light illuminated her back. "Just a bit more to the right."

From habit, he lightly touched her, to direct her where he wanted her to go. He'd touched beautiful women wearing far less than Tawny hundreds of times, but it was as if he'd never touched anyone before. And he hadn't. Not like this. Longing swept him, threatened his composure. He felt her indrawn breath, the sudden rigid line of her once-supple back.

He dropped his hand and backed away from her, gripping his camera like a lifeline. "You don't have to take off your top if you don't want to." That steady tone he'd prided himself on earlier was long gone.

"I want to take it off."

She reached beneath her hair and unhooked the top, and he watched the sides fall away and to the front. She lowered her arms and reached to the front. It was a wrap halter and tied in the front—beneath her left breast, he'd noticed. The material bisecting the elegant lines and curves of her back fell away.

"Brilliant. Truly stunning." He fired away. These would be incredible. "Lots of women with beautiful faces aren't lovely from this angle. Lift your hair once again. The way you did before."

She followed his instructions. He'd never gotten emotionally caught up in what he was photographing. It was art and it was his art and in many ways it was an extension of himself, but there was also still an engagement that wasn't personal, that didn't tie his emotions into it. But this was vastly different.

She turned slightly to her right, just enough to reveal the hint of roundness of her breast, the slight sag that meant they were real and not bought in a surgeon's office.

She dropped her arms and turned to face him, her silken curls curtaining the slope of her breasts and nipples, but the soft roundness of the bottom half revealed. Despite the fact she'd turned to face him, there was something more. A subtle shift in her body language, as if she'd discovered something, resolved something.

"Simon, do you have any idea why I've had doubts about me and Elliott?"

It had been one of those remarks he should've taken more note of but had been lost in the higher drama of the moment. He thought it through now. Elliott's turnabout in his sexual orientation had obviously surprised her, so that wasn't it. She didn't appear to have any ambiguity concerning her own. Which meant she'd been seeing someone else or had at the least met someone else. Rancor filled him. He didn't want to hear her confess to yet another attraction. Or perhaps that was exactly what he needed to hear to excise her from his heart, his psyche, his emotions. "My first guess is that you've found someone else, as well."

"Not exactly." Pathetic how glad he was to hear that. "Not the way you mean, anyway. I've developed an interest in someone else, even though it hasn't gone any further. Well, sort of."

She had his attention now. Who was he kidding? She always had his attention. She'd owned it from the first time he'd spotted her across the room. "Why don't you explain?"

"I promised you earlier I wouldn't fling myself at

you again. And I'm not. But it's time to be honest and I think you should know. It was you, Simon."

She could probably hear his heart pounding from across the room. Tawny had doubted her relationship with Elliott because of *him?* He didn't trust her words. Couldn't trust her words. What would possibly attract her to him over Elliott?

"Don't, Tawny. Don't go there. Elliott might've behaved badly, but I'm not a particularly nice guy and I don't want to be thrust into the role of payback pawn because Elliott's wounded your pride or broken your heart."

She jerked her head back, anger and hurt flashing in her eyes, caught up in the exchange and seemingly unaware that one plump, ripe nipple now peered through her hair. But he was aware enough for both of them. Hell, he was aware enough for an army.

"You think I'm making this up to get back at Elliott?"

"You're not trying to seduce me?"

"I'm trying to be honest, you thickheaded, arrogant, cold-blooded, sarcastic jackass, and you are really... pissing me off."

"Well, I can see, given that glowing description, why I'd be the man to give you second thoughts about marrying Elliott. Perhaps you felt the need to break it off based on the poor company he keeps."

She'd said she was pissed off earlier. She was bloody, wanking angry now.

"Here's the truth, Simon Thackeray, if you can handle it. I'll be damned if I know why, but I've started having dreams about you. About us. They began after we spent the day together for the photo shoot."

"What kind of dreams?" God, he could barely breathe.

"Sexual dreams. Explicit."

"They're just dreams, Tawny."

"I'm well aware of that, Simon. But those dreams, *you,* were beginning to take a toll on my relationship with Elliott."

Instead of gaining clarity, things were growing murkier and more tangled. It had almost been easier when she and Elliott belonged to one another. She'd been off-limits to Simon and his role had been clearly defined. "Why would you let a few dreams interfere with a real relationship?"

"It wasn't a choice and it wasn't just a few dreams. It was almost every night. At first I didn't want to go to sleep, because I didn't want to dream about making love to you." Heat surged through him. She looked down and studied her nails. "And now it's gotten to the point that being asleep is the best part of my day." She looked back up. "And I've felt guilty as hell with Elliott because it felt wrong to do the things with you that I was doing while I was engaged to him." Her gaze captured his. "And doubly wrong because what we had in my dreams was so much better than what Elliott and I had in reality."

Her words seduced him, fired along his nerve endings, tightened his body as surely as if she'd trailed her hands over him. "Maybe you won't have any more of those dreams."

She shook her head. "This afternoon I was napping when Elliott called. I was dreaming and just about to come. With you." And he wasn't so sure that if she went into enough detail he wouldn't come. She had him hard and throbbing. "I've felt like the biggest whore east of the Mississippi. Do you know the first thing that came to mind when he said you both wanted to come over this evening?"

Obviously her mind was an utter mystery to him since he had no clue she'd been having what sounded like very intense sex with him. "No clue."

"Ménage à trois. That's how depraved you've made me. I am trying to seduce you. Not to get back at Elliott. I need the reality of your touch to exorcise those dreams. Because as it stands now, I'm afraid you've ruined me for any other man."

WHEN SHE WAS SEVEN, frustrated by her lack of progress in her swimming classes, without really thinking it through, she'd sucked in a deep breath and jumped in over her head. And from that day forward her philosophy had taken shape: she'd swim or die trying. Obviously she'd swum.

And she'd just plunged in far out of her depth with Simon. But it was true. She feared he'd ruined her for any other man. And if she could offer him an outlet for his unrequited love, then why not?

Simon advanced toward her, beginning to click off picture after picture.

"Tawny, I'm sure that I haven't ruined you for other men, as you'll find when you get back into…circulation."

Circulation. Another man's bed was what he meant. And obviously he had no intention of or interest in being that man. Yet another dose of humiliation washed over her.

Why hadn't she simply kept her mouth shut? Why

had she let a few erotic dreams and one helluva live kiss convince her she and Simon had chemistry?

Obviously all the chemistry was in her head—as in chemical imbalance. Obviously he was willing to photograph her. Obviously he'd been offering her comfort earlier and she'd misread the situation. And now obviously she needed to put some freaking clothes on and try to maintain a few shreds of dignity until the power was restored and Simon was out her door. And out of her life.

"You're right. A little circulation will take care of that for me." She aimed for light and laughing, but it came out stiff and abrupt. She was precariously close to total humiliation. "Let me put some clothes back on."

She headed for her closet. Maybe she could spend an hour or so in there—except it was dark. She'd never let herself get caught without a flashlight ever again.

"Tawny—"

Simon touched her bare shoulder. She froze outside while heat filled her on the inside. "Simon, please don't touch me."

"That's not what you said a moment ago."

She ached for him. And what was the small matter of pride? She'd already humiliated herself. "You know what I mean. I'm not sure that I can stand for you to touch me and not take it any further. And since you're not interested in going there, it's best if you simply don't touch me at all."

His hand remained on her shoulder. Yearning like nothing she'd ever known before filled her. She wanted him with a desperation that bordered on obsession.

"I didn't say I wasn't interested." His fingers moved

against her bare skin in a featherlight caress. "I just don't want you to regret this tomorrow."

Moving in slow motion, she turned to face him. "I'm not looking for forever. I want you for tonight. I know you're in love with someone else. Let me be her for you tonight."

"You would sleep with me, knowing I may very well pretend you're someone else?"

She lifted her chin a notch. "Yes. You turn me on that much." She wasn't exactly shy and retiring to begin with, but there was a fantastic quality to being in her candlelit bedroom with Simon. She said things she would never have been bold enough to say in the harsh light of day. "I'll take whatever you're offering, except I don't particularly want to be a pity lay."

"You won't be standing in for anyone. This is about me and you. I wouldn't insult you by pretending you were anyone other than who you are." He tilted her head back with one finger beneath her chin and stared hard into her eyes. There wasn't a shred of pity in his eyes. They burned with a heat and a leashed passion for her. "And I don't want to be a revenge lay."

"Never," she said, winding her arms around his neck, feeling the corded tension of his body, already wet for him, hungering for his touch. "This isn't pay-back."

She wanted to quench this desire for Simon that consumed her and she wanted him to make her feel like a desirable woman. Right or wrong, she needed a little sexual validation.

He brushed his thumb over her cheekbone. "Is this really what you want, Tawny? Are you certain you want me? Because stopping will be torture once I touch you, taste you."

She leaned into him, unerringly fitting her hips to his. His cock was rock-hard against her mound, offering instant validation and stimulation. Her panties were drenched and her body was on fire. She rubbed her bare breasts against his shirt, delighting in the soft cotton against her aroused nipples. She breathed in his male scent and nuzzled his jaw. His breath quickened.

"Yes, I'm absolutely certain I want you. And I don't want you to stop. I want you naked on top of me—" she nibbled at his earlobe "—beneath me—" she teased the tip of her tongue along the rim "—beside me—" he shuddered against her "—behind me—" want thickened her voice and strummed through her body "—but most of all inside me."

HER WORDS AND HER TOUCH destroyed every defense he'd erected. He stood to lose the only friend he'd ever really had, Elliott, by sleeping with Tawny. But he'd trade his friendship and essentially his sense of honor, all of his tomorrows, for one night with her, to hold her, touch her, make love to her. And if he was a lesser man for this decision, he had the rest of his life to deal with it. Perhaps he'd dine on the bitter fruit of regret with tomorrow's dawn, but for tonight she was his.

He slid his camera to the floor, dropping the strap. "Tawny..."

He cradled her head in his hands. Without rushing, he kissed her gently, thoroughly, an unspoken promise that for the night, they belonged to each other. He told her in a kiss all the things that he couldn't or wouldn't say aloud—how much he wanted her, how beautiful he found her both inside and out, that among women she alone was the most desirable, that for years he'd carried the Hades analogy in his head and she had become his Persephone, but after tonight he'd release her, after offering and taking solace in her.

She returned his kiss, melded into him, connected with his soul.

The kiss heated, shifted to a higher intensity as she slid her hands beneath his shirt, greedily stroking his bare skin. Her touch ignited him. He reached between them and cupped her breasts in his hands, plying his thumbs against her nipples. She felt so good. Tawny pressed against him and moaned into his open mouth, and Simon was lost, gone. He sank onto the edge of the bed, pulling her down with him, between his thighs.

She followed, settling between his legs.

"It seems as if I've waited forever to touch you," she said. She pressed a kiss to the underside of his jaw while she explored his chest with her hands, bold strokes that fanned the fire inside him hotter and higher.

She reached for his belt and his jeans.

"Wait a sec. Let me take off my boots," Simon said. Tawny stood. He bent down and unlaced his boots— infinitely better than winding up with his trousers around his ankles. Tawny stripped out of her shorts and skimpy panties, dropping them on the floor in front of him. He pulled off the second Doc Martens and looked up.

He was glad he was sitting for his first view of her gloriously, spectacularly naked. She was every inch rounded woman, from shapely legs, to curved hips, to a small waist and full breasts. And obviously a proponent of the Brazilian wax.

Desire slammed him, tightened his balls. "You're so beautiful, you take my breath."

She smiled and there was a shyness about it that touched him. She slid onto the bed behind him and laughed softly, her breath warm against his bare shoulder. She smoothed her hands over his shoulders and nuzzled his neck, her breasts pressed against his back. Her touch sizzled along his nerve endings.

"I'm glad I'm not sending you running out the door," she said.

"Not a chance." He undressed and she pulled him back down onto the bed with her.

He rolled over and trapped her beneath him, his arms on either side of her shoulders. Her eyes darkened and she parted her lips, wetting the fullness of her lower lip with the tip of her tongue.

"The only thing that could possibly send me running is—" he lowered his head and tasted the sweetness of her neck, her shoulder "—if you tell me you've changed your mind."

"No. That…won't…happen." She arched her back, raising herself, inviting his kisses. Bathed in candlelight, her skin gleamed like a rare pearl. He licked the hollow of her throat and chased her shudder with his own. Her scent, the slight saltiness of her skin, the taste of her. He wanted to make love to her all night, learn every inch of her with his mouth, his tongue, his hands. But he'd wanted her so long, he didn't think he could wait much longer this first time around. He circled one plump nipple with his tongue. She moaned deep in her throat.

"Simon…" Tawny said in an agonized tone.

He flicked the other one with the tip of his tongue and then moved back to the first one—tasting her, tormenting them both.

They were both slick with sweat and her skin slid against his, her thigh cushioning the length of his erection.

She rolled him onto his back and kissed him as if she couldn't get enough. Her tongue dueled with his. Her hands explored him, almost frantic, and she made small whimpering noises in the back of her throat, leaving him hotter and harder. She seemed to want him as much as he wanted her. She rolled to her side again, pulling him with her, reaching behind her without taking her mouth from his. Simon broke the kiss.

"What are you doing?" he asked.

"Reaching for a condom."

He was such a dolt, he'd forgotten all about protection. That had never happened. He'd always been careful. That she kept a stock on hand wasn't particularly surprising, considering her battery-powered arsenal.

She looked at him, her eyes luminous, hot. "I'm so afraid this is another dream," she said. "I don't want to wake up. Because if I do, I'm going to be righteously pissed."

Simon laughed. She had the most unorthodox way of flattering him, but he was immeasurably flattered that she didn't want to wake up if she was dreaming.

"No. We're not dreaming," he said, stroking his hand down her back, over the lush curve of her bum. Reality had never been so sweet.

She held a condom aloft in triumph. "Strawberry

flavored." She tore into the package. "Mind if I do the honors?"

"Please. Feel free to," he said.

"My pleasure is—" she stroked the condom over him, her hand warm, with just the right amount of pressure, and he closed his eyes in a moment of *ahhhh* "—your pleasure."

So far she'd only just touched him. She tightened her hand and stroked again. His eyes flew open.

"Unless you want the shortest foreplay in the history of man, you don't need to do that again," he said, his hoarseness reflecting the strain of not coming.

"I'm ready if you're ready. I've had weeks of dreaming about you. That's been plenty of foreplay."

Simon knew a moment of performance anxiety. What if the real him didn't measure up to the dream lover he'd been for her? And the curious, mystical, magical woman that she was, she obviously saw it in his face.

"Don't even go there." She leaned over him and scattered kisses over his chest, laving his male nipples, down his belly. She lapped at his rigid length and took him into her warm, eager mouth. Simon called on every ounce of his self-control not to blast off as she fondled him with her mouth. She released him and he managed to breathe again. Her hair brushed against his belly, the strands teasing against his skin. "Actually tasting you, touching you, smelling you, is so much better than it ever was in my dreams," she said, her tone as hot as the passion glittering in her eyes.

She fell to her back, spread her legs and said with a sweet smile, "Now are you going to fuck me or do I have to beg first?"

It sent him totally over the edge when she said that. If he was any hotter, he'd melt.

He positioned himself between her legs and nudged at her with his sheathed tip. "No begging necessary."

Simon slid into her slowly, totally captured by the expression on her face, heat and pleasure suffusing her features. She felt so good, so right, and as he slid into her inch by inch, she gripped him, as if welcoming him home.

She wrapped her legs around him and hooked her feet behind his thighs. She lunged up to meet him. A few quick thrusts and they'd both be there. He drew a deep, shuddering breath and deliberately slowed them down. They weren't going for a distance record—they were both wound too tight, they didn't have a prayer of making it far—but he pulled back slowly until he was almost out of her and then treated them both to a slow reentry. Tawny gasped aloud and pushed into him, sending him plunging.

"You are deliciously wicked, Simon Thackeray."

Her honeyed Southern drawl wrapping around his name at the same time her honeyed channel wrapped around his cock nearly undid him. It was as if she'd woven some magic around them, bound them together in a union that went beyond the physical. As if she'd opened up a part of herself and invited him into the warmth and light that was more than skin-deep with her.

She was so open, so giving, and he wanted to give in return. He offered as much of himself as he could. He rode her harder and faster. Her head whipped back and forth on the bed, her hands fisted in the comforter and she urged him on until they were both caught up in the throes of a screaming orgasm—literally.

His Tawny was no wilting flower. She was bold and beautiful, and if he'd ever had a moment's hesitation that he might be standing in for Elliott, she dispelled that particular notion as she panted his name over and over as she shuddered beneath him.

Had she screamed Elliott's name the same way? Had she thrashed beneath him and arched into him as if she'd die without his touch? He absolutely didn't need to go there, yet he absolutely couldn't help himself.

She lay so still beneath him, her eyes closed, that if she hadn't been breathing heavily he might've thought her asleep. A slow smile bloomed on her generous mouth and she opened her eyes.

"That was…incredible…so much better than I ever dreamed it."

A strange sensation filled him. It took a moment for Simon to recognize it was contentment—utter bloody contentment. He answered her smile with one of his own. He didn't think he could not smile at this point—it was a totally involuntary reaction.

"Absolutely." And then because he wanted to share what he felt but had no clue how to say it, he kissed her, slowly, tenderly, an aftermath of passion.

He traced the curve of her side, his fingers molding against the softness of her skin. He had been painfully honest earlier—now that he was touching her he wasn't sure he could stop. Intellectually he knew skin was skin, an amalgamation of tissue and nerves and cells, but she felt like no other woman beneath his fingertips. He was so absolutely in love with her, loved her so completely, his whole being ached with it.

He lifted his head and looked at her. He dared so much more in the dark. Hiding in the shadows cast by the candlelight, he drank her in. Her hair spread in disarray across the bed, her eyes dark and mysterious, her lips swollen from his kisses, her body relaxed from his lovemaking. Without thought, he ran his fingers along the delicate line of her jaw, breathed in her fragrance. She captured his hand in hers, brought his fingers to her lips and feathered the lightest caress across them.

"Simon…" She hesitated.

"Yes?"

"I don't want to make you uncomfortable—" she glanced away "—but I…I'm not sure how to say this."

His heart, not fully recovered from their sexual calisthenics, began to pound again. "Just say it."

He was too raw and open to quell the surge of hope that she might profess newfound feelings for him.

"I…we… Oh, this is so awkward…."

He could barely breathe. Had she discovered, in the aftermath of making love—and that's what it'd been for him—deeper feelings for him?

"What, luv?" Endearments had never been a part of his vocabulary. They'd never been given as a child and he'd never cultivated them as an adult, but this one rolled off his tongue.

"I'm sweaty and sticky and I'm afraid I, well, stink. I need a shower."

Righto. He laughed at himself, at how off the mark he'd been. His brain must've still been centered in his willy. God knew, he knew he wasn't the most lovable guy on the planet. Not even his parents had ever loved him. That wasn't exactly the heartfelt declaration he'd built himself up for but she was right—they were both slick with sweat and although he might be a fool, he wasn't fool enough to turn down an opportunity tonight. "Need a back washer?"

7

"COME ON IN. THE WATER'S fine," Tawny said. She leaned back, welcoming the kiss of cool, smooth porcelain against her back.

"Give me a second." He strode out of the bathroom.

They might be here through force of circumstance, but it was very romantic with candles bathing the room in soft light and contrasting shadows. She'd placed votives in saucers on the floor around the tub. Nothing quite like being inventive.

The candlelight lent a dreamlike air. But it was more than that. The entire night was surreal. Simon Thackeray was about to climb into a bath with her after they'd just had fantastic sex that had been both tender and explosive. She'd discovered a consideration behind Simon's reserve she'd never anticipated, a quality that had never been part of her dreams yet had engaged her beyond the mere physical.

Simon returned, his camera slung around his neck. He should've looked sort of silly wearing only a camera, but there was nothing remotely silly about Simon naked. Impressive. Sexy. Drool-inducing. Heat flushed her body, regardless of the tepid water surrounding her. *Nice*—that was such an insipid word—muscular legs, nice package up front, totally nice ass. Wow.

Click.

She laughed. "Did you just take a picture of me ogling you from the bath?"

"Absolutely. Very sexy."

And there was a bonus to carrying on a conversation with a naked man. When he told you he found something sexy, well, you got visual proof to back up his statement. Simon wasn't lying—it looked as if he found her very sexy indeed.

"I'm not actually naked in the picture, am I?"

He grinned. "No. At this angle and with the water at that level, you can't actually see details—which is something of a shame since you possess very nice details."

"Careful, sir. You'll make me swoon," she teased in an exaggerated Southern drawl. Beneath Simon's sober exterior beat the heart of a flirt, and it was all the more potent because he didn't flirt indiscriminately the way some men did. She'd never seen this flirtatious side of him, even when she and Elliott had double-dated with him. Elliott. She didn't remotely want to dedicate a brain cell to Elliott at this moment.

"What do you think will happen when I get in the tub with you, Tawny?"

He was a devil to tease her in that low, suggestive tone.

"Keep talking that way and it'll be your own fault if the water's heated up by the time you get here," she said.

Simon laughed and kept firing off pictures. Tawny

had lost her self-consciousness in front of the camera. She simply ignored it and flirted with Simon.

"You're blowing your chance at cool and refreshing."

"Wet and warm sounds even better," he said.

"Getting warmer by the minute. Why don't you come on over and find out just how wet and hot it is?" She sat up, wrapping her arms around her knees. "Don't forget, you promised me a back wash."

"I plan to fulfill that promise thoroughly in just a minute. That's a great angle. Hold it for me."

At one time she might've been impatient, but she knew Simon would join her sooner or later. She eyed his smooth, firm erection—sooner from the looks of things. Anticipation hummed through her and she smiled her anticipation at him.

"Beautiful…oh, that's brilliant," he said, shooting photo after photo.

"I bet you say that to all the girls," she teased— however, a part of her rebelled at being just another photograph in a long line.

"I do say that to all the girls." The bottom dropped out of her stomach. That was *not* what she wanted to hear. He looked around the camera and grinned at her. He appeared young and carefree, which were two words she'd never thought to associate with Simon. Her heart did a funny flip-flop. "But I don't climb into a bath with them afterward."

Rat bastard. "I'm sure it's not for lack of opportunity," she said.

"Thanks…I think." He almost looked embarrassed. "I've had a fair share of invitations."

No stinking kidding. He was gorgeous and sexy. The

heat inside her grew hotter still—he wanted to climb in the tub with her, Tawny Edwards, as opposed to Chloe and the other exquisite, thin women he photographed. Of course, there was the matter of his dream woman, the unavailable, but Tawny wouldn't think about that because right now he was naked and here with her. Carpe diem.

"It's time to put the camera down, Simon."

He quirked his brows at her, amusement dancing in his eyes. "Do you think I'm just a puppet to be controlled? Are you always so bossy?"

She was. She knew it. "Only when I want something really bad."

"And I'm really bad?" His wicked sexy grin set her pulse fluttering.

"That's totally a matter of perspective. It's been my experience that you're especially good when you're really bad. And I can promise you I want you that way."

He placed the camera next to the wall. Anticipation notched tighter inside her as he crossed the small area. Once he lost the camera he carried himself with a measure of self-consciousness he hadn't had before. She found it endearing that despite his arrogance, he didn't strut around as if he and his dick were God's gift to womankind.

She'd had all those hot dreams about him, so the great sex was…well, great but no real surprise. But she hadn't anticipated actually liking him. And she did. He was tender and funny and sexy and… He stepped into the tub behind her and shot her train of thought to hell.

He sat down, sliding his legs on either side of her. He wrapped his arms around her, pulling her into the V of his body, as if it had been custom designed just for her. Her back curved against his belly and his chest, her head resting between his shoulder and his neck.

Despite their earlier flirtatious patter, Simon seemed equally content to enjoy the moment. She closed her eyes and absorbed the sensations. The rhythm of his heartbeat echoed against her back, his arms were strong yet tender around her. She'd had a boyfriend once who, when he'd put his arms around her, it had been like being locked in a vise grip. Eddie could take a lesson or two from Simon, who definitely knew how to hold a woman. He smelled enticingly of sex, sweat and his own scent.

Candlelight danced across the walls and ceiling. She was living one of those perfect, wildly romantic moments portrayed in movies and glossy magazines. She sighed, happy to be here, in this moment, now.

"Comfy?" he asked.

"Mmm. Very. You make a nice bath pillow."

"Great. Now I've gone from puppet to pillow," he groused.

Tawny smiled and pressed a kiss to his bicep. "But you're a very sexy bath pillow." Never had her dreams been this good. She was at the head of the line when it came to appreciating great sex, but there was also much to recommend this lazy, comfortable teasing with an undercurrent of anticipation.

He nuzzled his lips against her hair and Tawny could have sworn warm butter replaced all the bones in her body. She melted against him.

"There's a place near my grandparents' farm that my cousin Reg and I used to go to. There's a pool in the middle of the woods with a small waterfall. The pool's shallow enough that the sun heats the water. You can stretch out and sun on this huge flat rock. The water's clear and the air's sweet. When we were young, we thought fairies lived there."

He'd painted such a picture, she could see the place. She also saw a young, intense Simon looking for fairies. A warmth that had nothing to do with physical desire filled her. She knew from the amount of time she'd spent with him and through the things Elliott had divulged about Simon that he was an intensely private man. Maybe it was just the craziness of the night or the unusual circumstances, but she was certain he'd just shared a part of himself few had been privy to before her. And the notion of a young, romantic boy who believed in fairies didn't surprise her nearly as much as it would have at one time. He was a complex, complicated man. She'd wanted him in her bed, but now she found she wanted to know more about the man himself.

"It sounds lovely."

"It is. You'd like it."

"I'm sure I would." *Take me there.* The idea sneak-attacked her. "Do you go to England often?"

"I used to go once a year in the summer. Now I get over a couple of times a year. My father's parents died several years ago. My mother's parents still live in Devon. They're amazing. They're in their mid-eighties and they still keep a small farm going."

"You're close to them?" She'd only ever known her paternal grandparents, and they were even more starched and conservative than her father.

"As close as you can be with an ocean separating you. I spent glorious summers there when I was growing up." She heard his smile.

"Do you go with your parents?"

"No." The sudden chill in his tone was a stark contrast to his earlier warmth. His body tensed against her back, his arms tightened slightly. She intensely disliked Simon's parents even though she'd never met them. By virtue of how little he said, she had a pretty clear picture of two self-absorbed, self-important people who didn't make time for their son. She might be the odd man out in her family, but she still knew they loved her even though they often disapproved of her.

"I can't imagine you on a farm." She deliberately interjected a light, teasing note.

"I'll have you know I'm quite proficient at gathering eggs and milking a cow."

"No way. *That* I'd like to see." Despite her teasing, it was true. She'd like to see Simon unplugged. "Did you have a girlfriend there?"

"No."

"What's wrong with the girls in England? I can't believe you didn't have a girlfriend."

"Devon's not exactly a metropolis like New York or London."

"Are you telling me the countryside was totally devoid of young women? You never wowed a milkmaid one farm over with your egg-gathering technique?"

Simon chuckled, but it sounded forced. "There was one girl.... Her father was the vicar."

Sometimes he wasn't the most forthcoming with info. Fortunately Tawny didn't mind asking questions. "How British...the vicar's daughter. And her name was...?"

"Jillian. Jillian Carruthers."

"And whatever happened to Jillian Carruthers? Or do you still see her when you go to England?"

"I do still see Jillian, almost every trip."

"Oh." Oh. Crud. Suddenly her teasing and Jillian weren't quite so funny. In fact, Tawny felt sort of nauseous.

"She married my cousin Reg. They're expecting twins this fall."

"Oh." Surely that hadn't been pleasant to have his love interest marry his cousin. Was Jillian his unattainable woman? Yet, Simon had said his unattainable woman wasn't married. Tawny knew she was an evil bitch to feel so relieved Jillian was safely out of the picture. "Is it awkward when you see them?"

"Not at all. That was a long time ago."

She stroked her thumb over his arm, feeling the play of muscle beneath skin. "Did you ever tell her how you felt?"

"I did, in fact. But by the end of the summer, she decided I wasn't her cup of tea. She and Reg became an item and that was that."

Hmm. And there was more there than he was letting on. His tone was light and nonchalant, but she felt the tension in his body. "Were you devastated?"

"Only for a bit. They're well suited. It worked out that way for a reason. Life has a way of doing that."

She didn't want him to retreat due to a memory of a lost love. She deliberately brought the conversation back to them. "I for one am glad it worked out that way because otherwise I wouldn't be sitting here with you. Jillian has no idea what she's missing." She wriggled, pressing her buttocks against him, a not-so-subtle reminder of where he was, who he was with and the direction things were headed. "I think you're lots of fun."

"Do you now?" He pressed a kiss to the nape of her

neck, seeming to inherently know her most sensitive spot. He laughed softly at her intake of breath and the shiver she had no hope of hiding.

"Yes," she said. His teeth raked lightly against her shoulder and she shuddered at the exquisite sensation. "And I'm particularly fond of that kind of fun."

"I'm just getting started with the fun. I owe you a back wash." He released her and she passed him the soap. "Lean forward a bit."

She folded her arms over her knees and rested her head on them. He stroked his soapy fingers over her shoulders, traced down the line of her backbone and then rubbed small circles over her back. She almost purred, it felt so good. "Ahh. You certainly know how to wash a back."

"Your back has beautiful lines." He curled his fingers along her right side. "This curve. Very graceful."

Oh. The things he did and said—the way he made her feel. What was it about Simon that he unlocked more feelings, more response in her with a single touch than any man ever had with far more than a touch?

"Thank you. And don't even think about stopping and getting your camera."

"I'm not going anywhere." Heat underscored his teasing tone.

The water lapped around her as he gentled his soap-slicked hands up her sides, his fingertips barely brushing the sides of her breasts, to her underarms. My God, she'd never had anyone stroke her underarms, never knew it could feel so good.

She raised her head and uncrossed her arms when he cupped his hands and ran them over her upper arms. He stroked the length of her limbs and she leaned back into him once again, her breasts tingling, tightening in anticipation of where his hands would roam next.

He reached around, beneath her arms, and worked his finger magic across her collarbone, along her chest leading to the slope of her breasts and then the curve of her breasts, along the side, beneath them but never actually touching them or her nipples. Finally he cupped them and she dropped her head back against him, the thud of his heartbeat strong against her shoulder.

"Yes."

"Is this what you wanted?" His breath gusted against her neck. "Is this what you've been waiting for?"

"Yes."

"Me, too," he purred next to her ear while his fingers found her nipples. Warmth rushed between her thighs as he plucked and kneaded and caressed. Judging by the way his cock surged against her back, he enjoyed fondling her breasts as much as she enjoyed his "fun."

He cupped his hands and sluiced water over her front, rinsing off the soap.

"Now your back." She leaned forward and he rinsed. He settled her once again against his chest.

"Feel better?" He traced the shell of her ear with the tip of this tongue.

"Much." He expected her to think coherently… talk…when his tongue and mouth were…ooh.

"I think you can feel even better yet," he said, low and seductive.

She closed her eyes when he kissed her neck. She *loved* having her neck kissed. It tingled through her body all the way to her toes. He could spend hours kissing her neck and she'd be a happy camper.

"I don't know… I'm feeling…ooh…very good."

"We'll see about that," he said and anticipation coursed through her. He ran his hands over the rounded mound of her belly and she tried to suck it in, to flatten it. His warm breath teased against her ear. "Stop, Tawny. Relax. You're built like a woman's supposed to be built. Soft, with curves in all the right places."

Go to the head of the class for that answer, Simon. He was so tuned in to her, seemed to read every nuance of her body language. He trailed his fingers, the lightest of touches, along the tops of her thighs.

"Open your legs for me." His voice was as thick as his erection nudging her from behind and reminded her of her dream that morning. It was a perfect blend of fantasy and reality and left her all the hotter still. She spread her legs and cool water rushed against her slick heat.

Simon reached between her thighs, his arms and hands dark against her pale skin, and parted her with his thumbs. "Oh, luv, I like your bare style."

It had taken two margaritas of Dutch courage to actually work up the nerve to have another human being wax her *there* and it had hurt like hell, but when it was all said and done, once she'd gone bare she was never going back.

She inched her legs farther apart. "Me, too. The better to feel you."

And feel him she did—every screaming, craving nerve ending in her body centered between her legs. He traced her with a finger until he found her clit and brushed against it. She whimpered and pressed against his hand. Okay, maybe her neck wasn't her *most* sensitive spot.

"Easy. Relax. Not so fast. Sit back and enjoy it. Savor it. You liked it when I did that?"

"Yes."

"How about his?" He slid a finger into her and she forced herself not to arch into him, but she did clench her muscles around him.

"Yes."

"You feel so good. You're so much hotter than the water. It's like dipping my finger into warm honey."

His voice, low and sexy, his words, his touch, the feel of his body behind her, his arms around her, the feel of his breath against her skin when he spoke, the faint scrape of his whiskers against her shoulder, the cool water lapping at her hot skin, all centered in her, through her.

He alternated stroking along her slit and sliding a finger, then two fingers, into her, while his thumb worked magic on her clit. He cupped her left breast in his other hand, toying with her nipple, plucking, squeezing.

Tawny gripped the sides of the tub and spread her legs wider, pressing against his hair-roughened legs on either side of her. *Please.* She couldn't stand anything that felt this good much longer, but she also didn't want it to stop.

"Harder. Faster. Yes…yes…like that…oh…" She thrust her hips up to meet his fingers, driving him deeper within her, grinding her clit against the pressure of his thumb.

"That's it, luv. You're so beautiful. I want you to come for me. That's it…" Simon's voice sent her over the edge. She turned her head and bit into his shoulder, suckling him, tasting the warm saltiness of his skin against her tongue as she spasmed with pleasure.

She collapsed against him, quite simply because she didn't seem to have a bone left in her body. She felt as fluid and formless as the water surrounding her.

Simon pressed a kiss to her hair and wrapped his arms more firmly around her. "Oh, Tawny."

"Mmm," she murmured and rubbed her cheek against his arm, the only response she was capable of at the moment. Slowly she came back together, fully aware of his hard ridge behind her, the taut muscles of his belly and chest, the tension banding his arms.

She slid forward and turned around to face him on her knees. Sexual arousal and need etched his face, glittered in his eyes. With a slow smile she reached for the soap.

"Your turn."

"I CAN'T GET IT UP," TAWNY said, her frustration evident in the way she shoved her hair back off of her brow. "Do you want to try?"

"Sure. I'll have a go at it." God, this would be embarrassing if he couldn't get it up for her, but there was no guarantee. He put his weight behind pulling up on the window sash. "These older buildings have been painted so many times, sometimes the window's painted shut." He felt the smallest amount of give. "I think it's coming." Yep. The window gave and opened a few inches. He wrestled it the rest of the way.

"My hero," she said, teasing him with a smile, but her eyes shone with something that wrapped around his heart.

God, he was hopeless. He felt ten feet tall just because he'd opened the bloody window for her.

"It's no Arctic blast, but it's a bit cooler than in here." The drenching rain had brought little relief from the relentless heat. Steam rose from the pavement below.

"When it rains at home, it's steamy, too. But New York never smells fresh the way Savannah does after a rain," Tawny said on a wistful note. She swept back the comforter and top sheet and settled against the pillows propped against her headboard. "At least the sheets are sort of cool."

She obviously had no intention of sitting in the cloying confines of her den. Suited him fine. He stretched across the end of the bed, a towel around his hips. His damp clothes were draped over the shower rod in the bathroom. She'd had the benefit of fresh clothes and wore a pair of black panties, which were really just plain but very sexy, and a black tank top.

"Do you miss Savannah?" he asked.

"I miss certain things about it. The way it smells after a summer rain. The sound of a horse-drawn carriage on cobblestones. Spanish moss draping trees so old and sprawling they canopy the streets. Have you ever been there?"

"No. I'm not well traveled outside of New York and England."

She traced a lazy pattern on his calf with her toe. He liked the casual way she touched him, as if she needed to and had the right to. "The slower pace might drive you insane, but you'd love the city itself."

They lay in the flickering light, with the sounds of New York drifting in through the window, and she painted a picture for him of her birthplace, of the history and architecture and culture. Whether she knew it or not, her voice slowed, took on more of that honeyed Southern accent that always underlay her words. He imagined the two of them enjoying a horse-drawn carriage ride along cobblestone streets beneath moss-drenched oaks.

"You obviously love it. Why'd you leave?"

"I do love it, and in a way it was hard to go, but not really. I left because I needed to."

"Needed to or wanted to?"

"*Needed* to. I needed to step out of my comfort zone, discover new places, new things, discover myself."

She intrigued him with her mix of gutsiness, attitude, open sensuality and insecurities.

"And have you? Discovered yourself?" he asked.

"I thought I had. Tonight's sort of blown me out of the water. But I think I've finally figured out it's an ongoing process. Every day brings something new and different—some days more than others—like today. I know for certain I'm not the same person I was when I left, and that's a good thing."

How did she feel about today's changes? After this fiasco with Elliott, would she think about moving back home? She didn't strike Simon as the type to run home to her mother, but he had to ask.

"After this with Elliott, are you thinking about moving back?"

She shook her head and gave him a funny look. Tendrils of loose hair danced across her shoulders. "Not in the foreseeable future. I love Savannah and it'll always be home—I look forward to my visits—but New York has a pretty firm hold on my heart, as well. What about you? Have you ever wanted to live somewhere else?"

Tawny was easy to talk to and the dark didn't hurt either. Simon found himself telling her things he'd never told anyone else, perhaps never truly thought about consciously. "When I was a kid spending my summers in Devon, I wanted to stay there forever. When I got older, I realized it was my grandparents that drew me and not the place itself. Once I moved out on my own, New York felt more like home."

"My parents aren't exactly warm and fuzzy either."

They weren't even touching—well, except for her toe against his calf—but he felt closer to her emotionally than he ever had to anyone, even Elliott. He almost told her he hadn't said that about his parents, but he supposed he had. Indirectly. She had a way of seeing through to him. And as she'd said earlier, what was the point of prevarication?

"But you're warm and outgoing. How did that happen?"

"I'm an anomaly, the *which one of these doesn't belong.*" She laughed and the rueful note tore at his heart.

"I've always been the odd man out, as well." He'd thought it innumerable times. It was liberating to say it.

"What are they like?" she asked.

"My parents?" She nodded. "Clever, engaging, articulate. They're a self-contained unit. They made wonderful cocktail-party guests and lousy parents."

"No brothers or sisters?"

"Nope. Just me." And it had been just him in every respect. They hadn't been a family. Growing up had been such a lonely experience until he and Elliott became friends that he didn't particularly want to revisit it. "What was it like with two sisters?"

He switched the conversation back to her. She looked at him and he knew she was onto him, but she indulged him nonetheless, launching into tales about her siblings.

She was a natural storyteller. He loved the rhythm and cadence of her voice. There was a soothing quality to her speech even when she was regaling him with her childhood escapades.

"You might be the baby of the family, but I'm seeing a pattern here. You're definitely the instigator."

"Hmm. I told you…I'm the one who doesn't quite fit." Drowsiness exaggerated her drawl.

"You sound tired," he said.

"I am. What time is it?"

Simon checked his luminous watch. "Almost midnight."

"It's still early, but I think I'm emotionally exhausted and then too much fun…"

"Get some sleep."

"Mmm. That's a good idea."

They'd had sex twice, but there was such an intimacy to actually sharing a bed with another person, letting your guard down enough to drift into unconsciousness….

"Would you rather have me on the couch?" he asked.

"No. Stay with me." *Don't read more into it than she means.* "It's cooler in here…and I don't want you to go. I changed the sheets this morning, if that was… you know, if you felt funny about… I'm making a mess of this."

"You're not making a mess of anything." He slid up

the bed to stretch out beside her. She was one woman in a million—concerned that sleeping on sheets after Elliott would bother him. He ran his finger down the line of her nose and pressed a chaste good-night kiss to her forehead. "Thank you for telling me. Go to sleep and I'll be right here."

She smiled sleepily, hands-down the most beautiful smile he'd ever seen, on or off camera. "Try to sleep, too." She found his leg with her foot.

"I will."

He lay in her bed and listened to the muted sounds from a city that never slept, even in the midst of a blackout, and the soft cadence of her breathing. Without forethought, he lightly stroked her hair away from her face, wanting only to touch her while he still could, unwilling to sleep away his time with her. She uttered a soft satisfied sound.

"Simon?"

"Hmm?"

"I'm glad tonight happened." Imminent sleep slurred her words.

"So am I," he said.

Despite the suffocating heat, she shifted closer to him and—what the hell, they were both sweaty and sticky—he pulled her into his body. Her thigh slid between his and she curled her arm across his chest. She pressed a tender, drowsy kiss to his chest and he quietly fell a little harder, faster, deeper in love with her.

8

"No! Come back!"

Bloody hell! Simon jerked up, momentarily disoriented by the strange bed, candles and a screeching woman. Righto. Tawny. Her bed. Blackout.

"What's the matter?" He jumped to his feet and grabbed Tawny, who shook like a leaf.

"Peaches." She gulped air and motioned to the bedroom window. "He pushed through the screen and went out the window. He's on the ledge." She death-gripped his arm. "He doesn't have any front claws. What if he slips out there?"

She loved that cat. Simon didn't hesitate, didn't think, he just did. He worked the screen loose, tossed it back into the room and stuck his head out the window.

"Can you see him?" Tawny squeezed into the window opening. "Oh, God."

Peaches, now that the deed was done, apparently realized the error of his ways and huddled on the ledge several feet away.

She lowered her voice. "Come on, baby. C'mere,

Peaches. I've got a nice kitty treat waiting for you." Her voice shook.

Peaches yowled in kitty hysteria but didn't budge. Brilliant. If the people in the next apartment opened their window, the cat would probably be startled off the ledge.

Tawny gripped his arm again and Simon tried to reassure her. "Just stay calm."

"I'm going out there after him," she said.

"Bloody hell you are."

"I can't just leave him."

"I'll get him."

"No. I can't let you do that. And he doesn't know you anyway."

Over his dead body was she going out on that wet ledge. He looked down—all seven floors down—and it might very well be his dead body—but no way, no how was he letting her go.

"Panicked animals respond better to strangers in a rescue situation. I saw it on Animal Planet." Total, absolute codswallop—to borrow Grandpa Dickie's favorite expression—and he'd lie again to keep her off the ledge. He edged her out of the window frame and back into the bedroom.

"Wait here and I'll hand him to you." He didn't give her a chance to argue. He climbed out of the window and onto the ledge. It was far narrower than it had appeared from inside.

He gripped the window frame with his left hand and slowly stood, struggling to maintain his balance. He braced his right hand against the rough brick, wishing the ledge was made of the same instead of slick, wet marble. He hugged the building.

He made the mistake of glancing down. Vertigo rocked him. Head swimming, he teetered and then regained his balance. Fuck. Fuck. Fuck. He didn't like heights worth a damn.

"Simon, get back in here," Tawny said, her head shoved out the window, near his knee.

"I will when I get the cat." He kept his eyes trained on the building and Peaches.

"How are you going to do that?"

She'd picked a jolly time and place for a conversation. "I don't know. I'm working on a plan now."

"Don't you think you should've thought about it before you went out there?"

"I think best under pressure." More codswallop.

He edged toward Peaches, and his towel—the knot loosened by this climb out the window—inched down his hips. Lovely. He was only wearing a towel and it was falling off. Moving very slowly and carefully, he took it off and draped it over one shoulder. Better to hang his bare butt over a ledge than get tripped up by a towel.

Fuck again. He wasn't even going to die with dignity. Honor, perhaps, but no dignity.

Buck up. Grow a spine. He could do this. The key to not dying was to move slow and steady. At least, he hoped so.

And he had about a snowball's chance in hell of getting this cat. The bloody beast had swatted at him earlier when he'd tried to pet it. Simon did the only thing he knew to do—he kept sidling toward the cat and talked to it man-to-man…er, man-to-cat, in a low croon.

"Okay, mate. Just hang tight. See, this is the deal. You might have nine lives, but I've only got one...."

"What?" Tawny asked.

He carefully turned his head in her direction. "Just talking to the cat. Give us a minute, okay? And no noise and sudden movement would be most appreciated."

He looked back toward Peaches and pattered on. "Quite frankly, I think I'm too young to die, but even if I'm not, pavement-diving naked isn't exactly the way I wanted to go. And who knows, you might've used up your lives already."

The cat gave another hair-raising yowl. A whisper of a breeze chilled the sweat trickling between Simon's shoulder blades.

"Listen, I've got a deal for you. Just hear me out. I pick you up, we go back in there and I swear I'll get her to give you another name. Peaches... I might be out here, too, if I had to live with that. But on my honor, you'll be renamed as soon as my bare butt climbs back through that window with you."

Peaches flattened his ears. Te-bloody-rrific. That wasn't a good sign.

Simon was almost there...just a few more inches...

"I'm going to step over you, you know, to get to the other side."

Simon sucked in a deep breath. It was do or die and he didn't like door number two. He raised his right foot and stepped over the cat, which left him straddling Peaches on the ledge, somewhat spread-eagled but at least he could hold on to the window frame and screen of Tawny's next-door neighbor.

He glanced down at the cat. The cat looked up at

Simon. Or, more specifically, parts of him. Peaches eyed Simon's willy dangling in the wind with a wicked gleam in his kitty eyes, as if he'd just discovered a newfangled cat toy.

"Don't even think about it." Simon cupped a protective hand over Mr. Winky.

Suddenly an older woman appeared in the window.

"Pervert!" she yelled.

She yanked her window shade down, in his face.

Startled, Simon teetered. He dug his fingers into the window frame. Whoa!

Steady. Steady.

Only in New York.

He recentered and lifted his left foot over the cat. Whew! He unhanded the family jewels. Now for the really scary part—as if he hadn't been scared witless up to this point.

"I'm going to pick you up in this towel. Here's the tricky part. I need for you to be really still or I'm going to lose my balance and we're both going to splat—not a good ending."

He shifted the towel from his shoulder to his hands.

"Easy, there. Just remember, you get a new name. Something cool. Something macho. Something badass to go with your image." While he talked, he leaned down and oh-so-carefully wrapped the cat in the towel. "Stay cool. We're just a minute away from you having a new lease on life and me still *having* a life."

Amazingly Peaches offered no resistance and didn't squirm when he tucked him beneath his arm football-style. Simon had no idea how long it took—it felt like hours—but he continued to talk trash and edge toward Tawny's window. Finally he handed the cat through the window. Tawny snatched The Cat Who'd Earned a New Name and clutched him to her. Simon used his free hand to grip the edge of the open window.

"Do you need help getting in?" Tawny asked.

"Just give me some room." Simon climbed in feet-first.

With solid flooring beneath him and the windowsill behind him, his knees began to shake. Being confined by four walls had never felt so good! He turned around, slammed the window closed and locked it. They'd roast like swine in hell before he opened that window again.

He turned around just as Peaches…er, Him…lost his patience for being held, leaped out of Tawny's arms and shot into the other room.

He still hadn't recovered his breath when Tawny rounded on him, her eyes flashing, her hair sticking out at odd angles, as if she'd been in a brawl and it'd been nearly pulled out.

"That was the most stupid, idiotic thing I've ever seen," she yelled.

Huh? "What the hell? How about a thank-you?"

"Thank you? Thank you?" Her voice escalated with each *thank you,* which he really hadn't thought was possible. "I should *thank you* when you could've died out there, you idiot?" She flew at him and pummeled him on the chest. "You could've fallen. I was so scared. And you were naked. And you could've died."

God, she was nearly hysterical over *him.* He caught her wrists and tried not to hurt her. "Shh. Shh. It's okay. I'm okay. I'm fine. You're fine. We're fine."

We? Where had that come from?

She leaned her head against his chest. He ran his hand soothingly over her hair. She reached up and wrapped her arms around his neck, pulling him tighter, harder against her, as if she couldn't get close enough. "Never do anything like that again. I've never been so scared in my life. If you'd fallen…"

Her mouth latched on to his and she kissed him with all the passion aroused by fear and anger. She ground her mouth against his, unleashing his own post-window-ledge adrenaline surge. She waged war with her tongue. He kissed her back as if he was devouring her.

Dammit. He *could've* died out there. He hadn't been sure that he wouldn't until he'd slammed the window closed behind him. But he hadn't died and she was in his arms. And she cared, tremendously it would seem, that he'd risked his life.

They stumbled the few feet to the bed, both of them trying to eat the other alive. They fell to the mattress. This time Simon fished in the drawer for a condom, his hand shaking. He'd wanted her before, burned for her, dreamed of her, made love to her, but he'd never known anything like this—the overwhelming consuming need to bury himself so far and hard within her, to celebrate having come in off that ledge, to claim her.

While he put on the condom, she pulled off her panties and top and fell back, legs spread, sex glistening, ready.

"No. Roll over. On your knees."

She stayed on her back but closed her legs, a mutinous expression on her face. Wrong direction.

"No. Not until you blow out all the candles," she said.

She wasn't exactly the most logical woman he'd ever met. "But you're afraid of the dark."

"I'm even more afraid of how big my butt is. And

time's wasting." She reached out and wrapped her fingers around him and stroked.

Damn, it felt good, but he was made of sterner stuff than that.

He pulled away from her and dropped to his knees beside the bed. She eyed him with suspicion and a fair measure of frustration.

"I'm here to worship at the altar of your magnificent to-die-for bum. Why do you really think I crawled out on that ledge? For the cat? So that I could gaze into your green eyes afterward? So you could try to beat the bloody hell out of me when I completed my mission? Oh, no, luv. I climbed out there for this." He stroked the curve of her magnificent bottom and sank his hands into her cheeks. She looked torn between laughing and smacking him, but luckily she still had that I-want-to-screw-your-brains-out glint in her eyes.

"I said it earlier, this—" he stroked the curve of her rear "—could bring men to their knees. See. I'm on my knees. And I'd like you on your knees, in as much light as possible so I can enjoy not just the feel and the taste but the sight of this fine masterpiece in action."

He wasn't giving up on this. Not only was every word true—he wanted to see her jiggle and wiggle while he pumped into her from behind—but he also wanted her to get over this self-consciousness, wanted her to realize her behind was a cause for celebration, not something to hide in the dark and make derogatory comments about.

He nuzzled the soft flesh in question. Fully convinced actions spoke louder than words, he devoted himself to showing her how much he appreciated her assets. He took his time kissing…licking…sucking his way across her sweet terrain. She rewarded him with low moans of appreciation, squirming against his mouth.

He was on fire for her—he did have a major attachment to her rear and the musky scent of her arousal was maddening, the moisture seeping between her nether lips.... He culled a taste of her sweet nectar with his tongue.

"Simon..."

He looked at her flushed face from his vantage point between her thighs.

"Would you really deny me something that would make me so happy?"

Panting, frantic, hot, she rolled over so quickly it took him by surprise. He got to his feet and she was already on her knees, legs spread, her rounded cheeks thrust in the air, her bare sex glistening a wet invitation.

"You're driving me crazy. We'll do it your way. But just do it." She looked at him over her shoulder and slapped one full, luscious cheek. "If this is what you want, mount up and ride 'em, cowboy!"

Bloody right—he was a cowboy on a pilgrimage. Simon climbed on the bed behind her. He skimmed one finger between her cheeks. "I've approached the temple of the divine. May I enter?"

"Dammit, Simon. It's just not right for you to make me laugh when you've made me so horny."

He slid his condom-covered erection along her slick channel and rubbed it against her clit. "I'd like to offer up my sacrifice."

She thrust back against him and he finished the job, plunging into her, his hands grasping her hips.

"Yessss," she cried. "I'm happy. Are you happy now?"

She was hot and tight, and he settled into the rhythm of their ride and spoke while he was still capable of speech.

"No. I'm ecstatic."

"YOU WANT ME TO DO WHAT? Forget it. I'm not doing it," Tawny said and rolled to her back, huffing out her breath. Damnation, here she was feeling boneless and fabulous after really, really hot sex and now Simon had to go ruin it.

Simon rolled off the side of the bed, graceful, all leashed power and controlled muscles, and headed for the door. Annoyed with him or not, she'd be content to watch him walk around naked for a really long time—except he was walking out the door.

"Where are you going?" she asked.

"To get my camera."

"You need your camera to discuss this?"

"No. I need my camera to catch what you look like in a pout. Remember, I'm supposed to be capturing the real you."

"That was a jerk thing to say," she yelled after him.

"Sorry." Sorry, her well-ridden ass. He didn't sound sorry a bit. "It's my specialty," he called from the other room.

"What? Photography or being a jerk?" she muttered to herself, thoroughly put out with him.

"I heard that." He reappeared in the door, wearing his jeans but shirtless, camera around his neck. "Both."

"I'll second that."

He approached the bed, the camera whirring. She

tossed him a disgusted, haughty look, stuck her nose in the air and looked the other way.

"Perfect. Tawny in a sulk."

She whipped her head back around. "I am *not* in a sulk."

"Really? What would you call it?"

"Pissed. I'm pissed. You had no right to promise my cat I'd change his name. I love his name. You want to name a pet, go get one yourself," she said.

She could give a rat's patootie if she sounded rude. All her life she'd been told what to do, when to do it, how to do it. Finally she was on her own and she'd be damned if *anyone*—regardless how good he looked naked or how thoroughly he satisfied her in bed—was arbitrarily renaming her cat. Peaches was the first thing she'd ever had on her own that was all hers. Simon could stuff it.

"I was desperate. It was the only thing I could think of out there. And I gave him my word."

"Well, you should've checked with me first."

"What? I should've conducted negotiations from the window ledge, where I just happened to be hanging out naked?"

"There's no need for sarcasm, Simon."

"There's no need for irrationality, Tawny."

She *would* let that comment pass, 'cause the other option was to kill him. And to think she'd actually begun to like him. Ugh. He infuriated her.

"Did I ask you to go out there? No! In fact, I told you not to."

"You really thought I'd let *you* go out there?"

Tawny couldn't recall ever sputtering before in her life, ever being so spitting mad she couldn't verbally express herself. Not even that lifetime ago when she'd found out Elliott had swung to the other side.

"Uh…uh…you…you…absolute macho…do you think just because you're a man that you're braver?"

"Brave?" He threw back his head and laughed, but it didn't sound as if he was particularly amused. "Bravery had nothing to do with it. I was so bloody scared I couldn't see straight out there. And you can hang up the macho thing because Mr. Macho wouldn't admit that."

"And *I'm* irrational? Ha! If you were scared, why didn't you just let me go?"

"Because I couldn't… It just seemed like the thing to do."

He walked out of the bedroom. Typical male to just walk away in the middle of a conversation that wasn't going his way.

Tawny yanked on her panties and tank top and marched down the hall after him.

"Well, there's an explanation. That really clears it up for me. Thank you," she said.

"Can't you ever just drop anything?" Simon sat on the couch.

If he thought he could get rid of her or shut her up by holing up in this claustrophobic little den…well, he was wrong. She plopped down on the other end of the sofa.

"No, Simon, I can't. So shoot me if I like a little logic in my life."

"Righto! You're not exactly the most logical woman I ever met."

He *must* be kidding! That's rich—especially coming from a man who climbed out naked on a window ledge and promised to change my cat's name—without my permission, I might add—because it seemed like the thing to do. Oh, yeah. You're the king of logic."

"You want logic? Try this on. I went out there because if I didn't, you would, and I couldn't bear it if something happened to you." He snapped his mouth shut, as if he'd said too much. And well, really, he'd just said a lot.

Simon had gone out there because he was worried about *her?* Warmth that had nothing to do with sex and everything to do with emotion suffused her. It hadn't been all about him—making him look brave and macho. His climbing out on the ledge had been about *her.*

"Oh," she said rather dumbly.

"So I'm sorry that you're annoyed, but I promised him a new name."

Simon wasn't just a control freak intent on running her business. Guilt displaced her anger. "Maybe I did overreact just a little to all of that."

"Maybe you did. How would you like to be this big, bad-attitude cat with a name like Peaches?" He shuddered.

Really, he didn't have to sound so disdainful and he could drop the theatrics. "It's not as if I single-handedly emasculated him."

Simon reached along the back of the sofa and trailed his fingers along her shoulder. "No. The vet helped, but that name does a fine job."

"Okay. Let's hear you do better. Whatcha got?"

"Sorry?" His blank look struck her as rather comical and cute. She didn't think Simon often looked blank.

"Names," she prompted. "It was your idea. *You* come up with a name for him."

"It's your cat."

"According to some ancient cultures, since you saved his life, he essentially belongs to you now."

"But I don't want him." He looked horrified at the prospect.

"I'm not literally giving him to you. Think figuratively. I'm giving you the task of naming him."

"But I don't want to."

"Tough. You promised him a new name…so give him one."

"But I don't know anything about naming animals."

She rolled her eyes. God. He was sexy and insane and exasperating. "What do you mean you don't know how to name an animal? You just do it. Haven't you ever had a pet?"

He crossed his arms over his chest. "No."

He was pulling her leg. "No cats, dogs, gerbils, guinea pigs when you were growing up?"

"No."

She moved down the pet chain to a group she didn't exactly consider petworthy. You just couldn't cuddle a reptile. "Not even a lizard or snake or…maybe a frog?"

"No pets."

A lightbulb lit up in her head. "Let me guess…your parents."

"They weren't into pets."

Tawny ground her teeth, endangering thousands of dollars of orthodontia her parents had sunk into her pearly whites. What kind of people emotionally ne glected their kid and to top it off denied him a pet? Even the very proper Edwards household had included a dog, a hamster and several goldfish over the years. A frog would've been better than nothing. "Let me guess again. A pet would be too much trouble?"

"Righto."

"I really dislike your parents." She ached to give them a piece of her mind.

Simon looked startled, as if surprised she'd take exception with his parents on his behalf. Then he grinned. *Wow!* He should grin more often.

"Don't worry," he said, "they wouldn't be charmed by you either. You're too…unleashed for them."

"Unleashed? I like that." And she'd be frightened if those people *did* like her. "Don't think you're weaseling out of renaming Peaches. You either name him or he will forever be Peaches and you'll have reneged on your promise."

"You're a hard woman, Tawny Edwards."

"Humph. I'm just forcing you to put your…whatever…where your mouth is."

"Brutus." He smirked.

"Uh-uh. I can't live with a cat named Brutus. Try again."

"Magnus." An even bigger smirk.

Okay. She'd play his game…and beat him at it. "Forget it. I just had a stroke of genius. And it is a stroke of genius if you consider how ornery and standoffish and generally difficult he is. Instead of you naming him, I'll name him for you."

"Fine with me. What's his new name?" The smirk gave way to trepidation. He should be leery.

"Simon. I'm naming him after you."

"Didn't you just mention ornery and contrary and generally difficult?"

"Exactly. If the shoe fits…"

Oddly enough, Simon didn't appear leery or confounded or in the least put out. Who'd have thought it? The crazy man looked extremely pleased at having a cat named after him.

"HE SEEMS HAPPY WITH THE new name. What do you think?" Tawny said.

Simon the cat, formerly known as Peaches, sat atop the refrigerator, eyes closed, patently ignoring them. Simon the man thought Tawny was crazy, totally irrational and altogether adorable. "I'd say he's beside himself."

Tawny shook her head and sent him a chastising look. "I know him better than you do and I say he's happy."

"Whatever you say. I promised him a macho name and I'm fairly certain Simon doesn't fall into that category," he argued, knowing it was futile.

Tawny laughed and Simon mentally took a snapshot. He wanted to remember this moment forever. They were engaged in a totally inane conversation in her oven of a kitchen with no electricity and he couldn't recall ever feeling happier than he did at this moment.

"Like Magnus was boss? Yeah."

"You know, you could give a guy a complex," he said.

"Better watch out or you might turn out gay like Elliott," she said, obviously joking but obviously still smarting from Elliott's revelation.

"Not a remote possibility. I know you're having me on, but Elliott's sexual preference is no reflection on you." He smiled and allowed himself to look at her with the familiarity of a well-satisfied lover. "I know firsthand."

She stood on tiptoe and brushed her lips against his cheek, her hand resting lightly on his shoulder. "Thanks. Whether you like to admit it or not, you're really a very nice man."

Her tenderness shook him. "Didn't you call me a jerk not too long ago?"

"They're not mutually exclusive. You can be that, too."

The way she looked at him—as if he'd hung the moon—left his mouth dry and his heart pounding. She was wrong. She might think she knew him, but she didn't. He was 99 percent jerk 99 percent of the time. She was rebounding big-time and painting him to be someone he wasn't.

"You're going to have to talk to Elliott, Tawny."

"Technically I don't have to do anything…but I suppose I will."

"You'll need closure on it or you'll be tracking him down because you'll have that Prozac addiction," he said. She was too easy to be with. Too easy to tease.

"You know me too well." She threw a dish towel at his head.

He caught it one-handed. "You seem to be handling it well."

"I'm not prone to hysterics."

He quirked an eyebrow, recalling the scene she'd made when he'd come back through the window earlier. She'd verged on hysteria. Over him. He was still reeling.

"Okay. Well, thinking you're about to see someone you care—know—die, that's a little different. But as a rule I don't get hysterical." She looked him over from head to toe, her gaze lingering at the front of his trousers. "And you've definitely helped ease my rejection pain."

"Glad to be of service." And he'd be up for more service if she didn't stop eyeing his crotch that way.

"You may think, *yeah, right,* but I'm almost relieved. Not that Elliott's gay and not that he decided to screw around on me—that's a little tough to take—but I think both of us knew something wasn't working. And then when I started having those dreams about you…well, it does sort of make a girl think she's not quite ready to tie the knot."

He was still floored he'd been the object of this woman's fantasy—even if she had been unconscious at the time.

"Dreams are a pretty iffy indicator," he said. "Would you have called it off if Elliott hadn't gotten involved with someone else?"

She considered his question for a few seconds, her lips pursed, before she pushed her hair back from her face. "I don't know. Probably. Hopefully. I don't hate him, although I came pretty close when you told me. I'm less than impressed with his cheating and then dumping it on you to tell me."

"Do you still love him? You obviously did at one point." The question tied his belly in knots.

"I'm not sure." She nudged the spot on her finger where her ring had been with her thumb. He was sure she didn't realize what she was doing. "I did love him. Actually I think when I'm over being so pissed, I still do." His stomach plummeted. "But I don't love him the way I should to marry him. We have fun together, but there's no real passion between us—" her gaze snared him, trapped him with the banked fires within their depth "—no intensity. Do you know what I mean?"

He looked away before she saw the answering fire in his eyes. "The mention of his name ties you up in knots? You'd go to hell and back again if you thought he needed you? The sound of his voice sends shivers through you? I know exactly what you mean."

"Elliott and I don't have that."

Granted, she was a grown woman and could make her own decisions. But at one point she'd been sure enough to agree to marry Elliott. He knew firsthand she could be wildly emotional and illogical and he didn't want to see her make a decision she'd later regret.

"Passion doesn't last. It burns out and evolves into something else altogether," he said, playing devil's advocate.

"I'm not naive. I don't think people still have that after twenty years. Or—who knows?—maybe they do. But you should definitely have it in the beginning. Love shouldn't be totally comfortable, like an old pair of slippers. It should be like a pair of stilettos—sexy and exciting and worth the discomfort. And if that's what Elliott's found, more power to him." She shrugged and smiled.

Her smile was so her—natural, irrepressible, sunny—he couldn't help smiling in return.

"That's an original. I've never heard love compared to a pair of stilettos."

"I didn't realize I felt this way until…well, I think it started with those dreams, and now this with Elliott has forced me to reevaluate everything. And I can't help it if you think I'm being tacky when I say the sex between us, you and me, has been pretty incredible."

He'd have to be dead or stupid not to feel a surge of male pride that he'd rocked her world to a degree that Elliott obviously hadn't. He was fairly sure he wore the village idiot's grin. "It has been, hasn't it?"

"While we're discussing Elliott...I want you to know I have no intention of mentioning what happened tonight to him...you know...us."

That wiped the grin off his face. "Because you're ashamed?"

"No." She shot him a look that said he knew better. "Because he's your friend and I don't want to come between you. But even more than that, because I don't want you to think I slept with you to get back at him. I slept with you because you drove me crazy in my dreams and then when you got here...it was even worse."

"Worse?"

"You know what I mean. The sound of your voice, the touch of your hands on my shoulders, your scent." All the hallmarks of passion.

She aroused him without even touching him. And there was only one logical response to that.

Simon backed her up against the counter and kissed her.

9

TAWNY RAN HER HANDS OVER Simon's sweat-slicked chest. Making out had definitely raised her temperature, but it was like a furnace in the kitchen.

Something she'd read in a magazine once and filed for future reference came to mind. Now seemed like the perfect time to try it.

"How about a Popsicle? If the electricity's off much longer they're going to melt anyway. At least it'll be cool."

He moved so that she was no longer wedged between the counter and his hard—and some parts getting harder—body. "Sure. I haven't had a Popsicle in years."

"I keep them stocked when it's this hot. Sort of a sweet fix without all the calories." She opened the freezer and pulled out a box. "Great. They're still frozen. Cherry, strawberry or grape?"

"Definitely cherry."

She passed one to him. "That's my favorite, too."

She returned the box to the freezer.

She'd told him it would cool him down—but not

before she heated him up. She peeled off the wrapper. Slowly, making a sensual production of it, she licked up one side and down the other. "Mmm." Looking up at him, she deliberately took the Popsicle into her mouth and sucked, moving her head up and down over the frozen treat. She moaned in the back of her throat.

Simon stood transfixed, clutching his Popsicle in his hand. "I'm not sure I can watch you eat that without having a heart attack." He leaned against the counter, as if he was equally unsure his legs would support him.

Tawny smiled and nibbled at the tip. She was really getting off on how much she was turning him on. Turning both of them on. She slid her tank top down over her shoulders and pulled the front down, freeing her breasts. "Well, then, how does this work for you?" She trailed the Popsicle over her nipples. The icy cold felt incredible against her skin, the sensation shooting through her. "Wow! Guaranteed to cool you down quick."

Simon made a choked noise. "Tawny..."

There was a definite bulge straining the front of his jeans.

"Want to take our treat to the bedroom? I think it might be more comfortable in there." And she had no intention of having Popsicle sex—or any other sex, for that matter—in front of her cat. She snagged a bowl.

"Let's go." He grabbed her hand and damn near dragged her down the hall and into the bedroom.

"Mmm. I like a man with enthusiasm."

"You and your Popsicle have definitely aroused my *enthusiasm*," he said.

Laughing, she scooped up the towel he'd worn out

onto the ledge from the floor, spread it on the bed and sat down on the edge.

Simon reached for her and she backed him off. "Enthusiasm's one thing, but impatience is another. It's not time yet. We've only begun to enjoy our Popsicles."

She trailed it back over her nipples—God, it did feel incredible—and then over her belly and across the tops of her thighs.

"Luv, please…"

She felt like such a wicked woman. And she loved it. She was dripping wet and it wasn't sweat. "I can tell you where I really need cooling down…."

She lay back, leaning on one elbow, and spread her legs. She propped one foot up on the mattress, leaving herself open, giving Simon a visual of just how wet she was already.

"Tawny…" Simon said, part groan and all appreciation. His low, faintly accented voice slid over her, arousing her even more.

The kiss of the ice against her inner thigh zinged through her. Slowly she rimmed the frozen treat along her vagina, the sensation deliciously arousing.

She felt thoroughly wicked and thoroughly excited. She eased the melting Popsicle in and twirled it around.

"Ooh." It was hard and icy and she was so hot. Simon never looked away from her as he unzipped and took off his pants. She worked the melting ice in and out and licked her lips.

Simon walked over to the edge of the bed. "Suck on mine." She was so close, she could've come with very little effort when he used that erotic, commanding tone. He teased it along her lips and then slid it into her mouth. She moved the icy-cold Popsicle in and out of her vagina and he matched the rhythm in her mouth.

Tawny wasn't sure that she'd ever been so turned on in her life. She was so hot inside, she was melting the Popsicle in record time, deliciously cold against her inferno. And the look on Simon's face…

She slid her mouth off his Popsicle and licked leisurely down the length of it. "You look hot—" she eyed his straining erection "—and uncomfortable. I've got just the thing to cool you down. Cold on the surface, hot inside."

Simon didn't need a second invite. He rolled on a condom and in one smooth stroke he was in.

"Oh my God." Tawny wasn't sure which one of them said it. Maybe both. Maybe neither. Had anything ever felt as good as his hot cock against her icy-cold flesh? Hot and cold. Hard and soft.

It felt too good…she was so hot…she wasn't going to last any longer.

Popsicle sex with Simon—guaranteed to come in three minutes or less.

SIMON STARTLED AWAKE. It took him a second to figure out his cell phone was ringing in his pants somewhere on the dark floor. He slung his legs over the side of the bed and reached down, groping for his jeans.

By the time he found them, he'd missed the call. He glanced at his watch. Who the hell was calling him at this hour in the morning?

Tawny leaned up on one arm. "Hmm. Who's on the phone?"

"I'm checking now." He listened to his voice mail. "Simon, it's your father. Call me back at…wait, you can't call me here." He'd hung up. What the— His parents never called him.

"It was my dad," Simon said to Tawny, who had sat up, wide-awake now. "First he asked me to call him back and then he said I couldn't call him where he was. But I'm going to try anyway." Apprehension flooded him. Whatever this was, it couldn't be good.

Before he could hit Send to call the number shown on the display, his phone rang again. Same number flashed across the screen.

Simon answered. "Dad?"

"Simon, thank God you answered. I'm at City North Hospital. We think your mother's had a heart attack."

His father's words struck him like a physical blow. He sank to the edge of the bed. "Where is she now?"

"Here at City North."

"No." Simon bit back his impatience. "Is she in ICU?"

"No. They're running an EKG in the emergency room and checking her enzymes. She needs for you to come, Simon." There was a pregnant pause. "I need for you to come."

Simon didn't hesitate. For better or worse, they were his parents. They were all each of them had. "I'll be there. It may take me a while, but I'm on my way. I'll have my cell with me. Call me if anything changes."

He hung up. In a detached, remote way, as if observing another person, he noticed his hands were shaking.

"What is it? What's the matter?"

"My mother's had a heart attack." Speaking the words aloud left him nauseous. He dropped to the edge of the bed, uncertain his legs would support him.

"Oh, Simon." Tawny hugged him from behind, her

arms offering comfort from one human being to another. "Which hospital?"

"City North."

She released him and got out of the bed. She yanked open a dresser drawer and stepped into a pair of running shorts. Simon pulled on his jeans and T-shirt. Without any self-consciousness she pulled off her tank top and donned a heavy-duty exercise bra.

"What are you doing?" he asked.

"What does it look like I'm doing? I'm getting dressed. City North is northwest of here. I don't have a car and I don't know if we can find a cab at this time in the morning, but we could run it—" she glanced to where he sat on the edge of the bed lacing his Doc Martens "—if you think you can in those boots. Unfortunately none of my shoes would fit you."

"We?"

A few quick brushstrokes and she pulled her hair up into a ponytail. She looked at him in the dresser mirror. "I'm coming with you."

"That's not necessary." He stood and tucked in his shirt, zipped his pants.

"Yes, it is." She pulled on a running singlet.

"What if I don't want you to come?"

"Are you telling me you don't want me there?"

The trouble was, it frightened him just how much he *did* want her there. Scary how easy it was to want to lean on her when he'd stood alone so long on his own. And what did it matter whether he actually wanted her there or not? He knew Tawny. She'd be there regardless.

"Oh, hell. Come if you want to," he said.

"You're so gracious, Simon." She pressed a quick

kiss to his cheek. "But I forgive you. I know you're worried about your mom."

She buzzed around the room, pulling a small canister out of her seemingly bottomless bedside table and clipping it to her waistband. "Mace. A girl should never leave home without it." She shoved her feet into trainers and laced them up in quick order.

She stopped and looked at him. "You ready?"

"Yeah. You're sure you know where we're going?" He wanted to be there now.

"Positive. I've got a great sense of direction."

"That's good. I have no sense of direction." Simon lit a small votive and blew out the triple-wicked big boy. Votive in hand, he led the way to the front door. Tawny blew out the two candles she'd previously left burning in the den. Her apartment felt like an oven. They hadn't even started their run and sweat beaded his skin.

She joined him at the door, clipping on her cell phone. "Just blow it out and leave it here. It'll slow us down too much in the stairwell."

He grabbed her and pressed a quick kiss to her surprised mouth. She was scared to death of the dark, but she didn't want to slow him down in getting to his mother.

"You're one hell of a woman, Tawny Edwards. Let's keep it lit for the first set of stairs, so we can count how many are from landing to landing. Then if it goes out, we can count our way down in the dark."

"Sounds like a plan." They stepped out into the hallway and she dead-bolted the door behind them. "The stairwell's this way."

She grabbed his free hand and led him down the dark hall. Simon opened the heavy door beneath the dark Exit sign. The door slammed shut behind them, leaving them in the dank, cool and eerie quiet of the stairwell.

Simon gripped Tawny's hand even tighter. God, she must hate this. And it was about to get worse.

"Ready?" His voice bounced back at them.

"Let's do it."

He counted aloud as they went down one floor. Only six floors left to go. The candle had flickered precariously several times on the way down the last set of stairs and they hadn't even been moving that fast. It would take them forever at this rate.

Tawny stopped him on the sixth-floor landing. "Just blow it out, Simon."

"Are you sure?"

She took a deep breath. "You'll hold on to my hand?"

"I promise I won't let go of you, no matter what happens."

"Then let's move out." She leaned around him and blew out the votive, pitching them into absolute blackness. According to fire code, emergency exit lights should've shown up over the doorways. Obviously Tawny's building had compliance issues.

They made their way tentatively at first and then fell into a rhythm. Simon counted aloud, his voice echoing, but he thought it was some measure of comfort to Tawny to hear his voice and hold his hand in the inky black. Soon enough they'd reached the first floor. It hadn't taken long at all, but it had probably felt like a lifetime to Tawny, judging by her clammy hand.

Muggy heat assaulted them the moment they stepped out of the building. A few quiet voices drifted down from rooftops and fire escapes, and somewhere down the block a woman laughed. In the far distance a horn honked. The earlier party atmosphere had definitely dissipated.

"It's like a fairy tale where a spell's been cast, isn't it?" she asked, dropping into a lunge to stretch.

Simon moved through his own prerun stretches. He knew exactly what she meant. The city that never slept lay about them in uneasy slumber.

"It's like the proverbial sleeping giant, isn't it?" he said.

"Exactly. Listen, I know you're anxious to get there, but remember it's six miles. Let's pace it. I believe she's going to be fine, Simon. At least she's at the hospital and in good hands."

"You lead and I'll be right there with you."

Tawny headed east through the darkness toward New Jersey and Simon followed. At the corner, where a flower shop stood in silent bloom, she turned north. Simon reminded himself to match her stride. They ran in companionable silence for several blocks, only passing a few cars and the occasional pedestrian.

He needed this, to run, to push himself. Inside he was a mess. So he wasn't close to his parents. In many ways their relationship bordered on hostile. But he didn't want anything to happen to his mother. She wasn't exactly a nurturer, but he hadn't exactly tried to reach out to them either. At least, not in a long time. He'd summarily ignored their occasional overtures in the past couple of years.

Running through the dark, silent streets, he gave voice to the emotions racking his soul. Tawny would understand.

"I shouldn't feel this resentment. This situation should absolve it. I should let it go, Tawny, but I can't. Dammit, I can't let it go. It's always been the two of them, with me on the outside looking in. They had each other and I had my resentment. It was my companion during my childhood and while I was a teenager. All these years I've nurtured it, embraced it, and I can't abandon it now. But the really crazy part is, I love her so desperately...." He trailed off, conflicted, close to weeping.

"Of course you do. She's your mother. And you can resent the hell out of both of them, but it doesn't mean you don't love them. It's our job to be screwed up by our parents. They screwed us up. We'll screw our kids up. It's one of those unwritten laws of nature. But it doesn't mean they don't love you and it doesn't mean you don't love them."

Her words soothed his troubled soul as the night's oppressive heat absorbed the rhythmic pounding of their feet. Simon ignored the biting sting of a blister on his left heel. Doc Martens weren't optimal running footwear. Amazing how just talking to her made him feel better.

"How'd you get to be so smart?" he asked.

Her answer was lost when a spotlight fixed on them and a voice rang out.

"Stop. Police."

Tawny stumbled and Simon caught her arm, steadying her. They stopped and stood on the sidewalk, sides heaving, waiting.

Blinded by the light, they only heard the slam of a car door and approaching footsteps. "What seems to be the hurry? Kind of odd to be running in the middle of the night dressed all in black? You running from something or someone in particular?"

Piss if he needed some cop with a bad attitude. Didn't this guy have anything better to do? "Don't you have anything—"

Tawny stepped on his foot and cut him off. "Morning, Officer." Her Southern drawl rolled out, thick and sweet as molasses. "We're on our way to City North Hospital. Simon's mother's had a heart attack. I don't have a car and no cabs are out, so we've run all the way." Tawny smiled at the officer, who remained a faceless silhouette against the blinding light. "I know it looks odd, but Simon didn't have any running clothes at my apartment, which is why he's running in all black."

"Where are you from?"

Jesus, it was an ungodly hour, hotter than hell, they were in the middle of a blackout and this guy—this *cop*—was flirting with her. Give him a break.

"Savannah, originally."

"Ah, a Georgia peach."

Tawny laughed, that warm, husky laugh that crawled over his skin and turned him inside out. "And you sound like a New York boy."

"Born and raised. Hey, whaddaya say I give the two of you a ride to the hospital?"

Earlier she'd accused Simon of being macho, and really he never had been. But now he had the overwhelming urge to tell this guy to take his ride and shove it up...

"That'd be lovely. We'd really appreciate getting to the hospital as quickly as possible. Wouldn't we, Simon?" She stepped on his foot again.

"Uh, yeah. The sooner the better."

"I'm afraid you'll both have to sit in the back." The cop gave Tawny a look of apology. "Regulations. Only a badge can sit up front."

"The back is fine." She stepped over the uneven sidewalk and tugged Simon toward the car. New York's own Dudley Do-Right opened the rear door. Tawny offered him a smile that probably curled his insides. It would've curled Simon's if it'd been directed at him. "This is so nice of you," she said, climbing in the back, her running shorts hugging every delicious curve of her sweet bottom. And yeah, the dickhead wearing the badge noticed. Simon crawled into the backseat behind her. A steel cage separated them from the front. He'd never been in a police cruiser before. The radio squawked and the officer relayed his twenty—his location—and where he was heading.

Tawny held fast to Simon's hand while she carried on a conversation with Dan Berthold, their officer-chauffeur. With the streets virtually deserted, Officer Berthold didn't seem to mind breaking the law he was sworn to uphold, and within minutes they pulled up to the hospital that stood like a beacon of light in a surrounding sea of dark.

"Would you mind dropping us at the E.R.?" Tawny asked.

"No problem." Berthold swung around to the emergency-room entrance, threw the car in Park and jumped out to open the back door.

Simon didn't miss the way the cop eyed Tawny's legs as she climbed out. Simon quelled the urge to knock him flat. Assaulting an officer who'd just delivered him to his mother seemed a bad idea—even if he deserved it for looking at Tawny like that.

Tawny shook Berthold's hand. "Thank you so much. I know why you're called New York's finest."

"You want me to wait? I could wait."

"That's really sweet, but we don't know how long we'll be. Thanks so much."

"My pleasure." Berthold turned to Simon. "Hope she's okay, man." He held out a hand.

Simon took his proffered hand and shook it. Maybe the guy wasn't so bad after all. He hadn't really hit on Tawny and they had arrived a hell of a lot faster than running. "Thanks for the ride."

"Anytime." With a final appreciative glance at Tawny's derriere in her running shorts, Berthold got in his car and left.

"He had the hots for you."

Tawny rolled her eyes at him. "He got us here fifteen minutes earlier than if we'd run the whole way." She started toward the double doors. "Come on. When we get inside, don't worry about me. I'll wait in the lobby."

Simon stopped on the sidewalk outside the wide emergency-room doors. "No. I want you to come with me."

"I don't mind waiting in the lobby. I don't want to intrude."

He skimmed the line of her jaw with the back of his hand, needing to touch her, admitting what didn't come easily to him. "I'd really like for you to come with me."

She turned her cheek into his touch. "Then I'll go with you." She took his hand in hers. "Let's go find your mother."

They stepped into utter, overwhelming chaos, bright fluorescent lights—all the brighter after the dark—and the cool bliss of air-conditioning. Simon glanced around, at a loss as to where to go. Tawny dragged him behind her. "What's your mother's name?"

"Letitia. Letitia Marbury. She didn't take my dad's name when they married. Dr. Letitia Marbury."

Tawny marched up to a desk. Within minutes her smile and Southern charm had elicited his mother's location.

Tawny put her hand on his arm. "You go on up. I'd like to freshen up."

"I'll wait." Now that he was here he didn't want to go up, fear at exactly what he'd find stalling him.

"No. Go on up. You need a few minutes alone with them. I'll meet you there in ten minutes." She pressed a kiss to his cheek and pushed him in the general direction of the elevator bank. His sweat-soaked T-shirt chilled beneath the blast of air-conditioning. "I promise I'll be right up." She touched his arm. "Go on, Simon, she's waiting for you."

10

ONCE SIMON DISAPPEARED through the swinging double doors, Tawny headed for the exit. She followed two EMTs wheeling an empty gurney out the door. Ugh. The heat was even worse, coming out of the air-conditioning. She went from cool to sticky and sweaty in about two seconds flat.

She tried to ignore the strands of hair that had escaped her ponytail and lay plastered against her neck, and hauled out her cell phone. Cell-phone usage in an emergency room was one big no-no. She blew out her breath. She wanted to make this call about as much as she wanted another hole in her head. Double not.

She hit the speed-dial number.

He answered on the second ring. "Tawny?"

She jumped in without preamble. "We're at City North Hospital. Simon's mother's had a heart attack. You need to get here as quick as you can." She paced the sidewalk, past a couple sharing a bench and a cigarette.

"But I'm locked in at the gallery," Elliott protested.

"Then get unlocked. Didn't you hear what I just

said? Simon's mother's had a heart attack. He needs you. Here. Now."

"I don't know if—"

Elliott exhausted her patience. "*I know.* I know your very best friend in the world needs you now more than he ever has, and if you have to blow the damned door off the hinges, you better haul your butt down here pronto." An ambulance, lights flashing but siren silent, pulled up to the double doors. "Don't make me come get you, Elliott."

"Tawny—"

"Elliott, I'm not playing with you. If I have to, I *will* come and drag you out of there."

"Hold on a sec."

The back door of the ambulance opened and they wheeled out one very pregnant Hispanic woman. Very pregnant. Very distressed. Now there was something to be thankful for—that she wasn't *that* woman.

Muffled conversation came through the line and then Elliott was back on the phone.

"Richard's coming with me," Elliott said, defiance ringing in his voice.

Whatever. "I don't care if you drag in the whole rainbow coalition, just get here."

"But there aren't any cabs out and the subway's dead."

"Elliott, you're a New Yorker, for God's sake. Walk."

"Be reasonable, Tawny. I'm wearing my Bruno Ms."

If one more man told her to be reasonable tonight... Tawny barely held on to her temper. She wasn't at her most patient when running, literally, on maybe an hour of sleep. "Elliott, I know how fond you are of those shoes and I will personally pay to have them resoled.

Now listen to me and listen good. Pretend you aren't the center of the universe. Pretend you care as much about your friend as you do those damn shoes. You put Simon in a helluva position tonight and he covered for you. I don't care if you have to crawl, get here. You've got one hour to show up. I swear to you, if you don't, I will make your life a living hell."

"All right. I'm on my way."

His petulance didn't further endear him.

"And Elliott…"

"Yes?"

"Don't bitch about the shoes when you get here."

She hung up, fairly certain Elliott would drag in within the hour. Nagging him to come through for his friend hadn't been nearly as effective as promising him a life of misery if he was a no-show. And Elliott knew she would.

Tawny turned off her cell and made her way back through the sea of humanity lining the emergency room.

She ducked into a bathroom. Ugh. She hated public toilets. She wrinkled her nose at the antiseptic smell. Must be a prerequisite for hospitals that they use the cleanser with the nauseating stench. Why'd the urge to pee always strike at the most inopportune times?

She did her business and then stood in front of the sink washing her hands. Ew. She was positively frightening. No makeup. Sweaty. Scraggly, greasy hair. Dark circles from lack of sleep. She'd undoubtedly scare small children. She splashed cold water on her face and repaired her hair as best she could, but she still wasn't winning any beauty pageants tonight.

She left the bathroom behind and navigated the labyrinthine halls to the elevator bank. City North was clean and boasted a reputation for excellent care, but it was one of the older hospitals in the city and its elevators ran slowly. Eventually she reached the fourth floor, a relatively quiet hall that wasn't part of Intensive Care—a very good sign for Simon's mom that she was well enough to warrant a regular room. Two nurses sat engrossed in conversation behind the nurses'-station desk. Tawny followed the sign directing her left to the room number they'd been given downstairs.

Her rubber soles squelched on the spotless tile as she walked down the hall.

A distinguished-looking man who bore a striking resemblance to Simon stood outside the door. A little taller than Simon, gray hair, clipped goatee, chinos, a short-sleeved button-down and thick fisherman sandals. Distinguished didn't impress her. Her father and his colleagues were all distinguished and it didn't make them any more or less decent human beings than anyone else.

Tawny drew a deep breath. She needed to ditch the attitude. It wouldn't do anyone any good. This wasn't about her. She was here to support Simon, not mix it up with his parents. So this man hadn't exactly been the father of the year for Simon, but he was still his father. And Simon, despite their history and their obvious shortcomings as parents—definitely just her opinion—cared for them.

They were his parents, regardless of the fact that Simon deserved better ones. Of course, Simon could really use a better friend than Elliott, who'd needed intimidation to bring him here. Simon was sweet and tender and one of the finest men she'd ever met, and he deserved the very best life had to offer.

The man looked up as she approached, eyeing her blankly.

"Mr. Thackeray?" He nodded. "I'm Tawny Edwards, a friend of Simon's." She extended her hand and after a moment's hesitation he shook it.

"Very good. Very good. Charles Thackeray."

"How is Dr. Marbury?"

He passed a weary hand over his face. "Stable. She's resting comfortably now that Simon's here."

His obvious weariness dispelled some of her harbored animosity. Good parent or bad parent, here was a man worried about the woman he loved.

"He ran almost six miles to get here." She thought he should know.

He looked taken aback. "He ran?"

"Yes. Ran. In boots. The cabs weren't running and I don't own a car. He was worried sick." She thought it best not to bring up being stopped by the police. Simon really could use a lesson or two in diplomacy. She'd known as sure as rain that he was about to mouth off at that cop, and the only place that would get them was possibly arrested. The only place worse than her apartment to be in a blackout.

"Oh. He didn't say."

Charles Thackeray struck her as an academic who immersed himself in other times and places and didn't invest much in the here and now.

"No. He wouldn't, would he?" she countered.

"No, I don't suppose he would. Always been a bit of a loner, our boy. And a little standoffish."

Tawny managed not to gape and literally bit her

tongue to keep from mouthing off about the pot calling the kettle black and the apple not falling far from the tree. Instead she contented herself with saying, "You just have to work a little harder to get to know him, but he's definitely worth the effort."

He looked at her as if she'd just expostulated a new scientific hypothesis but didn't comment.

"So it was definitely a heart attack?" she asked.

"Yes. Chest pains woke her around midnight. Letitia's one of the most sensible women I know. She didn't know if it was the heat, indigestion or a heart attack. Instead of ignoring it, she told me to bring her to the hospital. Said she'd rather be embarrassed if it was indigestion than dead if it wasn't. Very sensible woman."

"I've seen the statistics. A frightening number of women die unnecessarily each year from heart attacks because they wait too long to seek treatment or simply ignore the symptoms," Tawny said.

Apparently Charles Thackeray wasn't as together as he seemed. Tears welled in his eyes. *Great, Tawny. Make him cry by driving home how close his wife had come to dying.* She awkwardly patted his arm.

"I'm glad she's fine now."

Charles nodded. "Something in my eye. Yes, of course. Good thing she's such a sensible woman. Let's go in so she can meet you."

Tawny thought that since she'd opened her big mouth about dying that he really just needed to reassure himself that his wife was, indeed, okay.

"I'll just wait out here till Simon's through visiting with her."

"Nonsense. Simon will want to know you're here and I'm sure Letitia will want to meet you."

Short of making a big stink, which didn't seem the thing to do, Tawny had little choice but to allow him to usher her into the room ahead of him.

In a quick glance Tawny took in the situation. Simon stood to the right of the hospital bed, looking terribly uncomfortable and self-conscious. She checked out his mother.

She'd mentally prepared herself for a Gorgonesque creature. She was quite surprised at how...well, *normal* the woman in bed looked, even though she was hooked up to the telemetry machine. A chin-length bob of dark hair shot through with silver framed an angular, wan face and eyes the shape and color of Simon's.

"Letty, this is Tawny Edwards." He paused significantly and then continued, "She's here with Simon."

Without thinking, Tawny moved to stand beside Simon and took his hand in hers, more for her benefit than his. She didn't know why she was suffering this sudden attack of nerves.

"I'm so pleased to meet you." Letitia Thackeray's crisp British accent was far more pronounced than her husband's.

"It's nice to meet you, as well—" Tawny paused to smile "—although I wish it were under better circumstances." She shifted self-consciously. Her Southern accent came across as thick as molasses in contrast to Letitia's clipped tone. "How are you feeling?"

"I'm fine. A little glitch in the system, but I'm going to be right as rain." She looked from Tawny to Simon and back again.

Charles smiled at his wife. The tenderness that passed between them nearly took Tawny's breath. Charles nodded. "It's that way."

"What way?" Simon asked. No one answered him. Tawny had no idea what Charles was talking about either. It was as if Charles and Letitia shared their own language.

"Oh, wonderful." Letitia beamed at Tawny from her pillow. "Simon's never brought a girl home to meet us before."

Home to meet them? News flash: they weren't exactly sitting in a drawing room sipping tea and munching crumpets. And they'd totally misinterpreted her and Simon's relationship. Heck, she and Simon didn't *have* a relationship. Talk about a wrong impression. She tried to let go of Simon's hand.

"But—"

Instead of releasing her hand, Simon squeezed it and glanced at the monitor beeping by his mother's bed. All righty, then. For right now they had a relationship. And it was whatever his mother wanted it to be.

Tawny smiled at the bedridden woman and hoped her smile wasn't as weak as it felt. "Yes…well, I wish I was meeting you both under different circumstances."

"No, dear girl." This was moving fast—she was already a *dear girl.* "This is wonderful." Letitia lowered her voice and took on a confiding tone. "Charles and I had begun to worry that he might be a bit of a poofter. You know, gay."

This family had some serious communication issues.

Simon uttered a choking noise and his ears turned bright red. "Mum…"

"He's definitely not," Tawny blurted without thinking. *Oh, crud.* She shouldn't have said *that* in such a knowing tone. Not to his *parents.* She, Tawny Marianne Edwards, was zipping her lip until they got out of here. She wasn't saying another word.

Far from offended, they seemed pleased by her outburst. Charles winked at Letitia. "See, I told you it was that way."

Tawny glanced at Simon. She saw the kindness and integrity in his brown eyes, the endearing tinge of red still burning his ears. She curled her fingers around his, his grip firm and sure. Her heart flip-flopped queerly as she realized that it was, indeed, that way.

"SIMON AND TAWNY RAN SIX miles to get here, Letty. And Simon's wearing boots," his dad said with a touch of awe and pride.

"You ran to see me?" his mother asked, a hint of wonder reflected in both her voice and her eyes.

Simon knew he was wading deeper into muck, but he'd sort it out when his mother wasn't lying in a hospital bed connected to monitors with an oxygen tube clipped to her nose. She'd looked so bloody pleased—they both had—when they'd misconstrued his and Tawny's relationship. And then when Tawny had looked at him as if she was somewhere beyond besotted...

"Well, not quite six miles. We managed a lift the last bit."

"In boots?"

He would've never guessed that he was this important to them. Emotion clogged his throat.

"I needed to make sure you were okay." It came out brusque and clipped.

His mother didn't seem to mind. "That's wonderful."

"He's a wonderful man. You should spend some

time getting to know him," Tawny said. Despite her soft voice, her look challenged both of his parents.

Her statement hung in the air, the bleep of the telemetry the only sound in the room. His dad stood a little straighter, his mouth pinched. No one took Charles Thackeray or Letitia Marbury to task. Simon nearly gaped when his father's face softened and he took his wife's hand in his.

"Perhaps you're right, young lady. I suspect our son is rather wonderful."

It was as close as his family had ever come to a Hallmark moment. And probably ever would. Simon was bloody close to blubbering.

It was just as well that Elliott breezed through the door, shattering the moment. "Dr. M, what are you doing here?"

What was Elliott doing here? Elliott brushed past them to hug Simon's mother. In the meantime, Simon glanced at Tawny and murmured, "You did this?"

She looked guilty but unrepentant. "I didn't know what you'd be faced with. I thought you might need him," she said quietly in his ear, leaning in under the guise of brushing something off of his shirt.

Elliott straightened and threw an arm around Simon's shoulders. "Simon. Thanks for taking care of my girl."

"Your girl? We thought…" His mother trailed off, frowning in confusion.

Elliott offered a charming smile. "Sure. Tawny and I are engaged. Didn't Simon tell you?"

"No. That particular detail wasn't mentioned." His father's eyebrows beetled together into a unibrow.

"But Simon and Tawny…" His mother verged on tears.

"Elliott's such a kidder." Tawny swatted at Elliott, angled so that only Elliott and Simon saw the serious glint in her eyes. "Quit teasing Dr. Marbury." She looked back at his mother. "We need to let you get some rest. In fact, come on, guys, we'll go get a coffee." She stopped just short of snapping her fingers at them.

His mother beamed her approval. "Ah, a woman after my own heart, one who knows how to take charge." She nodded at Simon. "You've done well, son. I like her."

"I like her, as well," his father said.

Well, bully, they were three for three, because so did he. This would be a fine mess to sort out later. "I'm a lucky guy."

"I'm the lucky one," Tawny said, casting an adoring look his way.

"But…" Elliott looked from one to the other, clearly confused.

Tawny cut him off. "An iced coffee would be heaven, wouldn't it? Let's go find the café." She grabbed Elliott by the arm.

"Ouch. You pinched me," he said.

"Oops. Sorry about that." She turned to Simon's mother. "Try to get some rest."

"I will. Thank you for coming with Simon." His mother looked at him. "You will stop back in before you leave, won't you?"

"Yes. Get some sleep."

Tawny led Elliott from the room. Simon followed. Tawny in charge was a formidable sight.

They'd barely made it to the hall when Elliott said, "What was that—"

"Put a lid on it, Elliott," Tawny snapped at him. "I desperately need a cup of coffee to make me close to human. We'll talk then."

She swept forward like a regal queen. Elliott deserved everything and anything she threw his way, and Simon was damned glad he wasn't Elliott.

Richard straightened from where he'd been leaning against the wall across from the nurses' station and approached Elliott. The look that passed between them was the unmistakable look shared by lovers.

"I see you *did* bring the rainbow coalition," Tawny said.

Richard glared at Tawny and linked his arm through Elliott's.

Simon found it fairly disconcerting to see his best friend arm in arm with his gay lover. But in the scheme of things, no more disconcerting than finding himself in Tawny's bed or discovering that his parents thought he might be gay. Altogether it had been a very curious night. And it wasn't over yet.

They took the next available elevator. At half past three in the morning they were the only passengers.

The doors closed and Elliott drew a deep breath, sniffing the air like a scent hound. He visibly paled, looking askance at first Tawny and then Simon.

"The two of you slept together." It wasn't a question.

"What are you talking about?" Tawny challenged.

"The two of you…you reek of sex." Elliott rounded on Simon. "I can't believe you screwed my fiancée."

Simon had known they'd have this conversation one day, he just hadn't anticipated it being quite so soon.

He looked pointedly at Richard. "You don't have a lot of room for outrage."

Tawny moved to stand directly in front of Elliott, her body screaming confrontation.

"Let's get a couple of things straight. I'm not your fiancée. Who I screw, when I screw and how I screw is no longer any of your business. I could do the entire NY Giants team for halftime entertainment and it wouldn't be any of your business. Once you dipped your wick there—" she stabbed a finger in Richard's general direction "—you were never coming here again. Literally or figuratively."

"Honey, his wick's no longer interested in anything you've got," Richard sniped.

"Which is a good thing," she lobbed back.

Simon bit back a laugh. Well said. She'd bloody well laid it all on the line. She really was a magnificent woman.

The doors opened to the first floor and Simon herded everyone off the elevator.

"I think we could all use a cup of tea…or coffee," he said, steering everyone to the right, following the signs to the café.

Tawny grumbled at Elliott. "You were supposed to show up to support Simon, not act like a jerk."

"Well, I guess if Simon doesn't like it you can always kiss it and make it better," Elliott said with a sneer.

Simon had a fairly good idea of how much willpower Tawny employed to ignore Elliott's comment. Doubtless, flaunting her and Simon's night in Elliott's face was tempting, especially considering Elliott had brought his new lover along. But apparently she'd been sincere when she'd said she hadn't slept with him to get back at Elliott. Instead she ignored his gibe.

"How did you get here so quick?" she said. "There's no way you got here in that amount of time from the gallery."

"My apartment's only a couple of blocks away," Richard said, letting the cat out of the bag.

Simon felt sucker-punched. Certainly he was a sucker. Elliott hadn't been locked in at the gallery. He'd used him. Lied to him and used him. Their friendship had weathered the occasional row, but never would he have believed Elliott would lie to him. He stopped outside of the café entrance, restraining Elliott with a hand on his arm.

"Thanks, Richard. I'd love for you to buy me a cup of coffee," Tawny said, very much tongue in cheek but obviously trying to get Richard to give Elliott and Simon a moment of privacy.

Elliott glanced at Richard. "Please. Do it for me."

"Well, since it's for you," Richard said, giving Tawny a look of distaste. He reluctantly followed her into the café.

"Were you *ever* locked in at the gallery?" Simon asked with quiet fury.

"Yes. It does go into lockdown mode."

"For how long?" Simon's anger rendered him nearly speechless.

Elliott shoved his hands into his pockets and looked abashed. "About an hour. The security-system people talked me through disarming it."

"Was this before or after you asked me to break your news to Tawny?"

"After. Definitely after. I swear to you, Simon."

He felt marginally better—*if* Elliott wasn't lying. For fifteen years they'd been as close as brothers, and in less than a day he no longer knew if he could trust Elliott. He no longer knew the man before him. The man he'd loved like a brother couldn't have betrayed his fiancée, wouldn't have left Simon to clean up his mess. "Yet when you got out of the gallery, you didn't think you needed to come over to Tawny's?"

"You were already taking care of it. I thought it would be best to let her sleep on it. I didn't know she'd be sleeping on it with you."

Simon's anger dissipated as quickly as it had swamped him, leaving exhaustion in its wake. He hadn't used Elliott, but he had betrayed him to some extent. Simon realized he'd come across as something of a sanctimonious bastard. Two women in scrubs walked past and he waited until they were out of earshot.

"Elliott, you put both of us in that position. Do you know she's afraid of the dark?"

"Of course I do. We were together for six months."

"Then why did you tell me to leave her there alone? That struck me as rather callous."

Elliott shoved his hands into his trouser pockets and avoided Simon's eyes. "Things have already been a bit rocky between us. I told you we haven't been setting any records in the bedroom—" Right, and Tawny'd pretty much said the same. "She says I whine and that I'm self-centered."

"You do and you are."

Elliott looked at him then. "I might a tad, but she's so damned bossy."

"She is." Simon considered it part of her charm. It rather naturally came with the territory. She was also smart and gutsy and brave as hell. He thought about walking down those seven flights of stairs without even a candle. He didn't harbor any fears of the dark and it had been rather creepy for him. But Elliott still hadn't gotten to the point. "And what's that got to do with you asking me to abandon her in the dark?"

"I don't know. I knew things weren't good between us, but I didn't want to think about her being alone with another man, even if it was you."

"A case of wanting your cake and eating it, as well?"

"I'm a self-serving bastard," Elliott said.

"In a nutshell, yes."

"You didn't have to agree with me so quickly."

"You merely said it before I could," Simon said.

"I think I went a little crazy tonight."

"Are you rethinking your decisions?" Simon asked.

"Not Richard and Tawny. I just regret the way I've handled it all. I made some very bad decisions tonight and I'm not sure how to fix this. I'm afraid I've jeopardized our friendship." It was more question than statement.

"You didn't ax-murder any little old ladies, did you?"

"Not that I recall."

"I think we're okay, then. Tonight…with Tawny… We didn't mean for it to happen. And if it hurt you… well, I'm sorry for that."

Elliott rested his head in his hands. He shook his head, as if to clear it. He looked at Simon in evident remorse.

"Simon, I don't deserve a friend like you."

"True enough."

"Would you let me self-flagellate without interrupting?"

"I'll try."

"I was being a jealous bitch. I knew once Tawny found out about Richard it would be over between us. I know her well enough to know that. But when I walked in and your arm was around her and…well, I know for a fact she never looked at me the way she looks at you."

Simon shook his head. It was late —everyone was tired and edgy. "That was for my mother's benefit. She and my father leaped to the wrong conclusion and I thought under the circumstances it was best to let Mum think what she wanted."

"How'd you know she was at the hospital?"

"Dad called."

The surprise on Elliott's face said it all. Simon laughed. "I know."

"You okay?"

"I'm fine. Sort of." He shook his head. "Tawny told them they ought to spend some time getting to know me."

"No kidding? What'd your father do?"

"I thought he'd go off, but he and Mum said they thought she was right or some other bit of rubbish."

"Maybe they're changing, Simon. It's about damn time."

"Well, it doesn't make any sense. I'm still the same person I've always been."

"See, that's where you're wrong, where you've always been wrong. I've been telling you for years… you think you've been the problem. Whether you're the same person or not is immaterial, because it's always been about them. They were the ones with the

problem, not you. Tawny read them the riot act." Elliott laughed. "I'm sorry I missed that part. I told you,
Tawny's a steel magnolia."

"She is a bit relentless. She said her nickname growing up was Bulldog."

"I can believe it. There's another thing you've got
wrong, Simon. I know Tawny. She's not an actress. She
wears her feelings on her sleeve. The way she was looking at you wasn't for your mother's benefit."

Elliott himself had said his judgment was skewed
tonight. "You're wrong."

"Simon, we've known each other for a long time
and you don't know how relieved I am that I haven't
totally botched our friendship."

"I feel a *but* coming and I've got an inkling I'm not
going to particularly like it."

"Probably not. For the life of me, I can't figure out
why you're so damned scared of being happy."

TAWNY NURSED AN ICED coffee that tasted like chilled sewer water—at least, what she thought sewer water would taste like—and ignored Richard two tables over. She wasn't pining over Elliott, but she wasn't quite prepared to embrace the new object of his desire. She was glad Elliott and Simon had stayed outside the café to talk. She needed a few minutes alone to sort out her head.

She wasn't sure whether to laugh or cry. She was in love with Simon. Somewhere between "Elliott's seeing someone else" and "It's that way between them" she'd fallen head over heels in love with him.

Damn if she hadn't gotten exactly what she'd wanted—a stiletto kind of love. There was nothing old-shoe comfortable about Simon. He was alternately caustic and tender and brave and vulnerable. She knew with a certainty that almost frightened her in its intensity that whether it was a year from now or twenty years from now or fifty, she'd still feel the same.

Maybe this had started when they'd spent the day together shooting the pictures for Elliott, and her erotic dreams had been trying to tell her what her head and heart weren't ready to hear.

Lost in thought, Elliott startled her when he dropped into the chair next to her. "Simon says we need to talk."

She had it bad, in a major kind of way. A thrill coursed through her at the mere mention of his name. Elliott, however, remained at the top of her jerk list. "So talk."

"I'm sorry," he said.

He should be. "I agree. You're a sorry excuse for a human being. You not only cheated on me but you lied to me tonight when I called you about Simon's mother. You deliberately let me think you were still locked in at the gallery."

"I know. It was wrong. You can't call me anything I haven't already called myself. I knew you'd be angry and if Simon found out so would he. I just didn't want to face it tonight. I didn't want to deal with it."

"You created the monster, Dr. Frankenstein. Deal with it."

"You're right."

"I am." How could you continue to berate someone who simply agreed with you? What she'd really wanted to say to him when she saw him face-to-face was that she hoped his dick would drop off, but now... he'd probably just agree with her, and where was the satisfaction in that?

"I'm sorry for so many things...for not having the courage to tell you how conflicted I was about my sexuality before things went further with Richard. Then I should've been man enough to face you alone and tell you myself. And I'm sorry for being a jerk earlier."

She'd never been a grudge holder. She forgave far

too easily. She wasn't sure whether she was cursed or blessed. And her ability to so easily forgive his betrayal also spoke to the fact that she hadn't loved him the way she should love a man to marry him. And despite the fact that her logic and rationale had been impugned tonight, she was a very logical woman. If Elliott hadn't behaved the way he had at every turn, tonight might never have happened with Simon. And she was immensely, intensely glad that tonight had happened with Simon. She had no regrets.

"That about covers it with us. I accept your apology and I no longer hope that your dick drops off."

Surprise, followed closely by relief, chased across his face. He chuckled. "I didn't want you pissed at me forever."

"I can't say I particularly like Richard, but if you care about him and he makes you happy, then I'm happy for you."

"Thank you. That's more than I deserve."

"Yeah, it is, isn't it?"

Tawny grinned and Elliott reached over and smoothed her hair behind her ear. "You're a kick-ass woman, Tawny. A part of me wishes things had worked out with us."

"It never would have, Elliott. And I have to say I'm glad it didn't," she said. "I'm okay, but have you made things right with Simon?"

Elliott nodded. "We're good. We talked about what happened earlier." He grimaced. "I've had to eat a lot of humble pie tonight."

"Only your fair share."

"Could you maybe go a little easy on me?"

"I'm not sure you deserve it, but I'll try."

"We talked about his parents."

"It's odd. I thoroughly detested them for the way they've treated him, but I couldn't help but like them when I met them."

"Welcome to my world. They've totally screwed up Simon's head—and it's a mess—but they're not deliberately cruel, just thoughtless. They've always been courteous. I never felt unwelcome in their house when we were teenagers, but there's always this distance. Fine if you're the friend, but it really sucks if you're their kid. Simon pretends it doesn't matter, pretends he doesn't care, but all he's ever wanted was for them to notice him." He looked thoroughly disgusted. "They didn't even make it to our high school graduation."

Tawny ached on Simon's behalf and thought more of him than ever before. "He didn't hesitate when his dad called and asked him to come. And from the sound of things, that's so much more than they deserved. He deserves better parents."

Elliott smiled faintly at her vehemence. "A lot of people do. But we have to play the hand we're dealt. Simon's one of the finest men I know, but they've scarred him."

She drew a deep breath and plunged into the deep end with both feet. "I love him, Elliott." It felt new and fresh and all the more real for giving it voice. Even now she was aware of him across the room with every fiber of her being.

The melancholy in Elliott's eyes touched her. He nodded. "I know."

"You do? How could you possibly...?"

"I knew the second I saw the two of you together in

Dr. M's room." Elliott creased the napkin on the table between them.

She laughed self-consciously. "Ridiculous, isn't it? Yesterday you and I were engaged and now I'm sitting here telling you I'm in love with him."

"I wouldn't say it's ridiculous at all. I'd say it's just the way it is, much the same as me winding up with Richard."

"You're his best friend. I need you to be okay with this." It wasn't particularly easy asking for his blessing.

"I have to be okay with it, otherwise you'll nag me to death *and* kick my ass in the meantime."

They both laughed. Elliott sobered.

"You'll have to fight for him, Tawny."

Her gut knotted. "I know he's in love with someone else…or at least he thinks he is. Who is she?"

"I know there is someone—someone he won't discuss, which isn't unusual for Simon because he's very self-contained. But that's not who I'm talking about." His blue eyes held a trace of pity. "It's Simon you'll have to fight."

"I HOPED I'D FIND YOU HERE. She's asleep."

Startled, Simon looked up from adding sugar to his coffee. It was time lapse at its worst—his father had aged ten years in the span of a night. Talking to his father was always more awkward than conversing with a stranger.

"Can I buy you a cup?" Simon offered.

"Any chance of scaring up a cup of tea?"

"Find us a table and I'll see what I can do," he said. In record time he returned with a steaming cup of water, a tea bag, cream and sugar. "It's the best I could do."

The table rocked when he sat down.

"Thank you. I seem to have found the one with the wobble."

"It's fine," Simon said. He didn't think they'd be here long enough for it to matter.

His father set the tea to steeping and an awkward silence settled between them, the same general stiffness he'd felt his whole life with his parents.

Simon cleared his throat. "Since Mum's fine and she's resting, we won't go back up. You'll explain it to her, won't you? Tell her I didn't want to wake her?"

His father nodded his gray head. "I'll let her know. Thank you for coming."

Had he doubted that Simon would? "Anytime. I'm glad you called me."

Silence stretched between them like a thin, taut trip wire. His father, with neat precise movements, prepared his tea. One sugar. A dollop of cream. No lemon. Stir twice. As a child, his father's tea-making ritual had fascinated him in its unswerving sameness.

Charles looked up from his cup, catching Simon unaware. "She wanted you here...and so did I."

"All you had to do was call." Perhaps it was exhaustion. Perhaps it was the courage to say things in the wee hours of the morning. But Simon said, "All I ever wanted was for you to love me."

His father's ever-erect carriage faltered. He looked like a tired old man. He shook his head. "I fear we've been terrible parents. I've always loved your mother so much, I didn't make room for anyone else. That was wrong, dreadfully wrong. When I thought I might lose her tonight, I realized how important not just she is to me but you, as well. To both of us. I believe Tawny was right—we've got a wonderful son we need to get to know."

The chill inside him had nothing to do with the air-conditioning. "I don't want to be the putty that fills the gap just because you think you might lose her."

"No. Never that. Your mother and I have missed you these last couple of years. But things have come full circle. Whether it was your intention or not, you cut us out of your life."

There was nothing to say, so Simon remained silent.

His father nodded in acknowledgment. "It was nothing more than we deserved. We can't change the past. All we have is the future. Your mother and I would like to be a part of your life."

He'd waited a lifetime for this. He should be ecstatic. But he'd built a wall around his emotions. Every hurt, every lonely hour had mortared yet another brick into place. One offer of intent couldn't tear down something so firmly in place. Simon rubbed at his neck, stiff with tension. "I don't know."

"Fair enough."

Charles sipped his tea. Simon finished his coffee. His father cleared his throat.

"Well, yes. What about Tawny? *Is* she Elliott's fiancée?"

Simon infinitely preferred to focus on Tawny and Elliott instead of his relationship or lack thereof with his parents. "Up until last evening she was Elliott's fiancée. I'm not gay and never will be. Elliott, however, just came out of the closet."

His father blinked. Twice. "This is rather akin to a racy BBC drama."

Simon smiled. His father never meant to be funny, but sometimes...well, he just was. Simon shook his head. "It gets rather complicated, but the bottom line is Tawny and I aren't an item. I got stuck at her apartment last night—well, this evening—and when Mum thought that...well, we just let her think it."

"Ah, that's just details and I really don't need to know all of that. All I need to know is the look on your face when she came through the door." He wrapped his hands around the cup and Simon noted the prominent blue veins that came with aging. "You and she share the same thing your mother and I have always shared. A current that runs deep, a connection few others get."

He'd explained they didn't have a relationship, but he bloody well had no intention of discussing his *feelings* with this man who'd never evinced the slightest interest in his feelings before.

"Wouldn't you say it's a bit late in the day to decide you're interested in my life?"

"That's ultimately up to you, but no, I don't. I can't change yesterday, but I can change tomorrow."

Simon didn't know what to say. He wouldn't promise anything he couldn't deliver on and he just didn't know if it was too little, too late.

His father looked disappointed. "Okay. Will you come back tomorrow, or rather later today, to see your mother?"

"I'll come back."

It was the most he could promise.

"You MUST BE LIVING RIGHT. What are the odds of finding a parking spot on a Manhattan street?" Tawny said as Simon eased his father's aged Jaguar into an empty space within half a block of her building.

"Must be all the poor sods stuck at work," he said with a slight smile.

Charles Thackeray had offered his car since he wasn't going anywhere and Simon would be returning in the morning…well, later today. She'd been more than content to ride home in air-conditioning as opposed to running. They'd driven the dark streets in companionable silence, each wrapped in their own thoughts.

"Dad said there's a flashlight in the trunk. Give me a minute to get it," Simon said, opening his door and getting out.

Fine by her. The worn leather seats were soft like a glove. It was no hardship to sit on her butt a little longer.

The trunk slammed and Simon appeared at her door, flashlight in hand, the beam of light making the surrounding dark all the thicker. He opened the door for her. "At least we don't have to tackle the stairs in the dark this time."

"I'm eternally grateful to your father," she said, climbing out of the car, Simon's hand beneath her elbow. He was a thoroughly modern man with an endearingly old-fashioned sense of gallantry.

The street lay quiet, deserted. She and Simon seemed to be the only two people awake in the city. Even the few voices they'd heard when they'd left earlier were now silent.

They walked to the front of her building. "It was nice to drive."

His teeth flashed white in a weary grin. "It did beat the hell out of walking back."

Once in the front door, Simon took her hand in his as they followed the swath of light across the lobby to the stairwell.

"I'm not so sure that Dad would've offered the Jag if it had been only me. I bet you've never met anyone that didn't like you," he said as they climbed the stairs.

Tawny felt sure he was talking to distract her from the dark. Even with the flashlight the inky black played host to her worst fears. She focused on the conversation and tried not to think about being swallowed up by the dark.

"That's not true. For the most part I get along with everyone. I like people. I think that's why it bothered me so much that you seemed to dislike me from the moment you met me."

"I've never disliked you."

She snorted but didn't argue the point. "And Mrs. Hinky doesn't like me."

"Mrs. Hinky?"

"My next-door neighbor. But she doesn't like anyone. Personally I think she's a bit of a nutcase, sort of paranoid. She's convinced people spy on her."

Simon made a choking noise. "Does she live to your right, if you're facing your building?"

"Yeah." How did Simon know Mrs. Hinky?

Simon recounted his earlier impromptu flashing on the ledge. Tawny laughed until she was gasping for air.

"Oh my God. That would've totally freaked out anyone, but especially Mrs. Hinky...." She dissolved into more laughter.

"Poor woman. I'm sure I was her worst nightmare come to life."

"I've seen you naked and it's no nightmare. But I'd better go over and explain tomorrow—well, later today—just so she's not totally freaked out."

"Probably not a bad idea." He tugged on her hand to stop her. "We're here."

It hadn't taken them any time. "You sure?"

"Yep." He flashed the beam onto the number stenciled on the door. "Seventh floor."

They were quiet walking down the dark hall. Reaching her apartment, Tawny unlocked the door and they stepped inside. Inside it was as hot now as it had been when they'd left.

"Hold on a sec and I'll have this lit," Simon said. A small votive flickered to life. He turned off the flashlight. "Don't want to run the batteries down."

With a meow, Simon, née Peaches, greeted her. Amazed, she scooped him up.

"Hey. Did you miss us?" She glanced over at Simon, who now had two pillar candles lit. "Wow. He's never greeted me before."

The cat batted at her chin with his clawless paw. She laughed and put him back down. "Okay. Enough already, huh?"

"It's the name change," Simon said, a ghost of a smile hovering around his mouth.

"Maybe. Or it could be my faith that he'd come around one day. Our perceptions become our reality." Wow. Where had that come from? She must be tired if she was spewing philosophical sound bites.

Exhaustion rooted her to the spot. Physically, emotionally, mentally, she was spent. She stretched and caught a whiff of her underarm. Ew.

"I could sleep a week, but I've got to shower first. Want to hop in with me? Just to shower," she tacked on, making sure he knew she wasn't offering sex.

"Sure." Simon laughed. "I'm not capable of anything more right now. I don't think I could get it up. Not even for you."

She smiled. That was one of the things she loved about Simon. He was so real. How many guys would admit that? She skirted the couch. "Good. I couldn't do more than lay there and I'd probably fall asleep, even if you could get it up."

He slipped his arm around her waist and she welcomed the support. "Okay, then. Shower only."

Votive in one hand, the other arm wrapped around her, he ushered her down the hall and into the bathroom. He put the candle on the sink, the mirror reflecting the light.

Tawny toed off her shoes and skimmed out of her shorts, panties and socks. Her top and bra joined the heap of dirty clothes on the floor.

She watched as Simon finished undressing—boots and jeans took a little longer to shuck. Absolutely lovely. Lean and muscular. He looked up and caught her watching him.

"What?"

"I'm tired, Simon, not unconscious. I'm just taking a moment to enjoy the view."

He grinned at her and walked over to turn on the shower. Those shoulders, trim waist, tight butt, muscular thighs. Arousal fluttered low in her belly. She felt the instant rush of desire that translated to slick, wet heat between her thighs.

"If I wasn't so beat, I'd try to seduce you into sweaty, nasty, on-the-floor, banging-my-head-against-the-wall sex," she said.

He quirked an eyebrow at her over his shoulder and she laughed softly. His expression was part hopeful and part weary disbelief. She shook her head. "It's a shame to waste the moment when you're all naked and—" she eyed his tight, bare buns "—well, naked. But I'm just too tired."

He laughed and stepped over his piled clothes to take her hand. "I may have to burn these clothes when I get home."

He led her to the shower. She didn't want to think about him going home. She didn't want the magic of the night to end. "I don't know about burning them… maybe just a fumigation."

She stepped beneath the shower's icy spray. The cold water felt delicious against her sticky, sweaty skin. An easy silence encompassed them as she and Simon alternated turns beneath the spray. When she'd shampooed and scrubbed every inch of herself and Simon had done the same, she turned the water off.

She swayed on her feet. Now clean and cool, she gave in to the fatigue weighing her limbs and numbing her mind.

"Hold on." Simon grabbed her towel off the hook and gently began to dry her.

"I can do that," she protested, but she made no move to take the towel from him.

"Of course you can," he agreed. He reached around her and blotted the water from her back. She gave in to temptation and rested her head against his strong shoulder.

"Hold on just a little bit longer," he said. He straightened and toweled her arms, chest and belly.

She stared, fascinated by the water clinging to his dark lashes and the drops caught in the stubble darkening his jaw.

"Mmm." It was nice to be coddled. "Believe it or not, I require more than an hour of sleep."

Simon chuckled as he knelt to dry her legs. The faint candlelight danced along the ripple of muscles in his shoulders, reflected off the sheen of moisture along the lean line of his back. He straightened, draped the towel over her wet hair and started doing some wonderful massage thing to her head. She groaned aloud.

"You've got to stop doing that or I'm going to fall asleep standing up."

He settled the towel around her shoulders and grinned. "That wouldn't be good."

He grabbed the other towel and made quick work of drying himself off while she stood there and watched like zombie-girl in la-la land. Simon stepped out of the tub. Before she knew what he was about, he placed one arm behind her shoulders, the other beneath her knees and scooped her up. His bare skin was cool and clean next to hers.

She should protest. Too heavy. Not necessary. But exhaustion muted her. Instead she linked her arms around his neck and pillowed her cheek against his chest, inhaling the scent of soap and Simon. The steady rhythm of his heart played like a lullaby beneath her cheek. Supported by his arms, his skin against hers, surrounded by his scent, she gave herself over to sleep....

12

SIMON WATCHED TAWNY SLEEP, the sun slanting across her buttocks and legs, her arm flung over her face, her hair an auburn skein across her pillow.

He rolled out of bed and padded into the bathroom. He pulled on his underwear and jeans. Walking around naked last night had been one thing but quite another this morning. The night's magic had vanished with the dawn.

He retrieved his camera and adjusted for the bright light streaming into the room. Neither of them had thought to pull the blinds when they'd stumbled into bed four short hours ago. She lay partially illuminated and partially in shadow. He took several photos, caught up in the play of sunlight over her skin. Retreating once again behind the safety of his camera.

She blinked her eyes open and smiled sleepily at him, and his pulse quickened. She eyed his camera. "Please tell me you aren't taking photos of me with bed head and no makeup."

She was a quixotic woman—undeterred by her nudity but worried about her lack of makeup. "You look beautiful," he said without thinking. And she did, with her hair tangled about her shoulders and her eyes soft and heavy-lidded with sleep.

"Right." She held a hand up between herself and the camera. "No more early-morning shots. Please."

"Okay." She did truly look beautiful, but she'd be self-conscious now. He walked over to the window and looked out at the city, offering her a moment of privacy without actually leaving the room.

The mattress creaked, announcing she was up. He heard her pad out of the room and the protesting squawk of the bathroom door.

Once again people crowded the street below, but very few cars were about. He fired off a few shots without any real interest. His heart wasn't in photographing the scene before him.

He heard the door squawk again and she walked back into the room.

"Thanks for going with me to the hospital last night," he said without turning around. They'd both been too tired to talk through anything earlier.

She opened and closed a dresser drawer. "I'm glad I got to meet your parents. What a relief your mom's okay."

"Yeah. It is." Simon winced inside. This was a bad case of *morning-afteritis*. They both sounded like characters in a poorly scripted play.

"I liked them better than I thought I would," she said, her voice muffled by the closet.

"They were…different." And that was an understatement. It was so typical that their decision to participate in his life revolved around their needs. They hadn't reached out to him because they were proud of him, or because they'd realized they'd missed out on knowing a great human being. No. They were feeling their mortality, their vulnerability, so he was their backup. Simon still played second fiddle to their agenda. And he didn't trust any of it. Now that his mum was fine, he fully expected they'd return to their insular world of two. "They certainly liked you."

"I tried not to be too unleashed for them." She peered around him to the street below.

Her hair brushed against his arm, her scent surrounded him and the urge to take her in his arms was almost unbearable, but the night's madness had ended.

"You charmed them," he said, stepping back from the window, away from her.

"Ha! They would've been thrilled with anyone who would've saved you from being—what was it?—a poofter."

Despite the heaviness of his heart and the general awkwardness dancing between them, Simon laughed. "Right. That was rich, wasn't it? If I've never brought a woman to meet them, therefore I must be gay. Face it, Tawny, you charm everyone."

"Ha! Don't forget about Mrs. Hinky. And I can guarantee you I didn't charm Richard."

"You and Richard got off to a less than stellar start." Bloody understatement. "You're square with Elliott?" Simon asked. He needed to make sure before he left.

"We're good. I've got closure, so I can forego the Prozac," she said, smiling. "And you guys kissed and made up?"

Simon shrugged. "We skipped the kiss—I didn't fancy Richard scratching my eyes out—but we're okay." He was making stupid, awkward jokes—definitely time for him to leave. He started toward the door and she stepped in front of him, stopping him.

She placed her hands on his bare chest, and his skin felt on fire. She wet her lips with the tip of her tongue. "Simon, I want you to know last night was the best night of my life."

He stepped back, away from her touch. "That's an unusual reaction to a broken engagement."

She dropped her hands to her sides. Her look chastised him. "That's not what I meant and you know it. *You* were the best part of last night."

"I'm flattered." And he was, but one of them had to be sensible. He walked out of the room. His camera case was still by the front door. It wasn't the pitch-black of last night, but a dark gloom curtained the room after the bright sunlight of the bedroom.

Undeterred, she followed him. "I'm not trying to flatter you. I'm being honest. Remember last night, when your father told your mother it was 'like that' between the two of us?"

He picked up his camera case without looking at her. "Yes. And I'm sorry that happened. I didn't want to upset her when she'd had a heart attack."

"I'm not sorry it happened. When he said that, well, I realized he had half of it right."

He snapped his head up. Had she guessed he was head over heels in love with her? "What do you mean?"

"I realized it is that way for me," she said, her voice soft in the shadowed room.

Simon clamped down on the ache inside him. She'd been raw and vulnerable last night. She'd very likely feel the same about any other guy who'd stepped in and treated her with any measure of decency. "No. Tawny, last night was extenuating circumstances. You were emotionally overwrought. Don't confuse the circumstances of the night with me."

"Are you implying I don't know how I feel?" This time her soft tone heralded an impending storm. But what he had to say needed to be said.

He'd already taken advantage of her to some extent last night. He'd be a total jerk to let her run with this now. And if he told her how he felt about her? Tomorrow or next week or perhaps next month, she'd realize how flawed he was, she'd see the darkness in him and he'd see the loathing in her eyes. It was far better this way.

"Last night was an emotional roller coaster for you. Give it a couple of days and it'll just be the night the lights went out in the big city."

"Don't you dare patronize me."

"I'm just being rational. One of us has to be." He knew the instant it left his mouth *that* was the wrong thing to say.

"Tell me I did not just hear you say that, Simon Thackeray."

He simply wanted her to see what was painfully apparent to him. Last night had been a space out of time. If she'd just be rational, she'd see that today it was back to the norm. But then again, maybe she couldn't be right now. Maybe it was that hormonally challenged time of the month.

"Are you maybe getting ready to start?"

"To start what?"

"You know...are you PMSing?" he asked.

The cat yowled from the other room.

"Luckily for you, I'm not. If I were, you'd probably be a dead man by now." She stomped into the kitchen. He heard her shaking cat food into the bowl as he walked past. He picked up his shirt, socks and boots. He pulled on his shirt. He sat on the edge of the sofa to put on his socks and boots. She came back out of the kitchen and lit a couple of candles without speaking.

"Listen, it's no wonder you're not thinking clearly, with Elliott coming out of the closet, the blackout, being dragged out to the hospital in the middle of the night. It's hotter than hell and you haven't had much sleep," he said, lacing his boot.

"That may all be well and true, but I have enough God-given sense to know how I feel."

"You'll see everything differently once the power's back on. A cool room, a hot shower, a decent meal and a good night's rest will make a world of difference."

She planted her hands on her hips, the heat and her temper obviously getting the best of her. "All the electricity in the world isn't going to change the fact that I love you, you arrogant…" She petered out, clamping her mouth tightly shut.

"No." He closed his eyes for just a second. "You and I both know you can't possibly love me. You don't go from being engaged to one man to being in love with another in less than twenty-four hours." And certainly not him, not the real him in the light of day instead of some romanticized version she'd created based on last night.

She raised her chin defiantly. "Stranger things have happened. For some people it's love at first sight."

"I know." He'd taken one look at her and he'd known. But she hadn't taken one look at him and fallen in love with him. He'd simply cushioned the impact of Elliott's betrayal.

Some of her ire vanished. "Oh, God. I got so caught up… I'm sorry I threw myself at you. I forgot that you have someone."

He shook his head. "There is someone, but… Some of us were meant to be alone."

"No. I don't believe that. You're wonderful and tender and…I refuse to believe you were meant to be alone. If you really love her, go to her, Simon. Don't wait until it's too late."

Perfect case in point that she was still overwrought and emotionally unstable. "Make up your mind, Tawny. If you love me the way you say you do, why are you sending me to someone else?"

She gentled her hand against his cheek, her eyes shadowed with a sadness that lanced him. "Because I can't make you love me if you don't. And pride's just a thing. I'm not ashamed that I've fallen in love with you. I got exactly what I wished for. This is definitely a stiletto kind of love." She lowered her hand and offered a halfhearted smile. "This is hard, Simon. Tenacity's always gotten me a long way. I've managed to get almost everything I've ever wanted by cajoling or nagging. I know that about myself. But unfortunately I can't bulldog you into loving me. But that's why we're here. It's part of our purpose in life, to love and to be loved. So if you're in love with this woman, you've got to let her know. I'm not some psycho who wants you to be miserable and alone just because you don't want me. I want you to be happy."

She only thought she loved him. He knew it just wasn't possible. "Tawny, you're very special…."

She shook her head and held up a hand to stop him. "I don't think I can listen to you fill me in on my attributes. And before you go there, let me say I can't feel the way I do about you and be friends."

He shook his head. "No. I don't think we can be friends. It was a great night and you're a wonderful person, but you had it right last night when you said our paths were unlikely to cross again. You'll make some lucky guy very happy one day...."

She averted her face, wrapping her arms around herself as if she were cold, despite the sweltering heat. "I think it's time for you to leave."

Simon slung his camera case over his shoulder. "I'll drop the photos in the mail when I finish developing them. Give me a couple of days."

She walked to the door and threw the dead bolt. "Send me a bill with them."

"No. We discussed that up front. No bill."

"If you don't bill me, then I owe you a party. It'd be neater and tidier if you'd just invoice me." She raised her chin a notch, daring him to argue with her.

"I hope you find the man of your dreams, Tawny."

She looked him dead in the eye. "I did."

He walked out the door and closed it behind him. She was wrong. And one day she'd thank him for this.

TAWNY'S CELL PHONE RANG. For one heart-stopping moment she thought it might be Simon. She hoped he'd decided that last night was something special, that whatever it was between them was something special. Nope. Elliott's number flashed on the display.

"Hi, Elliott."

"Tawny, is Simon still there?"

"No. Try him on his cell," she said. Why hadn't he just called Simon in the first place? She didn't have time to play operator. She was too busy being miserable.

"I don't need to talk to him. I just wondered if he was there. I need to come over." Excitement tinged his voice. She wasn't up for any of Elliott's drama.

"I don't think so, Elliott. This is bad timing. I'm just not up to it."

"I've got something you need to see." He sounded practically aquiver.

She was too lethargic and generally miserable to argue with him. Elliott, the self-absorbed, probably wanted to show her a promise ring he'd designed for Richard or something equally inane. "Whatever. Come on over."

"Can I bring Richard?"

At least he'd asked permission. "Are the two of you joined at the hip now?"

Elliott laughed. "Naughty, naughty, Tawny."

Ugh. Poor choice of words. "Forget I said that. Come over whenever."

She kept herself busy tidying up her apartment and tidying herself up until Elliott arrived with Richard in tow. She might be rejected and dejected, but she didn't have to look like a hag or live like a slob.

Elliott and Richard arrived bearing iced Frappuccinos and half a dozen bagels with cream cheese and a side of lox from Abrusco's. Caffeine was good. Food was better.

She took the proffered food and placed it on the chest between the sofa and chair.

"Abrusco's was Richard's idea," Elliott said. Obviously he wanted her to like Richard. She wasn't sure she'd ever like him, but she'd aim for civility. "Thanks."

"There's a raisin-and-cinnamon with your name on it in there," Richard said.

"My favorite. Thanks again." She dug out the bagel and smothered it with fattening cream cheese. The better to blimp up with. She bit into it. Even a day old and unheated it was delicious.

"Don't you want to know what it is Richard and I have to show you?" Elliott asked, pulling out an onion bagel.

"Elliott, this better be really good because I'm just not much in the mood." Bagels or not.

"Let me guess." He smeared lox over an onion bagel—now Richard could endure onion-and-lox breath. "You told Simon how you felt, he rationalized everything for you and then he left."

"How'd you know? Did you talk to him?"

She'd rather have this conversation without Richard, but really it didn't matter. And he'd been quiet. Not nearly as offensive this morning as he had been last night. Of course, she hadn't sniped at him either.

"I didn't have to talk to him. We've been friends for a long time." He gestured toward her with a plastic knife. "I told you you'd have to fight for him."

She felt empty inside. "I can't make him love me if he doesn't."

"If he loved you, would you fight for him?"

She winced. She'd known Elliott to be thoughtless often but never cruel. "If I thought he loved me, you know I'd fight."

Elliott smirked like the cat who'd just swallowed

the canary. "I found out this morning Simon's kept a big secret from me."

"Yes?"

"I knew Simon was in love with someone—I just didn't know who. And he's not the kind of guy you press for details like that. And, well, I can be a little caught up in my own life, so I really hadn't pursued it very hard."

Was that a glimmer of self-awareness on his part? "You know, there is hope that you're not a total narcissist."

Richard sniggered but Elliott ignored her comment.

"I found out this morning just who Simon's mystery woman is."

Her heart shattered. Knowing Simon loved someone else was one thing. But really *knowing*...

"I thought you hadn't talked to him," she said.

"I haven't, darling. But a picture's worth a thousand words. Remember our engagement party at the gallery?"

"Of course I remember it. It was only two months ago and I planned it." Why did Elliott have to spin everything out? "Does everything have to be a drama with you? Can't you just get on with it? Who is she?"

"All in good time, Tawny. Indulge me for a moment. Richard took photos that night at our engagement party. We were looking back through them this morning."

Richard pulled a photo out of a padded envelope she hadn't noticed before and handed it to Elliott. Elliott passed it on to her. "What do you think?"

Simon, obviously unaware he was being captured on film, stared at someone off camera. The stark longing etched on his face, the tenderness and pain in his eyes, felt like a knife to her heart. The expression on his face, in his eyes, was so private, so personal, she felt intrusive even looking. Richard had captured both the beauty and the sorrow of love. She looked away.

"I'd say that's the face of a man passionately in love," she said past the lump in her throat.

She felt sick. If that was at her engagement party, chances were she knew the woman he so deeply loved. Or perhaps not. Most of the guests had been Elliott's business acquaintances. It'd been a good opportunity for him to garner exposure for the gallery.

How could Elliott look so pleased when she felt like barfing?

"I agree," he said. "*That* was taken with a zoom lens. Richard took this one with the regular lens." He passed her another photo. "Take a look at the love of his life."

Tawny steeled herself to look down. The picture fluttered to the table, out of her nerveless fingers. Stunned, she stared at the photo of herself sitting alone at a table. Everyone had gotten up to dance and she'd needed a few minutes at the table alone. Simon sat one table over.

That yearning, that passion, was directed at *her*.

"But that's me," she whispered.

"Yeah. As I said, a picture's worth a thousand words. He loves you," Elliott said with a triumphant smirk.

Shock numbed her. "But it doesn't make any sense. This morning I told him how I felt, I told him I loved him, and he just walked away."

Elliott nodded. "He would."

"But why? I told him I loved him. He let me think he was in love with someone else and essentially told me to have a nice life."

"Ever since I've known him he's been emotionally neglected. Letitia and Charles aren't bad people and they're not cruel. And I think they've finally figured out what they did and want to make amends for it. They always had one another and Simon was left on his own. Thank God for his grandparents. If it hadn't been for them… But Simon's totally convinced he's unlovable."

She'd drawn similar conclusions from the little he'd told her about his childhood. But how could he possibly think himself unlovable? "Has he ever told you he's unlovable?"

"He doesn't have to. I'm falling back on clichés this morning, but if a picture's worth a thousand words, actions speak louder than words. He holds everyone at arm's length. I've been thinking a lot about Simon since we were at the hospital last night. I don't think he was always this way, although he was when I met him. I think when he was a kid, his parents just kept shutting him out and he finally decided it hurt less if he was the one who closed the door. His parents. Jillian, a girl from England. You. Even me sometimes."

It began to make a sad sort of sense. "Jillian married his cousin."

Elliott's eyebrows shot up. "You know about Jillian?"

"He mentioned her last night."

"I'm amazed."

"So, how did Jillian wind up married to his cousin?"

"She said once she got to know him that he wasn't her cup of tea," Elliott said.

As suddenly as they'd gone out, without fanfare the lights blinked back on.

"Well, I guess I just shed some light on everything," Elliott drawled.

It was corny and Tawny rolled her eyes but laughed nonetheless. "Things are looking brighter by the minute."

"Oh. That was so bad. I think I'll excuse myself to your well-lit bathroom on that one."

Elliott stood and left the room.

Simon loved her. Her. Not some nameless, faceless, skinny paragon. He loved her! If she didn't understand his twisted logic, she might be tempted to pinch his head off for walking out on her this morning.

Already her apartment felt ten degrees cooler, which she knew was impossible. Perhaps it was that her heart felt so much lighter.

Richard cleared his throat and Tawny jumped. She'd forgotten all about him.

"I owe you an apology. It was wrong…. I was wrong…." He sighed. "This isn't coming out right. I'm not saying being gay is wrong. I can't believe loving someone is wrong. But for it to happen the way it did…while you were still engaged…I'm sorry for that. I'm sorry for any pain I've caused you. I don't expect you to be my friend, but for Elliott's sake, I don't want to be your enemy."

Tawny busied herself with walking around the room blowing out candles. She straightened from the last candle and looked at Richard. There was no animosity in his blue eyes, merely a guarded wariness. "I don't believe the end justifies the means, but better that Elliott discovered this now than after we were married." She paused and smoothed her fingers down the front of her shorts. "I'm not sure I can be your friend, but

I'm not your enemy." She looked him square in the eye. "Unless you hurt Elliott—then all bets are off."

Richard blinked, obviously surprised. A smile crooked his mouth and he nodded. "Fair enough."

Elliott returned from the bathroom and looked from one to the other. "I feel as if I'm interrupting something."

"I'm just filling him in on all of your bad qualities, but I haven't had nearly enough time," Tawny said.

Elliott feigned amazement. "I was unaware I had any."

Tawny smiled angelically. "I could catch you up to speed if you had an hour or so."

"You're a sweetheart to offer, but I suspect you have better things to do with your time." Elliott picked up the photo of Simon and Tawny and studied it. "Here's the deal, Tawny. I think he's scared to trust that someone could actually love him. That it's not just a mistake. Simon knows all about how to love. He just doesn't know how to be loved."

She crossed her arms over her chest and smiled. "Well, he's about to learn."

He handed her the photo and grinned. "Feeling that way about you must scare the hell out of him. And for you to tell him you loved him...I'm sure he's terrified." Elliott shook his head. "If I didn't know you're the best thing that could possibly happen to Simon, I'd feel sorry for the poor guy...almost."

13

"JUST A MINUTE!" SIMON yelled. Couldn't a guy find a moment of peace in his own apartment? First his father called on his cell phone after he'd dropped him off, then Elliott rang with some stuff and nonsense about staying home, now someone at the door.

He clattered down the grated stairs of his loft. At least the electricity was back on and he didn't have to worry about what would happen to Tawny after dark. If the electricity hadn't been restored by dusk, he'd planned to show up on her doorstep so she didn't have to endure the dark night alone. It would've been awkward, but he didn't want her alone and scared in the dark. Now that wouldn't be necessary.

Despite the return of power, and hence air-conditioning, it hadn't put a dent in the heat. He'd showered without shaving and thrown on running shorts and a T-shirt. He was clean, but he looked grungy. Grungy suited his mood.

He threw open the door and then wished he hadn't. Tawny stood on the other side. He stared at her. A sundress clung to her curves. Her hair was piled atop her head. Sunglasses hid her eyes. A backpack purse was slung across her back.

"What are you doing here?" he asked. Rude and abrupt usually put people off.

"You might've had dismal parents, but I'm sure they taught you better manners than that. Aren't you going to ask me in?"

Of course, rude and abrupt didn't seem to work so well on Tawny.

"Come in." He ran his hand through his hair but stepped aside. He didn't feel particularly up to gracious, which wasn't his strong suit on a good day. And this wasn't a good day. "What are you doing here?" he repeated his earlier question. He left the door ajar as a not-too-subtle hint.

She closed the door and pushed her sunglasses to the top of her head. Her eyes sparkled. She looked positively radiant, and he was positively flummoxed.

"I'm here to collect on a promise."

She stepped closer, and the unique blend of perfume and Tawny triggered all those sensory things that made it bloody near impossible to think straight instead of thinking about having his face buried in her neck and his willy in her.... She *did not* need to come any closer.

"I didn't make any promises."

"It wasn't an exact promise. It was more along the lines of a promise of intent." She shrugged off her purse and held it in one hand. She looked him over from head to toe, sexual heat radiating from her, scorching him.

Simon shifted from one foot to the other, at a total loss. He'd walked out on her this morning and now she stood eyeing him as if he was a Popsicle on a summer day. And mother of God, he knew what she did with Popsicles. "Have you been drinking?"

Her slow smile simmered through him, heating him up. "Only a Frappuccino."

Focus, Simon. Not on her smile or Popsicles or the way her sundress hugged all of her curves. Focus on this conversation and getting her the hell out of this apartment before he did something really stupid like kiss her and beg her to stay. "What is this promise of intent?"

"You said if you had your lady love you'd know what to do with her." Another step brought her seriously into his personal space. Only a few inches of very hot air separated them. She smoothed her hand down his belly to the elastic band of his shorts, and his heart pounded like mad. "Well, I'm here, fully expecting to be—what was it?—oh, yes, fucked senseless for a week."

Bloody hell if that didn't catch Mr. Winky's attention. He had to get her out of here now. When she talked like that...

He sought to keep a cool head. Both of them. "What makes you think you're her?" She couldn't possibly know. He'd never breathed a word to anyone.

"Tell me I'm not." She pulled a photo out of her purse and held it out. Him, caught in a moment of weakness and utter misery, looking at her.

"Convince me this is a lie," she said.

He of all people knew the power of a photograph. How apropos. All these years he'd hidden behind his camera, only to be stripped naked, at his rawest in a photograph. He appreciated the irony.

He'd never convince her he didn't love her. But he knew she didn't really love him. She couldn't. He bracketed her shoulders with his hands and put her away from him. "Tawny, you're on the rebound. It's too soon. You don't really know me."

"Okay, I think you pulled out just about every argument you could. Now I'm going to debunk these myths you've created in that sexy head of yours. First, let's get it straight. Elliott wounded my pride." She stabbed at him with her finger. "You broke my heart. Second, it's too soon for what? Love doesn't come on a time line. It's not on-the-job training where you log in a certain number of hours for certification. And last, don't tell me I don't know you." She took her hand in his and brought it to her lips. "I knew you the second you climbed out on that ledge after my cat. I knew you when you held my hand in the dark. I knew you when you covered for Elliott. I knew you when you ran to your parents, literally, because they needed you, despite your history with them. I knew you when you dried me off and carried me to bed when I was too tired to move. There may be facets of you that I don't know yet, but don't tell me I don't know you."

It was one of the hardest things he'd ever done, because he really, really wanted to believe her. But he knew things she didn't. He knew that if she really knew him, knew that hollow core inside him, she couldn't possibly love him.

He pulled his hand away and put the width of the room between them. "Don't you understand?" He struggled to make her understand. "I'm like Hades. Lord of the Dark. You're Persephone. Light and beautiful. You don't belong with me."

Her mouth gaped open for a full five seconds.

"Please tell me you don't actually believe any of that hogwash that just came out of your mouth."

Just when he thought he'd heard all of her Southernisms. "Did you just say 'hogwash'?"

"Don't you dare make fun of me and don't think you can distract me. How about this—do you actually believe the load of crap you just shoveled my way? That's just wrong. And why would I want to be that mealymouthed Persephone? If you're going to draw some crazy mythical analogies, at least make me some kickass goddess like Athena or Artemis. Not some ninny whose mama had to come rescue her." She tossed her backpack onto the sofa. "You know, I was going to call a therapist on Monday for myself. You should make an appointment instead."

"I do not need a therapist," he said. "And if I'm so wonderful, why are you already trying to change me?"

"I'm not trying to change you." She threw her hands up in the air. "I'm trying to get some positive self-awareness through that thick skull of yours. And you definitely need a therapist if you keep spouting that kind of crazy crap."

"You think it's crazy crap and that should totally invalidate my viewpoint?"

"Listen, buster, you're the one who told me I needed to pack up and move back home if I was going to let my parents' opinion run my life. You take your own advice and stop letting a set of lousy parents ruin your ability to have a relationship."

That hit remarkably close to home. "Why do you need a therapist?"

"Just so you don't think you're getting away with anything, I know you're deliberately changing the subject. You have a habit of doing that when the conversation isn't going your way. But I needed a therapist because you were driving me crazy."

Simon crossed his arms over his chest. Next she'd be commenting on his body language. She had nerve saying he drove her crazy. She made him loony. "How was I driving you crazy?"

"Well, not you personally, but you in those dreams. I couldn't figure out how I could love Elliott and be having those kinds of dreams about you every night. But now that's easy enough without a shrink." She put her hands on his shoulders. "I don't love Elliott. Well, except as something that's a cross between a brother and a friend. Not the way I love you."

She made it sound frightfully logical. "Oh."

"That's it? Oh? After all of that, the only thing you have to say to me is 'oh'?"

"What would you have me say?" He uncrossed his arms and dropped his hands to his sides.

She closed her eyes, as if her patience stood on its last leg, and delicately banged her head against his chest. "Simon, I believe we have a long, happy future ahead of us. I know in my heart that you love me. But it would be nice to hear it without me having to drag it out of you." She cupped his jaw in her hand. "I love you, Simon Thackeray. Now is it really so hard to put this—" she looked at the photo "—into words?"

The photo all but shouted it, but he said what she so obviously needed to hear.

"I love you." The stark beauty in those three simple words, and the accompanying vulnerability, shivered through him.

"Thank you." She looked so happy it nearly ripped him apart.

What if he didn't live up to her expectations? What if he simply didn't have it in him to be the man she thought he was? "But it doesn't really change anything."

"Like hell it doesn't change anything. You are never getting rid of me, because I love you and I know you love me. Go ahead, retreat behind that wall of yours. If I have to go brick by brick and it takes me a lifetime, I'll tear it down. I'll crawl to hell and back if that's what it takes. All the other times I've been relentless and gone after what I wanted, that was just boot camp. This is the big event I've been training for. So be fore-warned, this is war."

"You'll get tired. You'll figure it out, sooner rather than later, that I'm not this romanticized version you've painted in your head."

"You are so wrong. Please, never tell me I'm irra-tional. I'm not harboring any illusions. You're arrogant and opinionated and sarcastic and really sort of bossy."

"You just called me bossy?"

"That's why we're so perfect together. You don't in-timidate me because I'll hand it right back to you." She sat on the sofa and pulled him down beside her. "You told me that you were scared when you went out on that ledge. It's okay to be frightened. That's what bravery and courage are all about. It doesn't require courage to face what you don't fear. It's okay to be frightened, but it's not okay to run away from it."

Hadn't Elliott told him, in the early-morning hours at the hospital, that Simon feared being happy? Maybe he'd been onto something.

"You don't seem to fear anything except the dark." Even as he said it he realized that though she feared the dark, she'd gone down those seven flights of pitch-black stairs with him, for him.

"That's not true. I'm scared to death I won't get through to you. I'm so scared of losing you I'm shaking inside." She held up her hand and he could see that it was, indeed, less than steady.

"And you really think that would be such a bad thing?"

"Infinitely worse than being trapped in the dark alone. Where else am I going to find someone to worship and adore this ass?" She flashed him a cheeky grin and then sobered. She held her hand out to him, palm up. "I'm standing here emotionally naked, Simon. Climb out on this ledge with me."

She was wearing him down, making him believe. There really was something akin to magic about her, because he found himself believing. Teetering on the brink of being convinced that she just might love him, warts and all. She'd gone into the dark with him, only needing him to hold her hand. And now she offered the same in return. He felt the dark emptiness inside him, that always seemed to hover at the periphery of his soul, slip away.

He placed his hand in hers and brought their clasped hands to his mouth, pressing a kiss to her hand. "You really do love me, don't you?" He didn't attempt to mask the wonderment in his voice.

She smiled as if he'd handed her the moon, and he was humbled that he had the capability to do so. "Hello. That's what I've been saying. You know, you have an attention problem."

He eased onto the sofa and she scooted onto his lap and wrapped her arms around his neck. Simon clasped her head in his hand.

"I love you," he said and kissed her, a tender promise. "I love you," he said again. It had a nice ring and it didn't sound nearly as frightening as he'd anticipated. He kissed her again, liking the pattern he had going. Except this time he kissed her longer, harder, deeper, mating his tongue with hers.

They came up for air and she wiggled her delightful bottom against his erection. She had him hot and hard with just a kiss. And before he totally abandoned himself to pleasure, he wanted an answer to something that had earlier seemed unimportant.

"Luv, I've got a question."

"Just for the record, I like that *luv* business. It makes me hot. Now ask away."

"Where did you get the photograph?"

"Elliott gave it to me." She nuzzled his neck. "You should check out my undies—I think you'll find them…interesting."

He slid his hand beneath her dress—"Elliott took that photo?"—past her thighs, anticipating a thong or sexy lace. Instead his fingers encountered hot, slick flesh surrounded by lace. Heat surged through him. "Oh, luv, these are *very* interesting." He traced the outline of her wet lips, bared by the lacy opening, with one finger.

"Crotchless. I came armed for heavy-duty battle." She smiled and teased the tip of her tongue against her lower lip. "It's Richard's picture."

He tugged her dress up past her thighs, exposing a

pair of black crotchless panties and her wet folds. "So Elliott ratted me out."

She laughed and spread her legs. "Yes. It was Elliott."

Simon slid a finger into her silky channel and she moaned deep in her throat, turning him on even more.

"I love it when you make those sounds. It makes my cock hard."

"And I love it when you talk like that and touch me that way. It makes me wet. But you know that firsthand."

Yes. He knew that intimately, arousingly. "Remind me to thank Elliott later. Much later. Next week perhaps. Right now I've got a promise to keep."

Epilogue

A year later

"Nervous?" Simon asked, taking her hand in his.

Tawny looked out from their vantage point in Elliott's office at the guests milling about the gallery. Everything was in place. Music. Caterer. Guests.

"A little. I've never planned a wedding before. Even an unofficial one. Why? Are you nervous?"

He rimmed his finger beneath the neck of his tuxedo shirt. "I'm not so fond of the bloody monkey suit and I'd prefer not to stand in front of a crowd, but overall I'm fine."

She eyed him from head to toe, flirting with him. "You clean up very nicely." And that was a gross understatement. He was mouthwateringly yummy in the formal black tie and tails. "I might have to get you into a tux more often."

His look sizzled over her, setting her hormones into a frenzy. Of course, with Simon it didn't take much to stir her up. "I'd rather you concentrate on getting me *out* of the tux."

"That can be arranged later. Do you think your parents will come?" she asked.

Simon shrugged with studied nonchalance. "I expect they might."

He still tensed, still had a stiffness about him whenever Letitia or Charles was mentioned. But he and they had made progress, albeit baby steps, in the past year.

"I think they genuinely regret your train wreck of a childhood. At least they're trying."

"I'm trying, as well. Do you really think people can change?"

"You know the answer to that. The only thing that limits us is fear and the boundaries we set for ourselves."

"Our relationship has helped me understand them better." He brushed his hand along her jaw. "I think Mum and Dad have a relationship similar to ours. Even after thirty years he's still head over heels in love with her."

Finally, after a year, he was beginning to believe, truly believe, in his heart and in his gut, that she loved him. That she wasn't going to wake up and decide there just wasn't enough substance to him or that the substance was too unpalatable.

He'd actually gone to Savannah with her a couple of months ago to meet her family, after the fallout from her broken engagement had cleared. It'd been an interesting weekend. While Elliott, with his outgoing personality, had charmed them, they'd actually liked Simon better—especially after they'd found out Elliott's sexual preference. Her father had pronounced Simon a man of depth. Her sister Betsy just thought he was weird, but then again, anyone not teeing off at the golf course or signing on at the garden club was weird to her sister, who lived in a microcosmic world.

And she knew for sure Simon was getting comfortable with their relationship when he asked her to go with him to England in the fall to meet his grandparents. Who knew? In a decade or so, her relationship-phobic love might actually decide to do something wild and crazy, like commit.

"Speaking of being head over heels…where is the happy couple of the day?" she asked.

Simon grinned. "Richard was nervous, so Elliott thought it best if they had a few minutes alone before the ceremony." He tugged again at his tie. "A gay commitment ceremony held in an art gallery—not exactly conventional. You'd think they would've picked something a little more avant garde than a tux."

"Would you like a little cheese with that whine? Anyway, Richard wanted tuxedos and Elliott wanted to make sure everything was the way Richard wanted it. I think it's sweet. Richard's been good for Elliott."

"Absolutely. He's much more considerate than he ever was before."

"And I think it's very cool they chose the anniversary of the blackout."

"Very sentimental. Very touching."

She shoved his shoulder. "Don't be a jerk." She knew better than anyone what a sentimental romantic he was at heart.

"But I'm so good at it." He smirked, sending her heart into a flutter and a heat blooming low in her belly.

"You're good at lots of things," she said and smirked back.

"Stop it. It won't do for you to go tenting the front

of my trousers with naughty insinuations before the ceremony."

"You know how to spoil a girl's fun."

"I'll make it up to you later, luv." And he would… and then some. "You know what today is, don't you? We've been together a year and we've got some unfinished business between us we need to wrap up."

"Business?" What was he talking about? And his timing left a lot to be desired.

"Right. I delivered your photographs, but you've yet to plan my party."

"You were supposed to bill me," she said, her mind wandering to her mental checklist. Had the caterer ordered the extra champagne Elliott had requested? Yikes! She thought they'd answered her email, but she didn't recall seeing the extra bottles.

"Now don't do getting all argumentative, luv. I need an event planned."

Men picked the weirdest times. She focused her attention on him. "What kind of event?" Simon wasn't a party kind of guy. He could've been voted Least Likely to Attend a Party in his high school yearbook.

"Something very similar to this. Except perhaps a bit fancier. Maybe something in a church and then a party afterward with a bit of dancing."

Was he saying what she thought he was saying? Her heart seemed to skip a beat. Perhaps he had impeccable timing after all. "Are you talking about a wedding and a reception?"

He snapped his fingers. "That's it."

"You're definitely sure? It's a lot of work if you think you might change your mind later."

"I've never been more certain of anything in my life."

"I presume you have someone in mind?"

"As a matter of fact, there's this enchanting creature who has me thoroughly besotted...."

"And have you asked her yet?"

"I'm working on it." He took her hand in his and dropped to one knee. "Tawny Marianne Edwards, would you marry me?"

She'd always thought it was sort of goofy when guys got on one knee in the movies. It wasn't. It was sweet and tender, and if he made her cry and her mascara ran she'd kill him. "I would love to do just that, Simon Trevor Thackeray."

He reached into his pocket and pulled out a velvet ring box. "I'd be honored if you'd wear my ring."

Oh my. He was doing this right. He opened it and pulled out an exquisite pear-cut diamond ring that was large...make that really large...forget it, they were talking *bling*.

"Do you like it?" he asked.

"No. I love it." He slipped it onto her finger. "It's beautiful." She waffled her hand back and forth, catching the light in the myriad facets of the stone. Call her tacky, crass, shallow and/or materialistic, but she'd always wanted a big ring, and her man had delivered. "It's a rock."

"It's as big as your sister's?"

She grinned at him. "Yeah. This'll blind her."

"And it's bigger than Elliott's?"

She presumed they were still talking about the ring. "Definitely bigger than Elliott's. It must have cost a fortune."

He slid his arms around her and pressed a sweet kiss to her temple. "You're worth it, luv. And anyway, it was easy money. I sold some of those photos of you in the bath to an internet porn site."

She grinned at his wicked, warped sense of humor and slid her arms about his neck.

The unmistakable click of a camera sounded. She and Simon both glanced toward the sound just as Richard fired off another shot.

"Now that I've caught the happy ending on film, do you think we could get on with this wedding?" Richard asked with a nervous smile.

Tawny laughed and didn't correct him. This wasn't a happy ending…this was just the beginning.

* * * * *

REQUEST YOUR FREE BOOKS!
2 FREE NOVELS PLUS 2 FREE GIFTS!

red-hot reads!

SPECIAL EXCERPT FROM

HARLEQUIN®

Blaze®

New York Times bestselling author
Vicki Lewis Thompson is back with three new,
steamy titles from her bestselling miniseries
Sons of Chance.

I Cross My Heart

"Do *you* like an audience?" Bethany asked.

If he did, that would help cool her off. She wasn't into that. Of course, she wasn't supposed to be feeling hot in the first place.

"I prefer privacy when I'm making love to a woman." Nash's voice had lowered to a sexy drawl and his blue gaze held hers. "I don't like the idea of being interrupted."

Oh, Lordy. She could hardly breathe from wanting him. "Me, either."

She took another hefty swallow of wine, for courage. "I have a confession to make. You know when I claimed that this nice dinner wasn't supposed to be romantic?"

"Yeah."

"I lied."

"Oh, really?" His blue eyes darkened to navy. "Care to elaborate?"

"See, back when we were in high school, you were this out-of-reach senior and I was a nerdy freshman. So when you showed up today, I thought about flirting with you because now I actually have the confidence to do that. But when you offered to help repair the place, flirting with you didn't seem like such a good idea. But I still thought you were really hot." She took another sip of wine. "We shouldn't have sex, though. At least, I didn't think so this morning, but then I fixed up the dining room, and I admit I thought about you while I did that. So I think, secretly, I wanted it to be romantic. But I—"

"Do you always talk this much after two glasses of wine?" He'd moved even closer, barely inches away.

She could smell his shaving lotion. Then she realized what that meant. He'd shaved before coming over here. That was significant. "I didn't have two full glasses."

"I think you did."

She glanced at her wineglass, which was now empty. Apparently she'd been babbling and drinking at the same time. "You poured me a second glass." When he started to respond, she stopped him. "But that's okay, because if I hadn't had a second glass, I wouldn't be admitting to you that I want you so much that I almost can't stand it, and you wouldn't be looking at me as if you actually might be considering the idea of…"

"Of what?" He was within kissing distance.

"This." She grabbed his face in both hands and planted one on that smiling mouth of his. And oh, it was glorious. Nash Bledsoe had the best mouth of any man she'd kissed so far. Once she'd made the initial contact, he took over, and before she quite realized it, he'd pulled her out of her chair and was drawing her away from the table.

Ah, he was good, this guy. And she had a feeling she was about to find out just *how* good….

**Pick up I CROSS MY HEART by
Vicki Lewis Thompson, on sale May 21,
wherever Blaze books are sold.**